GRAVE TRUTH

A SYDNEY BRENNAN NOVEL

JUDY K. WALKER

TITLES BY JUDY K. WALKER

THE SYDNEY BRENNAN MYSTERIES
(IN ORDER OF PUBLICATION)
Back to Lazarus (A Sydney Brennan Novel)
Secrets in Stockbridge (A Sydney Brennan Novella)
The Perils of Panacea (A Sydney Brennan Novel)
No Safe Winterport (A Sydney Brennan Novella)
Braving the Boneyard (A Sydney Brennan Novel)
River Bound (A Sydney Brennan Novella)
Grave Truth (A Sydney Brennan Novel)

THE DEAD HOLLOW TRILOGY
Prodigal
Founder
Heir

Cover design by Robin Ludwig Design Inc. http://www.gobookcoverdesign.com/

ISBN: 978-1946720153

For all the children who weren't believed, and the adults they became

Author's Note on Time: This story take place in the spring of 2005, after the events of River Bound.

1

"I didn't realize you were a woman," said the man in his late forties sitting on the other side of my heavy, wooden desk.

I knew what he meant—in my occupation and with a name like Sydney, it was a common mistake—but I waited to see if he'd dig himself a deeper hole. He'd come in asking if my boss was around, so it could only get better.

Deaf to his own verbal missteps, he continued, "I don't think my wife knows you're a woman, either."

He abused the hat in his hand, twisting it and tapping it against his leg. (Since when did men start wearing hats again? Men other than hipsters, that is, who aren't exactly thick on the ground in Tallahassee.) I wondered if there was a pile of gray lint beneath the chair, cast off when his hat struck the leg of his matching pants and gathering like dryer filter fuzz.

I tucked my red curls behind one ear and asked, "Is it a problem? That I'm a woman?"

The man blushed, looked at my face just long enough to confirm that yes, I was watching him blush, then looked back down at his hat. "No, I don't guess so. I mean... no."

I considered offering him a drink, but feared it would confuse him even more about my gender and vocational identity. "Why don't you tell me what brings you here. Mister...?"

He glanced up again, momentarily relieved to have a question he could answer. "Clint. Clint Spencer. I, uh, I actually live over by Ocala, but I had to come to Tallahassee on business. My wife figured while I was here, I might as well drop in..."

His voice trailed off. There's not much to look at in the front room of my office—some filing cabinets, bankers boxes crammed with additional files tucked under tables, my computer and printer, a couple of framed prints—but he was doing his best to find something.

Here on business, huh? His short, dark hair was simply cut, buzzed up the back and sides in what might be the #3 in a 1950s barbershop poster. The outdated style combined with his graying temples to make him look older; I revised his age down to mid-forties. He didn't have the confident demeanor or the wardrobe to be a lobbyist (his suit was well cared for, but definitely off the rack). This was personal.

"Mr. Spencer, what do you need from me?" I asked, sharply enough for him to focus on me instead of the cobwebs in my windows. (Note to self: clean the windows.)

"I'm sorry, Mrs.—Miss—Brennan. It's my niece. We need you to help us find her."

"How old is she?" I asked.

"Sixteen."

"Have you contacted the police?" I asked.

"No," Mr. Spencer said, and his hat fidgeting escalated to mangling. "It's complicated."

"How so?"

"We're not her guardians. And the people who are—the *person* who *is*—her foster parent... Well, let's just say she's not exactly doing a helluva job." There was a slight creaking sound as he dealt his hat a twisting, potential death blow, but I don't think he noticed.

"Mr. Spencer, why don't you start at the beginning."

He told me his sister-in-law had long been estranged from her family. "She died several years ago, and by the time Debbie—that's my wife—found out, our niece had already been taken into foster care. We had our hands full with our own kids, and they'd placed Addy with a real nice older woman, so we figured maybe it was for the best."

"Addy's your niece?" I asked.

He nodded. "But we contacted Addy's foster mother and started visiting. You know, just trying to get to know her because she'd never even met us before. This probably went on for a year, and things were going well. But Debbie has some health issues, and they flared up bad for a while. It took us close to six months to get her straightened out."

Mr. Spencer sighed, and for a moment I fancied his breath had made the Spanish moss sway in the live oak outside. Instead, a breeze had picked up. Whether it was the last gasp of winter or first of spring, I couldn't tell.

"Once Debbie got back on her feet, we realized we hadn't heard from Addy's foster mother in a long while. She didn't answer her phone, the house was empty, and there was a different caseworker that wouldn't talk to us—it was a mess. We finally found out the poor woman had fallen and broken her hip, and Addy had been placed somewhere else, with us none the wiser."

Mr. Spencer rubbed his nose in that I'm-a-man-with-allergies-not-feelings way. I pretended to make a note on the yellow legal pad next to me to give him a chance to recover himself. He pulled a handkerchief from somewhere and honked into it once, loudly, before continuing.

"It's all such a bles-sed mess," he said, pronouncing the word with two syllables like a proper Southerner. "We got a lawyer that didn't do us any good. Addy's been through three families and just as many caseworkers in the past two years. The woman who has her now won't let us see Addy, and she's got so many kids in her house she must have to do a head count every night. Except she doesn't, apparently, because Addy's gone."

"How do you know she's gone?" I asked.

He bowed his head, as if he'd done something nefarious. "One of my wife's friends is a substitute teacher, sometimes at Addy's school. She lets us know if Addy misses, and she gave me a call last week. I went by the house, and the foster woman told me Addy had chicken-pox. But she was lying. I know because we almost didn't visit Addy when our youngest was spots all over, but Addy said it was okay, that she'd already had them."

Now it was my turn to sigh. I felt for the man, but... "And she hasn't been reported missing? What about truant by the school?"

"They're off this week, so it's only been whatever days she missed last week."

There went that potential out. "Mr. Spencer, don't you think it would be better to hire someone who lives closer to Ocala? I could recommend someone—"

"My wife wanted you," he said.

I couldn't imagine why, since I'd never met the woman.

"And we're pretty sure Addy came to Tallahassee," he continued. "So far as we know, she's still here."

The Spencers had done some legwork on their own. A neighbor of the current foster mother didn't much care for the woman. Between talking with the neighbor, the substitute teacher, and a couple of Addy's friends (thanks again to the teacher), Mr. Spencer and his wife pieced together that Addy had been seeing someone. Someone older.

"Addy said she was moving to Tallahassee with this guy. One of her friends took a picture of them together. I don't know anything about that stuff, but she said she could email it or whatever," he said.

"Do you have a name?" I asked.

"Troy Cantrell. That's got everything we know about him," he said, sliding a few sheets of paper across my desk. The top page looked printed from a home computer. "And I put Addy's friend's phone number down at the bottom. The rest is anything else I thought you might need—birth certificate, foster mother's address..."

I skimmed quickly, trying to find anything that would justify me not taking the case. There was no father listed on the birth certificate. "What about her biological father?"

"He's dead. I think somehow he caused the split in the family, but I don't know any of the details. My wife's family never talks about it.'

So no immaculate conception, which meant I couldn't object on religious grounds. Were I religious. That still left me one solid area. "Mr. Spencer, since she is a minor, and you aren't her guardian, and her disappearance hasn't been reported to the authorities, I m concerned about some of the legal issues. I'll need to speak with my attorney before I can agree to look for your niece."

He nodded. "I understand, Miss Brennan. And I know Addy prob-ably just sounds like one more runaway, one more kid who finally found the trouble she's been looking for. I'm not going to lie; she can be disrespectful—never to us, but so I've been told. I don't think she's into drugs, but there's a good chance that loser she took off with is. But her life doesn't have to be like that. My wife and I would like to give Addy a home, a real honest-to-God family that'll stick with her until the day she dies."

He leaned across my desk with his secret weapon, a four-by-six photo of a lanky girl in denim shorts, squatting in the grass. She looked familiar, the way all kids look familiar until their faces set into adulthood. Long, brown hair hid half her face as she leaned forward, hand hovering over a cat with its paw extended in play. The camera had caught the moment she realized she was being watched, and the transition from an expression of innocence to wariness was unset-tling. I tried to hand the photo back to Mr. Spencer, but he backed away.

"That was taken three years ago. We don't have anything more recent, and I didn't have time to make a copy. I'm in town for another day, so if you could let me know by tomorrow afternoon, I'd appre-ciate it. I'd rather not leave her photo behind if you won't be needing it. Thank you, Miss Brennan," he said. Then he rose and exited my office with his mangled hat in hand.

I stood to watch him walk down the front steps, then pause and look both ways for his vehicle on the street. He never put his hat back on his head, just threw it on the passenger's seat when he reached his car, a light-blue sedan. I sighed, fanning the picture back and forth in my hands as if it were just another piece of paper, a flyer from the mailbox.

But those eyes... those haunted brown eyes.

"Well, shit," I said to no one in particular, picked up the phone, and dialed a familiar cell phone number.

The voice of my attorney and friend Roger Weber greeted me brusquely with, "Sydney, I hope you're not in jail, because I'm really not in the mood."

He was in a mood all right, one consonant with the gray skies and the increasing wind outside. "Not this time. Do you have a few minutes to touch base today, say around six or six-thirty?"

He was silent for a moment, presumably consulting his calendar. "I'll be at the office at six-thirty, but I can't stay long."

"That's fine," I said. "It won't take long. I just need a little advice about how to take a case without losing my PI license."

His sigh resonated over the phone. "Of course you do."

"I HOPE you're going undercover as a homeless person," were the first words out of Roger's mouth that evening.

Head bowed over his desk, scribbling notes in the margins of a thick, binder-clipped document, I'm not sure when he'd glanced up long enough to see what I was wearing. (For the record, a faded navy-blue T-shirt I couldn't recall buying peeked from beneath my jacket, over gray sweats with no holes.)

"I'm going from here to self-defense class," I snapped, feeling defensive already. I'd failed to grab a late-day snack, which meant I'd either drop to the floor or kill someone in class. "And I'm dressed fine. It's not at one of your fancy gyms with key cards and saunas and... juice bars."

· · ·

I HAD no idea whether Roger had a gym membership, but if he did, it would be a fancy one. Of course, I also didn't know what benefits fancy gyms actually offered, since I avoided gyms in general. And fancy things, come to think of it.

Roger glanced at me sharply. "You mean you have class with the outlaw?"

Outlaw was his way of referring to my friend Glenn. "You know he's not an outlaw. I mean, he might have been," —I wasn't sure what biker gang he'd been in back in the day, and *The Outlaws* wasn't out of the question— "but he's not anymore. He's a respectable businessman."

Roger rolled his eyes. Okay, Glenn owned a bar. But as a criminal defense attorney, most people would say Roger had no room to talk.

"What's on the schedule for tonight, advanced shiv technique?" Roger asked. "Molotov cocktails made out of Schlitz bottles?"

Hands on hips, I bit my lip against my first response, instead saying, "I'm not sure Schlitz ever came in bottles. So what crawled up your butt and died, counselor?"

Roger ran his fingers through his dark hair, worn a little longer than usual, before raising the fat document and waving it like a challenge. "A lying bastard of a witness. And a particularly ambitious and amoral assistant state attorney."

Flopping into a chair, I said, "I thought all the best ASAs already lived up your butt."

An almost-smile flickered across his face. "In their dreams." He tossed the paper back on his desk and added, "Sorry, Sydney."

I shrugged. "You're allowed. It's Monday."

"I should not be 'allowed' to be an asshole to you anytime," he said, meeting my eyes like a good adult. "And it's Tuesday."

"Whatever. You're forgiven," I said, sliding lower in my chair as my blood sugar continued to drop. Roger's loosened tie hung awkwardly, and the circles under his eyes matched his elegant gray suit. I asked, "Anything else have your boxers in a bunch?"

Roger and I have worked together for years, but he is a very private person. I'd only recently gotten a head count on his ex-wives (three). I wasn't surprised when he shook his head and asked me, "So what's the case that requires my considerable expertise?"

I told him about the Spencers and their tangled road to establishing a relationship with, and the safety of, their niece. When I finished, he leaned back in his chair, making it rock even though it wasn't designed to do so.

"The only thing worse than criminal law is family law," he said. "You have to deal with just as much dysfunction and drama, if not more. There's still a strong likelihood of somebody's life becoming irrevocably messed up. And your clients aren't in jail or prison, so you actually have to see them."

"*Most* attorneys have to see their incarcerated clients, too. They haven't learned that's what investigators are for," I observed, earning another almost-smile. Roger's refusal to see clients was legendary, and anyone who worked as a second chair attorney or investigator quickly learned what it was to become the Voice and Face of the Man.

"I'll need to talk to someone who specializes in family law," he said. "My instinct is that you're right to tread carefully. It's illegal to aid a runaway without notifying law enforcement."

"What if the niece were emancipated? How would that change things?" I asked.

Roger's mouth twisted and he shook his head. "Again, it's been a while since I was exposed to any of this stuff, but my recollection is that it's a lot harder to do in Florida than you might think. For a minor to be cut loose prior to the age of majority, generally, both parents have to consent. If the minor is orphaned... I don't know, I guess there'd have to be a *guardian ad litem*."

That meant someone appointed to specifically represent the child's best interests, and even more time spent in court to make that happen. "I hate to be a pain," I said, face squinting in anticipatory apology, "but the guy asked me to get back to him tomorrow afternoon."

"That's fine. I have to be somewhere," —he checked his watch and rose— "now, actually. But I'll make some calls after. Theoretically you should be okay looking for her, but if this girl is a runaway, things will get complicated when you find her."

"Of course they'll get complicated," I said, reluctantly standing from what had become a comfortable chair and following Roger to the door. "She's a teenager."

But I'd soon discover her hormones would be the least of my complications.

2
___

"**Y**ou're not doing it right," Glenn observed, gruff voice emotionless.

For some reason that annoyed me. Not that Glenn was critiquing my technique, but that he was doing it so calmly.

"It worked, didn't it?" I demanded, feeling a sudden impulse to grab the large man by the reddish-brown braid hanging down his back and swing him around the dojo like I was some bad-ass ninja superhero. I grinned at the image.

Glenn's eyes twinkled in response, either because he read my mind, or because he was teasing that he had other athletic pursuits in mind.

"It worked on Doug," he said, in the same tone of voice one might use to say you beat Charlie Brown. He pushed the cuffs of his long-sleeved T-shirt up to reveal fuzzy, golden arm hair, then reached down and pulled my chunky classmate to his feet. "That doesn't mean it'll work when you really need it to. No offense, man."

Doug had lost a few pounds since we'd started this small special class together last year, but it's true that he still was not the most physically adept person I'd ever met. He paused on one knee on the mat to catch his breath.

"No offense taken," he said, standing, face flushed. "I'm here to learn. And after all, she *is* a PI."

Doug believed my job was like an 80s television show with a catchy theme song. Bless his heart.

Our sensei Vince approached with another student, Maria, and said, "Glenn's right. Sometimes poorly executed technique is worse than no technique at all."

He motioned for the former biker to join him on the mat, and I felt a thrill of anticipation, as I always did watching the two men spar. Glenn had half a foot of height and fifty or sixty pounds on our pale, dark-haired sensei, but Vince always came out on top in the end. Sometimes it took some time, and a fair bit of trash talk, for him to get there, though. I wished I had popcorn.

This time was disappointing, all methodical demonstration of technique. Glenn and Vince faced each other, Vince in his black martial arts uniform and Glenn in dark-gray sweats. Glenn grabbed the smaller man's arm.

"You'll want to soften him up first," Vince said, slowly thrusting the heel of his hand toward Glenn's nose. "Head butt, kick, strike to the face. Whatever you can do in the situation. Then the wrist lock."

Vince moved from the strike to grab at Glenn's hand on his arm. "As you peel his fingers off, you're moving into the wrist lock. You need to get a feel for this. Your hand's probably gonna be sweaty, and it's probably gonna be smaller than your attacker's."

Glenn twisted away as Vince wrenched his wrist and used his other hand to push Glenn's arm, and with it the rest of his body, toward the ground.

"Be careful with the arm bar," Vince said, pressing his forearm against Glenn's upper arm while he gripped Glenn's twisted hand. "You have to control him—"

Vince slid his forearm lower, toward Glenn's elbow and then past it. Glenn demonstrated that the elbow was now free to move, flexing it first toward Vince's face, then toward his body. Finally, Glenn dropped the elbow, regaining the upper hand as he pivoted and faced Vince with a scary smile. "Or you'll regret it," Glenn said.

They walked through it again from the beginning, slightly faster, but this time Vince maintained control of Glenn's arm.

"Take him all the way to the ground, onto his belly. Then you can dislocate the shoulder," Vince said, demonstrating the motion, "or—"

He executed a series of blows to Glenn's back and head, slowly at first, then faster and faster, alternating flashing forearms, stiff hands and fists.

Glenn blinked hard when Vince offered him a hand up, as though something may have landed. "Show-off," he said.

I worked with Doug and Maria and a couple of newer students a little longer, but we'd hit our usual finish time and most of our energy was spent. Class drifted apart rather than officially breaking up ten minutes later.

"Remember, Red, this isn't theoretical for you," Glenn said, meeting me at the door.

"It's not theoretical for anybody in here," I said, avoiding his eyes while waving goodbye to Doug. "That's why we're the *special* class."

"Yeah, well, you're extra fucking special," he muttered.

I didn't want to risk stinking up my jacket by putting it on over my sweaty shirt, so when I stepped outside, the cool, humid night air slapped my damp skin like a pissed-off prom queen.

Walking next to me, Glenn drawled, "Who gets hijacked in a canoe?"

"On a first date," I added softly, tracing the dojo's brick exterior with my fingertips and trying to make out the vague, sweet scent of something blooming.

The once exuberant posters in the window of the Indian travel agent next door had faded to various shades of blue in the street-lights, making every destination look vaguely intergalactic. We'd both parked on the street, and though it was mostly deserted now, my little Cabrio, Cecil, was invisible tucked in front of Glenn's ginormous dark tank. Glenn reached out as we drew alongside his truck and gently held my arm to stop me. "How are you holding up?"

"Well," I said, turning to him, "Mike and I have been out a few more times, and we have plans for this weekend, so no real harm done."

Glenn shook his head. "I'm not talking about your goddamn love life. I'm talking about what's in here," he said, tapping a finger to my temple.

I resisted the temptation to lean into his touch, replying, "I'm fine."

"Uh-huh," he said, nodding, suddenly finding the pavement beneath us very interesting. "Did you tell him?"

"Tell him what?" It took me a moment to clue in (*oh, about our relatively recent absolutely illegal excursion that resulted in a dead bad dude but a still living us*). Blood and heat rushed to my face. "Is that what this is all about? You're afraid I'll *rat you out*?"

Glenn pressed his palm against the passenger door, my instinct said to prevent him from punching it. "You're the most goddamned, hardheaded... do you really think that? After everything we've been through, do you really think I'm worried about covering my own ass?"

"No," I admitted, my facial flush transitioning to one of guilt. Which is just as red as indignation, but not nearly as righteous.

"I'm not even saying you shouldn't tell him," Glenn said, leaning against the truck. "But be careful. Always consider the consequences a step past where you think you need to. I'm just trying to watch out for you, Syd. You're like the kid sister—"

"You had a wild night of passion with?" I asked, forehead wrinkling, voice faux confused.

A soft laugh fought through his mustache. "Yeah. I realized that wasn't the best metaphor as soon as it left my mouth. But you know what I mean."

I scooted next to him, resting my backside against the truck. "I do. Back at you, big guy."

We stood in companionable silence, nodding at Vince and Maria as they left the dojo together. Vince wasn't much taller than Maria, who was in the neighborhood of my own modest height. Both had dark hair, but Maria's tended to curl, and a few waves crossed her face as she leaned slightly toward Vince.

"What do you think?" I asked softly. I had the impression Vince and Maria had been spending a lot of time together lately.

"I think I maintain good relationships with my friends by not getting involved in their love lives," Glenn said.

His voice was even, but I thought I heard a hint of reticence that was not theoretical in nature, something specific to Maria. Maybe because she had a law enforcement background she never talked about. She was just as close-mouthed about her current job, which was probably still as a law enforcement officer. Glenn had a complicated relationship with LEOs, and the law in general.

Come to think of it, that relationship meant he often had good insights—or actual information—about other people who shared complicated relationships with the law.

"So I'm looking for this kid," I said.

"Go on."

"A teenaged runaway, in Tallahassee with an older boyfriend—"

"How much older?" Glenn interrupted.

My mouth twisted. "I don't know. I just got the case today, and I haven't decided whether to take it or not—"

"Ha!" he boomed.

I rolled my head on my shoulders, stretching out my neck, and didn't bother arguing. "I haven't had a chance to track down his particulars yet, but my impression is early twenties. He might be using or dealing, but if so, I'd say he's a bit player. Either way, they're up from Ocala, so he'll want to hit the party scene."

"And you want to know where they'll go," Glenn finished.

"The big man isn't just a pretty face," I said.

"Indeed," he replied, and I smiled as he smoothed his mustache ostentatiously, the moisture in his eyes and sweat at his temples reflecting the nearest streetlamp. "I can pretty well guarantee I won't be seeing your guy at Cooper's, but beyond that, it depends on whether he has connections. If he doesn't, he'll probably be like any other young man with more testosterone than sense and go for the flash."

That made sense to me.

Bars in Tallahassee occur in clusters, like an infectious disease. Some cater to the wine-and-cheese crowd (adults associated with state government and in denial about living in a college town), but more serve the I-swear-I'm-21 crowd. Although young when I moved to Tallahassee, I'd been past the first flush of legal drinking, so I didn't know the scene very well. Glenn suggested a couple of clusters, one almost equidistant from the Florida State University and Florida A & M campuses, and another out on Tennessee Street that made me shudder. It was an area of town I avoided.

"Don't suppose you'd want to go with me?" I asked.

He leaned in and raised his caterpillar brows. "You really think anyone will talk while I'm hanging over your shoulder?"

"Good point," I admitted reluctantly. More than a decade older than me and much scarier (imagine that, a grizzled biker dude who's scary), Glenn didn't exactly fit the club demographics. I pushed off the truck to stand on my own two feet. "All right, I gotta go."

"I hope you're headed for your refrigerator," Glenn said, circling his truck as I fumbled to get in my little hatchback. He continued, "Little as you are, you still scare me when you're hungry."

I tossed off a quick one-finger salute and heard his rumbling chuckle as I closed the door behind me.

3

Glenn was right about one thing. Okay, two things. I am scary when I'm hungry (though I won't cop to being "little"). And I hadn't admitted it to anyone other than myself, but I'd decided to take the case. *Conditionally*. If Roger later advised that the fires of hell would rain down upon me (or the fires of State Attorneys or ethics boards—same diff), I would listen to him. But in the meantime, some cursory digging couldn't hurt.

The next morning, I started by reviewing the material Mr. Spencer had given me. His niece's good-for-nothing boyfriend was, as expected, good for nothing. Fortunately for his niece, the guy wasn't exactly a kingpin, either. I ran a background check on Troy Cantrell and came up with a few possibilities, but only one that fit the demographics and location. He had a few arrests, including a trespassing, but nothing too serious. The only drug charge that had stuck was a misdemeanor possession.

I explored a few more digital avenues for both Addy and Mr. Good-for-Nothing Cantrell, as well as doing a cover-my-ass background check on my potential clients, the Spencers. There were no big revelations on any front, no screen flashing SHE IS HERE or BEWARE, THEY ARE PSYCHOPATHS. When my eyes began crossing, I transitioned to abusing my phone ear instead. I checked the local hospitals and put in a call to a friend with the police department. Addy Hastings wasn't being treated for anything catastrophic, nor was she in custody. Though I was beginning to feel like I was.

Too much office time always makes me antsy. An agitated hum vibrated through me, knocking everything just a bit off true. I hopped in Cecil and headed to the office supply store for some color copies of Addy's picture before making the rounds of the shelters.

The admin types at those facilities tended to be pretty close-mouthed about their clientele, but a few people were willing to talk with me. Having a background with the Public Defender's Office rather than law enforcement probably didn't hurt, nor did the fact that I was looking for a minor. Still, no one on staff admitted to recognizing her. I'd come back another day if necessary to talk to the "residents" with a plan of approach and possibly some help.

The hours slipped away without me eating lunch, and I settled for a late-day, freezer-burned burrito back at my office. The paper towel I'd wrapped the burrito in to nuke it had adhered to the last cheesy-beany chunk. I was picking at it, trying to work out how hungry I still was and whether it was worth the effort or the extra fiber, when I heard the metallic rattle of someone fighting my sticky screen door.

Cool air rushed inside as Roger opened the front door, then wrestled the screen door behind him until it was flush with the doorframe. He moved slowly, sweeping the room with bloodshot eyes that rested atop heavy bags.

I can count the number of times Roger has dropped by my office on one hand.

"So," he said, "this is your office?"

Maybe less than one hand.

I waved him to a chair with a Vanna White flourish before carrying the burrito bit to my kitchen trash, where it dropped with a size-appropriate thunk. "Can I get you anything?" I called out.

He didn't answer, but shook his head when I asked again on my return. "Are you alright?" I asked.

"Yeah, I just—" He stopped, rubbing his hands over his face as if to get the feeling back to a numb limb. He wore his usual work attire of a stylish suit whose provenance was lost on me. But like last night, the knot of his tie had inched away from his collar, and his hand crept up to loosen it more. "Honestly, Sydney, I could use some help."

"Okay," I said slowly, trying not to let my imagination get the best of me. Roger and I had worked on some challenging cases together, and it was hard not to wonder what would affect him this way.

He took a deep breath. "First, though, your runaway. We might have to get creative, but if we're careful, we should be able to take the case."

"We?" I asked. Roger rarely used pronouns—or any other words—without intention.

"I have some ideas about her situation, when you track her down. If the aunt and uncle are interested." I raised a brow, and he raised one right back at me, asking, "Did you tell Mr. Spencer you'd take the case?"

I glanced at the clock, realizing I was almost out of afternoon to do so. I called Mr. Spencer's cell phone, but there was no answer. I left a message on his voicemail, asking him to get in touch about a contract.

"Done," I said, turning my attention back to Roger. "So what is it I can help you with?"

He looked away before admitting, "My father is dying."

I reached across the desk to take his hand, but Roger leaned back, as if anticipating comfort and avoiding it. "I'm so sorry, Roger."

He nodded and met my eyes, but couldn't hold them. "It's been coming on for a while. That's why I had you track down Deidre's friend."

Deidre was Roger's sister and a former exotic dancer, as was the friend I'd located a couple of months ago. I'd never actually met Deidre, but I had borrowed one of her gowns for a fancy, work-related evening with Roger.

"Do you need me to find Deidre?" I asked.

He shook his head. "No. She's staying with me now, and she's seen him. I actually need you to talk with my dad."

I pretended not to notice when his voice cracked. "Sure, I can do that. When?"

"Now?" he asked.

I took a moment to survey the stacks on my desk and in my head. The latter were bigger, but there was nothing that couldn't wait until tomorrow. "Okay," I said, "let's go."

4

We took Roger's car. He admitted he didn't know when he'd last eaten, so I made him stop around the corner for a sandwich and we both grabbed some coffee. I offered to chauffeur, but the food and caffeine had kicked in enough by then for Roger to respond with stink-eye.

He is very protective of his car. Even drinking coffee inside it was pushing my luck.

Roger's father was residing in a hospice facility toward Thomasville, on the Florida side of the Florida-Georgia state line. Traffic was sluggish in downtown Tallahassee, but the worst of the evening commuter traffic wouldn't start for another half hour. Once we hit Thomasville Road, extra lanes dropped in and out like hungry pigeons at Lake Ella. These facilitated turning into an odd assortment of pale-brown brick office complexes, fast-food joints, and quick-oil-change parking lots nestled among ubiquitous green trees and shrubs.

The road settled into two lanes in each direction with a crepe myrtle-lined median down the middle. We passed through walls of indistinguishable green vegetation, anchored by larger, more established trees. Occasional breaks revealed houses or churches, and power lines traced delicate lines through the branches like deadly webbing.

Roger said, "So you know about Deidre, and you met Bridget—"

"Pixie Cut?" I asked, remembering an Amazon in boots and leggings who had once answered Roger's door. Pixie Cut was a pretty restrained name, considering what other physical assets were first to jump out at you. So to speak.

Roger glanced at me. "Yes, Bridget had a pixie cut when you met her. You know I have a lot of sisters."

"More sisters than ex-wives," I noted.

The rigid line of Roger's jaw made it clear my conversational interruptions were wearing on him. Damn caffeine. "Sorry," I said. "Go on. I'll shut up now."

He clenched his hands on the steering wheel and released them before continuing. "I grew up in foster care, like your runaway. I had a few short-term placements before I got lucky and landed with Amos Weber and his wife Loretta. They adopted me, along with Deidre and Bridget and several other children."

"I hope they had a big house," I said.

Roger smiled and finally began to relax, his shoulders easing away from his chin as he spoke. "They did, but it was still packed to the gills. And everyone trying to get to the bathroom... Dad had an extra one put in, but it was still a zoo. Ten kids—"

"Ten kids?" I asked, in disbelief.

"More than that in total, but I don't think we ever had more than ten at one time. We lived in a rural area on well water, and Dad always complained we'd run it dry, a house full of teenagers."

Roger signaled before turning onto a long, paved driveway. The entrance was flanked by a couple of live oaks, Spanish moss swaying. An egret stood alongside a small, man-made water feature, and a white-columned, red-brick building was just visible in the distance.

"Dad never yelled at us," Roger continued. "He's a gentle man, a softy. Mom was the disciplinarian. She passed away about five years ago. Even then, I knew there was something bothering Dad, something he didn't want to talk about but needed to."

We passed the brick building and continued to a mostly empty parking area, asphalt interrupted by the occasional small tree or shrub on the verge of flowering. Roger chose a spot away from the other cars and cut the engine.

"Now that he's so close, it's haunting him. Like it's his last chance to set it right." He unbuckled his seat belt and stared as a squirrel swished its tail on a nearby tree.

"Do you know what *it* is?" I asked.

"No," Roger admitted.

We crossed the parking lot to a building whose interior was as soothing as its landscaped exterior. The lighting was warm, as were the honey-toned hardwood floors and scattered rugs. An open area beyond reception had a fireplace (not lit at the moment) and comfortable furniture that could have come from someone's home. A television flickered through a window in a room off to the right, but the closed door kept its sounds inside.

The reception area was defined by a large, oval, wood-topped counter that reminded me of the check-in for a fine hotel. A black woman, early thirties like me, wearing a long-sleeved blouse appropriate for air conditioning, sat behind it.

"Hello, Roger," she said, as he signed us in.

"Hello, Dot. How is he?"

Her voice was kind—almost apologetic—as she said, "No change."

Roger nodded his thanks. "We'll find our own way back."

I followed him to a tiled hallway, and we paused before a door about halfway down the corridor. Roger took a deep breath before knocking, then led me in.

The elderly man in the bed had a face so ashen, I considered calling for a nurse, until his eyes opened and moved between Roger and me. He wore navy pajamas in a style that reminded me of old movies, button-front with a chest pocket and piped edges. A tube ran from an IV stand alongside his bed to his left arm. Whatever was in his IV probably accounted for the veneer of puffiness that lay across his otherwise sunken frame.

Roger pushed a button to raise his father to an almost sitting position, then brought a cup of water with a straw to his lips. His father sipped and cleared his throat.

"Thank you, son," he said, then looked past Roger to me. "You must be the infamous Sydney Brennan."

He inclined his head slightly toward a chair next to his bed, and I sat down carefully, afraid the vibrations would somehow cause his frail body pain.

"Please, call me Sydney," I said. "But I wouldn't believe everything Roger tells you."

He returned my smile and said, "If you think he's creative with the truth now, you should have seen him as a child."

"Destined to be a lawyer," Roger said, as if he were finishing a familiar punchline.

The elder Mr. Weber nodded. "Why don't you see if you can find Sydney something to drink?" Roger left without objection, and Mr. Weber continued, "Damned fine lawyer, too, but his head's too big already. Of course, I guess you know that."

"Agreed on both counts," I said, folding my hands in my lap to stifle the inclination to take his.

"Good. He needs people around him that'll keep him grounded." Mr. Weber paused a moment to get his breath. "He says you helped him find Deidre."

I hadn't done much except track down an old friend of his sister's at a strip club, but I nodded. "She's been to see you?"

"Roger brought her by yesterday. You know, he didn't have it easy growing up, even after he came to us. He was always trying to watch over the rest of the kids." He grinned. "We called him our little sheepdog. He still does that. Makes him a little high-handed sometimes, thinking he knows what's best for everyone else."

I considered Roger's three divorces. "I imagine his wives haven't appreciated it."

He chuckled. "No, they haven't. But it comes from a good place."

Mr. Weber closed his eyes against some unseen pain, and I suppressed the desire to offer him something, anything that might help. Instead I waited. Addressing the reason he'd asked Roger to bring me here would do more to ease his passing than any narcotic. Within a minute or two, he'd recovered enough to continue. He fixed his eyes on my face with the intensity of a man about to secure a promise, a dying man at that.

"Sydney, I have a terrible secret that I can't let die with me. But I know Roger. This knowledge will consume and destroy him. That's where you come in. We just met, and you don't owe me anything, but will you help Roger do what he can?"

My tongue stuck to the roof of my mouth, and he pressed, "Will you keep my son safe?"

A smarter woman would hedge, at least find out what this was all about. But being smart didn't matter. Closure did.

The parabolic glow from a tabletop lamp against walls the color of mild honey held us in a warm cocoon, as if no one else existed in the world. I reached for Mr. Weber's hand, careful of the IV. "I'll do my best."

He sighed and closed his eyes. "Thank you. Then you can get Roger."

On my way to the door, I heard Mr. Weber mutter behind me, "God forgive me, but we'll finally put them to rest."

ROGER FOLDED his suit coat over the chair by his father's head, and I took the next seat. Mr. Weber relaxed into his pillow and let his eyes drift into the middle distance. Into the past.

"I was working for a mechanic when Loretta and I got married," Mr. Weber said. "But my boss had a drinking problem, and I wasn't sure how long he'd be able to keep his shop going. The juvenile facility over near Vicksburg was looking for help—this would have been the early sixties. I can't say it was my first choice, but with a wife to support and high hopes for a family, I did what I had to do.

"I worked there for almost four years. And I saw a lot of things..." He paused, cleared his throat, then took a sip of water Roger offered before continuing. "It's true that power corrupts. There were men I was sure I knew, and knew what they were capable of, until they put on that uniform and proved me wrong. Now I'm not saying everybody was a bunch of psychos, but there were more people turned dark by that place than I ever would've imagined."

"What age range were the children?" Roger asked, voice soft.

Mr. Weber glanced at him briefly before turning his gaze away again, as though embarrassed. "Almost every age. I remember a little boy there once that was nine years old, but I'd say most were around eleven to sixteen. Once they hit the top end, they were putting them in adult prisons. And it was all boys. Which isn't to say they didn't have a place for girls—we just weren't it. Thank God, because I hate to think what would've happened to girls.

"But I didn't know what all was happening for a long time. Maybe I just didn't want to know, but I do think people hid it, knew I wouldn't approve. The duty roster, for example. They were careful about who they assigned me to work with and when."

"So this was something that went up the line?" Roger asked calmly, more like he was interviewing a witness than speaking with his dying father. "Not just a few bad apples rotting on the ground."

Mr. Weber's eyes finally focused on his son's face. "Oh yeah," he nodded. "I'm pretty sure it went all the way up the line. To the top, or darn near it."

Perhaps Roger knew some of the background already or was just speaking a shorthand with his father. Either way, I needed the men to be more explicit. "Mr. Weber, what went all the way up to the top? What was happening?"

He blew out his breath, then rubbed eyes that had started to tear. "We're talking about seriously hurting kids, maybe even killing them."

Roger leaned back in his chair, jaw working, but I moved closer, placing a palm on the edge of Mr. Weber's bed near his blanket-covered hip. "How were they hurting them?"

"The whole system was set up to hurt them. There was no question of rehabilitation except on paper. It was basically a work camp, with children providing free labor. Of course, so long as they were being taken care of, back then most folks probably wouldn't have objected to the children earning their keep." A sad smile touched the edge of his gray lips. "At least, that's what I told myself."

"But the working conditions were bad?" I asked, ignoring the voice screaming in my head, *What are good working conditions for a nine-year-old?*

Mr. Weber made a frustrated noise. "It was too hot to be out in the fields in the middle of the day, they weren't given enough water or food, and the discipline..."

He broke off, tried to sit straighter. "See, I didn't know. I usually worked on the main grounds around the administration building and the classroom—they did have *one* of those—so I didn't see what went on at the farm. Until one day, somebody called in sick and I drew the short straw. I like to thought I'd collapse out there, and *I* wasn't doing anything but standing around. My supervisor was not happy when I fetched more water for the kids, and the boys acted like they were afraid to thank me. At the end of the day, I went to the director—they never called him a warden, because that's not a *rehabilitation* type word—and told him what was going on."

"Were you reprimanded?" Roger asked.

"Not that time, not officially," his father said. "The director thanked me for my input, and I wasn't assigned to the farm again. But I heard plenty from the other officers, mostly that I needed to keep my GD mouth shut."

Under other circumstances, I would have smiled to hear Mr. Weber's coded profanity, considering what I'd heard from his son's mouth in the past. Instead, I brought us back to, "What did you mean about the kids' *discipline*?"

Mr. Weber's eyes drifted to the ceiling. I wondered if he'd answer or he'd relived as much as his heart could take, just as a nurse stuck her head in at the door. Mr. Weber ignored her, and she left us in peace at some nonverbal signal from Roger.

Then Mr. Weber continued. "There was another place they kept me away from, besides the farm. They told everyone the infirmary was off-limits because the sick kids could be contagious, or we could make them sick, or some such foolishness that seemed plausible enough at the time. Until that day in the fields, when I watched children bake and started looking around with fresh eyes."

Mr. Weber began coughing again, this time in earnest, simultaneously dry and hacking and full of phlegm. Full of pain. I winced to hear it and said, "I can come back again tomorrow."

"I don't have many tomorrows left," Mr. Weber said, shaking his head and sipping the water Roger offered. He breathed shallowly, the way you do when you're afraid you're going to start coughing again. "I waited about a week for things to die down before I went to the infirmary. Not sneaking, just walking in like I had business being there. No one challenged me. And that's where I saw the bad cases—the boy who lost a toe to a piece of machinery. The one who wheezed worse than you'll ever hear me, and I'm a dying man. And the one who... Well, there's no other way to put it. He'd been beaten within an inch of his life."

"For what?" Roger asked sharply.

"Depends who you ask," Mr. Weber said, grimacing. "A nurse tried to tell me he'd been in an accident. One of the other officers said he'd ratted out his buddies and they'd beaten him for it. I wasn't about to ask the child—even if he could speak, I sure as heck didn't want to put him in more trouble than he already was."

Mr. Weber smiled at Roger. "Your mother always was the brains of the operation. I'd held my tongue until then, but that night I told her everything. Together, we decided that I should go to the sheriff, job or no."

My stomach rolled with a bit of nausea around the edges. I had a bad feeling about what came next, like I'd heard this story before. Mr. Weber read more in my face than he should have after an hour's acquaintance.

"Uh-huh," he acknowledged. "You know what happened. First the sheriff said I must be mistaken. I told him I'd be happy to show him what I'd seen, and he changed tactics. Said he'd talk to the director and get to the bottom of it, nobody wanted a child punished who didn't deserve it. When I said no child could have deserved such a beating, he said that was awfully naïve for a man in my job. And if I wanted to stay in that job, I'd best be figuring out how the world worked."

Roger stood abruptly and circled his chair, standing over it and gripping its back. "Bet that went over well with Mom."

Mr. Weber tried to smile, but his lower lip trembled slightly. "Normally I'd have been pulling her off the man's back. But she was pregnant then. Her second time. That's why I'd waited to tell her what was going on as long as I did. She was still teaching then, too, and it was almost summer break. We figured we'd wait, see if the sheriff would do the right thing. For a while, it seemed like he might have done. I didn't get near the infirmary again, but everyone treated me polite enough, even if they were standoffish. I really thought it was okay."

Looking at his son, his eyes filled. "But it wasn't. A couple weeks later—it was toward the end of the day—my supervisor put me in a truck and we drove to another area of the property I'd never seen before."

Mr. Weber paused for breath. "It was all high grasses, and when we got out, my boss handed me a shovel. He told me to dig, and keep digging because..." He choked back a sob. "Because we had a boy to bury."

"Did you see the boy?" Roger asked.

Mr. Weber nodded. "Before they wrapped the sheet around for us to carry him, but I didn't recognize him. White boy, maybe twelve years old. The sheriff and the director brought him, saying he died of the flu, and I couldn't see a mark on him. But still... I asked if it was proper, burying him this way. They said he didn't have any family, and who else was supposed to bury him if not the state."

I looked away from the man and his grief, staring at the opposite wall to keep from crying myself.

"I might have believed them," he added, "if they hadn't lied to me so much already."

"So what did you do?" I asked.

"My mind was racing, deciding the best way to find out who the boy was and what had happened. But it didn't matter," he said, shaking his head as if he still couldn't believe it himself. "When I got back to the main building, they told me Loretta had been taken to the hospital. It was the baby, way too soon. The sheriff said he'd drive me, with lights and everything so we'd get there faster. But we were too late, she'd already lost our child. Again."

Elbows resting on his chair back, Roger dropped his head as his father continued.

"They kept Loretta overnight. The sheriff took me back to work for my vehicle, and he'd been all proper concern to that point. But when we got to the parking lot, he grabbed my arm as I was reaching for the door. Instead of something comforting, he says, 'Isn't life tragic. So many innocent lives just disappear. But y'all have another chance for a family. *So long as your wife's still alive.*' It was obvious what he meant."

"Who was sheriff?" Roger demanded.

"He's dead now." Mr. Weber said. "Long dead, from a bad traffic stop. When I heard, I couldn't help thinking he'd finally got what was coming to him. But Loretta and I were gone by then. We put the house on the market, moved to Tallahassee, and never looked back."

The nurse who'd popped her head in earlier appeared at the door. Her hair was an odd shade of orange, but her freckled face was kind. "Mr. Roger, I think you've worn your daddy out enough for tonight, don't you?"

"He and the young lady were just about to leave," his father said, managing a smile until she reluctantly left. Then Mr. Weber told Roger, "I've wondered almost every day since if that boy had family after all, people that never got to stand over his grave and say good-bye. I don't know what can be done for him or them, after so long. But I do know if anyone can figure it out, son, it's you."

5

I slipped my arm through Roger's free one as we crossed the parking lot. He didn't object. When we reached the car, he turned and leaned against its metal body.

Roger is not the leaning on cars type. Not even his own immaculate BMW.

I stared at his profile, trying to make out his expression in the fading light. "Your dentist is going to have words with you the next time you see him."

"You think?" he asked absently, before he resumed grinding his teeth.

Roger turned to me, dark brows pinched together, stark against his pale face. *Determined.* That was the word I was looking for.

"You sure you want to be part of this?" he asked. "You don't owe him—or me—anything."

"Really?" I said, trying to make my voice light. "I'll remember that the next time I call, asking for a favor."

"I'm serious, Sydney," Roger said.

"I know," I said. "Don't be a dumbass."

He glared at me, pretending anger. Well, *mostly* pretending. I raised a brow, and he gave in, mouth curling. To my surprise, he pulled me close and pressed me to his chest. Roger is not a huggy person. Neither am I particularly. But for novices, we faked it pretty well.

Face against his dress shirt, I decided Roger did have a gym membership after all, and he got to the gym much more regularly than I did (if you can properly make a comparison between any number and *never*). The silk of his tie was cool on my cheek. And he smelled good. Not organic hippie deodorant exactly, but not the manufactured chemical fakery of cologne, either.

"Are you sniffing me?" he asked.

"Would that be inappropriate?"

"Just a little," he said, releasing me.

"Then no, of course I'm not," I said.

Once in the car, he proffered a notebook his father had given him before we left. It was thin, spiral-bound and lined, the kind you see on sale in office supply stores at the beginning of the school year. I held it to the window for better light, but only got as far as the first page. *Dear Roger*, it began. I slapped the thin cardboard cover closed, thankful the darkness had kept my eyes from taking in any more, and handed it back to him.

"This is not for my eyes," I said.

Roger turned on the dome light to read. His breath caught, and I looked away. But I heard him flipping through the pages. A few seconds later, he said, "Here."

It took a while for my eyes and brain to calibrate to Mr. Weber's cursive handwriting, slightly slanted with distinctively simple capital W's, like inverted McDonald's signs. Maybe because it was one of the letters Mr. Weber had to capitalize the most. It was a list of names and titles, and the first name was Wilbur something (was that a *T* or an *F*?). Wilbur was identified as the Director of the Florida Youth Reform School. Next to his title in block capital letters was noted: DEAD.

We didn't have a name for the boy or, decades after his death, any easy way to get one. We did have a date of death, or at least an approximate one. Mr. Weber had remembered the day they'd lost their second child, as well as the first one. "How do you want me to start?" I asked.

He laid his head against the rest and closed his eyes. "I don't know," Roger said. "But we have to prioritize."

"Like a death warrant," I said. I hadn't worked many, but Roger had done plenty, and it was a shared context for a case short on time and high on stakes. Still, I regretted the words as soon as they left my mouth.

Roger opened his eyes, calmly met mine (*determined*), and said, "Exactly."

"Okay, then. I'll hit the newspaper archives, public records—the usual. See if I can get a line on the kid. And I'll work my way through the personnel list, from the top down. When I do find someone, you want me to approach or wait for you?"

"I'll do it myself," he said. "You just track them down."

Uh-huh, I thought. *That's what you think.* But I nodded, and Roger drove me back to my office.

It was true dark by the time we arrived downtown. Roger pulled off the street, up my office driveway so he was blocking my car. "You want to wait while I copy the list?" I asked.

"No," he said. "I have some other things to take care of tonight. I'll get the notebook from you later."

I opened the door, but paused when he spoke again.

"Listen," he said, "about our runaway."

I wasn't sure when she'd become *our* runaway, but I prompted him, "Yes?"

"The next time you talk to your client, ask if they'd like to file for custody."

I blinked in the cool air that rushed in through the gaping passenger door. For someone with no background in family law, Roger was awfully eager to open up a big, stinking can of it. "He said they'd like to give her a home. But why file for custody now?"

"It's a long-game strategy, helps us cover our asses," he said. "Gives us a little more control, or at least makes it so we're not the ones reacting."

Pleadings and hearings popped into my head, each one replaced by another, and another, but there was no way I could follow them to Roger's endgame. I didn't need to; I trusted him. But I also knew him.

"And what else?" I asked, leaning toward him.

His head backed away automatically, and he came dangerously close to blushing. Or so it appeared in the harsh, artificial light inside the car.

"And it sounds like it's the best thing for them and the kid," he admitted.

I patted his retreating face a tad harder than necessary. "Roger Weber, I do believe you're getting soft in your old age."

"You're not exactly made of granite yourself," he countered.

I shrugged, then shivered as I stepped out into the chilly night and watched him slowly back down onto the street, probably on his way back to his office. Not that I could talk. I was now working two cases on a short clock, with two kids on my mind. It was time to find the living one.

6

I hadn't spoken to Addy's friend yet, but while I was out, I'd gotten an email from the girl with the recent photo of Addy and her boyfriend. My pitiful color office printer made them both look jaundiced, but at least it was recent. Time to hit the clubs.

It was early enough to get decent parking and walk in without a cover charge at the first club in the Tennessee Street cluster, which meant it was too early for anyone I was looking for to be there. I did a quick walk-through anyway, familiarizing myself with the layout, especially the bathrooms and exits. A few young men huddled by the bar, but most of the space was taken up by a loud dance floor, which was slightly sticky and now eerily empty. The blasted 80s pop still rang in my ears when I returned to my car.

I did the same at two more clubs before I decided I'd hit the wall. I couldn't imagine how miserable I'd be when I actually had to contend with patrons and sloshing drinks. Still, it was time for my reward.

The crowd at my favorite by-the-slice pizza place was thick, but nothing like the typical lunch mob. I let my mind and eyes wander as I stood in line. It was a mixed clientele—not entirely overrun by college kids—and relatively well-behaved, though I could feel the energy escalating. The music in the background was alternative rock and a little loud for conversation, but nowhere near as deafening as the dance music had been at the clubs.

I perched on a stool at the bar with my mushroom and olive pizza (a slice as big as my head) and a glass of golden craft beer, enjoying the carbs and anonymity. About a third of the way through, I dropped my slice on my round, metal tray.

No way...

I leaned sideways for a better look, nearly flipping my stool because my feet didn't touch the ground.

Yes, way...

The investigator gods were smiling upon me. Sitting around the corner of the half-square bar was a young woman that looked suspiciously like the Addy Hastings in my photo. Minus the jaundice. She wore an oversized sweatshirt over faded jeans, no makeup, and a backpack sat on the floor by her feet. She sat alone, eating a slice of pepperoni with a can of Coke, and there was an empty seat next to her.

I grabbed my own dinner and weaved through the crowd. "This seat taken?" I asked.

She glanced at me like she wanted to say something smart-assed, and in that moment I knew it was Addy. Her face was leaner now, more adult, but its expression was so like the one caught by the camera in Mr. Spencer's picture that I felt a moment of déjà vu. Instead of a kitten, her attention returned to blotting her pizza with a napkin and she said, "No."

"Good," I said, settling next to her. "That guy over there kept accidentally brushing my ass every time he walked by. I mean, come on— how many times do you have to get up to check on your order?"

I felt bad throwing a stranger under the bus, but since I didn't specify which guy, the skeeziness was evenly diffused among everyone at the table I'd indicated. Each man was only a third of a skeeze. And it was in service of a good cause.

I tucked back into my slice, but kept dropping vegetable chunks on my lap while surreptitiously watching Addy. Her hair was still long, but she'd hacked some random layers into the front. It was also still brown, except where it was streaked with blue. Bluish-gray, really.

"What do you call that color?" I asked.

"Brown," she said, around a bite.

As I'd suspected, a smart-ass. My voice was flat with restraint as I clarified, "The other color."

"Distressed denim."

"Seriously?" I asked, getting into character. Fortunately I'd dressed casually. Jeans. Plain V-neck T-shirt under the button-down flannel I'd thrown on when it got cool. Boots.

She looked down at my feet, as if I'd given the universe—and her —a nudge. "Nice boots," she said, with genuine appreciation.

My friend Noel had given me grief for wearing the same boots to Cooper's a month or so ago. Brown leather, western style.

"Thanks," I said, pulling my pants leg higher to better admire them. "I lived in New England for a while. Took off when I broke up with my boyfriend. But it was almost worth staying, just so I could own a closet full of boots and actually wear them ten months out of the year."

She nodded, sipping her Coke through a straw tucked in the can. "I have friends who wear boots to—"

To school was my guess, but she caught herself, continuing after a brief pause.

"To work or out to clubs or wherever, with short shorts. I'm sorry, but that just looks stupid. Like you're trying out a new stripper act or something."

"True." I added, "I bet their feet reek, too."

Addy snorted. "Yeah. And their boots stink up the house. But they won't leave them outside because they're afraid something will crawl in them. Morons."

I tipped my glass high and watched the last foamy trickle of beer before it hit my thirsty tongue, then pointed at my plate. "You mind watching this while I get a glass of water?"

She shook her head and declined my offer to get her one. I meandered around the bar to the self-serve water station, surveying the restaurant the whole way. No sign of the no-good boyfriend Troy Cantrell. I chugged some water, deliberately splashing my sleeve when I refilled. Grabbing a stack of napkins, I blotted my cuff while heading toward a trash can by the door. No sign of the loser in the parking lot, either.

I reclaimed my stool with a sigh, only to realize I had to pee. No wonder—I'd just drunk a gallon of water on top of my beer. But my bladder would have to wait.

Addy ignored me, as though whatever camaraderie we'd established had withered in my brief absence. "So," I said, biting into my now-cold pizza, "what brings you to Tallahassee?"

She flashed wary eyes at me. Then she tried to look cool, but she didn't have enough maturity or experience at duplicity to pull it off. "What makes you think I'm not from here?"

"The way you keep staring at your pizza," I said, "like you're wondering if you stepped through a doorway into another dimension without realizing it."

"I have never seen a slice of pizza this big," Addy admitted, with a hint of child-like wonder.

"You know, they could fit a body in the oven, lying flat," I said.

Her eyes twinkled, forecasting a bit of snark. "Your body, maybe."

I ignored the urge to smack the little twerp and instead noted, "You're not exactly Manute Bol yourself."

"Who?"

I rolled my eyes. "A very tall dude who used to play basketball."

I took another sip of water, slowly, as though it were another beer and I was deciding whether it was too fancy-crafty for my plebeian palate. Really, I was wondering how I'd gone into this situation with no plan whatsoever. Obviously I never thought I'd run into the girl. But now that I had...

"I've always had a soft spot for really tall guys I look ridiculous standing next to," I confessed. "So how tall is the boyfriend who brought you here? The one you really want to ditch but haven't worked out how to do it yet."

With that comment, I blew past her being wary of me and into I'm-about-to-kick-you-and-run territory. Her eyes and mouth narrowed, a perfect visual representation of anger on a nonverbal communication flashcard. With a dash of fear. "Are you a cop?" she asked.

"Why? Are there cops looking for you?" I asked, matter-of-fact.

"No!" she protested, looking around involuntarily. As though she thought there could be.

Interesting.

"Good, because I'm not a cop."

She crumpled her napkin in her hand and squeezed it tightly. "Then what are you?"

"Someone who can help."

She snorted with disbelief. "What's that mean, you're a perv?"

"No!" I yelled, an energetic echo of her protest a few moments ago. Fortunately, a loud pizza joint is one of the better places to have a heated discussion about law enforcement and perverts. I took a deep breath, reminding myself not to let a teenager push my buttons. Even though it is their natural superpower.

What was their kryptonite... Honesty? Hearing the truth from me might throw the kid off her game. I leaned in conspiratorially. "Do you know the Spencers?"

Her brows wrinkled as she tried to place the surname out of context. "You mean Aunt Deborah and Uncle Clint?"

"They're worried about you," I said. "They've been trying to see you, but your foster mother won't let them."

"Of course not, Sylvia is a bitch," Addy spat.

"Does she hurt you?" I asked.

"You sure you're not a perv?" she demanded, voice sharp.

I ignored her attempt at provocation. "You think she reported you missing?"

Another snort. "Yeah, right. Maybe eventually, to cover her ass. But so long as she keeps getting checks, she could give a shit where I am."

"Well, the Spencers do. They want to know you're safe, so they hired me to find you."

Her face softened, and she looked like the child she'd been... when? Last week? Five years ago? "Really?" she asked.

"Really."

"So you're what, a detective?"

"Sure," I said, not wanting to quibble over terms. Especially when the ten-year-old in me thrills at being called a detective.

"And you know how to find people?" she asked.

I nodded, pulled out a business card and wrote my cell phone number on the back before handing it to her. "Where's Troy?"

Addy tossed her balled-up napkin on her tray, but I caught it before it tumbled over the back of the bar. Don't want to trip the bartender with recycled paper.

"Troy's around," she said. "You know, doing his thing."

"And your fake ID wasn't good enough to join him?" I asked. "Or he didn't want you around?"

There was a bit of puffy pout to her angry bottom lip this time.

"Remember, I know how old you are," I said, setting her napkin ball next to my own tray. "And I've been around enough Troys to know his M.O."

"Yeah, well, you don't know everything," she muttered.

"Then tell me," I said, leaning on my elbow on the bar.

She was quiet for a while, picking at the sleeve of her sweatshirt. A thread came loose, and she pulled and twisted it into some kind of knot art. "So what am I supposed to do?"

"What do you want to do?" I asked. She seemed dumbfounded that anyone was actually asking her. I continued, "How do you feel about the Spencers?"

She stared down at her tray and picked at its edges. Which was good, because I wasn't sure how much more her sweatshirt could take. "They seem okay. A little boring."

"Boring isn't always a bad thing," I said, afraid my sister Lisa was possessing my body as I heard the words pass my lips.

I checked the FSU Seminoles clock high on the paneled wall

above us. We were edging toward ten p.m. Too late to really work anything out with the Spencers. And I didn't want to bother Roger again tonight if I could help it. But I sure as hell couldn't leave her with her adult boyfriend, not to mention I didn't trust my luck to randomly stumble across her again.

I swallowed hard and forced myself to say the words. "For tonight, you can go home with me."

She raised an eyebrow. "You sure about that?"

I sighed. "You can crash in my guest room and we'll figure it all out tomorrow."

Her smile was tentative, shy, and made her look younger again. "Okay. Since you *claim* you're not a perv, I guess that'll work."

I rolled my eyes.

"I just gotta pee first," she said, sliding off her stool and heading to the back.

I still needed to pee, too, but no way was I shutting myself in a stall and risking her making a break for it.

Since Addy wasn't there to do it, I picked at my pizza while I waited. It was okay, but it was so much better hot. Or maybe just the thought of sharing a bathroom with a teenager in the morning had put me off food.

I ate a few more bites, thinking about the mess that awaited me tomorrow. Checked the clock again. Stacked our trays. Checked the clock again. Did the math.

Addy was gone. I knew she was gone. I didn't know how, but she'd snuck out. *Sonuvabitch*. I'd been complacent because I was in a place I sort of knew, but didn't go to regularly.

I walked to the bathroom to make sure.

No sign of her. The little brat had played me.

I sighed. At least I knew she was okay and in town. And at least now I could pee.

7

T here wasn't much I could do the next morning to find Addy. I needed to talk with her friends and the substitute teacher, Ms. Hallway, but I couldn't very well do either during school hours. Nor was there an easy way to find where she was staying, since she and her boyfriend had probably crashed with his friends. In the unlikely event they went to one of the shelters, the various staff I'd spoken with knew she was a minor, so maybe they'd call me. If not me, perhaps they'd call law enforcement to cover their asses on a runaway. In other words, as much as I hated the thought, my best shot at finding Addy was to hit the clubs again tonight and find the boyfriend.

That meant, after wrapping up a few things on outstanding cases, I worked on Mr. Weber's mystery without guilt or distraction. I soon found myself thankful I hadn't indulged in more alcohol the night before. Computer record searches make up the bulk of my work, but that doesn't mean I have to enjoy them. And one thing that makes the monotonous clicking and scanning even less enjoyable is doing so with a hangover.

The Florida Youth Reform School was closed down in 1998. Mr. Weber was right about the former director being dead. Wilbur

Richard had overseen operations at the juvenile facility for nearly forty years but dropped dead of a heart attack in 1991 while still on the job and possibly under investigation. His name had appeared in a Gainesville newspaper article earlier that year about a young man who'd died at the facility under suspicious circumstances. The family alleged the boy had died as a direct result of not receiving medical treatment, but the exact illness or injury wasn't specified in the article. Either the investigation went nowhere, or the state had settled with the family to keep it quiet; I didn't see a follow-up article.

The reporter whose byline appeared on the story no longer worked at that paper, but they gave me the name of his new employer. I left a message for him there, but with no prior relationship, I wasn't holding my breath on a return call. I had a journalist friend I could contact if I got desperate, but for now I'd focus on talking to whomever was left who might have direct knowledge of the facility. I didn't have time for tangents.

Mr. Weber couldn't recall the name of the number two man when he'd worked there, nor was that man mentioned in the investigation article or any of the other handful of stories I could find about the facility. Many of Florida's smaller newspapers had slipped into obscurity without being digitized. Only the big boys (with national circulation) were digitized back as far as the decades that interested me. Better to go to the source.

The Florida State Archives was bound to have something about the facility, maybe even copies of their employment records. Plus Frank, the head librarian, had a soft spot for me. No food or beverages—or pens, for that matter—were allowed in the Archives, but I often smuggled him a macadamia nut cookie. I called and let him know what I was interested in, and he said he'd pull some things for me.

That set in motion, I glanced at my calendar... *dammit!* My chair spun away and slammed into a bookshelf as I jumped up, scrambling to pack up my laptop. I'd forgotten I had scheduled maintenance for Cecil, maintenance that would hopefully remedy the funny noise he'd been making lately.

My regular mechanic, a friend of my teenaged neighbor Ben, was off on some sort of cross-country adventure, so I'd made an appointment at one of the chain places based solely on the criteria that there was a cafe with wifi next door. In my experience, an appointment at a chain mechanic meant you were choosing whether to give up an entire morning or an entire afternoon; the actual reserved time was meaningless. Unless, of course, you were late.

Someone had parked a beater truck on the street with its nose poking past my office driveway. Poor Cecil rocked as I bumped over the curb to get around the truck, steering one-handed while the other was busy gesturing obscenely at the absent owner. I avoided the main thoroughfares of Monroe and Tennessee, knowing they'd be clogged like a fat man's arteries, and stuck to one-way streets tight with parked cars and occasional overhanging canopies. I was only three minutes late handing over my keys, but the young woman behind the desk still gave me stink-eye.

It was midday, so I gave her the benefit of the doubt and attributed her crankiness to low blood sugar. It certainly wasn't doing anything for my mood, so I walked next door and ordered a caprese sandwich and what looked like a gallon of iced coffee. The round table I'd chosen was a bit too close to the door and a smidge too small to be eating and working at the same time. I struggled to not drop chunks of tomato or basil on my keyboard. (My jeans would wash, and the local mozzarella was so good I'd be tempted to pick it up off the floor.)

I TRIED a few variations on my juvenile facility searches, but turned up nothing new. Now what? My fidgety fingers tapping the edge of the table drew an annoyed look from a college student in an FSU hoody sitting nearby. See, this is why I needed to eat regularly. Twenty minutes ago, I would have stuck my tongue out at her. Instead I stopped tapping, sighed, and stood to bus my plate. And collided with someone heading for the counter.

"I'm so sorry—" I began. But I recognized my victim.

John Driscoll's navy uniform was still crisp with the start of shift. He'd gotten a haircut since I'd last seen him, which made him look closer to mid-twenties than thirty. He bent to pick up my dropped napkin, and I saw the hair in back was buzzed close to his skull, a sheen of pale scalp peeking through the golden-brown stubble.

"Officer Driscoll," I said. "You're early, aren't you? Or have you switched over to days now?"

John's official, stern Tallahassee Police Department expression softened into a smile. "Ms. Brennan, I didn't know you ventured out in daylight, either. Hunting sleeping vampires?"

"Something like that," I said. "Can I buy you coffee by way of apology?"

He leaned toward me. "Don't tell anyone, but they usually comp my coffee."

"Then I'll save you from taking graft and contributing to the public perception of law enforcement corruption." I stifled a laugh when he frowned at my remark, and asked, "Hot or cold?"

After closing my laptop (a paranoid PI's habits die hard), I purchased a hot coffee every bit as ginormous as my iced one, and John joined me at my table.

"How's Emma?" I asked.

Emma was John's cousin, and coincidentally the friend of Deidre I'd tracked down for Roger a couple of months ago. John and I had first met during a nighttime traffic stop, but I'd unexpectedly bumped into him again while looking up his cousin.

"Emma's good." He sipped gingerly through his lid.

"She still dancing?" I asked casually.

"Yeah," he said, but couldn't help the slightest shake of his head. She may not be breaking any laws, but he still didn't approve of his cousin's profession. "So what's up, Sydney? Sorry, but I don't have much time."

I retrieved the picture of Addy and her boyfriend from my bag. "You ever see this guy?"

"Should I have?" he asked.

"Probably not," I admitted. "But I'm trying to track him down. He hasn't been in town long. Might be a small-time dealer, and I figured he'd probably hit the clubs to get the lay of the land. I was wondering if you could shorten my list of potentials."

"And you think I'd know the clubs because I'm gay?" he asked, a hint of Southern drawl coloring a voice that was just short of challenging.

"No," I said, dragging out the syllable as I would with a recalcitrant child, then teased him with, "I thought you'd know because you're young and pretty. But more importantly, because you mentioned once you used to be the TPD's go-to guy when it came to keeping an eye on the clubs."

John blushed and—shame on me—it just emphasized his hazel-green eyes and full lips and made him prettier.

"Right," he said. "If he's small-time, he's probably not hooked into the meth or heroin or one of those scenes. Not yet. You have a sheet of paper?"

I found an envelope (unpaid office electric bill—*note to self*) and pushed it and a pen across the table. John scribbled down four places.

"Those are your best bets," he said, sliding the envelope back to me. I held out my hand for the pen, and he added, "I wouldn't go super late. People are too messed up by closing to be counting real money. Can you read it?"

I skimmed quickly and nodded. "Thanks."

"No problem," he said. "What about the girl in the photo? Can't she give you a lead on him?"

Stupid! It never occurred to me that he'd ask about Addy, and I really did not need her on law enforcement radar. I shrugged, hesitant to lie to his face, and glanced at the wall clock behind the counter. "Don't you have to go?"

He slid his cuff to check his watch, then almost spilled his coffee lurching to his feet. "Hell, yes. Thanks for the coffee."

I nodded, then closed my eyes in relief. I had to be careful. I had a feeling that was my one lucky freebie, and keeping Addy secret wouldn't be so easy in the future.

8

A fter picking up my car, I drove straight to the Archives for my juvenile facility information.

The Florida State Archives, under the jurisdiction of the Florida Department of State, is responsible for the collection and preservation of historically significant records. That can include documents, photographs, videos, etc. (I like to imagine holograms stored there in the future.) They also act as the repository for post-conviction public records in capital cases, basically a neutral clearinghouse for *a lot* of boxes as the State and the Defense battle over information in death penalty appeals.

With such significant responsibilities, you'd think the Archives would have its own building, if not its own block. Instead, it shares one of the less attractive government buildings in our capital city with the State Library and the Museum of Florida History. The exterior is all hard right angles and square columns that feel more industrial than inspirational to me. But once inside, the broad, open lobby with its clean, modern lines always makes me feel underdressed and as if whispering is the only appropriate form of communication.

A woman wearing a long, dark skirt and a tawny cashmere

cardigan over a dress shirt (very crisp, unlike Frank, who has a perpetual rumpled air) informed me that Frank was out, but he'd left a fat packet for me. A handwritten note on scrap paper read: *There's much more where this came from, but I'm short on time and this will get you started. Let me know what else you need.* I paid for the copies, thankful he'd only *gotten me started* rather than loading me down. I knew Roger would reimburse me for expenses, but I didn't want to have to shove my tab in his face anytime soon. He had enough to worry about.

Back at my office, I found the packet contained a couple of typed reports and a stack of handwritten forms. The shorter of the typed documents was a photocopy of a legislative committee's report from the early 1930s. The longer one was from the Florida Sheriff's Bureau (FSB) in the early 1960s, just a few years before it was merged into the newly created (and still operating) state investigative agency, the Florida Department of Law Enforcement (FDLE). Both reports included an overview of the center's history.

The Florida Youth Reform School was created in the late 1800s, ostensibly as a center for rehabilitation. As Mr. Weber had said of its later years, rehabilitation was on paper only. In practice, it was a working farm and labor camp. Officers were sent to round up "incorrigible children" if they lacked enough hands to bring in the crops at harvest time. Children were also rented out to businesses as laborers on private farms and in local phosphate mines. It was quite the moneymaking scheme.

The 1930s visiting legislative committee reported boys as young as five years old being held in chains, that children were beaten and malnourished, and that the designated "classroom" contained no desks or instruction materials. And yet the facility remained open, despite one newspaper calling it a "holocaust" and a governor lamenting that if people knew what went on there, if it were *their own children* being held and treated that way, they would take up arms and storm the facility.

This pattern persisted throughout the facility's life, with someone pointing at the naked emperor's dangling bits every few decades, asking how long such cruelty could continue. I skimmed many of the allegations; they were so horrifying I couldn't take them all in. I'd read things as bad or worse in individual cases when I worked for the Public Defender's Office, but I'd never seen anything so systematized and on this scale.

Sometimes reforms were mandated by state or federal authorities, but they never seemed to take. The second report suggested instituting changes to make the facility more in line with the aim of the Florida Sheriffs Youth Ranches, created in the late 1950s to help troubled boys become responsible, productive citizens. But the Reform School's track record made me skeptical that any real progress was achieved.

Finishing the second report, I dropped my pen on my note-covered legal pad and went to splash water on my face. Revulsion twisted my guts and a grinding ache had settled in the middle of my forehead. I needed to take a break, and maybe vomit, before reviewing the remaining documents. I closed my eyes and sighed.

And before hitting the clubs looking for Addy Hastings.

Forget a break; I needed a vacation.

Since that wasn't happening, clothing more appropriate for hanging out with the flashy young people tonight was in order. (Nothing makes one sound quite so decrepit as using the phrase *flashy young people*.) If I went home, I knew I'd never leave again. Instead, I found a black tank top in my office that, after some tugging and rearranging, looked more like a camisole than lawn-mowing attire. I also discovered some hair product in the bathroom that may have come with the office, but hadn't gone totally crusty yet. It would have to do. Finally, I grabbed a watch from my desk drawer, my emergency timepiece for prison visits and surveillance.

It was cool outside, but not quite cold, so I drove with Cecil's windows down to avoid asphyxiation. The cabin was congested with a cloying scent from the repair place, a knock-off version of car dealer smell. Twilight had enveloped the city. Downtown's streetlights, evenly interspersed with symmetrical, dark-leaved trees, were relaxing. Unfortunately, much of the rest of the city alternated between blinding bright islands of consumerism and pools of undeveloped darkness. The strobe-like effect made my head ache even worse.

I didn't consciously choose to stop by Cooper's, didn't even realize I was there until the sound of the gravel parking lot beneath my tires cut through my brain fog. But it didn't exactly come as a surprise, either.

It was still early for the Thursday night crowd. The booths and pool tables were occupied, but there were free tables and open spots at the bar. Glenn was in his usual position behind said bar, his red flannel shirt hanging open over a white T-shirt, sleeves rolled up to his elbows. I suspected that kept stool occupation down, since most people with any sense were a little afraid of Glenn. Plus, the man didn't exactly want to hear your life history, or tell you his, for that matter. A touchy-feely bartender he was not.

Glenn's mustache rippled in his version of a smile when he saw me enter.

"Hello, darling," he said, as I climbed onto my semi-regular stool. "What can I get you? The usual?"

"Just a Coke," I said. He started to open his mouth again and I added, "Not corrected."

"You're no fun," his voice rumbled, as he brought me a cold can and a glass with ice.

"I have a long night ahead of me with no fun and as little drinking as possible," I said. He cocked his head, and I found myself blurting, "Am I old?"

Glenn froze and stared at me, mouth twitching and eyes crinkling like a bad-ass biker Santa. I could see his internal struggle—innuendo? Takedown? Sincere engagement? I waited, eyes narrowed, to see which he would choose.

"What catastrophe has befallen you to prompt such a question?" he asked, his voice the cadence of a southern Renaissance Fest knight.

Ahh, charming flirt. I'd forgotten that possibility and smiled despite the evening that lay ahead. "I've been outsmarted by a teenager," I admitted.

Glenn nodded along as I told him my story of the previous night's investigative triumph (fine, investigative *luck*) turned tragedy. When I'd finished, he grunted and said, "Sounds like somebody I know."

I snorted.

"Think about it," he said. "What were you like at that age?"

I rolled my eyes, but dutifully performed the math. Me at sixteen... it would have been the year after my brother Allan died.

My sister, Lisa, was away at her freshman year of college, so I rarely saw her. Looking back, she must have felt incredibly isolated, and I suspect she suffered from depression. But at the time I'd envied her. Living somewhere different, somewhere no one knew you, or thought they knew you. Somewhere you could be anyone. And somewhere away from our parents.

Not that I ever saw my father, retreating to his backyard workshop as soon as he'd changed out of his work clothes. When he did emerge, he was inevitably bleary-eyed and blind to everyone around him. His clothes hung loosely, his belt a necessity rather than fashion accessory. Not surprising, since I don't know what he ate; the three of us never sat down together for a meal. Occasionally we stumbled over each other in the kitchen, wordlessly, at the coffee pot.

That's the year I began drinking coffee in earnest.

And then there was my mother... My mother and I were locked in a world of cold silence, punctuated by fiery arguments. I mostly kept my head down in school, but passed my evenings with young Glenn wannabes, full of fresh tattoos and stale ideas. Within a few months, Mom sent me away, unable or unwilling to deal with me anymore.

In retrospect, her concerns weren't unreasonable. She was afraid I'd get knocked up, or end up in jail, or die in a fiery crash like my brother. I can forgive her for my exile. But even years after her death, I can't forgive her for the rhetoric that accompanied it. Words so cruel, I cannot fathom inflicting them on my worst enemy.

I'd been fidgeting at the bar with my thumbnail and looked up to find Glenn watching me. "Sorry," I said, rubbing my hand across the wood where I'd marked the finish.

"You okay?" he asked.

I nodded, afraid if I opened my mouth, I'd ask him to correct my Coke after all. Or just skip the Coke and hand me the bottle.

Glenn's hands disappeared beneath the bar, appearing a moment later with his bulk bag of wasabi peas. He set them on the bar, pushing the mass of thin plastic away from the opening, and motioned for me to precede him. I popped a few, and kept filling my mouth until the fire shot to my sinuses, triggering an unladylike sniff and damp eyes.

Who needs therapy when you've got wasabi peas?

Glenn took his turn, and I fancied I could feel his jarring crunches in my own jaws. I lost count at eleven peas. The man was a wasabi machine. "You'd left home by then, hadn't you?" I asked.

"You mean, had I found my second fucked-up family by the time I was sixteen?" He paused to wash down the peas with his own corrected soda. "Yes, I had."

"How long was your hair then? I don't suppose you have any pictures?" I asked, feeling puckish.

He glared, tossed back the rest of his drink and began chewing the ice.

"You ever end up in juvie?" I asked, reaching for more wasabi peas.

He grabbed the bag from me, almost snagging my hand, and tied the top before tucking them away in another dimension. "Is this your constitutional curiosity, or professional interest?"

"Both," I confessed, licking the fiery corners of my mouth. "I'm working on another case, one with connections to the Florida Youth Reform School. You spend any time there?"

"Thankfully, no. I was a wily little hellion. And that place wasn't exactly a summer camp. It had a reputation," he said, as he wiped our nonexistent crumbs from the bar.

"What kind of reputation?"

"You'd hear stories about guys going there and never being seen again. Bad shit happening that nobody wanted to talk about. But it's hard to say what was urban legend and what was actually the implementation of antiquated ideas of juvenile justice." His arm slowed, paused, and his brows wrinkled.

"What?" I asked.

He sighed. "I might know someone who was there."

"Someone from the bad old days?"

He nodded. "It would have been—" his eyes went to a shelf above his head as he calculated, "—maybe the late sixties? Is that what you're looking for?"

"I'm looking for anything I can find," I admitted. "The facility is closed now, and I'm looking for old staff."

Glenn lay his forearms on the just-cleaned bar, leaned until his head was next to mine and spoke into my ear. "You gotta know, this guy ain't right."

I lowered my voice to match his, though we weren't exactly plotting the overthrow of democracy and no one would dare eavesdrop on Glenn in his own bar. "*How* not right?"

"Psycho would be an understatement," Glenn said. "And if he's a fugitive again, he'll be extra paranoid."

Again? I turned my head to look at him and caught a whiff of spicy, starchy roasted peas, overlaid by tingly Coke sweetness and whiskey.

"I can try to track him down. I just want you to know what we're getting into." Mouth set in a grim line, his expression reminded me of when I'd stumbled into Cooper's last year, set on a desperate mission with no plan except to throw myself at Glenn's scarily skilled (and well-armed, *ha ha*) feet. But this was just talking to a witness. Right?

And Amos Weber didn't have much time.

"Okay," I said. "Find him."

Glenn held my eyes as he drifted slowly back across the bar, as if he were waiting for me to change my mind. "Okay," he echoed.

A man standing at the bar several stools away lifted an empty bottle and Glenn nodded an acknowledgment.

I muttered at his back as he retrieved a fresh bottle, "If I can handle you..."

Glenn's face swung toward me in the midst of popping the bottle cap, and it pinged, disregarded, to the floor. "I got news for you, darling. The man makes me look like a pussycat."

9

The prospect of tracking down his scary friend put a damper on Glenn's mood, so I left to tackle John Driscoll's short list. The first club John had suggested was a bust, possibly literally. It was closed, and to be closed on a Thursday night, I figured something had to be busted, whether it was a water line or the entire establishment by law enforcement.

I hung out in the second club for over half an hour, nursing a too-sweet drink special at the bar. Should I have been relieved or insulted that no one except the frustrated bartender harassed me? It's true that I was too old to be a contemporary of most of the patrons, still wide-eyed with recently won freedom from adult supervision. I took comfort in the fact that I wasn't yet old enough (or, less comforting, *wealthy* enough) to be of interest as a cougar, either.

The third club's patrons were more demographically mixed. I was still on the old end, but not everyone looked like they'd be heading to a Greek party later or skipping class when they were hungover the next day.

Most of the men were casually dressed, as was typical everywhere, and many of the women had foregone the party makeup and sequined tops ubiquitous at the previous club. The central dance floor was respectably full but not elbow-to-elbow. Clusters of women gathered around its edges, shouting conversations over the music. Clusters of men populated the bar, a large, horseshoe-shaped affair with a wall down its center and scattered women waiting for drinks. I slowly, endlessly circled the bar, afraid I'd miss my prey on the other side if I stayed in one place too long. Good thing I hadn't worn heels.

Fake-sipping another vile, sugary, barely alcoholic drink, I glanced impatiently at my watch. Unlike the previous establishment, I hadn't seen anyone obviously underage, including Addy. However, as I set my drink on the bar preparing to leave, I caught a glimpse of someone who looked suspiciously like her squeeze Troy Cantrell.

The man stood alone at the far end of the bar, surveying the club as I had been, though (I hoped) with less subtlety. He wore a black leather jacket, the simple kind with a mandarin collar and no bells and whistles. It had to be too hot indoors (I was comfortable in my tank top), but he looked cool, and presumably that was what mattered. His dark hair was cut relatively short, but long enough for curl to creep in around its edges, and he needed to shave.

No strobing pyrotechnic show, but the club's ambient lighting was dim and blue-laced, so I still couldn't be sure of his identity.

I approached with my drink and wedged myself between him and the nearest other patron, staring patiently and waiting for him to notice my scrutiny. It didn't take long.

The arrogant smile of a young man who knows he's attractive crept across his face. "You know what you want?" he asked.

Yep, he was Troy Cantrell all right.

"I do," I said, mouth wrinkling with distaste as I took a sip of my drink before setting it on the bar. "But it's nothing I can find here."

I ran my eyes slowly up and down his body, appreciatively, but paused at his nearest jacket pocket, raising an eyebrow. "Or can I?"

"Maybe," he said. "Are you a cop?"

I slid up onto a stool. "Do I look like a cop?"

He displayed a lovely, charming, bad boy grin before sliding onto the opposite stool, bumping my knees as he did. I couldn't fault Addy's taste. I might have taken Troy home myself at her age.

"No, you don't look like a cop," he said, hand straying to the pocket I'd been eyeing. I don't even think he knew he did it.

I leaned in, close enough for me to feel the heat radiating from his jacket and for him to hear me without shouting, then put a hand on his knee. Honestly, it was to keep me from falling off my stool, but I didn't mind if he took it another way.

"Let me give you a tip," I said. "When you ask someone if they're a cop, don't let them sidestep your question like I did. Wait for an answer. If you care."

His smile disappeared so abruptly it was almost cartoonish.

"But I'm not a cop." I leaned back and traded a handful of knee for my drink. "Just someone who used to have a special friend, but doesn't anymore."

He recovered more quickly than I thought he would, saying, "No one wants to be friendless."

I raised my glass in acknowledgment. "You're new to town, aren't you?"

"New to here," he admitted, "but not new to the business. You looking for something in particular?"

"Yes and no," I said. "I have inclinations, but honestly, my friend knew me better than I know myself. I have a stressful job, and it's nice to be able to take the edge off in the evenings and on weekends."

"Is that it?" Troy asked, seemingly disappointed.

"Well, that's for everyday. I also like to set something aside for special occasions." I practically clutched the wooden seat beneath me with my butt cheeks, praying I didn't fall as I traced a zipper on his jacket chest. "Special occasions and special friends. Especially new, special friends."

I leaned back and rested my elbows on the bar, hopefully looking sultry rather than relieved I hadn't busted my ass, and he glanced quickly around the club. He was looking for his supplier, a contact, something or someone.

His eyes continued roaming the bar as he said, "So you want some X? I could help you with that."

"What about your little friend?" I asked.

"What little friend?" he asked, still distracted.

Wary of cracking our skulls if I fell, I tucked a foot on the rungs of his stool and said, "I'm talking about the girl."

That got his attention. He swung around so quickly I thought we'd take a dive together after all. "What about her? Do you know where she is?" he demanded.

"No," I sighed, as if I were now bored. "I just saw her around with you and wondered if she liked to play, too."

"Right now, I don't know what she likes," he admitted. "Would you excuse me for just a minute? I need to confirm something before we come to an understanding."

I nodded and he slipped into the crowd, thicker now than it had been when I arrived. Once I was sure he couldn't see me, I slid off my seat and made my way outdoors.

The cool, fresh air felt amazing against my skin after the fug inside. For about fifteen seconds. Then I started to shiver. I'd left my jacket in my car, and my arms were covered with goosebumps by the time I reached it.

So Troy didn't know where Addy was. Interesting—I'd called it right last night after all. I wondered if that's when Addy left him. Of course, just because she'd left him didn't mean she'd stay gone. She was only sixteen, and many women with much more experience and resources than Addy found themselves going back. Which meant I needed to know where Troy was staying.

I started Cecil's engine, blasted the heater, and drove around the block a few times searching for the optimal vantage point. I kept a pair of binoculars in my car, but didn't want to use them unless absolutely necessary. Relying on binoculars was an easy way to lose track of someone in the dark, not to mention getting a colossal headache.

I ended up parking on the nearest side street. There wasn't enough traffic to block my view, and I could see the club entrance without hanging out my window by my ankles. I left the heater on for a few minutes before cutting the engine, wary of sleep's warm embrace. I pulled my hair back while I was at it and slipped on a sweatshirt, hood at the ready. Like Troy would notice me anyway. He didn't strike me as a criminal savant.

Within fifteen minutes, I was blinking hard and had started in with shoulder rolls. It was barely past eleven p.m., and I wondered how long I'd have to wait. I stared at my cell phone on the seat next to me. Personal conversations may not be the most professional choice on a stakeout, but it would keep me awake.

Mike answered on the second ring. "Hey, beautiful," he said. "Are you home?"

"Are you?" I asked, in my best sultry voice. Or I tried, not realizing how much I'd strained it trying to be heard over club noise. I started coughing, which made me laugh. After a sip of bottled water, I continued, "In fact, I am not at home. I am currently surveilling a club so I can follow someone else home."

"I am at home," Mike said, "and wondering if I should be jealous."

"Hardly," I said. "The subject has the emotional maturity of a twelve-year-old, minus a twelve-year-old's ethics. He is a means to an end."

"Aren't we all?" Mike said.

"No, you're not." I paused as I squinted at a figure in the darkness. I might need those damn binoculars after all.

"Twelve-year-old is on the move," I said, watching Troy exit the club, with another man close on his heels.

"You need to go?" Mike asked.

"In a minute," I said.

Mike, who'd logged his own share of hours sitting in cars, waited silently while I focused on the two men. Troy jogged to the club's parking lot and got in a dark, four-door sedan. The second man was older than Troy, early to mid-thirties, and he ran toward my car.

"Shit," I muttered.

"Everything okay?" Mike asked.

"Just peachy," I said, checking that my door locks were engaged. It was too late to pull up my hood without drawing more attention, but the phone stuck to my ear would help.

The man hardly spared my car a glance, instead glaring up at the sky, now heavy with mist, as he fumbled to get in his vehicle. He'd driven a sporty little car parked directly in front of me, which made it easy to scratch down his Florida license plate.

"Sorry," I said. "I thought someone made me. Can I call you later?"

"Yes," Mike said. "In fact, I'd appreciate it if you did."

"Cool," I said, hanging up before we could get dysfunctional (*was that concerned or controlling?*) or my quarry could get away.

Troy exited the parking lot, pulling onto the main street rather than my side one. I waited a few moments to start my car, then fell in behind Troy's buddy, hoping he was as clueless as Troy. My tailing skills were a little rusty.

They drove to a neighborhood a few blocks away that was predominantly university students, but not the kind with keg stations on the sidewalks in the middle of the night. Most of the modest, one-story houses showed lights inside, and one was the source of music loud enough for me to hear through my closed car windows.

I did not miss college.

Both Troy and his buddy squeezed into a driveway, bumper to bumper behind another car. A long-haired head peeked around a curtain from inside the house, disappearing too quickly for me to be certain of gender. The two men walked to the front door together and Troy let them in as I drove slowly past. Once around the block, then I wedged my little Cabrio into a sort-of spot across the street. It was a phenomenal parking job if I do say so myself, but would get my bumper crunched come morning.

Good thing I wouldn't be there then. I slipped out of the car for a better look at the address and noted Troy's license plate as well, muttering the numbers under my breath the whole way. Once I'd jotted it down below his friend's, I headed for home and my empty bed.

Mike and I had only been dating for a few months, but we'd met during an investigation about a year ago and been friends ever since. We value our friendship, so we'd decided to take things slow. I was beginning to think that was a bad idea. The problem was that Mike lived a couple of hours west of Tallahassee. And we both worked hard, with intermittently insane hours when nothing else existed. When you're lucky to see each other a couple of times a month, taking it slow becomes *taking it s-l-o-w*.

However, Mike was coming to stay with me in Tallahassee this weekend, our first opportunity to pick up the pace. I was reviewing a list in my head (*clean the toilet, remind Ben not to show up unannounced, shave my legs*) when I reached my neighborhood.

Like many Tallahassee neighborhoods, it was wooded and fairly dark at night. There were no lights on in my house, but the motion light in my carport momentarily blinded me. I blinked as I gathered my purse and other random bits, dialing Mike while shutting Cecil's door with my butt.

"Hello?" he said, not sounding sleepy at all. It was an hour earlier in Central time.

"We're still on for this weekend, aren't we?" I asked, fumbling my keys at the door.

"I'm game if you are," Mike said. His deep-voiced tease was enough for me to picture him climbing into bed, wearing a Red Sox T-shirt he'd bought for me that lived at his apartment. (I blamed the word *game* for my imaginative digression.) My heart was still going all syncopated when he continued in everyday Mike voice, "I've got a case thing to wrap up Friday, but I'll leave first thing Saturday morning. What are you working on?"

"A couple of things. One I might ask for a little help on, and one..." Dropping my purse on the kitchen counter, I recalled what Roger had said about things getting complicated once I found Addy. "And one you're probably better off not knowing about."

He went quiet on the other end, I suspected to prevent him from blurting out what was on his mind. It was difficult for him to give me that kind of space.

"It's not dangerous," I assured him. "Except maybe to my career."

His soft exhalation was almost indistinguishable from the hum of my barren refrigerator. (I added grocery shopping to my mental list.)

Mike cleared his throat, and when he finally responded, it was in a mischievous voice. "Does that mean you'll be looking for another occupation? You could be my personal assistant."

"Really?" I said, turning on lights as I walked through the house toward the bedroom. "You sure you want to hire unskilled labor?"

"I highly doubt you're unskilled," he said. "But if that's the case, I'd be happy to teach you."

I laughed, and hung up after I'd secured a promise of some vocational training this weekend. And then I made sure I'd washed all my sheets.

10

The next morning I sat at my desk, bleary-eyed, mangling a paper clip and eying my long-empty travel cup from home. It felt like time for a refill.

I hadn't slept well the night before. I wish I could blame lascivious thoughts of my upcoming weekend, but it was always hard to settle down when I'd been out and about, doing my best Samantha Spade impersonation. Sitting on the couch with a cup of herbal tea, watching my fish Jackie and Bruce do absolutely nothing, had relaxed me. But the challenge came as I lay in bed.

Staring at the ceiling, my mind played movies of the juvenile center horrors I'd read about that day. Of children who knew nothing with more certainty than that they were alone. That no one cared. That no one would come to save them.

Eventually I'd dozed off, but I'd woken this morning with my pajama T-shirt sticking to me and the sense that dark images had followed me into my nightmares. A shower had helped, as had my generous cup of coffee (okay, half-pot), and the brisk air that greeted me outside.

But I was definitely slowing down now.

So far, I'd confirmed that the address where Troy was staying was a rental. It wasn't worth tracking down the lease. My money was on the guy who owned the car Troy had been driving—not Troy, I'd found out when I'd bit the bullet and paid to run its plate—and I had his name. I'd held off on running the other car's license, not wanting to go too far into the weeds.

Motion was good. I could drive by the house and see if anyone other than Troy was around and ask them about Addy. Except Troy didn't strike me as an early riser, and I wouldn't get anything with him there. I knew someone at the university who might be able to help me get Troy's friend's class schedule—assuming the guy was a student—but that was a big ask for not much return and might take a while. I could make the rounds of the shelters again, this time skipping the front desk and going straight to the patrons, but had no "in" to convince anyone to talk to me.

I was still considering my options, another sure sign I needed a caffeine top-up, when my phone rang. The cell phone, not the landline, which was unusual during regular hours. I almost missed the call, digging for the damn device in my pockets and bags.

I didn't recognize the number. "Hello?"

"You still up for seeing a crazy guy?" Glenn asked, his voice even more resonant over the phone than in person.

"You mean one other than you?"

It gave me pause that he didn't bother countering my tease.

"Earlier is better," Glenn replied. "He'll get worse as the day goes on."

"Worse meaning crazier?" I wasn't sure how that worked, although I was familiar with sundowning, when people with certain forms of dementia got more confused as the day progressed.

"I don't know about crazier," Glenn said, "but he'll be more fucked up, thanks to whatever his intoxicant of choice is at the moment. I can't imagine that helps his mental state, but it certainly won't do much for his mood."

"Okay," I said, "when?"

"Now."

~

I DROVE to Cooper's to meet Glenn. I'd never been to his home and
had no idea where he lived. In my imagination, it was something like
the Bat Cave, but with more booze and Commissioner Gordon potentially buried in the backyard.

Glenn was already waiting for me in his massive gray pickup, like
a bear tucked in a mountain cave. Yep, a Bear Cave, not a Bat Cave. I
locked up before jogging across the parking lot, dodging a light rain.

He almost smiled as I hung onto the oh-shit bar to ascend the
metal monstrosity and fell awkwardly onto the bench seat, saying,
"Watching you climb in my vehicle is one of those wonderful things
that never gets old."

"Like me?" I asked, aware that I was directly contradicting what
I'd intimated about my age last night. Optimism born of action had
helped me recover my PI mojo. "Thanks for doing this."

"Remember, your shenanigans help keep me young, too," he said,
before his truck rumbled to life.

I didn't think that was true. I may or may not have added wrinkles
to the man's countenance, but I had definitely added scars to his
already well-marked hide. Still, he'd been almost giddy when our
lives were in danger, not to mention the rush we'd both felt afterward.
But Glenn wasn't giddy now, nowhere close to it.

"That was quick," I said, struggling with a seat belt not designed
for someone of my stature or gender. There was no position for the
restraint that didn't mash a boob or choke me to death.

"What's that?" he asked, raising his voice over the engine roar as
we accelerated out of the parking lot.

I leaned toward the center, mashing my other boob. At least
they'd match. "I said, you found your friend quickly."

Glenn shrugged. "He's someone I keep tabs on."

"Why?" I asked.

"Various reasons," was all he would say.

Conversation would have been inaudible anyway, with the big
machine gearing up and down for traffic lights and turns, until we

reached one of the mostly wooded main traffic arteries out of Talla-hassee. It was a direction I rarely drove, and I was lost in no time. Rain was kind to the landscape, lending a gloss to pine needles and asphalt alike. Neither the trees nor the road would look so fresh and new once enough rain had accumulated to make the limbs sag, fill low spots in the pavement, and flatten grassy shoulders with its flow.

"How *prepared* are you?" Glenn asked.

It took me a moment to interpret his emphasis on the word. "You mean, am I armed?" I couldn't bring myself to say "packing" mid-morning on an otherwise normal Thursday.

I took his silence as an affirmative.

"No, I am not armed," I said. "Did you expect me to be?"

I didn't own a gun, but I'd carried—and used—one of Glenn's before.

"Probably best that you aren't," he admitted. "It'd just make things more complicated with Turtle."

"Turtle? That's the guy we're going to see?" I wanted to take comfort in the non-threatening moniker, but knew better than to make such assumptions.

Glenn frowned at the windshield, starting to fog, and adjusted the climate controls on the console. Or maybe he launched a shuttle. With that many bells and whistles, I couldn't be sure.

"Turtle Keane," he said. "You need to follow my lead with him. Don't speak unless you're spoken to. And don't be a smart-ass. Which, for you, means don't speak at all."

"Tell me about this guy," I said, although I almost didn't want to know.

We'd transitioned to a rural highway with no pretensions of being anything else. Glenn straight-armed the steering wheel and kept his eyes locked on the road. "Not much to tell. Or at least, not much that I know. Little older than me. Spent some time in the military. He doesn't talk about it, not even which branch, but I believe he was kicked out for almost killing somebody in his unit."

"What makes you think that?" I asked.

"Some things he said, things I saw him do."

"Like what?" I demanded when he didn't continue.

Glenn sighed. "Turtle was always good to me. He watched out for me, especially when I was just a little shit. But he generally doesn't play well with others, and he gets confused. Kind of a PTSD thing. When he gets like that... well, there's nothing you can do. You've got to let him think what he's gonna think—don't try to fight it—and get the hell out."

"But he's good with you?"

Glenn shrugged before downshifting to turn onto a smaller secondary road. "Mostly good. He's never tried to kill me."

I'd thought he was done speaking, but a moment later he muttered, "Not really."

Great.

Glenn slanted over the steering wheel for a better view of the road. It was paved, but narrow enough to feel claustrophobic in the wide, full-sized truck. Vegetation crowded the edges of the road, and I winced every time a stray branch scratched against Glenn's baby. The close canopy and now heavier rain kept ambient light to a minimum, but it wasn't dark enough for the headlights to do anything—the worst of both worlds.

Glenn hit the brakes and his heavy tires slid on the wet, leaf-strewn road. He muttered expletives under his breath and, once we'd stopped sliding, reversed carefully until we drew even with a gravel lane I hadn't even seen.

"I think this is it," he said.

It was as wide as the secondary road, but previous rains had cut deep, crisscrossing ruts in the lane. It was no challenge for the truck, but I would have been walking with my little hatchback. Assuming I'd made it this far. I clutched the oh-shit bar to mitigate the worst of the lurches. Glenn's truck had four-wheel drive, but hopefully we wouldn't need it. And hopefully the rain wouldn't get worse while we were in there.

Suddenly *there* was *there*. A reasonably well-maintained, fifties ranch-style house faced in pale-brown brick stood ahead of us. My shoulders relaxed slightly—I'd expected a shack with tin foil over the windows and a wolf tied next to the front door. That said, the woods came so close to the house in the back and on the sides, there might still have been a wolf waiting for us under cover. The free-standing garage was presumably a later addition, not built to the same standards. Its roof shingles were dark with organic growth, and piles of leaves atop one end gave the entire structure a sense of mushiness.

I wondered what, if anything, was stored inside. A blue sedan a decade or so past its prime sat in front of the house on a bare patch of ground. One of its back windows was covered by clear, heavy plastic and duct tape. Glenn pulled in behind it and cut the engine.

"Here," he said, handing me a faded denim jacket that had been lying on the seat between us. "Put this on."

I held it up, spread its sleeves with my hands, and tried not to examine its patches too closely. I wasn't exactly an expert on motorcycle gangs, but a couple of cases at the Public Defender's Office had given me enough passing familiarity with the world to want to avoid knowing what this would tell me about my friend.

"Are you serious?" I asked, dropping the jacket to my lap. It was so large, I could have made a pair of pants from the fabric and still had an appropriately sized jacket left over.

"Yes," Glenn said. "And I need you to—"

"I know, keep my mouth shut," I snapped.

"No, I need you to trust me," he said, squeezing my nearest hand, which still held a jacket cuff. "To trust that whatever I say and do in there, it's for a reason."

"Which is?"

"Finding out what you need to know, and then getting us out of here in one piece," he said, eyes drilling into mine. "I'm pretty sure I can do that. But I'd prefer to do it without hurting Turtle in the process. Which means making him feel safe by doing and saying exactly what his crazy mind expects."

I let that sink in for a moment, then glanced down at the jacket on my lap. "So I'm your bitch?" I asked.

Glenn didn't laugh, didn't even crack a smile. "Something like that."

Great. One-Percenter, biker bullshit. I sighed and shucked off my button-down shirt, trading it out for the denim jacket. My arms got lost, and my hands didn't emerge until I rolled the sleeves. I released my pinned-back hair, the fuzzy curls itching my face and neck where they fell, then shoved my hands in the tangled mess and gave it a shake to relax my scalp. Fortunately, I'd worn my boots again instead of sneakers or flats.

Glenn's expression had gone from scary stoic to something... hungrier. I tended to think of him as a big bear, but now he looked even more predatory. "Ready?" he asked.

I adjusted the collar on his jacket and caught the stale scent of storage. "Ready."

He patted my cheek with more force than I would have preferred. "You're something else, Red," he said, then rolled out of the truck.

I caught a glimpse of myself in one of the mirrors as I climbed down. I was something else all right. I was a crazy woman, and not just because of my hair.

11

Glenn knocked at the front door before hunching to drape an arm over my shoulder possessively. I was grateful for any shield from the rain penetrating my thick hair and trickling down the sides of my neck. I pulled Glenn's jacket tight across my chest. We stood for maybe ten or fifteen seconds, but it felt like longer. Finally, I heard the grinding and clicking of metal as someone disabled several locks.

The door opened in stages, slowly, a few inches at a time. The overhanging trees and lousy weather meant the interior of the house was relatively dark, and a window on the opposite wall backlit the figure opening the door.

All I could make out initially was a man shape. Slightly taller than Glenn, and more lean. As the door swung wider and my eyes adjusted, I saw shoulder-length dark hair hanging loose, not as curly as mine but just as fuzzy. Clean-shaven, or at least no intentional facial hair growth. The white glare of a cotton undershirt. His arms were nearly as pale, ghostly even, as was the face that hung back in the shadows. One arm braced high against the threshold, close enough to see round, dark scars clustered in its crook just above the

wrap of a tattoo. The other arm hung alongside his leg, hand gripping a dark shape that could only be a gun.

Glenn's voice was calm, but he crushed me closer as he said
simply, "Turtle."

I still couldn't make out his face, but I heard a surprising lightness
in the man's raspy response, "Baby Bear."

Wound as tightly as I was, I almost laughed.

Glenn released me and flung an arm around the other man. Their
foreheads collided so hard in their rugged embrace I was afraid I'd be
driving Glenn's truck back to Tallahassee. Assuming Turtle didn't
accidentally shoot me with his big-ass revolver (I had a good view of
it now) while hugging Glenn.

"Come on in," Turtle said.

Glenn didn't look to see if I followed. I reminded myself, as I drew
the door closed behind me, *Stay in character. Whatever happens, stay in
character.*

I jumped when I suddenly came face-to-face with Turtle. Well,
face to chest anyway. He pushed past me and cracked the door to look
out on the yard, scanning the landscape from horizon to horizon, gun
still held down by his leg. "You come alone?" the man asked.

I glanced at Glenn and felt his warning look as much as I saw it.

"Yep, all alone," Glenn said, and motioned me to join him.

Turtle closed the door, then sidestepped to the window and
pulled aside a curtain to stare for a while longer. The back of my neck
tingled in that primal way that should keep us safe but more often
than not gets ignored. Lately I was learning to not ignore it, but I was
grateful when Glenn hooked his arm over my shoulder again. The
pressure of his meaty arm eased the tingling.

"You sure nobody followed you?" Turtle asked, a slight, hissing
lisp to his voice as though he were missing a tooth.

"You're not exactly in the middle of town here, bud," Glenn
replied.

Turtle lingered a moment more, then nodded. "Yeah," he said,
seizing on Glenn's words as if he'd said something profound. I heard
a creak as he shoved the gun in a side holster. "Yeah."

Glenn surveyed the room and held out a questioning arm.

"Not there," Turtle said, when Glenn drifted toward a navy loveseat that faced the glaring picture window. "That's my spot."

The window was an older type with one big central plate of glass and smaller vertical sections on each end that cranked open. One section was open now, enough to let in cool, wet air and leave a little drizzle on the sill. Turtle gestured toward an armchair positioned to its right.

Glenn sat in the chair and gestured for me to sit on the floor. I bit back a protest, thankful Turtle kept a relatively clean if under-furnished house. A large rug joined the loveseat and the armchair in a group, so at least I wasn't stuck sitting on bare hardwood floor. Using the chair as a backrest, I leaned against Glenn's leg, feeling the edge of his boots through his jeans.

Turtle paid no attention to me. In fact, he barely had eyes for Glenn. Instead, Turtle sat on the loveseat and gazed out at the woods behind his house. Not in a philosophical, Thoreau way. In an *it's only a matter of time before they come for me* way. Turtle rose, angling for a better view, before sitting again. He was never still.

"You been good?" Glenn asked.

Turtle nodded. 'Good enough. You?"

Glenn answered with another question. "You hear about Randy?"

Turtle finally looked at him. "No, what happened? RICO?"

Glenn snorted. "RICO, my ass. He had a heart attack. Dropped dead in a titty bar over near Pensacola."

"No shit," Turtle said. "Well, I guess that's the way he would've wanted to go."

I tuned them out as Glenn engaged the other man in conversation about old friends, old places, things that reinforced their connection and helped Turtle settle down. Who knew the last time he'd had a conversation with an actual human being? I struggled with it myself sometimes, and I wasn't a loopy hermit.

I took in as much as I could about the house, as unobtrusively as I could. I couldn't see much beyond the living room, which I suspected came pre-furnished. The few pieces of framed art on the wall were very middle-class suburban. Farm scenes and landscapes. The wall opposite us held a fireplace, complete with screen and tools, but it looked and smelled too clean for me to believe it had been used this winter, possibly ever. The clock on the mantle was a brass one that swiveled under glass and brought to mind anniversaries.

What had I expected, babes bent over bikes with their ass cheeks hanging out? Leather chaps tossed on the floor. Beer bottles and condoms on every available surface? Okay, yes. That's exactly what I'd expected.

Some subtle shift in Glenn's tone or energy drew me back to their conversation. "You were there for a while, weren't you?" he asked. "At the Reform School?"

Turtle nodded, one arm reaching around to hug the other. The man was wiry, heading toward skinny. His cheeks looked recently hollowed, like an old man's, and bare muscles and sinews rippled and twitched beneath the tattooed skin of his forearm. I could easily imagine it swinging a length of pipe at someone's head.

But then, I've been told I have a very active imagination.

The arm Turtle gripped had fewer tattoos, mostly grouped around his wrist and hand and disappearing beneath his T-shirt on his bicep. Perhaps the thick, pink scar that ran the length of that forearm wouldn't take ink.

"What can you tell me about the place?" Glenn asked.

Turtle's head tilted, and he scrutinized Glenn sideways. A shiver ran through me as he said, "Why are you asking?"

Glenn shrugged. "I know bad shit happened there. But I don't know how bad. And I'm trying to track down some of the people who used to work there."

Agitated, Turtle stood again. One arm drifted to his holster, rubbing it as if for good luck. I noticed he hadn't secured the snap. "Why?" he repeated.

Glenn held out his hands in supplication. "Turtle," he said, stretching out each syllable, "I'm sorry. I know you don't like to talk about this kind of stuff."

"Why?" Turtle shouted, close enough to Glenn's face that the odor of Turtle's sweet, rotting breath drifted down to me.

I felt Glenn's calf tense, and a deep sense of foreboding overcame me as I wondered what he was about to do. Someone was going to get seriously hurt. Soon.

"Because we want to make the assholes pay!" I yelled. At least, I meant to yell. It came out something more like regular volume, but at least my voice didn't shake.

Turtle stared, as if seeing me for the first time. His face was stubbly, and a light scar sliced across his brow ridge. I wondered if the person who'd inflicted it had lived. He bent down, resting his hands on his thighs.

"Someone has to pay for what happened there," I said. "We supposed to wait for goddamned karma?"

Turtle's hand cracked across the side of my face. Hard enough for my teeth to cut the inside of my cheek, and hard enough to piss me off, but not quite hard enough to really ring my bell. I grabbed Glenn's leg instinctively, less for protection than to keep things from escalating.

"How the fuck do you know what they did?" Turtle demanded.

I thought of the guilt and fear Amos Weber had lived with for decades, and the pain I'd seen in Roger, wanting to fix it. And I thought of the people I'd loved most in my life, how I'd also wanted to fix them, but couldn't.

"You're right, I don't know what they did," I replied, chin held high and face defiant. "Because my brother never came back."

Turtle must have recognized some kind of truth in what I said. His gray teeth smiled, and I noticed one of his incisors was chipped.

"I like her," he said, and the same hand that had slapped me went to my hair, his long, slightly crooked fingers working their way toward the crown of my head. Turtle straightened, pulling me toward him. Toward his belt buckle.

The pressure against my scalp, the inexorable, creeping movement of my head, the powerlessness... together they triggered a sense of vertigo, the warning sign of a flashback trying to take hold. I focused on his buckle, but its raised image of a skull swam in front of me. The scarred and calloused fingers of Turtle's other hand strayed toward his pants while I dug my fingernails into my palm, desperate to stay *where* and *when* I was (*in a strange man's house, not in a strange man's pickup*), to keep my wits about me so crazy shit didn't happen again.

"Of course you like her," Glenn said. He gripped my shoulders, pressing me back toward him and the chair. I held in a hiss as the men's opposing forces tugged at my hair.

"Because she's mine," Glenn continued, and the edge in his voice could have cut glass. "She's not a pass-around."

Turtle removed his hand from my head slowly, but still tugged a few stray hairs free. I fought the involuntary tears that sprang to my eyes. Turtle stepped back, and I felt Glenn's arms on mine as he guided me up onto his lap. The chair was too small for it to be anything but awkward, and he shifted me to one side. I heard Vince's voice in my head, *He's keeping his dominant, weapon hand free.* That awareness helped me calm down and release my fingernails from my palm.

Turtle shrugged and returned to his loveseat. The moment his eyes were elsewhere, Glenn gave me a reassuring squeeze. Then Turtle was watching us or his favorite window again, I couldn't tell which. I sat motionless, but my mind raced.

"When were you there?"

My heart skipped a beat, slamming against my throat so I wanted to vomit, but it was Glenn asking Turtle, not Turtle asking me about my brother.

"I don't know," Turtle said. He faltered. "You know, my memory's not so great. Not with years and such. But I must've been... thirteen? Maybe not that old."

Turtle shook his head, more like he was pushing the memories away than that they weren't there.

"What do you remember?" Glenn asked, voice gentle. "You can tell me, Turtle. You can always tell me."

Turtle surprised me by closing his eyes. His fingers sought each other, trembling slightly. "I remember the smell of the dirt, first thing in the morning before all the dew had burned off. Before it got so goddamned hot it killed... a little nigger boy. I don't recall his name. He was in a different dorm. The dorms smelled like sweat, like dirty sweaty boys wanting to go home."

His eyes opened, but drifted back to slits as he leaned elbows on knees, then dropped his head. "Sometimes there were fights, but mostly they beat us."

"Who beat you?" Glenn asked, voice so low I felt its rumble next to me more than heard it.

"The guards. The warden. Whoever was there. Sometimes it was just lashes with the belt—they tied you down on your belly for that. In the Tar Shed. Except it wasn't really a shed. The floor was concrete, so they could hose it down. Still always smelled like blood and shit and piss."

"They ever take you in there?" Glenn asked.

Turtle's head jerked up, his eyes an animated mix of anger and pride. His voice had an almost flirty edge as he said, "What do you think, Little Bear? Have you ever known me to be able to keep my goddamn mouth shut?"

The corner of Glenn's mouth curled as he said, "Just once. For about a minute and a half after that Angel caught you square on the side of the head with a two-by-four at that place outside Delray Beach."

Turtle barked a laugh. "Yeah, but you took care of him for me."

Glenn said, voice hard, "*Adios*, motherfucker."

I clenched my jaw to keep from flinching. I felt like I was sitting on a stranger's lap.

Turtle nodded his head, mouth grim, and repeated, "*Adios*."

"I'd like to adios some of those asswipes you're talking about," Glenn said. "But I imagine a lot of them are dead by now. Do you remember other people who were there then?"

Turtle's gun hand went to his opposite arm again, scratching lightly, running long nails from his wrist to his elbow. "I don't think I want to talk about this anymore."

"The boss man's long gone," Glenn said. "But what about the guards, any of the rest of the staff?"

He shook his head. "But I'll never forget the infirmary. At first it was all smells, because you were hurt too bad to open your eyes, or you figured if they knew you weren't out they'd take you back and beat you some more. The smell of the disinfectant was strong, but it couldn't cover up everything else. Like this kid, Neal—*where the hell did that name come from?*—this kid Neal got his foot run over, and it rotted."

Turtle shot up from his chair to the picture window. The raw redness where blood had risen to meet his scratching was visible through the hair and ink on his arms. His scratching hand strayed to his gun holster again, caressing the leather. Staring out at the mixed hardwood and pine, he said, "The rot made it halfway to his knee before they finally cut off his leg. I swear to God I can still taste it in the back of my throat. Hear him screaming when I sleep."

Glenn shifted beside me. I inched off his lap, up onto the arm of the chair, and the movement caught Turtle's eye.

"Back in a minute," Turtle said abruptly, and loped down the hall, a door slamming behind him.

Glenn blew out his breath and said, "We need to get the hell out of here. Now."

12

I twisted on the chair's padded arm to face Glenn. "We can't leave yet. We didn't get a single name."

"And you think he can give us names?" Glenn shook his head, dumbfounded. "Have you been listening to the man? He's a goddamned mess."

I nodded, working myself up to saying something that would show just what a selfish, single-minded asshole I could be. *For the right reason.* At least, I told myself it was the right reason. And what else could I do? Turtle was broken too badly for anyone to fix. But maybe I could help bring down the people who'd broken him.

"What?" Glenn demanded.

I closed my eyes briefly (*yes, I am this person*) before asking, "What do you think he's doing back there?"

Glenn stared at me like I was an idiot. "Well, he's sure as hell not taking a dump."

I held his gaze, waited for him to realize I wasn't a naive idiot. Just a horrible person. Finally, Glenn's eyes narrowed as comprehension dawned. "You think after he shoots or snorts or smokes whatever the hell he's got back there, he'll have his head on straight, and he'll be able to access whatever memories he hasn't burned out yet."

Glenn pushed, "What happens to him when we leave here? Leave him with all the shit we opened up?"

I had no answer.

Glenn inhaled deeply through his nose and closed his eyes, much as I had a moment ago. Except I'd been working up my courage, and he was trying to control his temper. When he opened his eyes, the fire in them was so intense, I almost flinched.

"Fine," he growled. "Let's say his high gets his neurons firing. What do you think the chances are that instead of turning into a goddamned professor, the crazy sonuvabitch loses it completely? I can still see his handprint on your face."

I wasn't surprised; I could still feel it, especially as the heat flushed to my cheeks. "Didn't seem to bother you at the time," I said, even though I knew it was a low blow.

Glenn's hand was solid, not a tremble to be seen, as he pointed a meaty finger at me that could have punctured sheetrock. "Do you know how hard it was *not* to do something? I told you, I don't want to hurt him, and if I'd done what I wanted to do, things would've gotten out of control. I don't know about you, but I've got enough goddamn dead men on my conscience already."

I dropped my eyes.

Glenn was right. It wasn't worth it. Turtle's life might not be much, but it was his, whatever he chose to do with it. However he chose to end it.

"Okay," I said, and started to rise.

But it was too late.

Turtle burst through the door into the hallway, either surprised to find himself or us there. Glenn gave a small shake of his head, encouraging me to sit as Turtle advanced on us.

"You," Turtle said, shoving a bony finger in Glenn's face. Unlike Glenn, Turtle's hand shook, and he was sweating. He winced at the window's light, probably because his pupils were the size of dinner plates. "You said you're gonna get these fuckers. Is that right?"

"Yes," Glenn said, outwardly calm despite chewing me out a minute ago.

"You promise?" Turtle asked, one eye leaking tears.

"Yes, Turtle, I promise."

Turtle nodded his head and bent over his hands, almost a caricature of a villain. "Did I tell you about the Tar Shed?" he asked, but continued without waiting for an answer. "We called it that because they beat the tar out of us there. Usually the guards, especially this young guy—not much older than us—missing the end of his pinky finger."

He gripped his right pinky and pulled on it, as if to make his own hand match. Turtle paced to the opposite window, the one with the curtain that overlooked his driveway, and peeked out. "We used to joke he left it up somebody's ass. Except that wasn't funny, considering some of the stuff he did to us. Especially to the little ones... And he enjoyed every minute of it. Every minute of pain. Every minute of shit-scared terror. I still see that sick bastard in my nightmares."

Glenn cleared his throat, but before he could speak, Turtle whirled back around and said, "I don't remember his name, if I ever knew it. But sometimes somebody else came, like somebody in charge. And he'd watch the beatings. Him, I know."

Turtle pointed at his chest and tugged at the scoop neck of his T-shirt, pacing in front of us. "Always wore white, button-down shirts. They'd be nothing but sweat stains by the time they finished with us in the Tar Shed. He didn't help, he just watched. But it was that hot that he'd be drenched, too. He didn't do any of that, *we're hurting you to help you* bullshit either. He just stood there, not saying anything until the end. Even then, the only time he spoke was if he thought you didn't get enough licks."

"Turtle, did you say you knew his name?" Glenn asked softly.

Turtle almost jumped, he was so excited, walking that uncomfortable line between comical and disturbing in a fifty-something man who'd lived as hard as he obviously had.

"Dickie!" he shouted, then laughed, as if it were the most ridiculous thing he'd ever heard. "He was a dick so we called him Dickie. We even had a song—"

Turtle's voice broke off, and the euphoria vanished just as quickly.

He moved to the picture window and dropped to a squat, eyes scanning the trees in a jerky fashion. "The Tar Shed had a window," he said. "People would peek in to see how far along the beatings were. Adults mostly, but there was a little blonde kid..."

His hand strayed to the window crank. It was roughly L-shaped, but had a rounded knob on the end that he spun beneath his fingers. The hollow, wobbling metal sound strung my nerves even tighter. I couldn't help it—my hands strayed to hug myself, clutching my elbows. Turtle's eyes slowly tracked in our direction, toward the movement. Slowly toward me. And then, suddenly, not so slowly.

Turtle's hand flew to his holster as he lunged, and everything was motion. Glenn was rising, Turtle's arm was shoving my shoulder, and I was falling over the side of the chair to the floor. All at once. I fell flat on my back, grunting with the impact, and Turtle was straddling me. My brain tried to make sense of his stink (garlic and funky smoke and sickness), but kept overlaying it with the body odor of a man long gone, a man a year in the ground.

I turned my face away and felt his gun press against my temple.

"Was it you?" Turtle demanded. "Were you watching at the window?"

My throat worked to unstick my tongue from the roof of my mouth. But there was no point. Nothing I could say would stop him.

"Think, Turtle. She's a redheaded chick," Glenn said.

His voice was close, but I couldn't see him. All I could see was a ball of lint and a few crumbs gathered at the edge of the rug that looked like bits of Triscuits.

"And she's too young, Turtle," Glenn said, like logic could get through to the man. "Put the gun down."

Pain speared through my forehead as I twisted my eyes in their sockets, struggling to see Glenn without moving my skull. I needed to see him. But I couldn't. I'd have to trust him. And not lose my shit. My heart hammered in my chest, and when Turtle spoke again, I wasn't sure if I heard his voice or the drawl of a dead man.

"Are you sure you weren't there, watching through the window?"

he asked, pushing the barrel so hard I wondered if its edges were tearing my skin.

"I swear, it wasn't me," I whispered. I could smell it. I could smell the gun, oil and metal and the tang of recent firing.

"Turtle," Glenn barked, and the pressure against my temple eased. A hand joined Turtle's on my shoulder, and slowly peeled it away. "When I brought her here, I spoke for her. She's mine, so if you've got a problem with her, you've got a problem with me."

I recognized Glenn's touch as his hand crept slowly along my neck, up the side of my face. I held my breath as it pushed against the revolver's barrel, but a tiny whimper still escaped my throat. Then I couldn't feel the gun anymore, just Glenn's hand. But all I could think was, *his hand won't stop a bullet.*

"Hey!" Glenn said, and his hand felt more like the side of a fist, maybe gripping the gun barrel. "Do you have a problem with me, Turtle? Huh?"

Turtle didn't answer, and I closed my eyes.

"Turtle, do you trust me?" Glenn demanded.

Glenn's words struck me like Turtle's slap. *Do you trust me?* The echo with what he'd said to me in the truck soured my guts even through my fear.

Turtle's knees brushed against my hips as he climbed off me. I turned my head to see Glenn slowly, carefully taking Turtle's gun with one hand and sheathing his own knife he'd had ready with the other.

"I'm sorry, Bear," Turtle said. "I don't know what came over me."

"That fucking garbage you've got back there in the bathroom is what came over you," Glenn snapped. "We talked about this the last time."

Their words faded as they stepped away from me without another look, and I shut down, shut out everything around me. Tried to breathe again. Brought my knees to my chest before slowly twisting to a sitting position. Finally, I felt a tug at my consciousness. I looked up to see Glenn leading Turtle down the hallway, hand pressed to his back and looking over his shoulder at me. I couldn't read his expression, but a little hitch of motion was clear—*get your ass to the truck.*

He'd find no argument there.

Glenn had left his vehicle unlocked. I opened the passenger door and stood next to it. The rain had stopped, and my knees were shaking so badly I wasn't sure I could climb in. My tank top was sticky with sweat beneath Glenn's jacket. I took a deep breath, swung the door wide, and stretched for the oh-shit bar. My hand missed the first time, and fumbled with it the second. Another deep breath. Then I squeezed the sonuvabitch like it was Glenn's throat and slammed the door shut behind me.

When Glenn emerged from the house a few minutes later, he was alone. He didn't speak when he got in, just started the engine and swung the truck around on the bare ground until we were headed back to Tallahassee.

Neither of us bothered with a seat belt, but the truck didn't protest. Glenn drove through the forest until we arrived at a wide spot in the road beyond sight and sound of Turtle's property, then pulled over. Silence rushed to fill the cabin when the rumbling engine stopped. I watched the recent rain drip from the pine needles outside, imagined I could hear it hit the ground.

"Jesus Christ," Glenn muttered, as he slumped in the seat and rubbed his hands over his face. A long, juddering sigh rocked through his body. Then he faced me. "Are you okay?"

I jerked away as he reached for me. "No, I'm not okay."

"I'm sorry," he said, "but I told you we needed to leave. And I told you—"

"You didn't tell me he'd put a fucking gun to my head!" I snapped.

I instantly regretted my temper, not because Glenn didn't deserve it, but because the spike of adrenaline set me to shaking again. I tucked my hands out of sight under my thighs and rocked in my seat.

"Would it help if I told you the gun wasn't loaded?" he asked.

"It depends," I said, through a jag of teeth chattering. "Would you be lying?"

My eyes bored into his. They didn't falter exactly, but there was just a flicker. And then he caught that I'd caught it, and there was a little twinkle, along with the slightest flush to his throat. "Maybe," he admitted. "Just a little."

My glare wouldn't hold despite my best efforts—I had too much pent-up anxiety for any kind of stillness. I snorted. Glenn grinned. I laughed... and then my brain or hormones or whatever flipped the switch, and I found myself choking on a sob.

"Hey," Glenn said softly.

This time when he reached for me, I met him halfway. My face brushed against his cotton sleeve on its way to rest against his torso, but just for a moment. Before I could nestle into his shoulder, before my chest could start heaving in earnest, I pulled away. I pressed my palms to the dashboard, breathing in through the nose, out through the mouth.

"Red?" he asked.

I shook my head and took a few more calming breaths. "No," I said. "We're not doing this again."

He sat back, lips pressed so tightly they almost disappeared beneath his mustache. "Is that what you think of me? That I'd jump your bones right here in the truck?"

I opened my mouth to apologize—instinct, or feminine indoctrination—but caught myself. "No, I don't think that. But this isn't about you. It's about me, about me learning to deal with shit that's not going away anytime soon, in a way that's somewhere in the neighborhood of healthy. Without depending on you or anybody else."

I fought a feeling of self-consciousness as he watched me. Those were some big words coming from someone who wanted nothing more than to bury her face in a scary man's chest, content to know he would protect her from anyone who was scarier.

"Fine," he said, and started the pickup. "Just don't go confusing being dependent with accepting help from a friend."

13

Glenn and I hadn't spoken much on the way back, letting our adrenaline and emotions settle before saying anything else we might regret. It was hard to believe it was barely past noon when we arrived at Cooper's. I felt wrung out, like I'd experienced more than enough for an entire day already. An entire fricking year. I wished some magical, industrious creatures would finish my work for me while I went home, locked the doors and closed the curtains, and curled in my bed for a long nap.

Perhaps after a stiff, midday drink.

I abused my body in an alternative, culturally acceptable way and hit a drive-through. Back at my office, I arranged my desk carefully to avoid dripping fast food sloopy sauce on the envelope from the Archives. The typed reports could use another once-over, but the handwritten forms were calling to me.

I'd expected intake or incident reports or something directly associated with the inmates. Instead, Frank had provided an assortment of administrative paperwork from a six-month period, smack dab in the middle of Mr. Weber's tenure at the center. I even found a requisition form for an extra uniform for Amos Weber and tucked a sticky note on its corner for photocopying, in case we needed proof that he'd been employed there. I also added all personnel names and titles to my list. Maybe some of them would still be alive.

Not surprisingly, Wilbur Richard, the now-deceased longtime director of the center, had signed every form. People named *Richard* often went by *Dick*. It made sense that kids might transpose the two names. But could Turtle have confused the director and his second in command? Silly question—I had personal experience of Turtle confusing present reality with thirty-year-old memories. If he could think I was a little boy who spied on him while he was being tortured, then swapping the old director and his assistant wasn't a great leap.

I shuffled through the remaining pages more quickly: food, building supplies, sheets—all the day-to-day minutia involved in incarcerating children—plus weapons and ammunition. A request for restraints caught my attention, and I paused long enough for my eye to wander to the bottom and wonder, *what doesn't fit here?*

The shape of the warden's signature was all wrong—I'd seen it enough times by then to know. Examining the line more closely, I realized the shape didn't look right because it wasn't the warden's signature. Someone else had signed for him. Maybe the man was out sick, or attending a conference on advanced kiddie torturing techniques.

I squinted at the page and rubbed my aching forehead to make sure my tired eyes weren't deceiving me.

The form was signed by Milton *Dickey*.

I'd found Turtle's *Dickie*—and the center's Number Two —after all.

Within a few minutes I'd confirmed that, unlike his former boss, Milton Dickey was very much alive. Dickey owned and paid property taxes on a home in a small town about thirty miles from Tallahassee in neighboring Gadsden County. I mapped it out and researched the area. He resided in a neighborhood full of relatively high-value homes, but Dickey's was the most expensive, situated on the biggest slice of land. Property dollars generally go farther in Gadsden County than in Leon, and the home was assessed at nearly three times that county's average. I was looking forward to seeing what Dickey's hard-earned torture money had bought.

I continued working my way through personnel lists with databases, checking off a good chunk of the names as people who were now dead. A handful of others were scattered throughout the country. (Where do Florida residents go to retire? Anywhere but Florida.) Finding the remaining individuals would take deeper digging, and I wasn't sure that was the best use of my time. Roger didn't answer when I called to let him know what I'd found—probably in court, or in the midst of equally intense negotiations to avoid court—but my news could wait until this evening.

It was late afternoon already. My office building cast a deep shadow, and the dark-green canopy of a mid-sized live oak dappled the light beyond it as far as the street. I stood, rolled my neck, and shook myself all over like a wet dog to get my blood moving. Or at least settled in different spots, since I sat right back down. My neck protested (*you promised we were done with this*) as I picked up the phone again. I had two cases in motion, so now on to the other one.

My runaway Addy's friend back in Ocala was out of school by now. The teen answered her cell phone, but didn't have much to give me, and certainly nothing I didn't already know. At least, not over the phone. If something didn't break soon, I might have to spend a day in Ocala meeting people face-to-face. I hoped not. In addition to the annoying travel time, it wasn't without risks. Once I started interviews, especially with minors, the likelihood of someone officially reporting Addy missing would skyrocket.

But maybe that was best for Addy's safety and well-being. Maybe I was doing the wrong thing, essentially helping a child's closest family cover up the fact that she was missing.

Maybe. But my gut didn't think so.

Speaking of which, time to check in with my client Clint Spencer. He'd made it back home to Ocala following his conference and seemed surprised to hear from me so soon.

"What do you mean, Addy's okay?" he asked. "You saw her?"

It's hard to tell someone their teenaged niece gave you, *a trained private investigator*, the slip without feeling like a doofus. Fortunately, Mr. Spencer was too relieved to hold it against me. When I asked, he said he hadn't heard anything from the foster mother. According to their substitute teacher friend, Addy hadn't been reported as a runaway yet, which was consistent with what Addy's friend had said. That was good news, both for me (in avoiding complications) and potentially for our case.

"What case?" he asked.

This is what happens when I'm exhausted by a near-death experience at the hands of a crazy man, and also ready for more coffee. My mouth gets ahead of me.

"Mr. Spencer, you said you and your wife wanted to provide a home for your niece. Is that true?"

"Well, yes, but—"

"As you know, I've been speaking with an attorney about your niece's situation. He asked if you and your wife are interested in petitioning for custody of Addy."

"Are we interested?" he asked, voice faltering.

Was he asking his wife in the same room that question, or simply caught in a repeat-everything-the-lady-PI-says loop? I wasn't sure.

"Well, yes," he finally stammered, "we would be. We've talked about it. But... well, there are financial considerations."

"Could you take care of Addy if you had custody?" I asked.

"Yes, absolutely. We'd make sure of that. I meant, you know... lawyer money."

I could practically hear the poor man blushing with shame over the phone.

"We already dipped into our savings to pay for a lawyer who didn't do anything we could see. And then, with my wife's health issues, we had to dip in some more..."

I sighed. Roger dressed well, ate well, lived well. I wondered if his shiny car was paid off, though he struck me as the lease type. Well, I was about to throw his BMW under the bus. Or maybe my house payment, I wasn't sure which. "If it didn't cost you anything in addition to what you're paying me, would you be interested in filing for custody?" I asked.

"Of course, but how could that—"

"No guarantees, Mr. Spencer, but let me see what I can do. I'll be in touch as soon as I have news of Addy."

I hung up before the man could start stammering again and leaned back in my chair, propping my feet on the desk: the PI's thinking pose. Carefully, because it is possible to flip your chair that way. So I've heard.

It was time to take stock. Where was I, besides doing my best to avoid getting paid for any of my hard work? I'd tracked down my runaway and lost her. So far as I could tell, she didn't have connections of her own here in Tallahassee. That meant she'd probably make her way back to the boyfriend, and my best shot at finding her was through him. Either directly, by watching him, or indirectly, by watching the house where he was staying.

I didn't know how many people were living there, but if any of the guys had girlfriends—say, the peeking head I'd seen that night at the window—a closer look at the house might be a fruitful avenue. For young women still finding their place in the world, the arrival of an even younger female in their limited space typically triggers one of two reactions—resentment or empathy. Either could inspire a revelation about Addy's whereabouts.

Shifting gears, I'd also tracked down the second in charge Dick at the Reform School. Roger would want to speak with him, but now that we had a name and address, I felt as though I'd lost sight of the big picture. What did we hope to accomplish? What did Amos Weber need to pass on in peace? Just an acknowledgment of wrongdoing from someone who'd been at the top? Criminal charges? With the exception of murder, off the top of my head, I wasn't even sure of any charges that still fell within the statute of limitations for prosecution. That's why Roger was the lawyer.

Perhaps we could initiate a civil suit for the surviving children, or the families of those who didn't survive, based on newly discovered evidence of wrongdoing. Assuming we found some evidence. But Mr.

Weber would be lucky to live long enough to see it filed, much less succeed. Roger wasn't a fan of the media, but it might be the only avenue that worked for our timeframe—to sic someone we trusted on the story in the hopes of at least making the truth known and life uncomfortable for the surviving perpetrators.

My feet smacked back down to the floor when my cell phone rang. I assumed it was Roger. I was wrong. It was a woman's voice, with a fair bit of background noise.

"Sydney, are you standing me up?" she asked.

My eyes went to the calendar on my desk (*it's Friday*) and then the clock on my computer (*it's after 5:00, and I might need glasses*). "Crap! Sorry, Noel—I'm on my way."

I hung up on her "Uh-huh," and scrambled for my purse and jacket.

Lately my friend Noel and I had a standing date on Fridays at five p.m. for drinks at Cooper's. Somehow it had slipped my mind. I fumbled with my sticky screen door, then my even stickier front door lock. My hands shook as I thought, *Surely I get a freebie for absentmindedness on the day someone put a gun to my head.* Not that I would share that excuse with Noel.

On the day *Glenn's friend* put a gun to my head. And I was meeting Noel at Glenn's bar. Hmm... awkward much?

Yes, Glenn and I would eventually be okay, but would we be okay after just a few hours of fermenting?

I was about to find out.

14

Noel was chatting at the bar with Glenn when I arrived at Cooper's. The two could not be more different—a grizzled, long-haired, outlaw biker-turned-bar-owner white dude, and a perfectly mannered, conservatively dressed and coifed black woman banker—but Noel was on the short list of people Glenn would hang out with "on duty." I'd introduced them and provided the initial conversational bridge (*let's make fun of Sydney*). I was glad they'd moved beyond that to establish a relationship of their own.

I scanned the room (both pool tables and a few booths taken, but otherwise pretty thin) to avoid staring at Glenn. Because that's what I wanted to do, study him for cues and clues, figure out where we were. I knew we weren't meant to be a romantic couple, but there was something between us, something more than just shared, death-defying experience. His sibling analogy probably was the most apt. Sure, any decent therapist would have a field day with my penchant for attaching myself to older men after the early loss of my big brother. But at the end of the day, did it really matter? No matter what function or dysfunction had brought us together, I'd hate to damage our relationship.

Glenn's eyes were pinned to Noel's face until she glanced over her shoulder at me.

"There she is!" Noel said, grin wide enough to crease her eyes It was good to see her smile. Tragedy had brought us together (my investigation of her father's suicide), and she didn't smile enough.

"Sorry," I said. "I—"

"I know, you lost track of time," Noel said, in the tone of someone who's heard that excuse before.

Glenn finally turned to me and asked, "The usual?"

I climbed on a stool and rested my elbows on the bar, not quite ready to answer.

Noel looked from me to Glenn and back again. Then she raised a glass of iced, clear liquid, saying cautiously, "I'm going to go grab the corner booth. Take your time."

Glenn's lip curled beneath his mustache. "You think we scared her away?" he asked.

I still didn't answer, so he repeated, "The usual?"

I nodded, and he left to retrieve my Abita beer. I couldn't quite get my head around what I was feeling, but I didn't like it and I wanted it to stop.

Glenn set an icy glass on the bar and slowly poured the amber liquid. I could smell its rich yeastiness, and I imagined I could hear it frothing over the ambient noise. I reached for my drink, only to realize my hand had been resting at my temple, rubbing the spot where Turtle had pressed his gun.

The glass slipped a bit as I picked it up, so I used both hands. After a long sip, I raised my eyes to Glenn's and said, "I'm sorry."

He spread his fingers on the bar and pressed down, as if he were angry but not at me. "Sorry? What the hell do you have to be sorry for? I'm the one who almost got your brains blown out."

"But I'm the one who asked. And I'm the one who pushed." I was always the one who asked, who couldn't walk away, who didn't listen when someone tried to talk about consequences. I added, "I won't be pushing again."

Glenn opened his mouth, then shook his head. He sighed, and I couldn't read his expression. He shook his head again, took a sip from his drink, and leaned in like a proper bartender to say, "You know, pushing isn't always a bad thing."

"I know," I said easily, sliding off my stool before raising a brow and adding in my most provocative voice, "In fact, I seem to remember pushing being a *very good* thing."

Glenn barked a laugh and raised his ever-present glass. As I grabbed my own drink to join Noel, he said, "Just don't forget, Red. Pushing or not, you can *always* ask. For anything."

I nodded and turned away before he could see my eyes misting. Of course, Noel noticed when I sat across from her, even in the dim light.

"You two okay?" she asked.

"Yeah," I said, taking a sloppy sip from my beer and wiping my chin and the table afterward. "We're fine."

She glanced toward the bar, where Glenn was staring down a young, big dude who, until that moment, might have intended to be trouble. "He said to take it easy on you this evening, but that's all he'd say."

"And why do I not deserve polite conversation every evening?" I asked lightly. When Noel wrinkled her nose, I took the offensive. "So what's going on with you and Mr. Married Asshole this week?"

To my surprise, Noel didn't protest—as she usually did—that she never should have told me about her affair with the unidentified man. Instead she confided, "I'm worried about him."

I rolled my eyes, but she continued, "Sydney, I'm serious."

"Is he still... trying to stay in touch with you?" I'd caught myself before using the hot-button word *harass*.

Her gaze strayed to the table between us, and she fiddled with the corner of her drink's napkin. "He doesn't call that often. And I'm afraid to not answer. He doesn't even want to get back together. He just needs someone to talk to."

I burped, small but still unladylike, as I suppressed a snort. "I thought that's what his wife was for. But I'm guessing she doesn't really understand him."

Noel looked at me sharply. "It's not like that. He doesn't run her down. It's just... There's something else going on. He won't say what it is—to me or to her—but it's eating him up inside."

"I think that *something* is called a conscience."

She sat up straighter, lips pursed. Noel is not the most communicative person about her emotions, so this qualified as highly pissed off.

"I'm sorry," I said, to the second person in the space of a single beer. "But I just don't want to see you hung up on this guy."

"I'm not hung up on him!" she shouted.

Okay, so *that* was Noel highly pissed off.

"It's not about me," she said, glancing around self-consciously and lowering her voice. "It's about him. Actually, I was wondering if maybe you could—"

My cell phone rang, interrupting her. I didn't recognize the number and held up a finger as I said, "Sydney Brennan Investigations."

"So you really are a detective?" a young-sounding, feminine voice asked.

My mind raced, but came up with only one possibility. "Is this Addy?"

"Showing off, Miss Detective?" was her answer.

"That's Ms. Detective to you," I said, drawing an interested look from Noel. I rose, wary of involving her in my potential mess, shielding the phone as I left the booth. "So what's up, *Miss* Runaway?"

I meandered out of earshot and leaned against a lonely wall while I waited for Addy to tell me what she wanted, knowing that if I pushed her, she'd run in the other direction.

"I've been thinking about what you said," Addy admitted. "I need to see you again. In person."

"That's funny, because I've been thinking about the way you left me at the pizza place," I countered. "Do you have plans to leave me somewhere else, sitting alone like a fool?"

"No," she said, sounding more like a stubborn child than someone on the cusp of adulthood.

"I'm at Cooper's Bar right now," I said, waiting to see if she made an excuse. She may not have easy transport, and I was willing to go get her myself, but I needed to know how motivated she really was to meet me.

"Okay," she said. "I'll be there in a few minutes." And she hung up.

Well, well, well. I hadn't seen that one coming. I stared at my phone, wondering what she'd do next. It depended on her level of desperation, specifically whether she'd gone back to her boyfriend yet.

"So what was that about?" Noel asked as I returned to the booth.

I shook my head, unwilling to share. "You were saying?"

Her eyes dropped as I sat, focusing on her fingers interlacing on the tabletop. "I said, I was wondering if you could—"

And my phone rang again. "Sorry." Assuming it was Addy with a story about why she wasn't going to show up, I said, "This better be good."

"Sydney?" asked a confused, decidedly masculine voice.

"Roger?" I guessed.

"Yeah," he said. "I saw that you'd called, so I'm checking in."

"Just a minute." After an apologetic shrug at a frustrated Noel, I headed outside to the parking lot. This call required more privacy. It was nearly dark, and I strode around the corner of the building toward one of the streetlights sandwiched between trees and doing double duty as a utility pole before asking Roger, "Are you okay?"

"I'm fine," he said, sounding anything but. "Did you find something?"

I quickly gave him an overview of how I'd located Milton Dickey, the juvenile facility's number two man. I left out the part about the "witness" holding a gun to my head during the interview.

"That's good," Roger said. "Do you have the address?"

"I think so," I said, rummaging in my purse for my small notebook. "But the light's not great here. Can I email it to you later?"

"Sorry, Sydney, but I need it now. I want to go see him tonight."

I should have expected Roger would be fired up and ready to go immediately, but I hadn't. "Are you sure that's a good idea? Maybe you should—"

"Goddammit, Syd, I said I need it now!" He paused, getting his breath. When he continued, his mouth sounded closer to the phone. I pictured him hunched over the device, pacing in a parking lot of his own. "You still there?" he asked.

"Yes, Roger, I'm here," I said, keeping my voice as calm as possible. It was unusual for Roger to lose his temper.

"I'm sorry," he said. "I didn't mean to snap at you. It's just... We're out of time."

My hand went to my chest as I leaned against the wooden pole, afraid to ask. Finally, he said, "Dad's close. He's trying to hang in there... I spent all day with him at hospice, and he's really close."

That explained Roger not answering his phone.

I sighed. I couldn't risk losing a chance at Addy, but I also couldn't let Roger go on his own. I pulled up a map in my head, no small feat, because I'm not the most navigation-minded person. I believed that Milton Dickey's house was in the direction of the hospice facility, about twenty minutes beyond it.

"Fine," I said, "but I'm going with you."

Roger was one of the few people I knew as independent as I am and, a natural litigator, he lived to argue. When he didn't object, that put any reservations I might have had to rest.

"Thank you," he said, voice soft.

"No problem," I said, endeavoring to make it sound like any other case. "I'll meet you at the hospice and we can leave from there."

Roger cleared his throat. "Okay, that sounds good."

"It'll be a while, though," I said. "And I won't be alone."

I told him about Addy's promise to meet me, without ever explicitly using her name, so he technically had no direct knowledge of her identity. Yes, it was likely a fatuous effort, but it was one thing to endanger my PI license; it was something else to endanger Roger's law license. Not that I really thought it would come to that, or that if it did, my subterfuge would help. But it was all I could think to do under the circumstances.

Roger hung up, and as if on cue, headlights swept over the parking lot. A petite young woman wearing a hoodie stepped out of a car driven by another young woman. I didn't get a good look at the driver, but the passenger was definitely Addy. She hadn't seen me yet.

Now all I had to do was convince a teen who'd already ditched me once to trust me enough to ride with me to meet a strange man (Roger), so we could ride with him to another strange man's house (Dickey), who happened to be—to put it bluntly—A Bad Guy. To do I knew not what when we got there. Possibly restrain a distraught Roger from killing said Bad Guy.

I took a deep breath as I crossed the parking lot toward the unsuspecting teenager already climbing the stairs to Cooper's front door.

Piece of cake.

15

———————

I bounded up the stairs on Addy's heels as she fumbled with the front door, perhaps a little too quickly. The teenager glanced over her shoulder in alarm as she threw her weight against the door, stumbling over the threshold to enter.

"If I had a dollar for every time I tripped over that," I said, following, "I wouldn't need a tab."

Addy clutched the elbows of her sweatshirt, looking as though she still hadn't quite regained her balance. The schlumpy pack on her back probably didn't help. "You scared the crap out of me," she said, voice accusatory.

Part of me felt like I owed her for leaving me behind at the pizza place. Fortunately, a bigger part of me remembered that I was the adult in this situation and said, "I'm sorry. I didn't mean to."

Addy's long, dark hair was pulled back in a ponytail that had gathered in her hood. She looked like a kid who'd just finished basketball practice, frustrated because her mom was late picking her up. Except I doubted she'd ever played organized sports.

We stepped out of the way as a man opened the door behind us, and I surveyed the bar for the best place to speak with Addy. Not in the booth with Noel. I felt her gaze on me like a laser sight and gave a quick wave, receiving a curt nod of acknowledgment.

"Who's that?" Addy asked, wary and eyeing the door.

"The friend I was hanging out with when you called," I said, urging Addy forward.

She drew away when I tried to guide her with a hand, so I motioned her to the stool in the corner and positioned my own seat to shield her from view. I hated having my back to the door, but didn't want all eyes—*any* eyes—in the bar watching Addy.

"So you haven't gone back to Troy," I said, statement rather than question.

A single crease appeared on Addy's forehead. "How do you know that?"

"Remember, I'm the detective. You thought about what I said?" I prompted.

She nodded.

"Have you decided what you want to do?" I asked.

"I don't know," she muttered.

I held my breath to keep from releasing a melodramatic sigh. "Then how about you crash with me tonight, and I help you figure it out?"

She shrugged.

I didn't have time for this. "Okay, let me put it another way. Either you come with me, so your family and I know you're safe, or I will take you in to the cops as a runaway."

"You can't do that!" Her wide eyes went to the door behind me.

"Maybe not," I admitted. "Maybe you'll be faster than me when you run for the door and make it to the parking lot. And maybe, somehow, you'll run off into the night in a strange city, magically evading a trained investigator who lives here and actually owns a car."

I pulled my keys from my purse and held them up, jingling. Her attention locked on them, like a cat ready to eviscerate an unsuspecting bird.

"But even if you did get away, it would still be my legal obligation to report you as a runaway. Whether it screws up my client's chances of getting custody or not." I rose from my stool. "I'm going to get my beer now. You decide what you need to do."

My shoulder blades itched as I turned my back on her and returned to the booth, praying she wouldn't call my bluff. I'd busted my ass running for the door in Cooper's once before. Sober, I might add. I preferred to not meet the hardwood again while chasing a teenager.

I didn't bother sitting, just rested my palms on the tabletop with my back to the bar. "She still there?" I asked.

"Yes," Noel said. "Who is she?"

"It's best if you don't know," I said.

"How old is she?" Noel asked.

I opened my mouth to answer, but when words didn't immediately flow, Noel said in a wry voice, "Let me guess. It's best if I don't know."

"Exactly," I said. I picked up my beer and gazed at it with longing. I had a feeling I'd be ready to finish this one—and about half a dozen more—by the end of the night.

"Let me make another stab in the dark," Noel said. "You have to go now."

Her face was darker than usual, betraying a hint of angry flush. I opened my mouth, but she held up her hand. "No, don't bother saying you're sorry."

I was. But I didn't want to make her more angry. So I made a mute, penitent puppy dog face instead, blinking big eyes and twisting my mouth in a sorrowful grimace.

Noel didn't quite smile, but her face softened and she waved her hand in the air, the way you might dismiss an unruly child. "Go on. But remember, Sydney. Just because I work in a bank doesn't mean I have unlimited access to bail money."

I carried my beer back to the bar, where I found an equally unhappy Glenn. Glowering, he motioned me toward the far end with a peremptory head jerk. I dutifully followed.

Glenn's gruff voice dropped even lower than usual, and his face loomed. I could see individual hairs curling in his mustache, some of them gray. "I know you didn't bring a minor into my bar."

I felt bad about Noel, but although it wasn't a great survival strategy, there was something satisfying about pissing off Glenn. So long as it was just enough to annoy him and not enough to make him seriously angry. "Well, that's true," I said, "I did not *bring* her—"

"Sydney," he growled, head tilting in that way that said he was now dangerously close to actual angry territory.

I set my glass on the bar beneath his chin. If Glenn had a beard, it would've brushed the rim. "Don't worry, I'm working on getting her out of here right now."

"You damn well better be," he said, picking up my glass and wiping the wet ring it had left behind. "You know there are people who would like nothing better than to shut me down."

I hadn't known that, but I couldn't say it was surprising. I nodded and slunk away to the teenager. She'd been watching us closely, and she continued watching Glenn behind the bar as I approached her.

"So what's it going to be?" I asked.

"What's his deal?" Addy asked.

"No, sweetie," I said, voice cutting as I climbed up on the leather stool to block her view, "the question on the table is, what's *your* deal. Are you with me?"

She forced her eyes back to me. "Yeah, okay," she said, her tone more uncertain than begrudging, which was the only thing that kept my snark in check.

I gave a final wave to Noel, who was now talking on her phone and may or may not have seen me. "Do you have any other stuff?" I asked, holding the door for Addy.

"This is it," she said, tugging at the strap of the backpack she hadn't bothered to remove.

It wasn't much, and I wondered what she'd left behind. Certainly nothing important. If I could only carry one backpack, what would it contain? Keepsakes? Tank tops? Underwear?

I stepped on Addy's heels when she stopped at the bottom of the steps. She didn't complain, just moved aside and asked, "Where to?"

I pointed toward Cecil, parked on the lot's perpendicular end. "The little silver hatchback. But there's something I have to do before we can go home. We're meeting one of my friends and driving somewhere with him." I hesitated, struggling with the logistics. "You'll have to wait in the car, but Roger's BMW is really nice. Seat warmers for your butt and everything."

"This one's not so bad," Addy said. I could see a hint of grin as she no doubt imagined driving to the beach with the top down. That was always my daydream. Aside from the part where I spontaneously combust in the sun.

"Thanks," I said. "He's no spring chick, but Cecil's still got some life in him."

I unlocked the doors as she asked, "Your car's name is Cecil?"

"Of course. He speaks with a Cockney accent," I said. It occurred to me that everything Addy owned in the world could use a touch more security than my open back seat, so I unlocked the hatchback and motioned for her to toss her bag there. "The guy we're meeting is an attorney, and it's probably a good idea if you don't tell him your name."

"Addy?" A man's voice cut through the air.

"Shit," she muttered, as I noted, "Yeah, that name."

Troy Cantrell strode toward us, all indignant swagger. I hadn't noticed his car enter the parking lot, but I'd stopped paying attention once I had Addy in hand.

"Get in the car, Addy," I said, positioning myself between her and her ex.

Of course she ignored me. "Troy, go home. I told you we're done."

"The fuck we are," he said, now close enough for me to see he was wearing the same leather jacket he'd worn the previous night. He still hadn't shaved, either. "We're done *when I say* we're done. I came to Tallahassee for you."

This time, Addy didn't resist when I took her by the arm and led her to the adjacent line of cars alongside the bar. "Go back inside and wait for me there."

She hesitated. I gave her a gentle shove and said, "Go."

Troy's eyes followed her as she slipped between two cars and stepped over the railroad tie boundary, jogging toward the entrance. I trailed slowly, on the back bumper side of the vehicles.

Troy did a double take when he turned his attention back to me. "Don't I know you?"

"Do we ever really know anybody?" I asked, sidling around to block his direct line of Addy pursuit.

Troy stuck his hands in his pockets and tilted his head. It was both a pose and an effort to get a better look at me. Only a few yards separated us, but a large live oak cast shadows from the nearest streetlight. The exterior light at the bar entrance probably didn't help, either. He pointed at me as he came closer. "Yeah, I've seen you before. At one of the clubs. You still looking to buy?"

Troy Cantrell was not the sharpest knife in the drawer.

"No," I said simply.

Troy stopped, but couldn't seem to stand still, almost rocking, and I wondered if he was a bad businessman sampling his own product. The light from inside Cooper's flashed across the parking lot as Addy entered the building. He nodded and his face twisted as he finally put the two sightings of me together and figured out my purpose. "Sonuvabitch," he said.

"You know she's just sixteen, right?" I asked. "What's the matter, you can't find anyone your own age dumb enough to go out with you?"

He moved closer, within his striking range and possibly mine, and I widened my stance slightly.

"Why, are you volunteering?" he asked. "You're a little old, but you seemed pretty eager last night."

I gave a calculated laugh. "That's funny, I thought we'd worked out why I was there last night, and it certainly wasn't for your charms."

He took another step. My heart banged in my chest as I looked up at him (*at least he doesn't have a gun*), and I fought a powerful urge to gasp for more air.

"You sure? Because no one is that good of an actress," he said, tracing my arm with his fingers.

I pitched my voice low, hoping he'd mistake my fear for confident anger. "So says you and every other man too stupid to know the difference."

I tried not to flinch as his face lunged toward me. The sharp tang of alcohol on his breath made me want to vomit my own drink. "We'll see about that," he said, mouth twisting and fingers closing in a tight grip on my arm.

16

Soften him up, Vince's calm voice said in my head.

Tossing my purse aside, I kicked Troy in the shin as hard as I could without falling.

"Argh!" he cried out, bowing with the unexpected pain, but he still held my arm. "What the fuck!"

He drew back his other hand for a backhanded slap but, already moving, I ducked lower and barely felt the contact. Vince was right. My hands were sweaty and slippery, and they were smaller than Troy's. But they still managed to seize his hand and peel his fingers from me, twisting and pressing down on his wrist.

Troy cried out again, pulling and rotating his arm to ease the pain. Still gripping his hand, I pressed his upper arm toward the ground, and the rest of him followed. But his elbow kept flailing and I lost my balance trying to control him. Troy grunted as I fell on top of him, knees in his back. I climbed awkwardly to my feet while he was still catching his breath.

He braced his hands, rising slightly from the ground. I whaled on him as he rolled over on his side with a solid kick to his ribs that made my back twinge. Troy fell back to the gravel with a screeching moan. I kicked him once more before walking to Cecil and popping the trunk.

My tire iron was wedged beneath my spare tire, and by the time I pulled it free, I could feel someone standing behind me. I whirled with the metal rod—

"Easy there, Red," Glenn said, seizing my arm mid-swing. "I'm a friendly, and the man's still down."

Panting, I felt Glenn's hold ease and realized he was the only thing keeping my shaking arm aloft. He gently took the now-heavy metal bar from my hand and dropped it back inside the trunk with a ringing thunk. Then he faced me, resting a hand on my shoulders (*what was in his other hand?*), and asked, "You okay?"

My vision had gone a little dark around the edges and I felt a vague throbbing in my cheek, but there was still fire left in me that wanted to lash out at anything within range. "I had it under control!"

"I can see that," Glenn said calmly.

Addy's voice was decidedly less calm when she called out a warning behind us. "Hey! I think he's getting up."

I glanced past Glenn. Troy might be getting up, but it was a *process*, one with an aspirational destination. Glenn stopped me as I reached again toward the tire iron, slamming the hatchback shut. I hoped my keys weren't buried inside.

"He could have a weapon," I protested. Just because he'd assumed *I'd* be a pushover, didn't mean Troy wasn't prepared for someone else.

"I know," Glenn said, raising a hand so I finally saw the blade it held. The folding knife looked like a Boy Scout's toy in Glenn's massive hand.

I blinked, stared at Troy, then back at Glenn. When the hell had Glenn disarmed him?

"Look, I know you had this," Glenn said, "but it's my place. My business. Which means ass-wipes like him are my responsibility."

Troy had made it to all fours. Well, three of four anyway. One arm clutched his abdomen as he groaned. Glenn leaned over and placed a meaty hand between Troy's shoulder blades and pressed down, easily pushing him back to the earth. He said, "If you know what's good for you, you'll fucking stay down until I tell you to get up."

The younger man didn't move, except to turn his face out of the gravelly dust.

"Why don't you take the kid back inside while I explain the Rules of Conduct for patrons of Cooper's?" Glenn said.

It was a reasonable suggestion, but the way my body was humming, I still wanted to beat the crap out of someone. And I was afraid of what would happen once that humming stopped.

Another familiar voice called out my name, "Sydney?"

Noel stood just behind Addy, her expression hard to make out in the dark. Noel and I had experienced the emotional roller coaster of violence together when she was my client. She didn't know many of the crazy things that had happened since then, but if anyone (other than Glenn) understood what I was going through—and how not to make it worse—that person was Noel.

So when Noel said, "Let's go inside," I picked my purse up off the ground and followed her.

Addy followed me in turn. My legs felt strange crossing the parking lot and climbing the steps, as if someone else made them move. The temperature inside Cooper's had been comfortable before, but now it felt as though it could bake French fries. Or PIs. I began to sweat.

"Sit," Noel said, slipping behind Glenn's bar as if it were her own.

Addy and I complied, while Noel bustled around opening drawers and random containers, occasionally muttering under her breath. Once Noel's eyes went wide, and she replaced a tin lid carefully. Discretion prevailed over curiosity and I didn't ask.

Addy watched me while I watched Noel. She must have seen me take Troy down, but I couldn't tell how she felt about it. Maybe because she didn't know how she felt about it, either.

"So you ran inside and got Glenn?" I asked, my voice echoing strangely in my ears.

"Glenn is the bartender?" she asked.

"Bar owner," I said automatically.

Addy nodded. My logical mind knew she'd done the right thing, and I should probably tell her that, but my lizard mind still regretted not braining her asshole boyfriend when I'd had the chance.

"So you and Glenn..." Addy said, tentatively.

I gave her stink-eye, and she didn't finish.

Noel returned and set two steaming mugs in front of us. "Drink," she said.

Addy looked to me, uncertain, and I shrugged and took a sip. Hot, milky sweet tea. Sweat gathered at my brows, but I still closed my eyes in appreciation. "Thanks, Noel."

I didn't hear Addy say anything, so I opened my eyes and gave her stool a tiny kick. "Thank you," she muttered.

"You're both very welcome," Noel said, adding a bowl of peanuts to the wooden bar. "These don't quite go with your tea, but they're the only protein I could find, unless you count wasabi peas, which would be even worse."

I almost did a spit-take with my tea at the thought of the combination. Yep, there they were, those incipient giggles sneaking in around the edges. The first step in a potential meltdown. Which would be my second potential meltdown today, both well-deserved.

I needed a vacation.

For now, I'd settle for sweet tea and peanuts.

I tossed a handful of the salty buggers in my mouth, nearly choked when I didn't chew enough, then drank the rest of my sweet tea like I was at a knitting circle kegger. My throat burned, but it was a satisfying pain, like pressing hard against an aching tooth.

The three of us pivoted simultaneously as the door opened to admit Glenn.

He looked exactly as he had when I'd last seen him—no blood, dirt, sweat, or any other sign of having beaten the crap out of anyone. He pitched my car keys to me (*what was he, a fricking magician?*) as he strode toward the section that accessed the bar. Noel, looking self-conscious, started to leave, but he touched her forearm briefly and said, "You're fine."

Glenn disappeared for a few moments, then returned with a

familiar gel cold pack. He pointed at his cheek, then handed the ice pack to me without a word.

"I know," I said. "I didn't control him on the arm bar, didn't keep my face out of the way as I took him down."

He nodded and, instead of saying *I told you so*, said, "But you did take him down."

I pressed the pack directly against the skin of my face—the same cheek Turtle had slapped this morning—and experienced another form of satisfying discomfort. Noel regarded Glenn and me as if we were both heathens, then handed me a clean, still-folded dishtowel to wrap the pack. Five minutes behind the bar, and she already knew where everything was.

Well... I thought of the sliding section of wall in the back where Glenn kept his secret arsenal. Not *everything*.

Glenn stared at me as if he wanted to say something, but was reluctant to do so in front of Noel and Addy. Either Addy got the hint, or the excitement had finally caught up with her. "Where's the bathroom?" she asked.

"I'll go with you," Noel said, moving from behind the bar. "The faucet in there is a little tricky if you don't want to get soaked head to toe."

Glenn's eyes hadn't left my face. I fixed my gaze on the reddish-brown hairs curling free of his braid below the rubber band. A few gray hairs had snuck in, but not nearly as many as he had in his mustache. "I'm fine," I said, anticipating him.

"I know you are," he said, tossing the end of his braid over his shoulder, forcing me to find something else to look at. "But what about that punk in the parking lot?"

"I don't know. You tell me." The cold settling into my cheek made speaking awkward. "What did you do?"

"Just put the fear of God into him. You'd already done plenty." He leaned over the bar to look at my feet. "There's a reason they call those boots shit-kickers. My question is, what would you have done to him if I hadn't been there?"

"Is this about the tire iron?" I asked.

"It's not a tire iron; it's a lug wrench. Cars haven't used tire irons since the 1950s. They used to—" He shook his head. "Never mind. You didn't answer my question."

And I continued not answering, grinding my teeth instead. The hand not holding the ice pack still shook on my lap.

"Exactly," Glenn said. "You need to figure out how to ride the extremes, Red. How to do what you do without getting either so shit-scared you're paralyzed, or so banshee-pissed you kill somebody. Or you need to do something else."

Do something else. I set the ice pack on the bar with a thump. What would that even mean? Nothing but background checks, with no interviews? Stick to financial investigations? Not my strong suit.

But it hadn't always been like this. What had happened to make me go from having close calls I could share as funny war stories to... What do you call the stage beyond close calls? Where you're forced to do things you can't risk telling anyone for fear of going to prison?

Do something else... *Dammit!*

"I've got to go," I said, suddenly remembering, "I'm supposed to be somewhere."

Glenn glanced at Noel and Addy exiting the bathroom. His face was already so near, when he lowered his deep voice I could feel it vibrating in my chest. "This about the thing from this morning?" he asked.

"Yeah, it is. Believe it or not, I managed to get some sense from what Turtle told us." Then my train of thought veered sideways, as it so often did. "How'd he end up out there?"

Glenn shrugged. "I found him a place. Look, I'm not gonna lie to you and say he's just misunderstood, that it's not his fault. The man's fucked up, and he made his own choices. But..."

His voice trailed off as Addy climbed onto the stool next to me. Then he crooked a smile, whether for me or her I couldn't tell, and continued, "Well, it is what it is."

I nodded a farewell to Noel and gestured toward the door, telling Addy, "Come on, we have to go."

The teen gave a martyred sigh, sliding off the stool and pulling her hair free from her tangled hood.

Glenn picked up the cold pack from the bar, hefting it as if he were weighing it for shipping. "You need backup?"

I considered for a moment—despite my earlier vow, my day had been too long and screwed up already for me to be proud or stupid about help. "No, thanks. I'm actually acting as backup for my lawyer, so it's not that kind of situation."

"With you there?" he asked, as if I were a catalyst of chaos.

I stuck my tongue out at him, and Glenn tilted his head suggestively. Addy fell in next to me as he said, "That's okay, darling. You know you can be my backup in *any* kind of situation."

I couldn't help smiling at the innuendo, even though it hurt my cheek—yet another flavor of satisfying pain. I hoped the last pain of the night.

17

My legs pounded down the steps, moving as quickly as they could for still feeling like I'd borrowed them from someone else. I had to pause twice crossing the parking lot so Addy could catch up. Occasionally she stumbled, watching all corners and every parked car rather than where she was placing her feet.

"It's all right," I said. "Troy's gone."

Instead of moving more quickly, she stopped in her tracks. "Is he okay?"

"Does it matter?" I asked, before encouraging her, "Come on."

My body temperature was still running hot, so I held off on the heater when we were seated in the car. Addy shivered next to me, pulling up her hood as she finally answered, "I guess it does matter. A little. Troy could be an asshole, but he never hurt me."

"Really?" I asked, putting the car in gear.

She looked away, amending her answer to, "Well, not physically."

My mind was both sluggish and racing, moving in herky-jerky fits and starts. I took a moment to confirm the route in my head, making sure I knew which way to turn out of the parking lot. Then I said,

"Well, don't worry. He's not in a dumpster. Your ex got lucky and caught Glenn in a good mood."

"What about you?" she asked. "Was that you in a good mood?"

I smiled in the dark, making my cheek twinge.

That was me getting lucky... A thought I didn't share and tried not to dwell upon.

Addy fell quiet while I navigated through a few traffic lights and turned onto a narrow, canopy road. She leaned forward to look up at the obstructed sky through the windshield. The streetlights were less frequent here, but consistent enough to keep the overhanging branches of live oaks and their Spanish moss from looking too ghostly in the glare of my headlights and those of the car behind me.

"I'd be half afraid to drive on this road," Addy said.

"Because there's no shoulder?" I asked.

"That, and because it feels like a cave. Which seems really cool, until the ceiling collapses," she said, leaning back in her seat and hugging herself.

"Remind me not to watch horror movies with you," I muttered, turning on the defrost. Her proximity to the windshield had caused it to fog.

She either didn't hear my dig or ignored it. "This friend of yours we're meeting..."

I'd wondered when she'd ask. "Yes?"

"Is she black too?" Addy asked.

I glanced at her, but it was dark and her face was turned away to monitor the nonexistent shoulder. "You mean like Noel?"

"It's a good thing she didn't come out until after you beat the snot out of Troy," she mused. "He doesn't do well with niggers."

My body flew toward the steering wheel, the seat belt catching me, and Cecil twisted sideways slightly as he came to a sudden, screeching stop. The screeching sound continued even after we were motionless—the protesting brakes of the vehicle behind us. I braced myself for impact, but none came.

"What the hell was that?" Addy asked, breathless.

I had to reconstruct the events myself, in reverse order. Slamming the brakes. The moment of conversation that preceded it. My body already humming.

"What makes you think I would find that word appropriate?" I demanded of the pale blur that was Addy's face. "Do I look like a fricking idiot?"

A horn blared behind me. I waved the car around and rolled my window back up before returning to my rant. "Seriously. I asked you a question. Do I look like an idiot? Because the only people who use that word are morons and idiots."

I flashed back to Turtle this morning, his casual words and casual violence... That's my only excuse (admittedly a feeble one) for demanding, "Your mother teach you that?"

Only Addy's seat belt saved us from broken noses when her face lunged toward mine. "Don't you dare talk about my mother!"

"So she wouldn't approve either?" I asked, remembering too late I should have spoken in past tense. Remembering too late I was berating an orphaned teenager.

I jumped in my seat when someone banged a fist against the glass next to me. My heart pounded, but all I could make out through my fogging window was a dark shape. Muttering every expletive I could lay my tongue to, I slowly opened the door on the assumption that taking the person out preemptively with one big whump was inappropriate.

Squeezing out of the car, I found myself facing a very large, very round woman who was little more than a silhouette in her vehicle's headlights. *Avoid the words "moron" and "idiot,"* I reminded myself before speaking.

"Sorry about that," I said, pretending I was a normal person and not someone who could rip the heads off puppies. *Hmmm, puppies. Good idea.* I continued, "There was a dog in the road."

"I didn't see any dog," the woman countered.

"Well, you wouldn't have, would you?" I said. "Me being in front. And it was a small dog."

I pirouetted and bent around the front of the car. "I'd like to make sure the animal's not still here, so if you could just drive around us .."

My strained voice rose at the end like a teacher reprimanding a last period student, mentally counting the number of minutes before she can leave and drink her way through the weekend.

The woman shook her head but thankfully returned to her car, calling over her shoulder, "I got dogs of my own, but you need to be more careful."

Standing flush against Cecil, I waved as she drove past—with all five fingers, not just the middle one. The click of my seat belt was loud when I got back in the car. I didn't even look at Addy. I could tell she was still sitting in the car, still breathing, and I didn't need to know more than that.

Neither of us spoke for the ten additional minutes it took to arrive at the hospice facility. The parking lot was nearly empty on a Friday evening, and Roger stood in the cold next to his car.

Pulling into the nearest spot, I said, "My friend's not black. But he is a lawyer, so I guess that makes him a Jew." I cut the engine and added, "Get in the back seat of his car. And remember, keep your mouth shut."

My wrist twinged as I slammed the driver's door (more evidence of my less than perfect technique with Troy) before retrieving my purse from the back seat. I brushed off a piece of gravel stuck to its side and another caught in the strap like Velcro.

"Everything okay?" Roger asked.

I really wanted to vent to him. Roger has a no-nonsense way of being empathetic without being touchy-feely, combined with a willingness to call me on my crap when it's necessary. And sometimes when it's not. But I was okay, and Roger's father was dying. So Roger didn't need to hear me bitch, even if I needed to do it.

"Yeah," I said, voice hoarse. "Sorry, it took longer to get away than I thought it would."

I swallowed and cleared my throat. Had I been yelling at Addy? She had slipped into the back seat without a word, head bowed beneath her hood, and she tugged at the sweatshirt's long strings. I couldn't read her shadowed face, even if I'd wanted to.

I sank into the buttery soft leather of Roger's passenger seat, started to rub my tired eyes, and hissed when my fingers pressed against my cheek.

"You sure you're okay?" he asked.

I forced a smile and said, "I'm fine. Story for another time."

"Breakfast?" he asked.

Unlike Glenn, Roger wasn't flirting. We often talked business over breakfast.

"Only if you're buying," I said. And he always did.

He'd already programmed the address into his GPS, and a soft woman's voice announced we had twenty-seven minutes to our destination. That sounded like the perfect amount of time for a nap. The shakes had stopped and I'd begun to crash. But when I closed my eyes, I felt myself falling. Falling through space, and into places in my head that were better left alone. I sat up abruptly.

"You know where the seat warmer is, don't you?" Roger asked.

Maybe the shakes hadn't stopped after all. "I'm fine," I repeated, leaning against the cold glass of the window.

Roger glanced in his rearview window. "It's Addy, right?" he asked.

I sighed. So much for covering Roger's ass with pretense.

"Yes," she said, voice sounding small, younger than it had before.

"I'm Roger," he said. "Have you eaten?"

Have you eaten? His father was dying, he had an impossible task to perform before the man passed, on top of his usual insane criminal caseload, and he was asking a stranger if she'd eaten.

A strange sixteen-year-old runaway I'd just yelled at. Albeit not without reason.

"I'm good," she said.

We drove a few more minutes in silence before Roger asked me, "What do you know about Mr. Dickey?"

It was time to get my head in the game.

"Not much yet," I said. "He was the Assistant Director at the Reform School until the facility shut down in 1998. He worked as a lobbyist for American Correctional Enterprises for a few more years after that."

"Good money," Roger observed. Roger also lived well. He probably spent as much time working on pro bono cases as paid ones, but he made the paid ones count.

"He bought this house before he had the big-ticket job," I said, "so I'm wondering if he married into money. He certainly wasn't making enough running the facility to cover it."

"Anything on the wife?" Roger asked.

"Died about eight years ago. He's got two kids, a son and a daughter…" I paused to do math on multiple fronts. "Around your age. That's all I have on the family so far."

Roger nodded to himself as he drove. His GPS announced we were a couple of minutes from our next turn, which appeared to be the edge of Mr. Dickey's neighborhood. Roger seemed very calm, considering.

"Any change?" I asked.

He didn't need clarification.

"I think it helped," he said. "Knowing we have a next step seems to bring Dad some peace. I also made progress on our potential victims today. Spoke with a few colleagues who filed wrongful death suits on behalf of families whose children died in custody. One is bound by a settlement, but he'll be going through that with a fine-toothed comb. The rest were dismissed, but they may still be able to save us some legwork."

I pictured Roger multitasking, going back and forth between sitting at his father's bedside with a laptop and having hushed cell phone conversation in hallways. The man was a machine.

But of course he wasn't. And it was going to catch up with him.

Roger glanced in the rearview mirror.

"Addy," he said, "Have you ever heard of the Florida Youth Reform School?"

Seated directly behind me, she leaned toward the center to answer, "No."

"It's a place where they used to incarcerate kids," he said, signaling as we approached our turn. "And we think they did some bad stuff."

"Worse than locking up children?" she asked.

Roger's grim smile showed in a pair of metal filigree lamp posts as we entered the neighborhood. "Yes, worse than that. That's why we're here, to see what this man can tell us about it."

The subdued electronic voice advised that our destination was directly ahead in one hundred yards. She was off by a little, distance- and direction-wise, but not much. The Dickey house sat back from the road, with a gravel parking area cut into the grassy yard. A few tall conifers stood sentinel in front. Along the side and in back, the house was surrounded by woods thick enough to make it impossible to assess the extent of the property, especially in the dark.

"So you think the guy who lives here was part of it?" she asked. "That he was hurting kids?"

"Yes," Roger said, turning into the driveway and parking next to a modest, late-model sedan.

"And you think he's just going to admit it if you ask?" she demanded, incredulous. "Why would he do that?"

Roger parked the car and removed his seat belt, turning to face Addy. "Regrets," he said simply.

I glanced at Addy and raised a brow to let her know that I might have called her an idiot, but I shared her skepticism. Then I followed Roger to knock on the Bad Guy's front door.

18

The same model lamp post we'd seen entering the neighborhood highlighted a paved path to Mr. Dickey's entrance. The house was large, but not ridiculously so, painted white with black shutters and second-story dormers that gave it a traditional air. The bulk was one big chunk, with a smaller chunk to the right that was likely a later addition. A porch ran the length of the big chunk, wrapping around the corner to dead-end at the addition.

Mounting the front steps, recessed lighting illuminated ceiling fans and several wooden rockers that looked attractive but uncomfortable. Heavily curtained windows gave off a soft interior glow and a sense of occupation, but no revelations of movement.

Roger's arm stretched for the doorbell, the sleeve of his impeccable suit jacket rising to expose his designer watch. I suddenly remembered my own clothes had been through the Turtle drama this morning and the Cooper's ass-kicking this evening. At least I'd changed my tank top at the office in between. I was frantically brushing dust from my jeans when the door swung open.

"Yes?" asked a Latina woman in her late fifties, wearing tan slacks, a long-sleeved navy blouse, and tasteful jewelry.

She could have been the lady of the house, but she stood solidly in the doorway like a gatekeeper. The angle of her stance suggested she was protecting—or monitoring—someone inside.

Roger gave a token, professional smile, then said, "Good evening, ma'am. We have an appointment with Mr. Dickey."

He handed the woman a business card before glancing at his watch. "We may be a few minutes early. I wasn't sure how long it would take us to get here from the capital."

She examined Roger's card carefully, then stared at him and back at the card, as if she were checking a photo identification. "You don't have an appointment with Mr. Dickey," she said.

Roger ignored his proffered card and didn't even blink as he reasserted, "Yes, we do. *Ms.*?"

Instead of giving her name, she glanced over her shoulder down a hallway. "Do you mean you have an appointment with *Ms.* Dickey?"

Roger tilted his head and his mouth twisted, as though pretending to consider the possibility so he wouldn't appear an asshole. But not really. "I was under the strong impression it was with Mr. Dickey," he said.

The woman clamped her mouth shut, probably to cover a sigh, then nodded. "Follow me," she said, stepping aside.

The entryway was shallow, little more than a hallway extension. The woman led us past a closed door and an office with its door mostly shut, to a pair of sitting rooms. Each was demarcated by French doors framed in dark wood. The one to our left was closed and the source of the lights we'd seen from outside. It was the show-piece, with a large piano that I doubted was ever played and antique furniture more suited to admiring than sitting upon.

The opposite room was open, and it was there the woman gestured as she said, "Please have a seat. I'll be with you shortly."

This sitting room was smaller than its complement, and should have felt cozy with built-in bookshelves hugging the windows, a gas fireplace, and scattered rugs on the hardwood floor. But something was missing.

A loveseat, a pair of armchairs, and a small coffee table had been arranged to face a now dormant fireplace. Roger chose a chair and contemplated the artwork above the mantel. It was more vibrant than the prints on Turtle's walls, but still just looked like a boring country-side to me.

"What's the verdict?" I asked, wandering to the bookshelves.

"Not a big fan of pastorals," he admitted, voice low. Standing and moving for a closer look, he added, "But if this is an original, I wouldn't have it hanging over my fireplace."

Scanning the room, I realized part of what was missing—no tchotchke, just books, with the exception of a single shelf that held a few family photos. Apart from one stoic black and white group shot a generation or so removed, the rest featured only individuals. A man in a suit accepting an award. A faded blonde child sitting on a picnic blanket. A darker-haired child in a sports uniform. The subject of a more recent and better-preserved photo was unrecognizable, a solo skydiver clad in a jumpsuit and full-face helmet against a blue and white sky. Perhaps it was the missing matriarch.

I knew as little about valuing books as I did about valuing art, but surveyed the titles anyway. Most were hardcovers, with similarly styled leather binding suggesting they'd been purchased in sets: classics, history, encyclopedias, law, etc. I pulled a few free at random and confirmed they were real books with printed, paper pages and not just shelf filler.

Shoving a book on contracts back between its neighbors, I noticed a more eclectic mix of paperbacks and hardcovers on a bottom shelf. I slid a chair away from the wall to get at the books, cringing as a leg escaped the rug and scraped the floor with a squawk.

"Sydney, what are you doing?" Roger asked, sitting again, more curious than concerned.

"Just looking," I said, squatting beside the chair.

They were children's books, arranged by series. *Curious George. Frog and Toad. The Chronicles of Narnia*, still framed in its box and looking new. *Nancy Drew, Hardy Boys, Encyclopedia Brown*. All looking pristine, except for one. The matte yellow hard cover of a Nancy Drew mystery was mashed at the top, and its spine had a dark stain.

I was leaning for a closer look when a masculine voice boomed behind me, "Don't touch Ellie's books. Hurt her books, and she'll hurt you."

I swayed sideways, the chair catching my weight. Regaining my balance, I turned to see a man who was elderly but trim, his gray hair still thick with a slight wave on one side. Clean-shaven, a cleft chin gave him a youthful, almost naive appearance, while his light-brown cardigan over gray slacks made him look like an academic. What had I expected, heavy brows and knuckles dragging the floor?

His voice was sly as he continued, "She thinks I don't know how her brother really broke his arm, but I do."

Focused entirely upon me, Mr. Dickey was startled when Roger stood from his chair. They were about the same height, with Mr. Dickey's shoulders only slightly stooped.

"Mr. Dickey," Roger said, holding out a hand, "I'm Roger Weber. I'm an attorney, and I'm here to talk to you about—"

Mr. Dickey spun from Roger, calling out, "Ellie?"

Roger looked at me questioningly. I stood and shrugged—I had no more clue than he did—and joined him to present a united front.

The woman who'd let us into the house appeared, shooting us an angry look, and said, "Mr. Dickey, I just tried to call her. I'm sure she's on her way. Why don't we go back to your room and wait for her there?"

Mr. Dickey jerked away when she reached for his arm. "Don't touch me—I am not a child!" he protested. "I am not..."

His voice trailed off as we caught his eye again, as though he'd already forgotten we were there. Confusion crept into his features and a slight tremor infected his voice. "Who are you? Who let you in?"

"Sir," Roger said, voice calm and even, "I'm Roger Weber. I came to talk to you about—"

"The facility," Mr. Dickey finished, suddenly lucid. Canting his head, he even looked cunning. "Of course. You're here about the boys. Why else? Rosa, you can leave us."

Rosa abandoned her wrangling efforts, but I doubted we'd seen the last of her.

"Please, have a seat," Mr. Dickey said, indicating the grouped chairs.

"Thank you, sir," Roger said. As soon as his back was to the man, Roger raised both brows in an expression I recognized: *I don't know what the hell this is, but we're running with it.*

I sat directly across from Mr. Dickey and Roger chose the loveseat between us. Mr. Dickey directed his attention to Roger and asked, "Is this about the incident at the farm? Because that's been taken care of."

"Elaborate," Roger said, relaxing in his seat and casually adjusting his jacket.

Mr. Dickey's half-smile made my skin crawl. "I thought Wilbur didn't want me to elaborate. But I can assure you there is no evidence of wrongdoing by our staff."

Roger's smirk matched Mr. Dickey's. "Well, sir, that's a nice sentiment. But not a likely one. If someone dogged were to search for evidence, where might they find it?"

Mr. Dickey's face transformed abruptly, becoming hard and angry and his body rigid. "I said, there's no evidence."

Roger leaned forward confidentially. "Mr. Dickey, it's my job to prove you wrong, before someone else does. The question is, where do defenses need to be shored up? What are your weaknesses?"

The older man appeared confused, briefly, before he nodded appreciatively and rested his chin in his hands to consider. "The usual places, I would think."

"Which would be?" Roger prompted.

"The infirmary. The farm. And the sadist," Mr. Dickey said, voice low. "Though he usually cleans up after himself."

Roger hummed a warning. "But it's always the cover-up..."

Mr. Dickey nodded and raised a shoulder in acknowledgment of the possibility.

"So you think he could be a liability?" Roger asked.

"I think he could be a goddamned psychopath, is what I think," Mr. Dickey admitted. "And I've warned Wilbur, multiple times. I don't believe in sparing the rod, but no sane man does the things I've seen him do."

Roger closed his eyes briefly and snapped his fingers next to his temple, as if to jog his memory. "I'm sorry," he finally said ruefully. "That was Officer…"

Mr. Dickey opened his mouth but paused, eyes drifting as if he'd lost the thread of the conversation. His hands tugged at the cuffs of his sweater sleeves. And we waited.

I didn't realize how far forward I'd hunched in anticipation until my neck twinged. Or maybe that happened when the commotion started.

Women's voices—Rosa and someone else—rang out from the entryway, raised in argument.

Moments later, the unidentified woman burst in upon us. My approximate height with a slim build, she wore a black power suit and spike heels that should have gouged marks in the hardwood floor. Her dark hair was cut in a chin-length, shaped bob and her curved brows were so sharp they could slice paper. "What the hell do you think you're doing in here?" she demanded.

Roger attempted to introduce himself, but she interrupted him. "You do *not* have an appointment with me *or* my father, and you lied your way into his home. Give me one reason I shouldn't have you arrested."

Roger's equanimity frayed as he stepped into her space and said, "Give me one reason I shouldn't have *your father* arrested."

Her mouth dropped open in astonishment (makeup still flawless late on a Friday evening), then she laughed. "This is ridiculous. Rosa, call the police."

Roger asked, voice grim, "Are you sure you want to do that? There's no statute of limitations on murder."

The woman stared at Roger, whether considering his words or the man who said them I couldn't tell. Finally, she raised a manicured hand, and the woman she'd called Rosa paused mid-stride.

Mr. Dickey had remained sitting during the exchange, speechless, as had I. But comprehension finally dawned on his face. He looked over his shoulder at Roger, then rose from his chair.

"Now I know who you are," he said.

"Daddy, shut up," the woman said.

Mr. Dickey moved toward Roger, hand held out cautiously as if the lawyer were a hot stove. I reluctantly stood and joined the group. I didn't know how this would shake out, but I was pretty sure I could take Mr. Dickey's daughter. Unless she tried to stab me with one of her heels.

"Daddy, it's time to go to your room," she said.

Mr. Dickey took Roger's sleeve in his fingers and said, "*I know you.* Weber, you said. You're Amos Weber's boy, aren't you? That guard at the Reform School." Mr. Dickey released Roger's sleeve and turned to his daughter. "He tried to cause trouble."

My heart skipped a beat, but the woman appeared unaffected. Too unaffected. She took her father's hand in hers and said, "Go to your room, Daddy, and I'll take care of this."

"He doesn't look a thing like his father," Mr. Dickey said.

Rosa hovered, waiting to escort him, but Mr. Dickey was unwilling to move. That is, until his daughter squeezed his hand hard enough to make him wince.

"Now, Milton," she said, proffering her father's arm to Rosa.

His gait was uncertain as he left, and even with Rosa's assistance, he nearly stumbled. The man still launched a parting shot as he reached the hallway. Voice dripping with disdain, he said, "Amos Weber always was a pussy."

The tiniest fissure appeared in his daughter's stoicism as she briefly closed her eyes and sighed, then closed the French doors behind us. She asked, "Are you Amos Weber's son?"

"Yes, I'm Roger Weber," he said, holding out his hand. "And you must be Eleanor Dickey."

She nodded as she took his hand.

"My colleague, Sydney Brennan," Roger continued.

Her grip was cold, wiry, and strong, perhaps a hair stronger than custom and manners dictated. I returned her nod and held my tongue.

Ms. Dickey gestured toward the hallway. "I'm sorry about that," she said. "He's... not himself anymore. Not for quite some time, in fact."

"I'm afraid my father's health is failing as well," Roger said, taking his former spot on the loveseat. "That's why I'm here, and why this really can't wait."

I returned to my chair, but Ms. Dickey hesitated, calculating. Watching her mind work was like watching Roger.

"And the *this* you're referring to would be?" she asked, sitting in the chair her father had vacated. "I can understand your urgency, but murder is a serious accusation. Hyperbolic, even."

Roger leaned forward, elbows on his knees. "Serious, yes. Hyperbolic, no."

I didn't wear heels regularly, but I felt some serious shoe envy when Ms. Dickey crossed her legs. She said, "I assume these allegations—which you still haven't shared—are associated with the old Reform Center. What kind of evidence do you have?"

It struck me as an odd progression, going from *that's crazy talk* to *but can you prove it?*

"We're working on that," Roger said.

She turned her attention to me for the first time, scrutinizing me from head to toe. Not quite dismissive, but her expression still conveyed that I was found wanting. "I suppose that's where you come in," she said.

I gave one big nod.

"Do you speak?" she asked.

I almost didn't answer, just to piss her off. "When the occasion calls for it. But I don't talk just to hear my own voice."

She raised an interested brow.

Roger continued. "We can prove a child was buried illegally at the facility."

She shrugged at his bluff, as though unconcerned. "People weren't so careful about such things in those days."

"We can't prove he was murdered—*yet*—but the child died under suspicious circumstances," he countered, "and he was disposed of like garbage. No autopsy. No marker. Nothing to show he ever even existed or mattered to anyone."

She didn't respond.

"Ms. Dickey, you know that's not right. You wouldn't want that for your own child. Or for your father," he added. "I'm not saying Mr. Dickey was calling the shots. That was Wilbur Richard. But your father knows what happened. And he can help us put the boy to rest. Before it's too late."

Her face softened. "But he can't. You saw him." She rose and said, "So I'd like you to leave."

The house was silent save for a whisper of central heating hum as we followed her to the door, and I couldn't help wondering about Mr. Dickey. I had a flash of Rosa stuffing him in a straitjacket with a ball gag. Although if anyone had such maltreatment coming, surely Milton Dickey did.

Headlights shone through a pair of narrow, leaded glass sidelights at the entrance while Ms. Dickey disengaged the lock. She didn't comment on them, or the approaching vehicle. Roger motioned me out ahead of him, and Ms. Dickey stretched out lithe fingers to trace his arm as he passed. Leaning against the heavy wood door, elbows held close to her body in the cold, she said, "I am sorry about your father."

"And I yours," Roger replied from the porch, voice neutral and face expressionless.

"Do be careful getting to your car, Miss—" She gave me one of those *I'm so sorry you're so forgettable*, faux apologetic expressions.

"Brennan," I said, smiling as if I actually believed she'd forgotten. My cheek twinged from the day's adventures and I wondered if I had a shiner.

"Miss Brennan. I was saying, they may be quaint, but I hear cowboy boots make for difficult walking." She retreated across the threshold into the house. "If either of you return to my father's house, I will call the authorities. Good night."

19

Heat rushed to my face and snark bubbled in my brain as I stared at the closed door, refusing to look at Roger. He let out a sound that might have been a snicker, if he did *snickers*, as he motioned for me to proceed.

Head down, staring at my *quaint* feet on the shadowy, paved path, I nearly fulfilled Ms. Dickey's wishes for my demise by walking into a wall. A human one, that is.

"I'm sorry," said the enormous man-flesh barrier. His chest and shoulders were so broad, he put me in mind of a professional wrestler in an expensive suit. At least it felt expensive when I grasped it in the dim light to keep from falling. "I didn't realize the Dickeys had company."

It seemed a disingenuous thing to say, considering he'd have seen Roger's vehicle.

"Pardon me," he said, disengaging my hands to step sideways and continue past us.

I shuffled the rest of the way to Roger's car without incident and stared at the house while waiting for Roger to let us in. Light flashed as someone opened the door to admit fancy-wrestler-dude, but whether it was Rosa or Eleanor Dickey, I couldn't say.

"I don't suppose you know who he was," I said.

"No," Roger said, opening his door. "You mean, you had insufficient opportunity to ascertain all his vital statistics?"

"Very funny," I said, getting in the car.

Addy leaned, sleeping, against the window, and had twisted her hood to buffer her face from the cold glass. Her snuffling, startled inhale echoed through the car as our doors closed simultaneously.

"It's just us, Addy," Roger said. "I hope you didn't get too cold."

"M'okay," she mumbled, still waking.

"Feel free to go back to sleep," I said, noting the SUV the man-wall must have driven. "We'll be driving for a while. But put on your seat belt."

"'Kay," she replied, settling back against the window after snapping the safety device closed on her third try.

She was asleep again before we reached the main road.

"Poor kid," Roger muttered, glancing in his rearview.

I could make out the motion, but not his expression.

"Yeah, 'cuz she's stuck with me tonight." And what about tomorrow? Or the day after? I knuckled my aching forehead. First things first.

"So what do you think?" I asked.

"About Ms. Dickey? I don't know," he said.

"I don't like her," I said.

Roger chuckled softly, as if trying not to wake Addy. "Tell me something I don't know."

"I don't trust her, either. She's lying, at least by omission. And am I the only one who found the whole situation with her father creepy?"

"You mean, *Ellie* and her *daddy*?" he asked, enunciating with distaste. "No, you are not."

"If she is lying, why? Is she just protecting her father's reputation? Is she protecting him from a criminal murder charge, or just worried about civil liability?"

Roger shaded his eyes as a vehicle approached with blazing high-beams. "Maybe she's worried about something else entirely. Something we don't even have an inkling about, but could if we continue our investigation."

"Exactly," I agreed. "Which brings us full circle. One of the big reasons I don't like her is because *she didn't want me to*."

Roger's head nodded slowly. "She was pushing your buttons."

"Like she was channeling my dead mother," I said, pulling out my cell phone. "I'm calling Ralph."

"Good idea," Roger said.

Ralph Abraham, my old boss and mentor at the Public Defender's Office, may be semi-retired, but he still kept his nose in everything criminal justice-related. His home phone rang several times before he picked up.

"Hey old man," I said. "Did I interrupt your dinner?"

"We just finished, but we're about to have dessert, so make it quick," Ralph said, before lowering his voice to add, "Supposed to be some kind of low-sugar crap."

"This'll just take a minute. So Roger's got this case," I began.

Ralph grunted at the mention of the attorney. I turned to Roger and said, "Ralph sends his best."

Roger echoed Ralph's grunt.

They'd known each other for years and always feigned indifference. It was mostly show, but the three of us had worked a tough case a few months ago that had been a significant strain on Ralph. Also on his wife Diane, who still hadn't forgiven me for the fallout. Much of it was Ralph's own fault, but it was a lot easier for Diane to stay pissed at me than at her husband.

"What can you tell me about Milton Dickey?" I asked.

Ralph yelled, "That sonuvabitch!"

I winced and stared at the phone. I was prepared to drop it if necessary to save my hearing. "I take it you're familiar with the man's work?"

Ralph harrumphed. "I was involved with one of those Reform School wrongful death lawsuits. Not much, but enough to know that asshole, and Warden Richard, had to be slicker than owl shit because they sure as hell didn't get what they deserved."

"I dropped by his house—*nice* place, by the way—and Dickey has dementia now," I said.

Ralph said, "Good. The man was an evil sadist. He didn't just turn a blind eye to what was happening, I'm pretty sure he directed it. Including the beatings. Personally."

"You ever hear anything about a guard missing part of a finger?" I asked.

"What is that, some kind of *Fugitive* bullshit?"

I rolled my eyes at the phone, even if he couldn't see them. "So that's a no?"

"I don't remember him, but that doesn't mean anything. I was there more for big picture than details." Ralph paused for a moment, then continued, "Also to help keep an eye on the local situation. That place did not go quietly."

I glanced at Roger in the dark, but he was watching the road. "What do you mean?"

"The area's whole economy was based on that prison and its farm, so a lot of people were willing to turn blind eyes to what was going on. With all the investigations over the years—state and federal—they got pretty entrenched."

"Was there violence?" I asked.

"I don't recall anything major. Threats, vandalism, that kind of thing." He paused and doubled back. "You know Milton Dickhead was involved with American Correctional Enterprises after the Reform School shut down, right?"

"I did know that."

"Bunch of greedy, dirty bastards. I tell you..."

And he did. I let Ralph's angry diatribe wash over me, a river of righteous indignation. I'd heard it all before and possibly even said it, since I share Ralph's issues with the privatization of our prisons and jails. Don't get me wrong—I understand Joe Schmoe getting pissed and wanting to know where his tax dollars are spent when he hears a story about some random dude getting cable TV in prison. (Generally *not* on cable TV.) But in my experience, bad things happen when profit is the driving factor behind incarceration. For privatized prisons, there's no money in empty beds or lower rates of crime and recidivism. There's no profit in people feeling safe.

The outskirts of Tallahassee appeared as scattered fireflies in the distance as Ralph wound down. "Sydney, are you sure he's not faking it? Dickey, I mean. He's the kind of guy who'd fake anything—*do* anything—if he thought it would keep him out of prison or court."

I considered. As much as my inner conspiracy theorist loved the idea, I didn't buy it. "No, I'm pretty sure he wasn't faking it. And his daughter didn't seem to think he was, either."

"You met Eleanor?" Ralph demanded.

"Yes, and she's a real piece of work, too," I said. "Why, do you know her?"

"Yes…" Ralph said, dragging out the word in a way that made me wish I could lay my hands on him. Finally, he prompted, "Eleanor Powers."

Powers… I pressed my hand against my forehead, working it in circles. "Sounds familiar, but I can't place it. Eleanor Powers is her married name?"

"I think she was married for about five minutes. Can't blame her for not going back to the name Dickey," Ralph said. "She followed in her daddy's footsteps."

"Meaning?"

"Corrections," he said.

I recognized a staticky sound on the line as Ralph rubbing the gray, late-day scruff on his dark, dimpled chin. He continued, "I personally never had occasion to interact with her. Florida's a big state. And I think most of her muckety-muck positions have been in juvenile facilities."

My seat belt dug into my neck as I sat up abruptly. "Seriously?"

"Oh yeah. Right now, Eleanor Dickey-slash-Powers runs that place west of here, not all that far from where the Reform Center used to be…" Ralph paused while he flipped through the Rolodex in his head. "Brummel Youth Academy."

ROGER ROLLED his hands on the steering wheel, processing what I told him about Eleanor's career in corrections. The one she'd neglected to mention, even casually, in our conversation with her about her father's kiddie prison legacy. "Wow. That took some..."

He trailed off.

"I think *gumption* is the non-testicle word you're looking for," I said, and glimpsed Roger's smile in the now-intermittent streetlights. "Eleanor had to know we'd find out at some point and be pissed. So, was that more messing with our heads, or just doing the best she could, thinking on the fly?"

"No idea," he admitted.

We stopped for dinner on the edge of town at a chain Italian place. Roger had never struck me as someone who liked kids (to be fair, he wasn't fond of most adults, either), but he did a good job engaging with Addy. Of course, Addy wasn't exactly sitting in a bumper seat, eating grilled cheese off a paper placemat. In some respects, she was more adult than child, living on her own for most of her life. On the other hand, there were choices she couldn't legally make for herself. And no matter what her experiences, she wasn't quite there developmentally, either.

It was a fine line to walk, for Addy and anyone interacting with her. I'd fallen off that line and landed hard on the adult side when I chewed her out in the car. I told myself that when I was her age, I'd rather have been treated as an adult than as a child. But Addy wasn't me. And I *was* an adult now. I needed to start acting like it.

Addy stood, excusing herself for the bathroom. I watched her cross to the restroom alcove. Fortunately, it was nowhere near an exit.

Roger shook the lonely ice in his glass, but he'd already drunk enough tea to keep him up all night. "How about that debriefing I never got?" he asked. "Tell me about the witness who gave you Milton Dickey's name. You get anything else?"

"He confirmed the poor living conditions at the center, and the abuse. The worst beatings occurred in a place the kids called the Tar Shed." I glanced around. No one sat nearby, but at the risk of ruining someone's meal—including my own—I settled for a grim, "It was *really* bad."

Roger knew what that assessment meant coming from me and shook his head, disgusted. "Who's the witness?"

"A crazy biker guy Glenn took me to see this morning."

Roger's brows narrowed. "How crazy?"

"Crazy enough to greet us with a gun." I stared down at my own iced tea, suddenly blushing. "And, crazy enough to put the gun to my head when he lost it."

"Jesus, Sydney!" Roger's lips compressed with frustrated anger. Finally, he inhaled loudly through his nose and said, "I warned you about him."

"I can trust Glenn," I shot back.

Roger's head rotated, somewhere between nodding and shaking. "Just not the people he runs with?" he scoffed.

I slid my plate sideways so I could get in Roger's face without saucing my boobs. "Don't be an arrogant asshole."

His neck extended to meet me, expression hard, marinara wafting on his breath. "But I do it so well."

"Well," I said, equally implacable, "you are a lawyer."

We didn't smile, but our faces and posture slowly relaxed. "Write it up for me," he said, meaning the interview.

I nodded, then caught sight of Addy chatting with our waitress.

"Is that what happened to your face?" Roger asked, holding up his glass of ice as an offering.

Great. Now I'd have to go to the bathroom to look at it. "Partly. That, and Addy's boyfriend," I said, giving him a thumbnail sketch.

"You did have an interesting day," Roger said.

"Considering what Ralph told us, Ms. Dickey obviously knows more than she's sharing. Tomorrow, I figured I'd see what I can do to nudge her toward Jesus." I folded my napkin and jammed it under the edge of my plate. "What else are we doing?"

"I'll keep working the lawsuits angle," Roger said.

Distracted, I watched Addy and the young waitress laughing.

Addy was still smiling tentatively as she joined us, saying, "I hope it's okay, I ordered dessert."

It was a glimpse of the child again, like the moment just before Mr. Spencer's photo was taken, just before she instinctively protected herself from anyone who may be watching. And I held my breath, waiting for her to shut down.

"Good," Roger said, returning her smile. Then he rubbed his eyes with the heels of his hands. Maybe the gallons of iced tea wouldn't keep him awake all night after all.

I rolled ice cubes around my mouth with my tongue, trying not to crunch. Our plan on the Weber front didn't seem like much. Just plodding investigation, checking things off the list. That was fine, normally, but this wasn't a normal case. We were on a clock, striving to accomplish in a few days what decades of state and federal investigations hadn't.

I set my tumbler down forcefully enough to rattle the remaining ice. "What is our pie-in-the-sky, wish-on-a-magic-lamp, best-case scenario for this investigation?" I asked.

"If dad was right..." Roger considered while the waitress set a decadent slice of chocolate cake in front of Addy.

He hesitated, glancing at Addy, but she only had eyes for her dessert. Not that I could blame her. The frothy, between-cake layers were chocolate mousse. I motioned for Roger to continue.

"Find the boy's body," Roger said. "Have his remains identified, returned to his family, and given a proper burial."

"Then let's do that," I said.

Roger stared at me. Through me, really. I just happened to be in front of him while his brain spun off in fifty directions at once calculating, *could we really do that?* He said, "We'll need a map of the complex."

"Discovery from one of the lawsuits?" I suggested.

"Maybe," he conceded. "But none of the cases I've been able to get a line into so far. And tomorrow's Saturday."

Which limited easy public records access to whatever was scanned and online. That didn't cover a lot of ground.

"I'll bet they have a copy in the State Archives," I said, reaching for my fork.

"Also possible, but they're closed tomorrow, too," Roger said.

"Don't worry." I grinned as I speared a corner of Addy's chocolate cake with my fork. "I know a guy."

20

It wasn't that late when we picked up my car, but it had been a long day, and I was about to have an overnight house guest. Before my mind could spin out too far—*a teenager in my house*—said teen spoke from the seat next to me.

"Tallahassee is kind of a weird place."

"In what way?" I asked.

"I don't know," she said, sounding self-conscious now that she'd spoken her opinion aloud. "Like it can't decide if it's a city or a suburb."

"Most of Florida feels that way to me," I admitted. "Suffering from an identity crisis. Too many growth spurts, too many people from too many places, supposedly reinventing themselves but recreating the familiar."

Now *I* felt self-conscious. I tried to avoid being philosophical while I was sober.

"Did you grow up here?" Addy asked.

"No," I said, signaling onto the final "major" road before reaching my neighborhood. The surrounding trees made the sky darker, thicker. Almost claustrophobic. "I grew up near Orlando."

"I've been there once," Addy said.

"Disney World?" I guessed.

"Yeah," she said, and snickered. "It was awful. Some special *help the poor foster kids* trip, so we left in a couple of vans at a crazy early hour in the morning. One of the brats puked on me on the drive, so I got to smell that all day. And we couldn't split up, so after he puked I didn't even get to go on any decent rides. Because who puts a car puker on a roller coaster?"

"How old were you?"

"I don't know. Maybe nine." She paused, then added softly, "It was right after my mom died."

Oh yeah, the mom I recklessly invoked while yelling at you. I hesitated. Should I offer sympathy? Share that my own mother was dead, other details about my messed-up family? Was that bonding, or hijacking the conversation and making it about me? I was beginning to think it was easier interviewing outlaw bikers than teenagers.

"About this evening," Addy began.

Which part, I wondered? *This evening* covered a lot of ground, but I kept my mouth shut and let her finish.

"I'm sorry about what I said, about your friend. I don't really think that way," she said. "I'm not, like, a racist."

I figured it was a good sign that she'd brought it up, but now that she had, I wasn't inclined to go easy on her. Especially since I wasn't the one who deserved an apology. "Then why did you use the word?"

"It's complicated," she said.

As I turned onto my street, my eyes were drawn to the flickering blue of a television at Mr. Ginley's house. It filtered first through the crack in his curtains, then through delicate Japanese maple tree branches recently filled out with leaves. Lights glowed from my own living room on the opposite side. Ben had started letting himself in again, with my permission, feeding my fish when he knew I wasn't around. Hanging out and watching my TV.

Ben was a teenager and we got along perfectly most of the time. It struck me that I was overthinking relating to Addy. I just needed to talk to her the same way I would talk to Ben. That boiled down to, *tell the truth*.

"I'm sorry I yelled at you like that," I said, pulling into the carport slowly in case Ben had left a yard tool in the way that would go crunch. I cut the engine and continued, "But you think life's complicated now—it's only going to get worse. So why did you say it?"

Addy sighed. "I know you'll find this hard to believe, but Troy isn't a total asshole."

I snorted, and she glanced at me in surprise before laughing softly herself. "Okay, fine. He mostly is, but he was a way out. So he's got some stupid ideas, about black people and Mexican people..."

"Basically, anybody who's not a straight white dude," I guessed.

She didn't bite. "To be around Troy, and people like him, you say things sometimes. To blend in. Because they don't like people who don't blend in." She hesitated, then added, "If you don't blend in, they turn on you."

I stared ahead at the back wall of the carport and rested my hands on the steering wheel to give her as much space as I could in the small car, mentally and physically. "I get that," I said. "But Troy wasn't in the car with us when you said it."

"I know that!" Addy yelled, defensive. "I just... I didn't think."

"I get that, too," I said. "But—and I speak from experience here—that's why you have to be careful who you hang around. Their dumb shit seeps into your brain, and they bring you down to their level. If you're not careful, you'll end up as stupid as they are."

Addy unclipped her seat belt and muttered, "Like you never hooked up with somebody like Troy."

I laughed. "God, no! I never went for white supremacists, or wannabe drug dealers. Drug *users*, yes. And lots of other kinds of wannabes. I definitely went through a bad boy phase."

"Went through, past tense?" Addy asked significantly. "What about the guy who owns the bar?"

My traitorous fair skin blushed, and I was glad for the dim light. "Glenn and I are just friends."

"Too bad. He's kind of sexy," Addy said.

You don't know the half of it. But I kept that to myself, protesting,

"He's old enough to be your..." As usual, the math escaped me. "At least your father. Probably your grandfather in some states."

"Not *yours*," she said.

Now that we'd both loosened up a bit, I decided it was safe to press her a bit more on Troy. "So what did you see in Troy? I mean, he's an attractive enough guy, but if he's that much of an asshole..."

"I told you, he wasn't all the time," she said. "And he was a way out. A way to get to Tallahassee."

Something about her answer tickled at my brain, reminded me of something Troy had said. But before I could grasp it, the carport light flashed on overhead.

"Do you live with somebody?" Addy asked as the kitchen door flew open.

"No, that's my neighbor. Listen, why did you—"

But she'd already exited the car. I tapped my forehead against the steering wheel, resisting the urge to tap harder.

At least Ben was age-appropriate. And not a racist, misogynist dumbass.

I stumbled through my open door, shoulders laden with bags, and found the kids being awkward. Addy's hands were tucked in her sleeve cuffs while she tugged at her hood strings, and Ben had shoved his hands in his jean pockets.

"Don't mind me," I said. "I don't need any help."

"Oh, hey. Sorry, Syd. I was just asking Addy if you guys had eaten," Ben said, closing the door behind me. He pronounced "Addy" precisely, as if he were still getting used to saying it.

"We did eat," I said, "but there's some leftover pizza in the fridge if you're hungry."

Ben's eyes flicked to Addy, and he blushed. "Yeah, I found that already."

I refrained from my usual dig at his eating habits to avoid embarrassing him even more. Ben's growth spurt had slowed, but his height was creeping steadily toward his father JD's. I gave him an assessing look as I dropped a bag on the counter. Scratch that—I suspected Ben was now taller than JD, and over six feet. He needed a haircut, which was his usual state, and light-brown stubble dusted his cheeks. It was mildly disturbing how much he looked like his father, minus the evidence of life experience on JD's face—creased skin, crooked nose, small scar.

Thank God for small favors. Addy stole glances at Ben now, but she'd be jumping his bones in my kitchen (as I had JD) if Ben had his father's bad boy edge.

I shuddered at the thought.

Addy's backpack was still slung over one shoulder.

"You can put your stuff in the guest room," I said. "Through the living room, down the hall to the right, the only room that's not a bathroom."

Addy's eyes met Ben's, glancing over her shoulder as she rounded the counter.

"How long is she staying with you?" Ben asked.

Too long, I thought.

"Just a day or two, until we get her squared away. And she's not really here," I warned. "Not that anyone will want to know."

"Got it," Ben nodded, face serious.

He may only be a junior in high school, but he was far more dependable and trustworthy than most adults I knew. In fact, I might need his help over the coming days. "What are you doing after school tomorrow?"

Ben gave me a *have you taken your medication today* look. "Syd, tomorrow's Saturday. Dennis is still gone, so I'll be spending the morning over at his garage, but other than that I don't have much in the way of plans."

Saturday. I knew that. I also knew Ben's friend was out of town; that's why I'd gone to the chain mechanic. So, if tomorrow was Saturday...

"Dammit!" I said, burying my face in my hands, then adding a "Dumbass!" for good measure.

"What's wrong?" Ben asked, leaning on my counter. "Wait, I thought you wanted me to stay out of the way this weekend because of Mike..."

I nodded with a bitter smile. Yes, this was the weekend Mike was supposed to come over. *The* weekend. I laughed out loud at the absurdity.

Ben winced. "I'm sorry, Syd. That sucks. You have to work?"

"Something like that," I said. Work, and host a minor sleeping a few feet down the hall in my spare bedroom. Not exactly conditions conducive to Mike and me getting our freak on.

"Well, listen, Addy's welcome to hang out with me at the garage if you need somebody to keep an eye on her while you're gone—"

"I'm not a child," Addy said, striding back into the kitchen and glaring at Ben as if he'd kicked a puppy and then stepped in its poop. "I don't need babysitting."

Ben stuttered, but quickly abandoned whatever words he would have spoken. Wise man. He meant well, but there was no right thing to say at the moment. I was torn between giving Addy a high five and telling her to get over herself.

"I have to make a phone call," I said, heading toward my bedroom. "Ben, you know where the remote is."

Know where it is... he was probably the last person to put batteries in it. I kicked off my shoes, grabbed my landline, and flopped on the bed, staring at my recently repainted walls. The woman at the counter had sworn the pale aqua that now adorned them would be calming.

Maybe she worked on commission.

By the time the call went through, I'd given up on serenity and closed my eyes.

Mike answered by saying, "Tell me this isn't bad news."

"I thought our goal was to have an honest relationship," I replied, rubbing the heel of my hand against my forehead. "So which do you want? Honesty, or sparkles and unicorns?"

Mike groaned. "Give me the bad news."

I did, without going into too many details. Mike tends to be more optimistic than I am, but even he was speechless. Finally, he grunted, "Hunh."

"Yeah, my thoughts exactly," I said, shoving my pillow against the headboard to raise my head. That made my lower back ache, so I raised my knees. I needed to have words with the person who sold me my mattress, too. He definitely worked on commission. "What's your schedule look like *next* weekend?"

"Depends on how a hearing goes during the week," Mike said. "I may have to prep witnesses for a murder trial."

I listened to him breathe. We did that a lot, listening to each other breathe over the phone. Sharing silence when we couldn't share space.

When Mike spoke again, his voice was lighter, tinged with his trademark optimism, false or not. "Let's play it by ear. Maybe you'll wrap up sooner than you think, and I'll be racing down the interstate, knocking on your door before you know it."

It was my turn to grunt.

Mike lowered his voice in a parody of sexiness, "Promise you'll greet me at the door in a robe and nothing else."

I laughed. "Promise," I said, and smiled at the phone as the seconds ticked away. I was almost disappointed when I heard a deep inhale that foreshadowed him speaking. I loved hearing Mike's voice, but knew we'd be wrapping up the conversation and hanging up soon.

"I'm telling you. Everything will go smoothly. Clients will not lie. Witnesses will be where you expect them *and* they will cooperate. Documents will magically appear with crucial bits of information." Mike added as an afterthought, "And your opponents will not play dirty."

"Maybe," I said, just to humor him.

Because I definitely didn't believe it.

21

I got Addy settled easily that night, probably because she was as exhausted as me. She tried to help make the bed, but stalled out on the pillowcases so long that I finished it myself. (The one good thing to come from my aborted weekend with Mike—a dryer full of clean sheets.)

The first thing I did upon waking Saturday morning was check that Addy hadn't snuck away in the night. I heard her cooing snores as soon as I opened the guest room door. It was still relatively early, so after showering and starting coffee, I got on the phone to the Spencers. No one answered, either on Mr. Spencer's cell phone or their home landline, but I left a message on both. I didn't explicitly say I had Addy, but made it clear I had something important to share.

I was staring at the clock, wondering if just after eight a.m. on a Saturday was too early to call the Spencers' friend, when Roger called to beg off breakfast. We settled on a later lunch instead. That gave me more time to get stuff done, and Addy seemed content to sleep.

Biting the bullet, I dialed Faith Halliway and found her awake and functional and far more coherent than me. The first question out of the substitute teacher's mouth was, "Have you found Addy?"

"I know she's safe," I hedged, glancing self-consciously toward the guest room. "Do you know Addy very well? Can you tell me a little more about her?"

"I can't say I know her well, but I've met her a few times. And of course I hear about her, from the Spencers and when I substitute at her school. She's always very polite, a good student but not exceptional. Of course, considering what she's been through and the instability in her life, that in itself *is* exceptional."

"So not a wild child?" I asked, drawing on the typical runaway stereotype.

"No, I wouldn't say she is at all," Ms. Halliway said. "Certainly no more than the usual amount of teenaged rebelliousness."

I braced myself as I asked the dreaded question, "Do you know if she's been reported missing yet?"

"She has not," she affirmed. "And I'm keeping an eye on that."

I breathed a sigh of relief. "Will you please let me know as soon as she is?"

"Absolutely," she said. "Clint and Deborah are good people. I really hope they can do something for that poor girl."

Ms. Halliway had known the Spencers "forever" (in human terms, that translates to fifteen years) and was ready to swear on a stack of Bibles that they were of good character. I cut her off when she began telling stories of their Christian charity. Not that I didn't appreciate compelling character testimony, but it wasn't my current priority. What I needed now was reasons for a court to rule Addy was safer in the immediate short-term with her aunt and uncle than with her foster family. In other words, bring on the dirt.

Unfortunately, Ms. Halliway couldn't give me any additional information about Addy, her boyfriend, or her foster mother except, "That Sylvia Maddox is no better than she ought to be." Perhaps an accurate character assessment, but not exactly something we could use in court against her.

"I tried to reach the Spencers this morning, but had no luck," I admitted. "Do you know of anything they'd be doing now?"

"Did you try their house? Clint often forgets his cell phone."

When I confirmed that I had, she said, "Maybe they were working in the yard. If I see them, I'll tell them we spoke."

Having put it off as long as I could, next I called my friend Frank at the State Archives. He'd already set aside additional records for me and planned to hit the farmer's market anyway, so he was happy to meet me downtown this morning.

I didn't feel comfortable leaving Addy behind. As luck would have it, I heard the shower kick on just as I was about to wake her. I fixed some toast and set out my limited slathering options—butter, peanut butter, and jelly; I really needed to go to the grocery store. I was working on my second (or was it third?) cup of coffee when Addy emerged. Wet-haired, she wore a T-shirt I'd loaned her last night, but her own threadbare jeans.

"Didn't fit?" I asked.

She shook her head. "They about to killed my crotch."

"Thanks for sharing," I said, but knew what she meant and didn't want to contribute to any body issues. "They don't fit me right either. Have some toast."

She chewed in silence as I told her about my attempts to contact her uncle, and about my impending appointment. "You can go with me to the Archives, or—" I hesitated. Ben was a good, responsible kid. Of course, he wasn't the one I was worried about. "Or I can drop you off to hang out with Ben at the garage, and we'll meet up later."

She shrugged and said, "Yeah, sure," and rose to get her backpack.

It didn't take a degree in child psychology to know she was agreeing to the latter.

"Just bring what you need," I said, suppressing a cringe as I added, "You can leave the rest here."

It wasn't even nine a.m., and I'd already resigned myself to having a teenager in my house for another twenty-four hours. And sacrificing getting laid in the bargain.

Our first stop was a coffee shop in the same neighborhood as the garage. Frank deserved at least two mac nut cookies for dealing with the unwashed public on his day off. I also picked up a bagel for Ben and mochas for Addy and me. Caffeine doesn't count on Saturday, right?

Concrete block painted brick red, the garage was set back from the street in a designated commercial area that nevertheless clung to some green space. A leafy sycamore infringed upon the parking in the front, asphalt buckling around its base. I'd barely stopped the car before Addy jumped free with her drink and Ben's bagel and barreled into the office area. Moments later, the two of them emerged from an open repair bay and waved me on. But I still sat, idling, when they disappeared inside again.

Take her or leave her, I told myself. *But make a choice, and stop second-guessing.*

I sighed, reversed out of the parking lot, and headed toward the Archives. Downtown Tallahassee is mostly government business and not a lot of retail, which meant it was quiet on the weekends. It only took a couple of minutes for the ugly, flat rectangle of the state building to come into sight. "Ugly" is my entirely subjective but nonetheless entirely accurate opinion. I will admit, however, that most buildings would suffer in such proximity to the grand, Greek revival-style Florida Supreme Court.

Parking was weird with one-way streets and restrictions, even on weekends, so I reluctantly pulled into the nearest multilevel lot. I hunched my shoulders against a cool breeze and walked quickly down the street toward the Archives entrance. I was a little surprised there weren't gaggles of young students lining up outside the Museum of Florida History. Perhaps gaggles were restricted to weekdays.

Sticking my face to the door, I squinted in the over-bright sunshine. I was about to call Frank when he appeared on the other side, seemingly out of nowhere. His broad smile shone even through the reflected glare, and I found myself grinning back at him.

I wouldn't say Frank and I were close, but he was one of the first people I'd met years ago when I arrived in Tallahassee. His welcoming face had been a relief then, and it still was. His wavy white beard, tinged with yellow, was as thick as ever. A formerly white canvas boat hat, buttons corroded to a bluish silver, covered Frank's thinning hair. He'd changed out his workday khakis for jeans, but still wore his trademark sneakers.

"Sydney!" he gushed, wrestling a set of keys free from the lock as I passed. "Are those for me?"

"You know they are, Frank," I said, handing him the bag of cookies. "How's it going?"

Frank peeked in the bag and beamed with appreciation. "Oh, I can't complain. Especially since I'll be retiring soon."

"Uh-huh," I said. He'd been claiming he was on the verge of retirement almost as long as I'd known him. "Thanks for coming in on a Saturday—I owe you."

"I was just looking for an excuse," he admitted. "I left my book here yesterday, about the history of the Pensacola and Atlantic railroad. You know that was the first railroad built in the Florida Panhandle..."

I pretended to listen, my head rotating on my shoulders to goggle, as it always did, passing through the high-ceilinged lobby. They'd hung a strange piece of artwork overhead that looked to me like the remnants of an auto accident. I wondered if it was associated with a current exhibit, but didn't dare ask. Frank was one of those people who knew something about everything and felt duty-bound to share. His lectures were always interesting, but generally went down better with beer. It was too early for beer, even on Saturday, and I didn't have the time to spare.

Frank led me through an open work area that was off-limits but within view of the public, dropping the cookies on a desk as we passed. We continued down a hallway to a small, pristine room where I'd often reviewed records. Several neat stacks of files rested on a long laminate table. Frank slipped on a pair of white cotton gloves.

"Ohh. Does that mean you have really old, juicy stuff for me?" I asked.

Frank shrugged. "Habit. I'd already made copies of these records

I'd pulled for you," he said, indicating a couple of the stacks, "but I think what you're really going to want is in here."

He retrieved a large binder from another pile and carefully maneuvered a sheet of paper free. It appeared approximately legal size, until he unfolded it to three times that and spread the page flat on the table.

"Is that a map?" I asked, incredulous.

Frank's eyes flicked toward the acoustic-tiled ceiling as he considered. "I believe it's more properly called a site plan. Not sure if it was ever filed anywhere, but it was created in 1958 when they added a free-standing tool shed here." He indicated with a gloved finger. "I take it your enthusiasm means you want a copy?"

"You better believe it!" I said. "Frank, you're a genius."

"You're just now realizing that?" he asked, affecting a faux appalled expression.

The man was a goof, but his energy was infectious.

Frank carefully folded the *map* (call me a philistine) and said, "Back in a minute. Your invoice is on the copies. Just add in the oversize."

I tugged the invoice free from the rubber band securing the stack and scratched down an addition from memory. Then I did a little more mental arithmetic as I pulled my checkbook from my back pocket. I was pretty sure the check would clear...

Frank returned, tucking the oversized copy and my paper stack into a thick accordion file. "Much obliged, ma'am," he said, taking my check. "Now let's get you out of here, before someone gets the wrong idea."

"And thinks I'm stealing something?" I asked.

Frank laughed. "No, thinks we're open. Someday your active imagination will get you in trouble."

I left Frank locking up.

The breeze had dissipated while I was inside, but the sunlight was still blinding and I'd left my sunglasses in Cecil. I blinked, glancing at the sparse vehicles across the street outside the Supreme Court—a couple of mid-sized sedans and an SUV—and wished I'd parked there instead. The nearest ground-level spots were reserved, but I probably could have gotten away with using one today.

I clutched my files beneath one arm and shaded my eyes with the other as I walked to the parking garage. I didn't park there often and, once inside, it took me a moment to get oriented. Stepping sideways out of the path of an oncoming vehicle, I finally caught sight of the elevator next to me and wondered whose brilliant idea it was to paint the metal door the same dull taupe as the surrounding walls.

Entering the empty elevator, I glanced casually over my shoulder to watch the vehicle park farther up the ramp, just beyond a white pickup that blocked my view. The structure was as sparsely occupied as the parking lot across the street had been.

I set my new files in the back and dropped heavily into Cecil's driver's seat before hunting down my sunglasses. It was a little dark in the garage, but I put them on anyway. They always gave me confidence for clandestine operations, whether performing or exposing them.

On my way out, I took a good, hard look at the vehicle that had passed me in the garage. A dark-gray Mercedes SUV, it looked vaguely familiar, but the windows were tinted so heavily I couldn't make out the figure inside. I wouldn't bet my life on it, but I was pretty sure I'd seen it parked behind the Supreme Court when I emerged from the Archives.

Pulling onto the one-way street, I dug awkwardly in my pocket and plucked a hairband free. (I swear, they multiply in my washing machine.) I drove slowly, barely moving, until I saw the SUV exit the parking lot behind me. Then I edged to the right as far as I could (there was no shoulder, just lane), put my hatchback in park and punched on my hazard lights.

Nothing to see here, I projected. Just a ditzy woman trying to be responsible, parking on a basically empty street long enough to get her hair out of her face. I battled my untamable red curls as the SUV drove past.

The second—no, it was the *third* sighting—was the memory charm.

I had seen the SUV in the lot across the street a few minutes ago. But I'd also seen it outside of the Dickey house, parked alongside Roger's car. The hulking shape behind the wheel must be the human wall I'd walked into last night.

My imagination might be active, as Frank claimed, but it certainly wasn't *overactive*. So why was Ms. Dickey's visitor following me?

22

W ho was this guy, and when had he started following me? We'd taken Roger's car to the Dickey home, so even if he was the same man from last night, he wouldn't have casually recognized Cecil. Had he seen me (and my distinctive red hair) on my morning cookie run? I'd stopped by my office this morning before the coffee shop, just long enough for me to run inside and grab something. Perhaps he'd been watching then, tucked off-street at one of the neighboring law offices, and gotten lucky.

Which still begged the bigger question: *why me?*

I didn't like this development. There was no reason to think I was in any danger, but it'd be nice to know if he was still around. And I preferred to find out in a public place. Both the library and farmers market were nearby, and either would do.

Every Saturday except during the dead of winter (yes, Tallahassee has winter, though it is not entirely dead), vendors with white awnings occupy a few blocks of appropriately named Park Street. It's a beautiful area, the broad median bisected by brick pathways and hosting occasional pavilions, lined throughout by Spanish moss-draped live oaks and smaller trees and shrubs whose names escaped me.

Today was a Goldilocks day: cool but not cold in the shade, a mix of vendors with early produce and arts and crafts, and enough people to feel like you were in a crowd but not enough to make you claustrophobic. Plus plenty of parking. I chose a spot in the center of a block where I could wander a bit without ever losing sight of my escape route.

FRANK WAS NOWHERE to be seen around the market, nor was my new, large friend.

My gaze drifted beyond the broad green median, across the street to the multistory brick building that was the main branch of the Leon County Public Library. I grabbed my files and a notebook from the back before setting off, crossing both lanes and the median to the opposite sidewalk. The library was built on a slope (I hesitate to say *hill*, since it's Florida and you won't believe me). The Park Street entry gave admission to the second floor, but I'd circle the block and enter via the main entrance and parking lot on Call Street. The roundabout path prevented any tail from being absolutely sure where I'd gone without increasing the likelihood of showing himself.

I took a moment to admire a pair of fat-trunked palm trees at the corner, noting no pursuer, then turned downhill at Duval Street. The massive brick church across the street cast a shadow that fell short of my sidewalk, and I felt exposed and hot. The sun was blazing when I ducked around the corner of the building, grateful for the oaks and crepe myrtles bordering the large parking lot.

I surveyed my surroundings a few more times as I ascended a mountain of stairs that would have done Rocky proud. Once inside, air conditioning chilled the thin layer of sweat on my skin, and I paused near Circulation to acclimate and choose a secluded table for reading. And maybe catch my breath.

With an hour before I needed to leave and meet Roger for lunch, I got right to it. The first fifty pages or so of documents Frank had just given me were the kinds of administrative things I'd already seen—requisition forms, scheduled maintenance, payroll authorizations, etc. from a couple of months in the fall of 1963. Nothing earth-shatter-ing, but they added more names to my list of people to track down, mostly staff but a few juvenile detainees as well.

I'd scribbled about a page and a half of notes when I flipped to the next document to find a handwritten note: *To Be Shredded.*

My brows rose like a cartoon character's. That sounded promising.

Disciplinary records for several children followed. This portion of the stack was twice as high as what I'd already reviewed, so before digging into the hundred or so pages, I begged a few paper clips from the Circulation desk. I separated records into sections by individual and noted any identifying information. The boys ranged in age from eleven to fifteen. Pulling out the birthdates, it quickly became clear that the children had stayed at the facility at different times across *three* decades. So what was the unifying factor?

One of the names sounded familiar, Kenneth Gerard, but I didn't know why. Too bad I hadn't brought my laptop. I grabbed my stuff, list on top, and made a beeline for the library's computers. There wasn't much demand around lunch on a Saturday and I didn't have to wait. I started with the familiar Kenneth Gerard. Nothing obvious on my first search, so I tweaked it, then tweaked a little more... and there it was: *Wrongful Death Alleged After Teen Dies in State Custody.*

It was a 1987 article from the St. Pete Times, detailing the boy's death at the Reform School a day after a fight with two other boys. Gerard's mother alleged there was no fight, that her son was beaten by the staff and subsequently died from an untreated head wound suffered at their hands. There was a single additional follow-up arti-cle, and if Gerard's mother had filed suit, it hadn't been reported. I could check later, or Roger may know. I glanced at one of the library clocks—I needed to leave to meet him soon.

I continued working my way through my list. Of the seven names, I was able to confirm five boys, including Kenneth Gerard, had died in custody at the Reform School. I couldn't find anything on the other two, possibly because their names were too common and I was doing a rush job. Two of the dead boys were said to have died during a flu epidemic in the 1950s. One more died in a fire at the facility in the 1960s, and the remaining confirmed death was an escape attempt in the 1970s. The boy had been struck by a vehicle in the dark and died from his injuries.

Back at the table, I flipped to the escape attempt first. The day before his death, the boy had been placed in solitary confinement for being disrespectful to one of the corrections officers. It was the middle of July, and the report noted that "After six hours in the Box, inmate was found unconscious and carried to the infirmary for observation."

I didn't realize I'd closed my eyes until a pile of books dropped with a bang on the other side of my circular table. I jerked my eyes open to see a teenaged boy in a hoody ignoring me. My eyes returned to the photocopied page, caught by a pair of evocative words. *Subsequent seizures.* How the hell was the kid supposed to have attempted escape when he was having seizures?

Glancing down at my cell phone, I saw my time was up. My stomach rolled with revulsion as I straightened the stack of papers and shoved them back into the accordion file. Even carrying them made me feel dirty, like they'd transferred their nastiness to me and Frank and anyone who had contact with the information in them.

Walking upstairs to the Park Street exit, I took in the handful of teens scattered about with their heads down. What about Addy? Had the runaway been contaminated by proximity, by the things Roger and I were investigating?

There was no sign of the man from Milton Dickey's house outside, and I tried to shake off the horrors I'd read while walking through the market on the way to my car. I passed an organic farm stand, with carrots and lettuce, peas and leafy items I didn't recognize. Teenagers need veggies, right? But they'd rot in my car before I made it home. Addy and I had used the last of the bread for toast, so when I saw a bakery tent, I headed in that direction. I sniffed their lavender scones, drawing annoyed looks from the bakery staff, before grabbing a loaf of sliced whole wheat.

The proliferation of pastries and sight of ordinary people milling in their weekend casual clothes relaxed me a bit, gave me some distance. Perspective. I realized I'd probably been paranoid. Understandable, considering the crazy day I'd had yesterday with Turtle and Troy. The things I'd been reading for the past few days. But practically every other vehicle on the street now was a dark SUV. That didn't mean the drivers were out to get me, just that they didn't care about gas mileage.

My mind wandered with my feet, and I wished Mike were with me. I valued his opinion, on cases if not my mental state, not to mention (as I passed another produce stand) his skills in the kitchen. Would he have cooked for me this weekend—I smiled and blushed—or would we have subsisted on whatever we could grab and growl between bouts of ecstasy?

The distinct, earthy scent of sandalwood drifted from a nearby table where a young woman with long, loose hair and layered, flowing skirts sold handmade candles. She proselytized about auras to a woman with short, white, no-nonsense hair wearing capris and a blue fleece. The graying man next to her was built like an athletic coach, the kind who actually made it to The Show, albeit briefly. Wearing jeans and a much more threadbare fleece, he could have passed for her Mr. Bean or Crew.

Except... something didn't feel right. I caught a glimpse of his solid jaw, but I could never see his face. And his posture seemed wrong, hunching next to the woman but not toward her, as if using her body for cover rather than sleeping with it every night.

Paranoid, Brennan, I thought. *Remember, you're just paranoid.*

But as I turned toward my car, he reached for a candle. His right hand was missing the tip of its pinky.

My heart pounded in my chest. I fought powerful, warring desires to move in for a closer look, or run. Instead, I kept walking casually, as though there were nothing more important on my mind than whether it was too early to buy tomato plants.

Coincidence. It had to be. Just because the man had lost a third of a digit and was in the right age range didn't mean he'd tormented Turtle decades ago. When a couple of laughing, rambunctious teenaged boys bumped me, I took the opportunity for a circumspect glance behind me.

The white-haired woman was still there, but the man was nowhere in sight. I was right; they hadn't been together.

I clutched my loaf of bread too tightly, wishing I'd purchased a hard baguette or something with a little more heft. Particularly when I saw a gray SUV on the downhill side of the median, directly across from Cecil on the uphill side. No one—large wall of man or other-wise—sat inside.

So two strange men may or may not be following me, and may or may not be together. Was that a better or worse scenario than them working independently?

At least Addy wasn't in the car with me now. But what had I gotten her into?

23

I didn't see either of my friends (who were anything but) while pulling out of my spot. But it was hard to keep an eye out for the men with the added distraction of so many pedestrians who couldn't bother to look before crossing the street. I continued going straight past what should have been my first turn, then made a complete circuit around the block until I was headed in the proper direction. Still no gray SUV. And no one waving nine and three-quarter fingers.

It might be time to bring in some more manpower (person-power?), at least investigatively. If Roger didn't object, I'd ask Mike if he had some free time for digging. I couldn't be our constantly moving feet on the ground and keep up with vetting everyone we might be pissing off. Besides, Mike's background was in computers, so he was much better—and faster—at that part than I was.

Roger and I had agreed to meet at a Thai place with okay food but excellent privacy. I found him sitting in our usual red pleather booth in the back corner. A plate of spring rolls sat in the center of the table, and a Thai iced tea sweated at my place. I dove into my seat and sucked down a big jolt of caffeine and sugar before speaking. "Sorry."

"No Addy?" Roger asked.

He was looking civilized, drinking hot tea from a small ceramic pot. It made me want to order another plastic tumbler of my creamy concoction, with an extra straw, just on principle.

"Left her with Ben. Which is good, because she doesn't need to hear the sick crap we'll be discussing," I said. "And because I also seem to have a secret admirer. Or two."

I told him about seeing the large man in the SUV at the Archives and the market, as well as the pinky-impaired guy.

Roger's brows wrinkled, but he held his tongue until the waitress had finished arranging our pad Thai and stir-fry on the table. Hunger trumped my now fading fear. I scooped generous portions of noodles and rice onto my plate as Roger sat pensively. Pad Thai was one of the few dishes I could reliably eat rather than wear while using chopsticks. All bets were off on the stir-fry, so my fork was at the ready.

"Did either of them make you feel unsafe?" Roger asked.

"Yes," I admitted, rolling my just-snapped wooden chopsticks between my hands. "Especially Pinky Guy. Whether that's justified or me being paranoid, I don't know. Hell, I might have even imagined him."

Roger's face twisted into a wry smile. "Sydney, you know as well as I do that all defense people are paranoid. But it doesn't mean they're not out to get us."

"I'm not a defense investigator anymore," I said, contradicting my status but not his assessment of the defender mentality. That was spot-on.

"Don't be stupid," he said. "It's in your bones. It's who you are, even if it no longer pays the majority of your bills. So tell me about these files you got from the Archives."

I'd brought my notebook in, but avoided nitty-gritty details while we ate. I've been known to peruse crime scene photos over pizza at home, but I try to maintain some sense of decorum in public. I could see Roger's wheels turning when I gave him the list of dead children. He removed his napkin from his lap, preparing to get up and pace, before remembering where we were. I stopped talking and gave him a moment. In other words, I ate while he stared at the ceiling and figured out shit.

I was just beginning to regret my second helping of pad Thai when he clenched his fist and bowed his head. "What is it?" I asked.

"I bet it was discovery," he said. "That those records were requested by the plaintiff in a wrongful death suit—I think it was in the 90s, filed by Cliff Rangowski. I was talking to one of his associates yesterday, and she mentioned a couple of those names."

"That wasn't about the Gerard kid?"

"No, it was later," he confirmed.

I leaned back in the booth, hands on my full belly. My thinking pose. "So you think Rangowski's crew subpoenaed the records on previous deaths, and... the Reform School was still open then, right?"

Roger nodded. "On its last legs."

I continued, "They subpoenaed the records, and the Reform School provided a sanitized version."

"Or nothing at all," Roger countered. "The Reform School fought everything, every step of the way, dragging it out. Which was their usual M.O., but they had even more incentive in that case. The dead boy's father was dying of cancer, and there were no other survivors with legal standing—or the will to pursue it—once he was gone."

"But someone at the facility couldn't bring himself or herself to destroy the dead boys' records, and tucked them in amongst innocuous stuff going to the Archives at shutdown," I guessed.

"Seems as good a theory as any. This is good," Roger said, but his voice was subdued. "Someone *might* be able to use this to vacate a summary judgment, say it was a fraud upon the court."

"Sounds like you think that's a big maybe."

He shrugged. "There are a lot of variables, and it's just a first step..."

"And while it suggests the place was run by psychopaths for decades, it doesn't get us any closer to finding the body your dad helped bury," I said. I tried to keep a straight face and play it cool, but I couldn't stop a betraying grin.

"What?" Roger asked, expression vaguely hopeful.

"I saved the best for last," I admitted, and pulled the map out with a flourish.

Flourishing is safe with a photocopy.

Roger's eyes went wide, and he shoved dishes out of the way. Our waitress came to see what kind of fit he was having, catching the left-over pad Thai just before it hit the floor.

"Sir," she said, sharply, but still showing remarkable restraint, "if you'll wait just a moment, I'll take care of these. Do you want this boxed up?"

"Yes, please," I said.

I don't think Roger even heard her. I also don't think he does "boxed up." He placed his napkin across the bare section of table, then motioned peremptorily for mine. Soon he had a mini tablecloth that accommodated most of the oversized paper and kept it free of sriracha sauce.

"Sydney, you're brilliant," he said, butt rising from his seat for a better view of the map.

"Duh," was my reasoned response. "So, do you think your dad will be able to figure out the location?"

"Let's find out," he said, folding the map as he scooted from the booth.

I stretched out an arm to restrain him. "Easy there, Tex. We need to pay first. Actually, that's your job. I'm too brilliant for those ordinary kinds of transactions."

Roger threw a napkin at me. Fortunately, *his* napkin, which was always less messy than mine.

But he still paid the bill.

"I DON'T KNOW," Mr. Weber said, voice whispery and rattling with phlegm. I'd noticed his IV was gone today. "A piece of paper with lines on it doesn't look like the real world. It's been so many years, and the whole time me trying so hard to forget."

"That's okay, Dad," Roger said, mostly hiding his disappointment.

Roger hated to lose as much as he loved to win—it's one of the things that made him such an amazing litigator. But this wasn't about his ego. It was about giving his father peace.

"Mr. Weber," I began.

"Please, sweetie, call me Amos," he cut in.

I smiled and continued. "Amos, let's try something different. I want you to close your eyes, go back to that day, and tell me what you see. You said you rode in a truck to the place where the boy was buried. Where were you when your supervisor came to get you?"

"I'd just come out of the main admin building," he said. "Old Miss Lewis—long gone now, she was elderly even then—she was the secretary, and it was a pretty rough bunch working there. I stopped in most afternoons, to make sure she was doing okay and see if she needed anything."

"And did she?" I asked.

"I don't know," he said, brows creasing with anxiety. "I imagine—"

"I'm not asking you to imagine," I said gently. "I can do that. Don't overthink it. What was the last thing she said as you left the building?"

"That if I happened to trip over an extra glass of iced tea, to be sure and bring her one," he replied. His face cleared and mouth fell open with surprise after he'd finished.

"Don't go cheating and open your eyes," I said.

He smiled. "What else?"

"So you walked outside the administration building," I prompted. "Then what?"

"My supervisor... I can't recall his name," Amos said.

"That's okay. It's not important. What did he say?"

"He drove up in a pickup. One of the beater ones they used with the farm. The windows were down and he leaned across the front seat and said something like, 'Mr. Weber, I need you to come help me.'"

Amos laid his palm flat on the bed, as if to quell a shaking. It was so hard not to press it between my hands. I glanced at Roger and saw he had the same dilemma. Roger stood, quietly, and moved a few paces away.

"Was the road he took paved?" I asked.

"No, it was gravel," Amos said. "Big, tall grasses grew up to the edge of the path, smacking the truck, and sometimes you had to lean in or roll up your window."

"Which direction did you go from the admin building?"

His hand lifted from the bed, as if he were using it to point the way in his mind. "Back toward the main road at first, but then it curved around to the left and kept going a ways."

"Did you pass any other buildings?" I asked.

Amos shook his head so slightly I almost thought I'd imagined it. "No, I don't believe we did. At least, not once we got beyond the main part of the complex, with the dorms and such." A moment later, his entire body flinched with realization. "Except for a shed. A real simple wooden one, not much bigger than a carport. I believe they kept it there for times when they weren't taking the farm machinery all the way back to the main garage, but wanted it under some cover."

"Do you remember any other landmarks?" I asked. "Maybe a tree, or some abandoned equipment..."

"No, there weren't any trees more than palmettos, and they wouldn't still be there anyway. That's how it was, the whole way until we stopped."

Amos paused to get his breath. I gently placed his sippy cup in his hands, unable to listen to his gurgling phlegm any longer.

Once he'd had some water and cleared his throat, I took the cup and Amos continued. "It was a big field where he parked the truck, like it had been cleared way back and maybe used for grazing. But there were trees in the distance, big trees. Looked like oaks. And there was a patch where the grass didn't grow so well."

I prompted him. "That's where you dug?"

He nodded, and his hand strayed to his bottom lip. "But it wasn't right next to the truck. It was at least fifteen, twenty yards away. I remember because the shovel felt so heavy to carry afterwards."

He held his breath, fighting a sob. "He was wrapped tight in a sheet, all proper like. Thank the Lord they didn't make me cover him up. I couldn't have done it."

Roger pushed past me to take his father's hand. Amos opened his eyes, and Roger said, "It's okay, Dad. You've said enough."

His father nodded, and tears trickled from his bloodshot, rheumy eyes. Roger sat on the bed next to him, using his free hand to stroke his father's thin, white hair back from his temple. "You can let it go now, Dad."

And he did, with wheezing breaths that hurt my heart.

It seemed an appropriate time to leave, so when I heard my phone buzzing in my purse, I took advantage of it. Catching Roger's eye, I held up my cell and headed out the door, answering in the hallway.

It was Ben. "Hey, what's up?"

"Syd, I'm sorry. I know you're working, but I didn't know what else to do," he babbled. "Except call the cops, and I couldn't do that..."

My chest seized. I covered the phone while I sucked in air through my nose until I could speak. "Ben, just stay calm. What happened? Is it Addy?"

He made a grunting noise of assent. "Everything was good at the garage this morning. Then we ate at the falafel place, and everything was cool. But I had to get gas. And I was going to pay at the pump, but Addy said the falafel made her thirsty. So I figured I'd pay inside and get us some drinks..."

"Oh, no," I groaned, seeing where this was going.

Ben continued as if he hadn't heard me. "And I come out of the convenience store, and the car's not there." Ben let out an exasperated sigh. "Syd, Addy stole my car! She's gone."

24

I gave Roger a whispered heads-up with a promise to check in later before racing to the parking lot, dodging a couple of saintly staff on the way. I tried the phone number Addy had called me from previously, but got no answer except a strange woman's voicemail. What the hell was she thinking?

Sometimes I found it helpful to start with absolute worst-case scenarios and work my way down the pyramid of potential catastrophes. Worst case: either the man in the SUV or Pinky Guy had something to do with it. Fortunately, that was hard to swallow. So far as I knew, there was no relationship between either of them and Addy, and there was no reason for them to necessarily think she was a way to get to me. Assuming they even wanted to get to me, which was a big fat paranoid assumption based on possibly seeing Pinky Guy in my vicinity *once* and Ms. Dickey's friend twice.

I still hadn't heard back from the Spencers. Maybe there was a connection between their silence and Addy's disappearance. As much as the thought of speaking to them at this moment made me cringe, I tried all the numbers I had for the Spencers. No answer, and I didn't leave a voicemail. If I didn't hear back from them by tonight, I'd have to follow up with their friend Faith Halliway.

So what were the other dark scenarios? Addy could be playing us. I was pretty sure that wasn't the case, not just because I was a decent judge of character, but because I couldn't see the gain in it. It's not like she'd gotten anything more than a few meals and a night in a clean bed. Well, that and Ben's car. Him reporting it stolen would have been a worst-case scenario. Once the cops were looking for Addy, we'd have no chance of keeping her with us under the radar. And the Spencers would have no chance of getting a leg up on her foster parent when it came to filing for custody.

Ben looked miserable standing outside the convenience store, both five years younger and fifteen years older than his chronological age. The cause? Vulnerable uncertainty combined with a deep-seated need to take responsibility, all writ large upon his face for someone who knew him as well as I did.

He didn't wait for me to cut the engine and barely waited for the car to stop before jumping in the passenger side.

"How do we find her?" he asked.

Having made my way through the greater potential catastrophes, I'd decided one of the lesser ones was more likely. "We'll see if she went back to the boyfriend."

Ben's body hummed with energy as I drove. Once I had to call him out on his tapping leg; I could feel it shifting my little Cabrio's course. Embarrassed, he stopped.

I'd tracked Troy to the same general area of town, so it didn't take long to get in the right neighborhood. "Ben, I need your eyes. I've only been here once, and it was late at night."

I didn't really need help navigating, but it gave him something to do, and I appreciated a few extra seconds of warning. I told him the address and gave him a general description of the cars, though I couldn't be sure of color since I'd seen them by streetlight.

Darkness had been kind to the neighborhood, and it looked tatty in daylight. Not quite dumpy, but like the owners couldn't be bothered to do better because there was no point with student renters. The car Troy had been driving was in the driveway, along with an unfamiliar car. I parked across the street again, not wanting to risk being boxed in if someone arrived after me.

"Stay in the car," I said.

"No. What if it's not safe for you to go in alone?" he protested.

Dear, chivalrous child. Good thing he didn't know about my altercation with Troy the night before. "Ben, I appreciate the concern, but this is my job. It's what I do every day, usually without backup. I know how to handle myself."

I had to admit, the young man had almost mastered glowering.

"But I will ask you to sit in the driver's seat," I said. "So we can make a quick getaway if necessary."

Having a job, and perhaps the prospect of being a getaway driver, placated him. "Fine," Ben said. "But yell if you need me."

"Don't worry," I said. "They'll be able to hear me in Pensacola."

But my smile was forced and faded quickly as I strode toward the front door. My experience was that one's voice had a bad habit of making itself scarce when most needed. Like screaming for help.

I rang the doorbell, didn't hear anything, and knocked on the dingy white door of the brick house. While I waited, I pulled out my cell phone and again dialed the number Addy had previously called me from.

The door swung open to reveal a sweats-clad young woman. "Yeah?" she said, adjusting the ponytail on the back of her head. "What do you want?"

At that moment, the pouch pocket on the front of her hooded sweatshirt began to ring. She pulled her phone free and answered, "Hello?"

"So it was you," I said into my phone before hanging up.

The young woman's brows wrinkled. "What is this?" she asked, staring at her phone as if she still weren't sure whether to disconnect.

"You gave Addy a ride to Cooper's," I said, smiling. "That's what a good friend does."

She nodded and looked over her shoulder, distracted. "Yeah, I just—"

"But you're also the person who told her asshole boyfriend where you'd taken her," I added. "That's what a backstabbing bitch does."

Her face flushed. (I had to admit, I was a little taken aback to hear the double-B word come out of my mouth as well.)

"What did you say?" she demanded, stepping toward me. It was hard to quantify numbers in sweats, but she definitely had a few pounds on me. "Just who the hell do you think you are?"

As she spoke, unaware, Troy Cantrell appeared behind her. We must've woken the man of the house. Or at least, the guest man of the house.

I nodded in Troy's direction and said, "I'm the one who knocked him on his ass."

She flinched, stepping sideways, and I felt a moment of remorse for taking my frustration out on her. I had no idea what the dynamics were like in the house.

"It's okay," Troy told her. "I got this."

Dismissed, she disappeared inside. Troy pulled the door closed behind her, but left a foot or two gap to stand in. He seemed uncertain about why I was there and how to proceed, so I went on the offensive.

"Where is she?" I asked.

"Who?" he asked, his vacant voice sounding as stupid as the question merited.

"The Queen of England, dipshit. Who do you think? Where's Addy?"

"I don't know where—"

I pushed past Troy, surprising myself almost as much as I surprised him, hitting the front door hard enough for it to swing back against the wall. "Addy?" I called out. "Addy?"

The young woman who'd answered the door was sitting on a worn couch in the living room, knees tucked, watching a talk show on TV. She looked up as I passed through, blinking rapidly, shoulders hunched with alarm, but didn't say anything.

The living room was separated from the kitchen by a passthrough. Unless she was hiding in the oven, Addy wasn't there, but I marched in anyway, riding my adrenaline high. That might have been a strategic error. Troy, who'd now had time to progress from confused to pissed off, blocked my path on the way out.

"What the hell do you think you're doing?" he demanded.

My eyes flicked sideways in a quick assessment. No handy tenderizing mallet or block of carving knives on the counter. Not even a coffee pot or mug. Just a bowl of soggy cornflakes. I took a small step back and turned sideways, in case I had to engage with him physically. "Tell me where she is, Troy."

He put a hand to his forehead, and I noticed the bruising on his face with satisfaction. Until I did the ass-whooping math and realized I hadn't caused it. Apparently, I wasn't the only one who'd taken a turn with Mr. Cantrell. He shook his head, and the anger seemed to transform to exhaustion. "She's more fucking trouble than she's worth."

My cell phone buzzed from my pocket, but I ignored it. "Then help me find her," I said.

Glancing over his shoulder, he fixed his gaze on the woman who'd let me in, until she rose from the couch and disappeared down the hallway. Then he leaned against the counter on his elbow. The gesture emphasized his considerable height, and how lucky I'd been to catch him by surprise in the parking lot.

"Addy know anybody else in Tallahassee?" I asked.

"Naw," he drawled, waving a hand, "she practically doesn't know anybody back home. She sure as hell doesn't know anybody here."

"What about her?" I asked, nodding my head in the general direction the chick in the sweats had disappeared. "She helped Addy get out."

"That's Donnie's girlfriend. She practically lives here, probably just wanted to be rid of Addy," he said. "Thinks it's getting too crowded."

I took a good look at Troy, whose even-featured, chiseled (if scruffy) face was even more attractive pouting and bruised. He didn't look like quite as much of an ass without the leather jacket, but he was still the classic underachieving loser dating an underaged girl.

He looked miserable. I thought of Ben sitting in my car. Addy did seem to have a certain effect on men.

"Maybe it is too crowded," I said. "Maybe it's time for you to go home."

I expected him to protest, but instead he said, "You don't think she's coming back, do you?"

Troy might be older than Addy, but he was still awfully young. I took a chance and brushed by him, heading casually toward the door. He didn't try to stop me.

25

W ary of an attack from behind (loser ex-boyfriend or angry co-ed, either was a contender), I didn't relax my guard until I reached the car.

"Scoot over," I told Ben.

"Not there, huh?" he asked, grunting as he banged his head crawling across the center console.

My grunts echoed his as I fought to free my cell phone from my pocket. I didn't recognize the number, but the recent caller had left a voicemail. *Ms. Brennan, I think I recognize your friend, if you get here expeditiously.* It took me a moment to recall which shelter the pedantic woman ran, and a moment longer to decide she wouldn't report Addy to the cops. Probably.

By design or happenstance, many of the shelters and social services organizations were located in the same general area of town as the majority of off-campus student housing. I didn't waste any time crossing the half-mile or so between us, as evidenced by Ben alternately clutching his seat belt and the door handle. My driving might also have been impaired by an equally racing mind. Why was Addy at a shelter? The director hadn't said in her brief message.

It was a relatively small, privately run facility, and soon the pair of modest houses-turned-businesses were in view.

"There!" Ben said, pointing down the street. "That's my car!"

Cecil's small frame slid easily into a metered spot, and Ben was out before I'd even cleared my seat belt. I cringed as he bolted across the road, praying he had enough sense to look or enough luck to not get hit. I waited, standing flat against Cecil while a truck passed, its slipstream throwing my hair into my mouth. By the time I darted through traffic, Ben was already yelling at Addy.

"What the hell were you thinking?" he demanded. "Do you even have a driver's license?"

"Yes, I have a license!" she retorted, as if he were a moron. "And I know how to drive."

The two teens faced off on the sidewalk next to Ben's car. The blue streaks in Addy's hair seemed brighter since they'd dried from her morning shower. Ben held his arms and shook his head as he stared down at her. When he continued, his voice was less angry than mine would have been. "Why?" he asked. "Why would you *steal* my car?"

"I had something I had to do," Addy replied, trying to hold her ground but not doing a very good job of it.

It was reassuring to see she had a conscience.

He hesitated, brows wrinkling his otherwise unlined face, as though he was truly attempting to understand her point of view. Unsuccessfully. "Why wouldn't you just ask?"

"Okay, guys, let's do group therapy later," I said, glancing around to see if anyone was watching. The shelter director. The cops. My possible stalker(s). "Addy, give Ben his keys. You're coming with me."

Now her mask slipped entirely, or she began acting very well. Her eyes filled, and her lower lip trembled. "I'm sorry," she said. "I didn't think."

"I know," I told her, surprised at the calm in my own voice. Maybe Ben was rubbing off on me. "It's okay. Just get in my car."

I stood next to Ben and watched Addy dodge traffic, ready to give chase if she ran, until she climbed in Cecil and slammed the door. The sun reflecting off the pavement was a smidge too warm to be comfortable. A slight queasiness settled in my belly, and I told myself that was why. The heat and glare. *Yeah, right.*

"I'm sorry about this," I said.

Ben shrugged. "It was my fault for buying into her crap."

I shook my head. "No, it wasn't. And I wasn't kidding about 'group therapy' later. Can you make it for dinner?"

"You know me," he said, feigning more upbeat than he was as he circled his car. "I never say no to free food."

"Yet another thing we have in common," I said, forcing a smile before giving a last wave and dashing across the street.

Buying into her crap, huh? Is that what I was doing?

Maybe a little bit.

Addy was staring out the window, fidgeting at one of her fingernails with the thumb on the same hand. Once I'd closed the door and blocked out the traffic sounds, a snapping sound was audible every time she flicked the nail.

"Are you turning me in?" she asked.

"No."

"Taking me back to Ocala?"

"No."

She looked at me, surprised. "Why not?" she asked.

Instead of answering her question, I asked one of my own. "Addy, why did you come to Tallahassee?"

"Because that's where Troy was going," she said. She lied better than she had previously, but she was still no pro.

That night in the parking lot at Cooper's, Troy had said he'd come to Tallahassee *for Addy*, implying it was her idea. Of course, he'd also just told me she didn't know anyone here. Maybe he was wrong. But, with the exception of the recent car theft jaunt, now Addy was sticking close to me. If there *was* someone Addy knew in Tallahassee, someone important to her, she didn't know *where*.

"Addy," I said, voice firm, "Who are you looking for?"

Her face abruptly went pale, her long hair seeming darker in contrast.

"Addy, remember, this is what I do. I can help you, but you have to trust me."

She didn't answer, but she hadn't denied it or run into traffic, so I continued. "Is it a friend of yours? Someone from home?"

Addy nodded, mashing her lips together until a narrow band of color appeared that highlighted their pallor.

"What's her name?" I asked.

I heard her tongue unstick from the roof of her mouth before she said in a small voice, "Carly Whitmore."

"Tell me about Carly." When she hesitated, I pressed. "Addy, tell me, or I can't help you help her."

It was stuffy in the car, but Addy tucked her hands inside her sweatshirt sleeves and hugged herself. Finally, she said, "I met Carly in foster care. We were never placed together, but we had some... overlap in between."

"And you stayed in touch?" I asked.

She nodded. "About six months ago, things started getting too weird with her foster family, so Carly bugged out for Tallahassee. I know she made it here—I got a couple of postcards. But she was supposed to let me know when she got settled."

Resting my hands on the steering wheel, I looked out into a distance I couldn't see. I didn't like where this was going. "You're sure she's not back in the foster system?"

"Positive," Addy said. "See, she's older than me. She turns eighteen in a couple weeks. That's another reason she left. She figured, being so close to her birthday, nobody would bother with her."

No doubt because so few people had bothered with her thus far in her life. "She know anybody here?"

Addy shook her head. "No, she was like me, except she didn't even have Troy. But, with all the college kids, she thought it was a good place to get lost. And it's not scary dangerous like a lot of other cities."

I raised an eyebrow. The scariest places I've ever been weren't cities, but this wasn't the time to share that observation. "And you thought she might be at one of the shelters?"

Addy shrugged.

I sighed and started the car.

"All right," I said. "Let's see if we can find her."

WE SPENT the rest of the afternoon going over much of the same ground I'd covered earlier in the week looking for Addy. She had a year-old photo of her and Carly, but it wasn't particularly helpful. The two girls stood shoulder-to-shoulder in front of an asphalt basketball court at an outdoor park, almost silhouetted by an overcast sky. The friend who'd taken the photo was long gone. Addy didn't know where, but they'd never been that close anyway.

Addy went in with me everywhere because she refused to part with her photo. Which was fine, since I didn't trust her enough to leave her alone in the car. Addy's presence also encouraged wary young people to speak with us. Not that it mattered. No one recognized Carly or knew anything about her. So they said.

"That last girl," Addy said.

"Young woman," I corrected, mostly because I was attempting to train myself.

"Whatever," she said. "With the ratty hair. Do you think she was lying about Carly?"

"Not exactly."

Addy paused by the passenger door, gazing across the hood of the car at me. "I think she was scared about something," she said.

I raised an eyebrow. The kid had good instincts, or maybe just similar life experience. "I believe you're right," I said, getting in the car.

Addy flopped into the seat so hard the car moved. "You think she figured we weren't being straight with her? About why we were asking questions."

"Maybe," I said. "What would you do if someone you've never seen before showed up out of the blue and started asking you questions about Carly?"

Her lips tightened, and she blinked hard. I started the car and belted up before she answered. "I'd keep my mouth shut."

"There you go," I said, merging into traffic. Though I still thought there might be more to it than simple distrust this time.

"Well, crap," Addy said. "How do you ever get anyone to tell you anything?"

"Sometimes I don't," I admitted. "And it's frustrating. The key is to make the person you're interviewing understand that what you're doing is actually in their best interest. Or, in the best interest of the person they think they're protecting."

"But what if it's not?" Addy asked.

I had no answer, at least not one I was willing to share.

I was tempted to ask my new bestest cop buddy John Driscoll to do some checking on Carly—he could find out far more than I could, and far more easily. But I didn't dare let him get sight of Addy. The last thing I needed was to put him in an awkward position, or find out it wasn't awkward as he immediately threw Addy and me under the bus by reporting her. I'd call him from home instead, which is where we were headed now.

My cell phone rang before we quite made it. Reaching for the device, I knocked it to the floor on Addy's side. She handed it to me just before my voicemail kicked in.

"Yeah," I said, drifting toward the center line as I nearly dropped the damn thing again. This was why I usually pulled over for phone calls—I know my level of coordination all too well.

"Everything okay, Sydney?" came Roger's crisp voice. "Any luck finding Addy?"

"Yeah," I said, echoing my earlier professionalism. "She's right here next to me."

"Good," he said. "Is she coming with us tomorrow?"

Tomorrow... It took me a moment to recall we were searching for children's graves tomorrow. Did I really want to take Addy with me for something like that? Plus I hadn't heard back from the Spencers yet.

"We'll see," I said. "Are you okay with Mike meeting us at the Reform School?"

Roger had agreed to Mike helping out with some background at lunch, but I hadn't run it by Mike yet. So why not volunteer him for even more tasks without asking? Sounded like the perfect way to build a healthy relationship.

"I think Mike meeting us would be an excellent idea," Roger said. "We could use an extra pair of eyes."

I hoped Mike's eyes was all we'd need.

Roger and I set a meet time and place as I pulled into my carport. Clouds had rolled in, and dusk was approaching, so I wasn't surprised to see a light on in the house. Ben would be waiting inside.

Correction: I *assumed* Ben would be waiting inside. Or I would, except I didn't assume things like that anymore. Which is why I made Addy wait in the car, taking my keys with me. If Addy made a break for it on foot, Mr. Ginley or one of my other nosy neighbors would see which direction she'd gone. Hopefully without calling the cops

I knew Ben was in a bad headspace when I found him listlessly watching crap TV on my sofa. I didn't know how much was because of me and Addy, versus how much was his flaky mother, his part-time job, his classes, and the rest of his complicated teenaged life. When he didn't speak or look up as I entered, I also knew he wasn't going to tell me. At least, not right now.

I sat next to him on the couch and asked, "Where's the duct tape?"

He looked at me, confused.

"I've got Addy in the car," I said. "I figured if we duct tape her to a chair, she can't run."

A smile touched the corner of Ben's lips, and I felt a pang as I saw his father JD there. Someone else for Ben to worry about.

"She swears she won't, but we could do it anyway, just on principle," I added. "And yes, you can tape her mouth."

His face split into a genuine grin. "Next time, I will," Ben promised.

I sighed, giving his leg a gentle pat. "You do realize, she wasn't trying to screw you over."

He blinked hard and gave the slightest head shake, surprised at me rather than the sentiment. "I know that, Syd."

Of course he did. Sometimes I forgot that Ben had what neither of his parents could match (although JD came closer): an almost scarily perceptive sense of empathy. "Then what?" I asked.

His eyes dropped, and he stared at a worn spot on the thigh of his jeans and picked at it. "I don't get why she didn't trust me."

"I can guess," I said, "but I think that's something you need to ask her."

As if on cue, I heard the side door to the carport open. "Sydney?" Addy called out. "Is it okay to come in now?"

I raised interrogatory eyebrows, and Ben rolled his eyes. "Okay," he said.

"We're in here," I answered, rising from the couch reluctantly. My stomach rumbled as I waited for Addy to join us. She made it as far as the living room threshold and hesitated, hands shoved in her sweat-shirt sleeves again.

When Ben met her eyes, Addy's gaze faltered, but only for a moment before she cleared her throat. "Ben," she said, "I'm sorry I stole your car."

Good job, kid, I thought but didn't say out loud. My influence was not needed here. In fact, I didn't think I was needed here at all. "Can I trust you guys not to kill each other if I go pick up something for us to eat?"

"There's Chinese food in the fridge," Ben said.

My mouth gaped like a baby bird's. "For real-sies?" I asked, as pleased as I was surprised.

Ben blushed. "I picked it up on the way home."

"Gold star," I said, giving him an enthusiastic double thumbs-up. "In that case, I'm going to make a few quick phone calls, and we can eat in... say, twenty minutes?"

Neither teen answered, but I pretended they did. "Cool," I said. "Yell if you need anything."

Or when the stabbings start, I thought, retreating to my room with one of my notebooks.

John Driscoll promised to check whether Addy's friend Carly had been picked up in the past few months by the TPD. I wasn't crazy about owing a cop a favor, but maybe this just made us even? I needed a scorecard to keep track.

I still couldn't get through to the Spencers, and it was starting to worry me. Supposedly they wanted to take care of their niece. Either Mr. Spencer had lied about that, which I doubted, or some kind of shit was hitting the fan in their lives. I tapped my pen against my notebook. I couldn't help wondering if their absence was an indication that, regardless of good intent, they were incapable of taking care of Addy at the moment.

I was also unable to reach their friend, Faith Halliway, which did nothing to allay my concerns.

"Don't borrow trouble," I told myself, channeling my grandmother and pushing my fears to the side for the moment.

Now it was time—past time, really—to check in with Mike. Unlike my clients, he was available.

"You want me to be your body-hunting buddy," he said, after I'd brought him up to speed. His tone was hard to interpret. His humor was often dry, but I wasn't sure it was that dry.

"It's an offer you're not likely to get from anyone else," I said, going for light.

"Still trying to top our first date?" he asked.

Good. That was humor. "God forbid," I said. "Are you in?"

"I wouldn't miss it," he said, and I gave him directions to meet us.

I hadn't mentioned SUV Guy or Pinky Man. It wasn't a conscious omission, but having summoned them in my mind, I walked to the nearest window facing the street and peered from behind the curtain. Nothing. No stalkers. No strange cars or anything else on the quiet, residential street. The only thing to draw the eye was the impressive mass of pampas grass next to my mailbox. It needed pruning. The texture of winter dead and fresh spring leaves contrasted with the inky shadows beneath the trees, pooling at the edge of the street and bleeding around Mr. Ginley's house.

I was starting to think I'd overreacted about the men. And yet. . a feeling like a finger lightly tracing the back of my neck gave me a shiver. And yet, maybe not.

26

The old Youth Reform School was just across the Central Time Zone line, giving us an extra hour with our travel, but it still felt early when we met Roger the next morning. Addy fell asleep in the back seat within minutes of finishing her morning mocha and tucking the cup safely in the trash bag Roger provided.

At least he let us drink in the car.

Roger glanced at her in the rearview mirror. "This is getting to be a habit," he said.

"A runaway sleeping in your car," I asked, "or the three of us bonding American-style, burning fossil fuels to hurtle a hunk of steel?"

"We do look like a family out for the proverbial Sunday drive, don't we?" he observed.

"Except for the German car."

"And the fact that none of us are related, by blood or romantic entanglement," he added.

"I assume that's not a proposition," I said, fighting the foggy listlessness always prompted by green-edged, monotonous interstate.

"No, it is not," he said, smiling almost wistfully.

My butt slid down the seat until the lap belt stretched tightly across my belly. "So how did you propose to your wives?"

Roger shook his head.

"Come on," I pleaded. "It's a long drive, and you have three stories to choose from. I'm only asking for one."

"I'm afraid you won't get any of them without alcohol," he said, then added, "Don't feel like you have to stay awake on my account."

"Fine," I said, leaning against the cool window. "I can take a hint."

The car's motion was soothing, and I dozed until we reached the outskirts of nothing. That's what it looked like anyway. Stretches of highway where the speed limit dropped to forty-five or even thirty-five miles per hour with rarely more than a business or two in sight. I hated these areas, not just for their speeding capriciousness (they were infamous for aggressive ticketing), but also because they were ugly. Flat ground, anemic grass, and pale asphalt, with only the occasional tree. Exactly the kind of place you should be able to drive quickly to pass through.

"Mike's meeting us there?" Roger asked, softly as if he didn't want to wake Addy.

"Yeah," I confirmed. "He said he'd call if he had any issues."

We were finally passing through something that approximated a small town, with a local gas station and convenience store, a mechanic, and a couple of other small businesses. I pulled out my cell phone. No messages, but practically no signal either. Not that Mike would have problems finding the place. Being navigationally challenged was my special gift.

"You think she's up for this?" he asked, eyes on Addy's sleeping form in the rearview mirror.

"Why didn't you ever have kids?" I asked.

He shot me a look, and I raised my hands in apology before answering him. "I didn't have much choice but to bring her. And if it gets too weird, we can always send her back to the car."

"Why would it be too weird, hunting for the graves of dead kids?"

he asked. He was probably going for deadpan, but his voice was obviously strained.

"Are you sure *you're* up for this?" I asked. "We can stick with the usual legwork. Go back and dig into the Archives, I can keep on tracking down the kids, maybe get lucky with a guard—"

"No. Thanks, Sydney," he said. "I'll be fine. And we're almost there."

The road had entered bedraggled forest, composed mostly of tall, straight pines. Chain-link fence occasionally peeked through the trees, but there was no sign, no plaque, nothing to indicate the significance of the upcoming nondescript driveway. Roger braked—we'd have missed it entirely if the roadside weeds had done a better job of shielding Mike's bright-yellow Jeep from view.

I hadn't considered that the property itself might be secured, but a broad metal farm gate blocked vehicular access. That's when it hit me that what we were doing may not precisely speaking be legal.

"Do we have—do we *need*—permission to be here?" I asked. I don't know why, since I already knew the answer.

"Really, Sydney? You don't trust me to talk our way out of a simple trespass?" Roger asked, rolling down his window as Mike approached.

"Better to beg forgiveness," I muttered, paraphrasing Roger's motto. I had a feeling we were about to go beyond a simple trespass.

Mike's quick smile at me through Roger's window made the air around me go thin. In a good way. Then he extended a hand to Roger, all business.

"Mike," Roger said. "Thanks for helping us out on this."

Mike nodded, and in the taciturn way of males, their pleasantries were complete. "The gate's not locked," Mike said, "but I haven't been in yet. I didn't know how you'd want to proceed."

"Not locked, huh?" Roger asked, staring while he brushed rusty dust Mike had transferred to his hand onto his fancy pants. (Cargos made of a quick-dry fiber, they could probably do double duty as a tent on Mars.) Mike held his gaze, and Roger finally said, "Well, then, we'd better get to it."

Addy stirred at the clanging noise when Mike uncoiled a wrapped chain from round, gray crossbars. He pushed the resistant gate open, then waited for Roger to drive through before following and closing the gate behind us.

A couple of live oaks and a single, squat, rotting palm tree flanked the potholed driveway. The path split fifty yards or so ahead of us at a modest, single-story building. The shingles of the building's low, pyramid-shaped roof were worn, with a few missing, and the original color of its walls was indistinguishable from faded dirt. But the structure was still standing. The driveway wrapped around the structure to become a parking lot on the right side and lead onward into the complex to the left. Roger veered to the right.

Roger parked, and we found ourselves staring at a landscape that was green without giving a sense of life, like mold. The immediate area was the ecological equivalent of a junk drawer: scattered tall pines, unrecognizable shrubs, snarling vines both leafy and gray-stalked, and grasses ranging from formerly domestic to Jurassic Park escapees.

Scattered, haphazardly constructed buildings reinforced the sense of disorder—brick, wood, and cinder block, ranging from relatively intact to all but swallowed by the land—and that was just within sight of where we stood. A couple were ringed by chain-link fence and ragged bits of razor wire.

"Are we here?" Addy asked, voice fuzzy.

"Yes," I said, and we gathered next to the vehicles. Though what being *here* meant remained elusive. It felt as though we'd taken a step back in time. Or maybe forward, just past the age of man.

The sky was the glaring white of socked-in overcast, the air heavy with humidity and something more... I'm not the most superstitious person, but it was hard to shake a pervasive sense of wrongness clinging to every molecule that touched my skin. It felt like bad things had happened here, and the place itself had been pushed beyond caring.

The heavy air also had a hollow quiet, with no birds or rustling leaves and just a hint of white traffic noise in the distance. The sudden, abrasive sound of Mike brushing his hands against his pants startled me. He was dressed much as Addy and I were, in jeans and a long-sleeved T-shirt. He wasn't wearing his glasses, but a hat covered his chestnut hair, which seemed a little shorter than when I'd last seen him.

"You must be Addy—I'm Mike," he said, extending a now slightly cleaner hand toward Addy.

Addy shook it awkwardly, blushing at the attention.

Mike reached into his Jeep to retrieve a Red Sox cap I'd left behind during our last visit. He offered me the hat, and once I'd donned it, his gallant arm. "Shall we?" he asked.

I was grateful for the garment and the gesture. The glaring sky hurt my eyes, and the paved walkways were buckled with yellowing, wiry grass crowding the cracks. Plus, I appreciated the warm solidity of his body next to mine, no matter what the excuse.

Sighing, I patted his arm and spared a glance for Addy half a step behind me. Eyes downcast, her hands had once again retreated into her sleeves. We all seemed to be dragging under the weight of the place's atmosphere. For me, it was a pressing sense of hopeless isolation.

But I wasn't actually alone, and Addy was.

Addy was always alone.

I placed a palm on her back, gently bringing her forward to walk next to us. She didn't look up, but she didn't resist, either.

Roger stopped, removing his sunglasses to rub eyes shadowed with worry and lack of sleep. Replacing the dark lenses made him instantly formidable, almost invulnerable. To someone who didn't know better.

"Okay," he said. "It's time to find out what evil was done here."

MIKE'S JEEP was the obvious choice to make our way to the farm area of the property, though a small, puckish part of me would have paid to watch Roger drive his Beemer baby over the cracked road into the unknown. I did my usual shorter legs kindness, getting in the back with Addy, and Roger navigated with his annotated map.

The landscape was a surreal time capsule. A lone, faded chip bag blew across the road in front of us as we cruised past the administration building. Following the road to its left, the next structure was a fenced compound, its single-story brick building and the fence itself appearing time-worn but whole.

"They locked people up here?" Addy asked, voice soft. "Kids?"

It was a desolate space now—as you'd expect, having been long abandoned. But with no trees, no construction that was anything other than purely functional, I couldn't imagine it ever having been otherwise.

Roger fought his seat belt to look at Addy as he answered. "Yes. I believe that was a dorm. By the time it was in use, supposedly no one younger than thirteen was incarcerated there."

I recognized his Skeptical Voice.

A mirror image of the building sat on the opposite side of the road. We continued past it, our silence unbroken save for Roger's rustling map and the back seat creaking as Addy turned to watch the structure's retreat.

Beyond the first two compounds, the road lost all claim to the word *paved*, giving way to rutted gravel and shell. Addy and I braced ourselves against the doors and the seat as the Jeep rumbled forward, and we all rolled up our windows to avoid the chalky-tasting cloud that snatched at our slow-moving vehicle. Nameless scrubby vegetation appeared, scattered among tall pines whose branches were no longer than stubby fingers until they neared the top and became a crown.

Not thick enough to constitute a forest, the trees' presence gave me a sense of unease. There weren't enough to provide shelter, just enough to crush your house—or your passing car—come high winds.

The next building hadn't been victim of a falling tree; it had just given up. The facing wooden wall gaped open, and jagged pieces pointed outward like splintered brown and gray guts. More fragmented boards piled inside, so many I couldn't imagine how any walls remained standing. I blinked, trying to make sense of spots of color, but they persisted as blurs of red and blue and orange.

Leaning into Addy's space for a closer look, I grunted as the Jeep jolted and my seat belt jerked painfully across my chest.

Addy glanced at me, then back at the ruined scene before us. "Chairs," she said.

She was right. Classroom chairs with metal legs and plastic seats, flung haphazardly rather than stacked. The building must have been a schoolhouse.

As before, the derelict building had a mate on my side of the road in a comparable state of disrepair. At least, I assumed it was comparable; much of the structure was buried under kudzu. The leaves hadn't filled in completely yet, or I wouldn't have seen more than a massive lump.

"Why do they come in twos?" Addy asked.

"I'd imagine the legacy of segregation," Roger said. "Blacks and whites were separated by law, so there were often black and white versions of everything—dorms, classrooms, cafeterias..."

The Jeep slowed even more. Addy and I bumped heads angling for a better view between the front seats. Mike waited for Roger to give him directions at a split in the road.

"Left," Roger said, and we continued on.

The pine trees fell away, and the broad surrounding field and even broader sky made my neck prickle. Grasses and vines dominated, and the "road" further devolved into *whatever path has not been consumed by vegetation.*

Our wheels slammed into a particularly deep rut—*front! back!*— and Addy emitted a sound somewhere between a squeak and a squeal.

"Sorry," Mike said.

"Slow down," Roger said, though we weren't exactly speeding. "What do you think?"

Mike stopped and let the vehicle idle while he surveyed the area and the map Roger handed him. "I think that's the equipment shed," Mike said, pointing at about ten o'clock.

I knocked my hat askew on Mike's seat belt, looking over his shoulder. A portion of a single wall stood in the field ahead of us, weathered gray boards disappearing into mounds of greenery. Presumably the other three walls were feeding the plants as well.

"We're nearly there," Roger said, taking the map. "Dad said they drove half a mile or so past the equipment shed."

Roger's eyes were bright with anticipation, and chin motion betrayed his jaw rotating back and forth ever so slightly. We all scanned the surroundings compulsively, fruitlessly, as the Jeep crept forward. It had been decades since Amos Weber helped bury a boy in ground that even then was indistinguishable from the earth around it. Staring intently into the glare made my head ache.

Soon Mike stopped again, noting, "That's four-tenths. We can leave the car parked here." He stepped out, his long legs saving Addy and me from a potential tumble when he discovered a six-inch drop from the road into the surrounding field, invisible beneath the grasses.

"Ladies," he said, offering us each a hand down in turn.

Roger wasn't the most outdoorsy person, but he was methodical. He directed us to walk as an evenly spaced line, with the men on the ends and Addy and me in the middle. After seven minutes, Roger stopped us, based upon some math about our walking speed and distance and terrain. Or maybe he just liked the number seven. The end person stayed put, becoming the first person in our new line as we swung around to cover the next section, walking back toward the road. Walk and repeat.

Mike carried a machete on a sling over his shoulder, but the vegetation rarely extended past our knees. I was still paranoid about snakes and wished I was wearing my cowboy boots, though I was glad of my long, denim pants and long sleeves. Stray branches and blades brushed the fabric, irritating my ears with a heebie-jeebie sound and releasing a pervasive, earthy funk that made my lungs constrict and my throat itch.

Mr. Weber had said he'd placed a flat stone the size of a dinner plate on the boy's grave to mark it. Even if someone waved a wand (or a weed eater) over the field to clear it, it would be difficult to spot a single stone. Fortunately, after a few transects, we began crossing ground with bare patches, tufts of scraggly grass sticking out like a bald man's ear hair. I grew hopeful, remembering what Mr. Weber had said about the grass not growing well there. Of course, he'd also noted big oaks in the distance, and those trees were now long gone. Nothing grew taller than me, and in the plant kingdom, I'd definitely be a shrub.

The sun had crept high overhead and I was sweating beneath my shirt when we gathered around the Jeep for a break. Mike broke open a case of bottled water.

"What, no sandwiches?" I asked.

He pulled a bag of granola bars free from the piles in the back with a flourish.

"Oh, thank God," Addy said, grabbing a couple and following Roger around the front of the Jeep.

I was still watching her when I felt myself being swung around and pinned to the side of the Jeep. My heart leaped into my throat in a not entirely pleasant way, but I forced myself to relax.

"Why, good morning, Ms. Brennan," Mike said, flipping my hat around so the brim guarded my back. "I don't believe we've had a proper greeting yet."

"I believe you're correct, Mr. Montgomery," I said, flipping his hat as well. "Let's fix that."

The back of his neck was warm and sweaty, and the buzzed hair at the base of his skull tickled my hand as I pulled him toward me for a chaste, close-mouthed kiss. After all, we were grave hunting. Except once his warm lips hit mine, it was hard to restrain myself. Mike's mouth parted deliciously... and the Jeep began rocking behind me.

"Ouch!" I said. Or rather, gnarled a sound of protest meant to communicate that sentiment as my teeth banged painfully against Mike's.

Mike grunted, backing away, then yelled, "Hey! Easy on the paint."

"Sorry," Addy said, "but I took my shoes off."

I blinked, eyes unfocused and blood residing in non-brain portions of my body. Addy was standing on the hood of Mike's Jeep.

"See anything?" Roger asked, exhibiting a Zen-like calm. After all, she was standing on Mike's car and not his.

"I don't know," she said, voice uncertain. At some point, she'd pulled her hair into a ponytail and threaded it through the back of a cap I didn't recognize. But she still shaded her eyes against the glare. "Maybe over there?"

Mike gave me a quick kiss on the forehead, then opened the driver's door and hopped up on the frame next to the seat with the agility of a twelve-year-old. He flipped his hat back around to gaze where she'd been pointing.

"Excuse me," he said.

Addy slid down to make room, and Mike was around the windshield and on the hood of the Jeep before I could figure out how he'd done it. *Show-off.* Such feats were easier at six-foot-two than at... considerably less.

"Well?" I asked impatiently.

"Maybe there's something there," he said, jumping down and looking to Roger. "Hard to say."

Roger swigged from his water bottle before saying, "We'll hit it on the next set of transects anyway. Ready?"

We'd marked the spot where we'd emerged from the field so we knew where to carry on. We walked slowly, deliberately, eyes on the ground, but when we reached the far end of the line (recognizable by a kicked-up section of darker dirt), Roger said accusingly, "That wasn't remotely seven minutes—five at most."

Standing next to him, I put a hand on my hip. Since Roger was on the leading end, he more than anyone else had determined our pacing.

"Fine," he said. "Let's bring it back."

Mike said nothing, but rolled impatiently on his heels as we all passed him to claim our new positions.

It didn't take long.

The vegetation was sporadic in this section, revealing a pile of rocks between Roger and me about fifty yards from our start point. I didn't exactly run when I saw it, but I did walk quickly. Of course I tripped, falling to one knee within throwing distance of the mound, and Roger beat me to it.

"You okay?" he asked when I joined him, but his eyes never left the ground.

"Yeah," I said, taking in the rubbly heap about three feet long, composed of stones that looked like they could have come from the surrounding earth. "What do you think?"

"Dad said he left a single, flat stone," Roger said.

I shook my head and lifted a fist-sized rock. It left a reddish-brown, dusty mark on my palm when I dropped it. "You can't be saying that's a natural occurrence."

"No, I'm not."

So if the pile wasn't natural, what else wasn't? I glanced over my shoulder. *What did I trip over?* Standing slowly, my lips went numb as I staggered, zombie-like, back the way I'd come.

"Sydney?" Roger said.

My knee had left a depression in a patch of scrubby grass when I fell. I knelt there and pushed aside a leafy green weed. Its abrasive surface made the skin on my fingers burn.

The object I'd tripped over was a single, flat stone, partially sunken back into the earth.

Roger knelt next to me and ran his fingers across its surface.

I opened my mouth to say something, but I couldn't. Roger pressed a wrist to the corner of his eye and sucked in a breath. I lay my hand on his, still resting reverently on the stone. Roger nodded, continued drawing breath audibly through his nose.

We'd found Mr. Weber's grave.

"Sydney! Roger!" Mike called out.

I blinked away dirt and emotion and lifted my head. Mike stood twenty yards away—no more—next to a kneeling Addy.

"I think we've got something here," he said.

My mouth still hung open as I stared at Roger in horror.

"If this is where Dad buried the dead boy," he said, voice rough as he lifted an arm to gesture slowly toward Mike and the stone pile we'd just left, "then who are they?"

27

Y ou know those optical illusion drawings, where if you turn your head and look at just the right angle, a young woman's portrait becomes an old woman's profile? And then, having seen it, you can't *unsee* it.

Once we stumbled upon the first three potential graves, we couldn't stop seeing them everywhere. We found four other cairns and two simple, half-rotted wooden crosses, fallen to the earth they'd once stood upon.

"We need to stop," Roger said.

I agreed; I'd just been waiting for him to suggest it. Completely wrung out and overwhelmed, I couldn't imagine what Addy was feeling. She'd said she didn't want to stay in the car, but that was about all she'd said beyond, *Is there more water?* or *I think there's another grave here.*

Mike threw an arm over my shoulder and gave it a squeeze. I leaned into him gratefully as he asked Roger, "Do you have a plan?"

Roger swished a mouthful of water before answering. "Of sorts. Some of the attorneys from previous wrongful death suits prepared a writ of mandamus to compel recovery of the boy's body—they're updating it to include all remains on site. We've got a forensic anthropology team on standby, so if we can get someone to sign off, they're ready to mobilize. I want to make sure this is done right."

Of course, there might be nothing and no one to recover. Just the rock equivalent of crop circles. As Roger had said, that was for the experts to determine. We'd avoided doing anything to alter potential crime scenes (decades of neglect had done enough already), simply marking potential burials with stakes and pink surveyor's flagging tape. Roger had also brought a digital camera fancy enough to befit his bank account and photographed the area extensively.

I left Mike and Roger discussing logistics while I fetched Addy, standing just beyond the last burial spot we'd flagged. She wasn't physically far away but seemed in another world, gazing into the distance. A breeze lifted the ends of her hair and set the grass to rustling around us.

"Roger's dad said there used to be huge oak trees over there," I told her.

She didn't respond.

I moved forward, within her view but not blocking it. "We're stopping for now."

Addy finally focused on me, and my heart cracked again at the warring innocence and world-weary cynicism on her face. "So we're just leaving them?"

"Roger will see that they're taken care of. I promise." I watched pink flags flutter in the breeze over Addy's shoulder. "And he'll make sure—*we'll* make sure—someone pays."

"Good," she said.

The physical and mental exhaustion was palpable back in the Jeep. I felt the weight of the dead, and of my words to Addy, as we drove away from the graveyard. Roger and I would make someone pay—we *needed* to make someone pay. But it wasn't going to be easy. And if I were brutally honest with myself, I wasn't sure it was possible.

Roger's phone rang as the entrance parking came into view. He mostly listened to the person on the other end, getting out as soon as Mike stopped the Jeep to pace the lot with his phone.

Mike's eyes met mine in the rearview, brows peaked with concern. Addy hadn't spoken again, and Roger may have a plan of sorts, but the rest of us didn't. I checked my phone. No messages. I excused myself, clambering out the back and retreating to the opposite end of the lot from Roger, still on the phone and listening more than talking. I hoped that was a good sign.

The Spencers should be done with church by now, and I couldn't reach them. Again. I tried to remember the last time I'd spoken to Mr. Spencer—Friday? Not that long ago. I wondered if they'd signed the custody papers. Maybe they'd changed their minds about Addy.

I left a message for them, and then another message for their friend Faith Halliway. Barring something more ominous than silence, Roger had enough on his mind right now without worrying they were MIA. If need be, I could go to Ocala tomorrow. The thought of the three-hour drive (each way) made me want to sit on my bare ass in the parking lot and cry, but it could be done.

"Any luck?" Mike asked when I got back in his Jeep.

I couldn't remember how much I'd shared about what was happening; he'd at least intuited that I was in problem-solving mode. I shook my head, and Roger joined us in the car a moment later.

"Okay," Roger said, sighing as he dropped into his seat. "Things are in motion."

I leaned between the seats. "Meaning?"

"Meaning, I don't know how on a Sunday, but they got a judge to sign off—"

"No," I interrupted, touching his arm gently to forestall the wave of legalese about to wash over us. "We can talk details later. I meant what does this mean for us right now, today."

"Oh," he said, momentarily at a loss, noticing Addy again.

"I'd say it's time for lunch," Mike suggested, sensibly and to my own stomach's grumbling satisfaction. Mike might have heard it, adding, "Past time."

"Right," Roger said, then made a gesture that from another man would have been a plebeian head smack. "Someone from the forensic team is on his way to get the lay of the land. He was in Panama City for the weekend... You know what, I'll just stay here."

He opened his door and started to roll out of the vehicle.

"Roger," I began, "we can—"

"No," he said, landing almost solidly. "I want to make some notes before he arrives, while things are fresh in my mind."

It wasn't unreasonable for him to want or need some alone time, but I still glared at him sideways, raising a warning, don't-make-me-teach-you-sense eyebrow.

"I'll be fine," he said, corner of his mouth twitching. "I promise. And we'll check in with each other in a few hours."

Addy stretched an arm past his seat belt to wordlessly hand him a granola bar.

"Thanks, Addy," he said, this time with a full smile. "Make sure they feed you something good."

AN HOUR LATER, we sat at a rustic table one woodcrafting step up from a picnic bench, on a cafe deck looking out at a forest wetland of gray-trunked cypress—or was it tupelo? I'd never learned to tell the difference between their ridged, swollen bases. Lovely as it was, there was a slight odor akin to decomposition, the kind of tang that might just put you off your food on a hot summer's day.

"What river is this?" Addy asked. She sipped her soda like a kid, stretching her neck and nearly piercing her top lip with the straw.

With Mike in the restroom, I shrugged my ignorance (*Apalachicola? Suwanee? Styx?*) while shoving another thick, wedge-shaped fry in my face. We'd gotten to the cafe too late for the catch of the day, but their cheeseburgers were nothing to sneeze at and the iced tea was real *brewed* tea, not lemony sweet powdered crap. I raised a glass that was about the same color as the river.

"You ever been this far west?" I asked.

She shook her head, stabbing an ice chunk with her straw. "I'd never even been to Tallahassee until Troy and I left. I've never been anywhere."

"Except lovely Orlando," I said in a sarcastic tone of voice that earned me a grin.

"I've never even been to the ocean," she said.

"No shit?" I said, more loudly than I'd intended. Mike gave me a sharp look as he sat down. It's possible someone had spiked my tea, but more likely a surreal day had made me punchy.

"No shit," she confirmed.

My phone rang before I could comment—Roger.

"I'm so sorry, Sydney," he said, skipping the greeting.

"What's up?" I asked.

"There's no way I'll be able to go home tonight. Or at least, not at a reasonable time."

"Do you need help with something?"

Mike watched me questioningly and I mouthed, "Roger's stuck here tonight." Right about the time I figured out that meant Addy and I were, too.

"Thanks, Sydney," Roger said, "but there's not really anything you can do. The forensic guy is assessing the site now, and a couple of the attorneys are on their way so we can put our heads together. Listen, I'm happy to cover a rental car, if there's anywhere close we can get you one."

"Hold on," I said, covering the phone and filling in Mike.

"That's stupid," he said. "Just stay the night with me."

"I don't know," I waffled. "It's a sweet offer, but..." I glanced at Addy. She was enough of an adult to have moved with her boyfriend (though not legally), and she didn't seem weirded out by the idea, but it still didn't seem right. Plus Mike's guest room had an awful little futon.

"You ladies can have the bedroom, and I'll take the couch," he said, anticipating me. "You know I've slept on it before."

Actually, he'd been a true back martyr and slept in his recliner while *I* slept on the couch. Hopefully, someday soon we'd both sleep on the same piece of furniture at the same time.

Addy shrugged. "Fine by me."

Mike glanced at his watch, and a sly grin played across his face. "And if you're staying, we've got just enough time to find a beach before sunset."

Addy's face lit up and her hands clutched into excited fists like a child's. "Can we?" she asked.

I didn't have a chance.

We weren't exactly within spitting distance of the ocean, so it was nearly dusk when we reached some nameless spot on the Gulf Coast, free of condos and crab shacks. Mike pulled over at a wide patch of road, and we scrambled over the rocks and fill that shored up the edge of the coastal highway. Until the next hurricane.

After clambering down, we took off our shoes and rolled up our pants. The air held a slight, fishy tang of algae, and the dropping tide left a band of wet, packed sand, golden-brown in the fading light. Swell was nonexistent, and the ocean reflected the sky's colors like an artist's glass.

Addy was quiet, almost reverential, as she crept to the water's edge and touched it with trembling fingers.

"It's cold," she hissed, but gradually worked her way in to her ankles, then her shins. The salty water soaked the cuffs of her pants.

We meandered down the beach, Addy and I paired and Mike lingering behind, no one speaking. The rhythmic, trickling advance and retreat of the water was soothing, and my breathing slowed gratefully to match it. The intermittent, punctuating waves of passing cars mimicked organic white noise.

Our sand walk disappeared at a jutting rock bend, and we swung around to return. The horizon had melted from pale yellow to livid orange to the pinks and purples that portended night. Addy drew a pace or two ahead of me. At some point, I felt Mike's fingers in mine, uncertain how long they'd been there because it felt so natural.

By the time we arrived at Mike's Jeep, its bright-yellow body was a dim beacon in the near-dark. Mike used his keychain flashlight to locate our shoes (and make sure they were empty), then handed the light to Addy, first up the bank. I followed on her heels, giving Mike a hand up onto the buckling section of asphalt and rock we perched upon. He had parked so near the edge, standing on the same level as the vehicle was a challenge.

Addy and I shivered in the cool air and stared out at the dark water while Mike unlocked the vehicle. Clouds formed a solid, pale line where the ocean met the horizon.

"Mom told me my dad loved the ocean," Addy said, turning to open her door. "She didn't tell me much about him, but she said that more than once, so it must be true."

"I'm sure it was," I said, helping her up into the Jeep. "Can you blame him?"

Mike stood behind me and prevented me from breaking my neck when I closed Addy's door too enthusiastically on the narrow ledge. He gripped my hand, and I squeezed it and pulled him to me, whispering in his ear, "Thank you."

28

I jolted awake at a sigh of breath on my cheek.

"Hey, sleeping beauty." Mike's soft lips on my temple calmed my racing heart. "Sorry, but Roger's on the phone. And he's being cagey."

It took a moment to get my bearings. Daylight, barely. Distressed pine nightstand with a dark metal lamp and not much else. South-western-style comforter draped over me. Photo collage on the nearest white wall featuring people I wouldn't know even if my bleary eyes could see. Except one person.

Mike's bedroom. Mike stood over me; the warm presence on the other side of the bed was Addy. I sucked air through my nose, trying to stifle a yawn as I rolled out of bed and headed toward the living room.

"Nice pants," said the man wearing khakis.

I wasn't wearing pants, just yesterday's underwear and a Red Sox shirt that covered my butt and not much else. I'd loaned my longer T-shirt to Addy, and wearing a pair of Mike's boxers had seemed a little too intimate with a teenaged guest in the house. Though in retro-spect, perhaps better than no pants.

Mike pointed at the kitchen counter. "You left your cell phone out here."

I squinted at the clock on the microwave. 6:11 a.m. Why the hell was Mike awake to answer? I leaned on the counter, rubbing the heels of my hands against my eyes. Because it was Monday. People worked on Mondays.

And apparently every other day, if those people were me.

I reluctantly picked up the phone and said, "Yeah."

"Addy's papers are being filed. And if you're going back to Tallahassee with me, I'm leaving now," Roger said.

I groaned. "Any chance you could add a few more words for the person who's been awake for half a minute?"

Roger made a noise that might have been frustration, though with me or himself I couldn't say. "My apologies. Good morning, Sydney. I got word that the Spencers' custody petition will be filed—" there was a pause while he did math "—in less than an hour."

"Good," I said. The Spencers must have signed after all, which made me feel slightly less stressed about not hearing from them. "What else?"

"The head of the forensic team asked me to stop by the Reform Center this morning," Roger continued, "and as soon as I finish up there, I need to return to Tallahassee. Hospice says my father is declining."

Having seen the man recently, I knew he didn't have far to go.

Standing next to his coffee maker, Mike held up an empty mug. I nodded.

"I'm so sorry, Roger," I said. "I can get a car if need be. What's best for you?"

He sighed. "I'd value your eyes at the facility. And honestly, I think I could use the company on the drive home if you don't mind."

Roger said he'd pick us up. I handed the phone to Mike so he could give Roger directions while I splashed some water on my face and brushed my teeth, dressed, then got Addy out of bed. She didn't complain, but I'm not sure she was awake enough to invoke the power of speech.

I left her in the bathroom and found Mike still in the kitchen. A plate full of English muffins sat on the counter, and he was filling the toaster again. Snugging behind him, I nestled my cheek in the divot between his shoulder blades. "Thanks for making breakfast," I said.

"Oh, you mean you wanted some, too?"

I gave him a punitive flick. Just two fingers, not that hard. Okay, fine, hard enough to make my fingers go numb. And his butt happened to be the nearest target. I squeaked as Mike spun and lifted me, breathless, onto the counter. I wrapped my legs around his waist, pulling him closer... then stopped as I had an unexpected flash of the last time I'd gotten frisky with someone while sitting on a counter.

It had not been Mike's counter, or Mike.

"What's wrong?" he asked.

Pushing the image from my mind, I said, "You're too far away."

"Really?" He leaned in and gathered my hair, lifting it. I shivered as he put his mouth to the back of my neck before whispering, "What if I—"

"Is there any coffee?" Addy asked.

If Mike hadn't caught me, I would have fallen off the counter. I wriggled back down to the floor, one butt cheek at a time, heart hammering in my chest. My legs nearly gave way when I landed.

"Sorry," Addy said. She didn't seem especially sorry, but then she didn't seem especially invested in any human emotion, just desperately in need of caffeine.

Mike stood close enough for me to feel the heat of his body, one hand on the counter and the other raking his flushed face. His lips were deep pink and slightly swollen, his eyes unfocused. "Coffee's over there," he said, pointing when he'd finished abusing his cheeks.

Addy passed by without another word or glance at either of us, pouring herself a mug and taking a grateful, slurping sip.

"Sorry," I whispered.

Mike pulled me to him, kissing the top of my head. "You're worth the wait," he said. I sighed and relaxed against his chest, just as he amended it to, "Probably."

I gave him another flick.

~

DESPITE THE COFFEE, Addy was asleep before we even made it to the main highway. I couldn't blame her. We'd stayed up later than we should have watching a soccer game on TV. Pretending we hadn't discovered a secret graveyard full of children that day.

That it was a graveyard had yet to be verified. The forensics team had done a quick survey of the area yesterday, but wouldn't start excavating for a while. Someone was arriving with ground-penetrating radar today, the first step in determining what—or who—was there.

"I think we all know what they'll find," Roger said.

I had no idea how long it would take, but significantly longer than processing a regular crime scene. Days? Weeks? Months? "What about identifications?" I asked.

"Obviously I said I'd share what we've found. They have a couple of names from previous lawsuits—neither went anywhere—and a few more from an unpublished FSU research project. But even those, they'll have to track down next of kin and get DNA samples for any chance of confirming identity."

He didn't sound hopeful. I wasn't either, but Roger didn't need to know that.

"Hey," I said, touching his arm briefly. "It's only a matter of time. This is the first step, and you made it happen. Your dad can..."

I struggled for the least bad euphemism, grateful Roger's gaze was back on the road. "...He can have some peace, knowing this is taken care of. And eventually, families that you've never even set eyes on will be able to—after decades of not knowing—*finally* put their sons and brothers to rest."

Roger nodded, staring straight ahead, throat working. One hand swiped at the corner of his eye, but his voice was clear when he said, "I know, Sydney. But it's not enough. I will see someone in prison for this."

Again, not a time for sharing pessimism. "Yes," I assured him. "Yes, *we* will."

The question was who.

The gate was already open at the Reform Center and Roger drove through slowly. "How many people were here yesterday?"

"By the end, maybe half a dozen," Roger said. "I'd expect twice that today."

A few vehicles sat in the lot by the administrative building where we'd parked yesterday. Presumably ones carrying equipment had been driven deeper into the complex.

Roger parked next to a ten-year-old sedan that looked as if it hadn't been washed since it was bought. I couldn't even be sure of the color. "The head scientist said she'd meet me before hitting the field, so she should be around here somewhere. Feel free to wait in the car."

I was surprised when a wakeful Addy spoke from the back seat. "I'd like to take a look around, if that's okay."

"Yeah, so would I," I added. "I'll take my cell phone, in case you're ready to leave before we get back."

Roger agreed and strode toward figures milling outside another building in the distance. Addy and I lingered, leaning against his car. The air I inhaled through my nostrils was frosty enough to give me a throb of brain ache. Addy pulled her hood over her head and tucked her hands in her pockets. Shoving my hair in a hat left my neck exposed to the cold, but that was better than frightening innocent bystanders with my fuzzy, red morning hair.

This portion of the complex, within hearing distance of intermittent highway traffic, didn't seem as ominous today. The neglected landscape and abandoned structures were depressing, but no longer actively threatening. Perhaps it was the presence of other people, or perhaps it was the knowledge that what lay beyond our sight was so much worse.

Being somewhat acclimated to the miserable place made it easier to look at objectively. For example, the variety of the structures. Were some of them in better condition because they'd been used and maintained longer, or simply because they were more solidly built to begin with? The nearest main administration building was among the best preserved.

"You want to start there?" I asked Addy.

"Sure," she said.

The peaks of the hip roof looked rounded with wear rather than capped, but it seemed unlikely to imminently collapse. Addy and I climbed the front steps and stood warily beneath a small entry portico. I'd be leery of leaning against either of the two columns supporting it, and the already dirt-colored walls showed water stains beneath the two windows on either side. A pair of heavy wooden doors guarded the entrance. Mike had tried them yesterday, but I couldn't help checking for myself—yep, still locked. And putting a little weight into it didn't get me anywhere.

Addy looked at me, then at the locking mechanism. "Well, you're a PI, aren't you? Why don't you pick the lock?"

Where do people get these larcenous ideas about my occupation? I rolled my eyes and said, "Come on."

We proceeded back down the handful of steps and around the side of the building. There was no landscaping near the walls but enterprising weeds and a fair bit of scattered garbage.

"Don't even think you're gonna push me through a window," Addy warned, stumbling over a bit of debris that might have been the rusted remains of a metal bucket.

I said, "Of course not. I'd stand on your shoulders."

Not that I really would climb blindly through a window. I couldn't remember the last time I'd had a tetanus shot. And I didn't really *need* to get in; I was just curious. That said, I've noticed a dangerously direct relationship between exposure and curiosity; the longer I hang around something, the more curious I get.

We turned the back corner and found another door, this one a single, cheap laminate suitable for interiors.

That wasn't the odd part.

The door was secured *on the outside* with a low-tech security bar, basically a two-by-six resting in a metal brace. A metal hasp was mounted above it, but I didn't see a padlock.

Brows wrinkled, Addy asked, "Is that normal?"

I shrugged. What constituted normal in a place where children were buried in unmarked graves?

I lifted the board free and leaned it against the exterior wall. The door stuck, so I motioned Addy out of the way before bracing a foot against the doorframe. A screeching, tearing sound filled the air. I wasn't sure if it was the door yielding or my shoulder vacating its socket.

It was mostly the former.

"Sonuvabitch," I muttered, rubbing my arm.

Logically I knew no one would lock us inside, but the possibility almost creeped me out enough to carry the board with me. Instead, I used it to prop the door open.

I crossed the threshold into the dim interior and turned to see an unmoving Addy, chewing her lip so hard I was afraid she'd bite it in half. "You want to stay here, make sure I don't get accidentally locked inside?" I asked.

She hesitated, but I could tell she was barely on the uphill side of terrified. I added, "Honestly, the door gives me the heebie-jeebies."

Addy nodded and made a sound that might have been "Okay."

I patted her forearm and said, "I won't be gone long."

I found myself in a hallway with nasty industrial carpet of an indeterminate, dark shade that had degraded to the consistency of smelly, nylon dirt. The only illumination came from the doorway behind me and a few open doors along the hall. I stepped carefully inside the first room on the right. A striped mattress lay on the bare floor, and the dismantled door to the hallway rested alongside it, overlapping slightly.

The room across the hall, its door partially closed, was a former office. A cheap laminate desk missed its chair. Its matching bookcase was empty, as were its drawers, save for a few manky paper clips. Yes, I am that nosy.

I left the office and followed the hallway toward the front entrance. My feet kicked little scraps of lumber, I thought mostly trim, but I couldn't be sure in the dim light. At the midpoint of the hall, the doors on either side were closed and locked. I touched the wall tentatively as a guide, but it was a revolting sensation, like grainy, thick dirt and cobwebs with a hint of sticky dryer lint. I quickly pulled my hand back and wiped my fingertips on my pants.

The hallway ended at an open reception area, brighter thanks to windows bracketing the entrance and a few others set high on the walls (though not nearly as bright as I would have liked—the glass must be filthy). An industrial metal reception desk sat slightly off-center, with a bank of three-drawer filing cabinets nearby. I went straight for the cabinets. The chances of anything juicy being left behind were slim, but since I was here…

The filing cabinets were the heavy, old kind fashioned from a retired tank. They stood flush against each other with the final one snug to the wall. I flinched at squawking metal when I opened the herky-jerky drawers. The first two cabinets were empty, but the third one on the outside—I yanked on the handles—was locked. Why lock something that was empty?

Habit, said the pessimist in me. The optimist went to work banging her knuckles against the side, listening.

The optimist was usually the one who gave me sore knuckles, and many other injuries.

The cabinet was much heavier and less hollow-sounding than a contemporary office store model, and I couldn't tell if there was anything inside or not. I stared at the lock in the upper corner and yanked on the handle again in frustration. I'd be lying squashed on the floor with the cabinet atop me before the damn thing came free.

Maybe I could find the key.

I started with the metal desk. "Vintage" was the word you'd use to describe it if you were selling it on eBay. There were three deep drawers on either side of the knee well—empty—and one shallow one beneath the laminate-sheathed worktop. I tugged it out as far as it would go, then wedged my hands inside, getting grit under my nails as I ran my fingers along the back edge.

Nothing. I mashed my forearms painfully, grunting as I wrenched my hands free.

The knee space under the desk had a backing, flush with the drawers at the bottom. I crawled into the metal cave on my hands and knees, suppressing a cough. My hands explored the floor tentatively, and I told myself its texture wasn't rat pellets.

"Eeep!" A soft squeak escaped me when my fingertips felt the solid, toothy edge of a palmetto bug's legs.

Or did they?

No. Fricking. Way.

There was an actual *key* on the floor. All nastiness was forgotten as I scraped at it, flipping it onto my palm. I squinted, but all I could tell was that it was the flat metal kind that opens small locks. And possibly filing cabinets. I tucked it into my jeans pocket and backed carefully out of the cramped space. I was nearly free, when—

"Hey!" a woman yelled behind me.

I slammed the back of my head on the underside of the desk. "Ouch!" The enormity of the pain hit me in earnest a moment later and I added a heartfelt, "Sonuvabitch!"

"What do you think you're doing in here?" The woman's voice sounded unexpectedly familiar. I wondered if I was hallucinating from skull-ringing head trauma.

Knees aching, I sat on my butt and scooted out to face the music.

Early thirties, her black hair was pulled back in a long ponytail that revealed a face just as luminous but slightly less brown than the last time I'd seen her. She must not have been working in the field lately. She would be today, as evidenced by the cargo pants covering covetously long legs, her typical cool weather field attire.

Shocked, it took me a moment to find my voice, but I finally answered, "I'm looking for a can opener."

Laney Singh, my longtime friend and former housemate I hadn't seen for years, peered down at my typically graceful posture on the floor. "Sydney? Is that you?"

I lifted my hat to reveal a flash of fuzzy red hair, and she clapped her hand over her mouth before giggling with delight. "It is you! Come here!" she demanded, pulling me by the dirty hand to my feet and into a lung-crushing hug.

I peeked over Laney's shoulder to see Addy standing uncertainly behind her, still chewing her martyred lip and looking none too happy to be inside the building. Disengaging all but one arm from Laney, I spun us both around. "Have you met?" I asked.

Addy nodded.

"Wall full of degrees, one of the best forensic anthropologists in the country, but this brilliant woman could never put the can opener back in the same spot twice," I said, smiling. "My favorite was the freezer. How did you manage that one?"

Laney shook her head but laughed, squashing me to her side. "Making chili fries, of course," she said.

"Oh, of course," I said, rolling my eyes at Addy and earning an almost-smile. I gestured for her to precede us out of the building, and she wasted no time, almost jogging back to open air.

"How long's it been?" Laney asked.

"Too long," I said. "I didn't know you were back in Florida."

She nodded. "Gainesville mostly. But consultations take me everywhere." She stopped, waiting for Addy to pull ahead of us to ask, "Is she part of this Reform Center mess?"

"No. Different mess."

"Thank God," she said. "But you are."

My face twisted with reluctant acknowledgment. "Roger Weber brought me in. His father is the one—"

"He told me, though he didn't mention your name," Laney cut in. "Are you and Roger close?"

"Why, do you want to date him?" I asked, grinning. Roger was an attractive guy, but I wouldn't have thought he was her type. A little too buttoned-up.

Laney didn't answer, and her jaw had a determined set I recognized. I added, "I don't know how close Roger is to anyone, but I'd say we're good friends. Why, what is it?"

She stared at the mangy carpet by the back door. Laney didn't like to speculate about sites, and I could tell she was struggling to find words that wouldn't violate her principles. Eventually she sighed and settled for, "You'll need to be ready, both of you. I'm afraid this is going to get bad."

Then she gave my hand a final squeeze and marched outside to get to work. I followed her, all thoughts of the key in my pocket forgotten.

29

Roger was waiting for us at the car, and once Laney and I said our goodbyes, we were on our way. I was surprised Roger didn't ask about our relationship, but he was distracted, quiet. When we reached the interstate, he said, "My sister is with Dad now."

Before I could ask which one, he added, "Deidre. Everyone else is on the way. Everyone who'll come, I mean."

It sounded like his family dynamics were as complicated as my own. No wonder, with so many siblings from so many different backgrounds. "Do you want me to drive?" I asked.

"Nice try," he said with a ghost of a smile.

Conversation tapped out, I pulled my notes from my bag to review. Yes, I am one of those privileged souls who does not get carsick while reading. It's a handy skill for an investigator, even more so when I worked at the Public Defender's Office as part of a team rather than driving myself all the time.

I'd actually been staying with Laney when I was hired by the PD's office. Laney and I were college roommates in Boston. Later I found myself passing through Tallahassee while she was attending grad school at FSU, and I'd stalled out on her couch. Hard to believe I'd never left the city.

My mind wandered, back and forth between my scrawled pages and the past, eventually falling into the future. I should have asked Laney what to expect time-wise on the excavation. Not that she'd have had a solid answer. It all depended on what she found and whether legal wrangling came into play. So far, Roger hadn't mentioned objections to the proceedings by any State agencies, but I had no doubt that once the possibility of recovering human remains became real, CYA (cover your ass) mode would kick in.

We'd crossed into what passed for a moderately hilly area in Florida, mostly grassy with a few pines and notoriously iffy cell reception, when Roger's phone rang. He snatched it up from the console, as aware as I was that his call was living on borrowed time.

"Yes?" he said.

I strained to make out the other side of the conversation, but he'd rested the phone against his opposite ear. Even his fancy car, with its purring engine and velvet tires on asphalt, made too much noise for me to hear anything.

Finally he said, "Soon," then, "Okay," and hung up.

I stared at his profile, practicing amateur divination. Was it his father? Had Laney found something already? Or maybe one of his many criminal cases had just gone south. *Way* south. Because that was the one thing I *could* divine—that the news was not good.

Roger glanced in his rearview mirror.

I twisted in my seat to see Addy, head resting against the window, but eyes open.

"Addy," Roger said, "Your foster mother has reported you missing."

Shit. I was afraid something like this would happen, but lately I'd forgotten to worry about it. Life had just gotten very complicated.

Addy's face went pale and she sat up straight. "What does that mean? Are you taking me back?"

Roger was focused on Addy more than the road, and I nearly asked him to pull over. He said, "She claims you stole from her."

Addy's face instantly transformed from a sickly white to an angry pink flush. She shook her head and turned to stare out the window. "Of course she does."

I started to speak, but Roger held out a hand to stop me. The edge of the road and then a hint of gravel shoulder rumbled beneath our tires. Roger slowly guided his car back to the center of the lane and asked, "Have you heard from the Spencers lately?"

I tried not to squirm as I answered. "I spoke with Mister on Friday, but I couldn't reach them this weekend."

"When's the last time you tried?"

"Last night, and I've left messages everywhere I could think of." He didn't answer, and anxiety compelled me to fill the silence. "I didn't want to worry you unnecessarily."

Roger nodded, lips working, contemplating. "They signed off on the custody petition this weekend, so it must not be serious."

"That was my feeling," I said. Though I'd gotten less optimistic as the morning passed and I still hadn't heard from them. And it was obvious from Roger's tone that he was no more convinced than I was. I pulled out my phone and saw that we were back in a dead zone. "No reception."

I scrunched my neck for a glimpse at Addy through the side window. She was rocking a little and chewing her nails. Unless she was eating her fingers. I hadn't seen her do either one before. The car slowed and I glanced at the oncoming exit sign.

"Should have gotten gas before we left," Roger said apologetically.

But when we reached the gas station just a few hundred yards from the exit, instead of pulling in next to the pumps, Roger parked in front of the small convenience store. He cut the engine and turned to face Addy. Her eyes were red and she looked like she was trying not to cry.

"Addy," Roger said, "it's my understanding that you don't want to go back to your foster mother."

She shook her head vehemently.

"And I assume you don't want to be taken into custody by law enforcement," he continued.

She looked confused, so he clarified, "To a shelter, or a juvenile detention center."

Her eyes went wide and she yelled, "No!" before clambering for the door handle.

Of course it was still locked, and there was nowhere for her to go anyway. The only other building in sight on the lonely rural road was a long-shuttered antique store.

She lunged across the seat and tried the driver's side.

"Addy," Roger said, voice firm. "Calm down. I won't take you anywhere you don't want to go—I promise. Do you trust me?"

She slammed a hand against the door in frustration, and he repeated, "Addy! Do you trust me?"

Her shoulders slowly lowered and her head turned incrementally toward us as she sat down properly. "Yes," she said, voice hoarse.

"Do you want me to be your attorney?" he asked. "To help you figure out where you'll be safe, and help you get where you belong?"

She nodded, tears trickling down her cheeks.

"I'm sorry, Addy," Roger said, "but I need you to answer with words. Do you want me to be your attorney?"

She took a deep breath that hitched a bit before saying, "Yes, please. I'd like you to be my lawyer."

"Then consider me hired," he said, smiling gently and handing her a folded bill. "We've got another hour or so of driving. Would you mind getting us some drinks and snacks? Sydney and I will have water, and get whatever you want. Okay?"

She nodded, wiped her eyes and wet cheeks with the hood of her sweatshirt, and said thank you.

The door locks clicked and the car shifted ever so slightly as Addy got out. Or maybe that was just my mind spinning.

"How long can you shelter a minor before notifying her guardian or law enforcement?" I asked.

"Twenty-four hours," Roger said, not looking at me.

Which I'd already been doing for... More than three times that, since Friday night.

"Unless she's a runaway," he added. "Then no aid is permissible."

Great. I closed my eyes and rolled my head on my shoulders. "And what's the penalty?"

"First-degree misdemeanor, up to a year in prison," he said. "But it won't come to that."

No, it probably wouldn't. But it didn't have to. We were screwed. We'd both pissed off enough people over the years who were just looking for an excuse; we'd be lucky to not lose our Bar and PI licenses.

"I'll petition to be her *guardian ad litem*," Roger said.

I was speechless for a moment. Or maybe it was the spinny brain thing slowing me down. Eventually I sputtered, "You can't do that!"

"Why not?" he asked calmly.

The door handle jabbed my back as I lined up for my best, most earnest *help your friend realize he's an idiot* face. "Because you're up to your neck in this already. There's got to be a conflict of interest or... something!"

"My name's not on any of the Spencers' pleadings," he said. "I just gave them a referral."

"Because you don't know shit about family law!" I pointed out. The more frustrated I became, the calmer Roger became. Which of course just made me more frustrated.

"Who's the smartest lawyer you know?" He smiled, but there was a stiffness in his expression that made me think he was faking his arrogant confidence. "Sydney, I can figure it out."

"Yeah, well, what happens when *the court* figures it out? That you were chauffeuring her all over the Panhandle for days *before* requesting the appointment?"

He shook his head. "It'll never come to light."

I literally threw up my hands—not a great idea in a sedan, which is why I chipped a fingernail on the window, but I didn't have it in me to care. "So am I supposed to just hide out with Addy until you get a hearing date, then magically bring her to court because I'm psychic? If you want to maintain this charade, we can't have any appearance of being in contact."

That's when another paranoid possibility popped into my head, one that involved me being led away in handcuffs instead of just losing my license. "Or maybe I just drop her off in front of the courthouse so they don't arrest me for kidnapping."

His smile vanished. "Sydney, I don't blame you if you don't want to be part of this. Investigation is what you do—it's *who you are*—and I understand if you don't want to jeopardize that. But I will ask that if you have to report Addy, give her to me rather than turning her over. And give me a few hours to get some things in place before you call it in."

I struggled to process the fact that he was absolutely serious. I was used to Roger caring about his clients—and other human beings in general—in an abstract way. Doing what needed to be done to make sure they had the best possible outcome, but without ever engaging in real, human interaction. Now, in the midst of his father dying, Roger was willing to risk his livelihood for a kid he barely knew.

I glanced in the store, where Addy was still wandering the junk food aisles, tugging at the string to her sweatshirt.

And, I guess, so was I. Risking my livelihood, that is. But there was a difference between calculated risk and throwing your life away.

"Don't be a dumbass," I said. "I'll bet you know someone else who could do this, someone who—*as unlikely as it sounds*—would be *better* than you."

Something flickered across Roger's face. "You do!" I pressed.

He responded with a nodding, shrugging hybrid. "I do, but I'd prefer not to ask her."

"Yeah, well I'd prefer to be three inches taller, but that's not happening," I said. "Call her."

His fingers traced the steering wheel. I wondered if I had time to beat him into submission before Addy returned.

"Fine, I'll call her," he said. He picked up his phone and dialed, then stared at me, straight-faced, while he waited for his call to go through. "Only three inches?"

I raised an eyebrow, and then a middle finger.

30

Roger dropped us at the coffee shop, where Cecil was thankfully still in one piece. It helped that the place was open twenty-four hours and I was a regular customer who tipped. I grabbed a couple of sandwiches from inside before driving us around the corner to my office. Addy settled into a chair with her lunch and a catalog she'd found abandoned on some flat surface while I did some quick catch-up.

In all of the Reform Center drama, I'd forgotten I'd asked John Driscoll to check with the TPD on Addy's friend. He'd left a detailed message on my office voicemail.

"Sydney, we picked up a Carly Whitmore last month," he said. "I can't tell you what the charges were, but nothing serious enough to request prosecution as an adult. Ms. Whitmore was transferred to a secure juvenile facility pending court disposition. The strange thing is I can't see where anything happened after that, and she should have had a hearing by now. You might want to follow up with the facility, Brummel Youth Academy. I hope this helps."

It helped me progress a step toward... something. But I was beginning to fear that something wouldn't end with me finding Carly.

Hopefully the past couple of days hunting dead kids was just making me morbid and pessimistic.

But why did the name of the facility sound familiar? I grabbed my legal pad and quickly skimmed my notes. Of course—Ralph had said Brummel was the juvenile center Eleanor Dickey currently ran. That woman's stink was popping up everywhere.

I leaned back in my chair, considering the best way to get information about Carly. I didn't often deal with juvenile matters, but I was pretty sure simply calling and asking if the girl was there wouldn't work. Especially once Ms. Dickey got wind of who was asking. Maybe Ralph would know someone, or Mike might have some experience—

"Sydney!" Addy said, crumpling her sandwich wrapper.

I'd zoned so far out I'd forgotten she was there and nearly toppled my chair attempting to right it. It's a gift. "Yeah?" I asked.

"Will we be here much longer? Since I didn't get a shower this morning, I was kinda hoping..."

"I wouldn't say no to a shower, either," I admitted. I shuffled through the stack of mail on my desk, then gathered a few things— including my uneaten sandwich—and said, "Okay, let's go."

It was less than a ten-minute drive to my house in light traffic. Not long, but more than enough time for me to angst about whether to share my Carly findings, such as they were, with Addy. I didn't want her to expect too much, but I didn't want to give her any excuse to not trust me. The moment she stopped trusting me was the moment I stopped trusting her, and not so coincidentally the moment my life got to be even more of a pain in the ass. I'd have to go back to watching Addy like a hawk.

It was the thought of being joined-at-the-hip bathroom buddies again that clinched it. "So, Addy," I said, "I might have a lead on Carly."

The naked hope on her face was almost painful to witness.

"Nothing solid yet," I hastened to add, "but she was picked up by the Tallahassee cops a while back. She have a criminal history?"

Typical mercurial teenager, Addy rolled her eyes at me angrily and turned to stare out the window. "Oh, because she was a foster kid, so she must be trouble."

"I didn't mean that at all. Addy, I've helped guys who *killed* people, and guys who—believe it or not—did a helluva lot worse. I don't judge," I said. "I'm just trying to help. I promise. And the more I know about her, the easier it is to find her."

Addy looked at me, albeit with a scowl. "Yeah, well, it doesn't matter anyway. So far as I know, she was never picked up for anything. Not even shoplifting."

"Okay," I said. "Thank you."

I hadn't realized how much tension I was holding in my neck and shoulders until the road curved to reveal my neighborhood. Quiet and mostly still forested, its modest but well-kept homes interspersed with Spanish moss-flecked canopy calm me. I became aware that my back wasn't actually flush against my seat and forced myself to relax into it. Once I'd done that, my shoulders crept away from my ears, too.

Until I saw the fancy gray SUV parked on the street beneath said canopy, just around the corner from my house.

"Shit," I muttered, taking my foot off the gas but fighting the inclination to slam on the brakes.

"What?" Addy asked, sitting up straighter.

Which was exactly the opposite of what I wanted her to do.

"Get down!" I said. "Slump like you're tired. Put your hood up, and make sure your hair's not showing."

Addy did as I'd ordered before asking in a low voice, "What's going on?"

"I'm not sure," I admitted, driving slowly past the SUV.

Our lots were relatively large on a short block; to get any closer he would have had to park next to Mr. Ginley's property. All I could make out through the distant, dark windows was the large shape inside. He'd already seen my car (the Cabrio was almost as unmistakable as my hair), and he obviously knew where I lived.

So far the man had only followed and watched me. But I hated the idea of bringing him home, and of him possibly approaching while Addy was with me.

Today was Ben's early day off school, and his car was parked next door, but that didn't necessarily mean he was at home. As we drifted slowly toward my driveway, I said, "I want you to jump out as soon as we hit the carport and sneak next door to Ben's. Stay out of sight, and if you can't do that, slouch and keep your hands in your pockets. If the door isn't unlocked, check the back. The key's under a flowerpot somewhere."

"What about you?"

"I'll be fine," I said, but after a moment's reflection recalled it was unwise (some might even say dangerous) to be overly optimistic. Pulling into my driveway, I added, "If you don't hear from me in fifteen minutes, call my cell phone and I'll tell you what to do."

Though not a full garage, my carport is tied into my house and mostly enclosed, with walls at the back and opposite side. Person-sized gaps where they meet at the corners blazed with sunlight, and once Addy slipped through the one closest to Ben's house, she was out of sight. I cut Cecil's engine and fumbled for my cell phone—not in the console; it must be in my purse in the back.

I got out, opened the back door and heard the gray SUV rolling up my driveway. It came to a stop as I slammed my car door, parking close enough to block my escape. I glanced at the cell phone in my hand, anger and fear warring within me. *Come on, Brennan, what are the chances this guy will harm you in broad daylight outside your own house?* And anger won.

I sat on Cecil's bumper to wait. The man got out with none of the awkwardness I displayed with SUVs and could have done the same exiting Glenn's monster pickup. He was over six feet tall, though it was hard to say by how much because he had the breadth to match. A navy suit stretched across his broad shoulders and strained the single waist-level button securing it as he closed his door. No obvious weapon, though the way his suit was cut I doubted I'd see one unless it was pointed at me. He was reasonably attractive, if too beefy for my tastes, clean-cut with a full head of short, brown hair that was neat without being fussy.

"Ms. Brennan," he said, removing sunglasses as he entered the shadow of my carport, "I was wondering if I could have a moment of your time."

"You already have," I said.

The corner of his mouth twitched. "Perhaps we could speak inside."

I crossed my arms in front of my chest. "I'm not in the habit of taking strange men into my house. Especially not stalkers."

His mouth opened, but his reply was far from instantaneous. "I'm afraid I don't know what you mean."

"You were following me Saturday. Downtown," I said.

He blushed slightly. "In fact, I was downtown Saturday running errands, but I can assure you I wasn't following you."

I didn't believe him, and, arms still crossed, didn't bother trying to hide it.

"My apologies for any misunderstanding," he said, moving toward me, "but I thought you knew who I am."

I straightened and held my ground as he reached inside his suit jacket... and pulled out his wallet. He extended a business card between two fingers. As I took it, I noted his enormous hand could almost have engulfed my skull.

I shook my head as I read the card: *Blake Tucker, Brummel Youth Academy, Assistant Director.* "You got a photo ID to back that up?"

He reached in his jacket again and handed me a laminated ID from the facility, attached to a lanyard. Even in his headshot, you could tell he was enormous.

"Were you ever a wrestler?" I asked.

"Football," he said.

I didn't love the idea of inviting the man inside, but I loved the idea of him accidentally seeing Addy even less. Grabbing my stuff from the back seat, I nodded toward the side entry and said, "Come on."

Tucker held the screen door open while I unlocked the main

one, but I wasn't sure if his goal was chivalry or intimidation. Intentional or not, it was hard for him to not look intimidating. His bulk loomed over me even after I'd climbed a couple of steps. Then there was the matter of blocking my car, though if I were honest, I'd often done the same to interview witnesses. I'd just done it more subtly.

I chucked my purse and sandwich on the counter and headed straight for the coffeemaker, waving Tucker toward my kitchen table. "Have a seat," I said, as I started a pot. "I need coffee. Can I get you anything?"

I opened my fridge as he settled uncomfortably in a too-small wooden chair. "By anything, apparently I mean water. And hopefully milk," I said, sniffing the container, "since I require it for my coffee."

"Black coffee would be great," he said.

I nodded and sat across from him. "So, what brings you to Tallahassee?"

When he crossed one leg over the other, ankle to knee beneath my almost too narrow table, he did so carefully. Almost as carefully as he smiled. "I work in town nearly as often as I work out at the center. And I live in Tallahassee."

"Do you?" I asked. "You're not one of the Dickeys' neighbors?"

That microscopic mouth twitch again. Hopefully he wouldn't have a seizure in my kitchen. "So you do recognize me?"

"Yes, of course. Oh, you mean from outside Milton Dickey's house?" I raised an eyebrow. I've been told my eyebrows are lovely (*not really—who would say that?*), but they did not invite the man to confess that he had followed me after all. "So why are you here, Mr. Tucker?"

He did not suggest I call him Blake.

"Since you weren't at your office this morning, when I found myself having lunch on this end of town, I thought I'd stop by on the off chance you were at home."

I didn't bother asking how he knew where I lived (it would be easy enough to find out). I did, in a small act of annoyed defiance, serve him coffee in a Public Defender's Association fundraiser mug.

"Thank you," he said. "And please don't let me keep you from your lunch."

I grabbed a plate for my sandwich (no, I wouldn't have used one if he hadn't been there) and brought it to the table.

"Fine. But if you haven't explained why you're here by the time I finish my sandwich—and I'm damn hungry so it won't take long—we have nothing else to *not* talk about. And you can leave." I motioned him to start by waving my sandwich and then shoving it in my mouth.

Always classy, that Sydney Brennan.

"Fine," he echoed. "It's Ms. Powers's understanding that you've found something at the Reform Center. Enough of something to call in a forensic team."

I nodded.

"And?" he asked.

I finished chewing and wiped my mouth with a napkin before replying, "Hunh-unh. This is your show."

Then I went back to my turkey sandwich. Tucker should be thankful it wasn't creamy, no-chew hummus, or he'd be out the door by now.

A deep exhalation that would have been a sigh if he'd opened his mouth rocked Tucker's frame. "As you saw Friday night, Mr. Dickey is no longer capable of—"

"Looking out for his own interests? Or his daughter's?" I asked.

Tucker gave me a disappointed look, as if the comment were beneath me. Or maybe it was because I spoke while chewing. He countered, "Of engaging with the world around him in a meaningful way. In a way that would be helpful to your investigation. But Ms. Powers found a box of records among her father's belongings that might be useful," he said.

I'd finished my sandwich except for a crusty ring of too-dry bread, but Tucker's satisfied expression said he knew I wasn't going to kick him out. I sipped my coffee, considering. "And in return, you want me to keep her apprised of what's happening with the forensic investigation."

He gave a single nod. "Nothing confidential. The same information she could get through other channels, but would prefer direct from the source to avoid any misunderstandings."

I didn't doubt she could, so I had no real qualms about sharing. "Deal," I said. "On one condition."

He motioned for me to continue.

"I'd be grateful if you could check on a Brummel inmate for us."

"Oh?" he said, raising both brows. "Someone currently incarcerated?"

"That's what I'd like to know. And if she's not, anything else you can tell me about her potential whereabouts." I watched him carefully as I added, "The name is Carly Whitmore."

He didn't seem to recognize the name.

"As you said of our investigation, it's nothing confidential. And it's information I could get through other channels," I smiled, "but why involve someone else if we don't need to?"

I was surprised when he said, "Deal," and returned my smile, though his seemed forced. "I take it the forensic investigation will be focused on the grounds and not the buildings?"

"So far as I know."

"That's probably fortunate," Tucker said, then shook his head. "Anyone spending any significant time in and around those structures would be taking his life into his hands."

"So you've been there before, to the Reform Center?" I asked.

"Once. Ms. Powers took a group of senior staff from Brummel, soon after she was hired. She thought it was important for us to have a sense of history."

"Does that mean you don't have Ms. Powers's legacy of corrections?"

"No," he said, mouth crooking. "My family were more likely to have been incarcerated than to be holding the keys."

I wiped my mouth a final time before noting casually, "It must be a burden, growing up with those kinds of expectations. And knowing what went on at the Reform Center, what her father did to those boys... I don't know if that would make it easier or more difficult."

"You'd have to ask Ms. Powers about that," Tucker said stiffly, and rose from his chair. "Thank you again, Ms. Brennan."

The kitchen door to my carport burst open as Tucker adjusted the standing drape of his suit.

"Hey, Syd!" Ben exclaimed, standing with his hand on the doorknob, quickly taking in the tableau. "Sorry—I didn't realize you had company."

Tucker said, "I was just leaving. Ms. Brennan, if you'd like those records, they're in my car."

Ben stepped back far enough to let the older, larger man pass and not an inch more, with a frank, appraising expression on his face just short of downright challenging. It struck me, as it had so often, that teenaged Ben was a better man than many of the "adult" males I knew.

Still, I gave Ben a good solid bump and a flash of stink-eye when, focused on the big bad wolf, Ben didn't move out of my way, either.

Tucker offered to carry the records inside for me, but I'm an old hand at lugging bankers boxes and it wasn't full. I perched on the steps, holding the box, while he backed down my driveway onto the street. I watched his SUV continue out of sight.

Ben held the kitchen door wide for me. Addy must have shared what little she knew about the situation, and he'd come—he thought —to the rescue. *I didn't realize you had company,* Ben had said when he burst inside. His words were almost identical to Tucker's when we literally bumped into each other outside the Dickey house.

So what had Blake Tucker thought he was rescuing his boss from?

31

"I don't like that guy." Ben said.

I wasn't sure what I thought of him. I certainly didn't trust Blake Tucker, but it felt like he was part of something bigger I couldn't see yet. Which meant I couldn't see how he fit, either.

I set the box on my desk before returning to find Ben watching out one of the street-side windows, though Tucker was long gone. "Ben, I appreciate you checking on me, but Addy's the one we need to be worried about. Where is she?" I asked.

He glanced toward the kitchen door, and his house. "Probably on her way. She told me not to call the cops," he said, then added, "Not that I would have."

"Calling the cops would not be my first choice," I acknowledged, sitting at the kitchen table to sip my lukewarm coffee. "Which isn't to say there aren't times when it's appropriate. Look, Addy's in the middle of some complicated stuff right now—"

Ben interrupted me with a snort, joining me at the table. "I'm not a moron, Syd. I know that. And I know sometimes there are things that I'm better off *not* knowing. Just tell me, is she in some kind of danger?"

"No," I said quickly. Then added, "Not the *physical* kind."

He nodded, obviously catching my hesitation. "Maybe the *legal* kind?"

I lifted a brow suggestively as I took another sip of coffee. Ben rolled his eyes, then stood and went to the door. I couldn't imagine how he'd heard Addy, but a moment later he let her inside.

"She's okay," he said. Presumably meaning me.

Hands hidden in the cuffs of her sleeves, Addy slowly nodded. I stood to top up my coffee and held the pot high, but both teens shook their heads.

"Good," I said, setting it back without pouring. "It'll stunt your growth. And no comments from the peanut gallery."

Addy ignored my attempt at banter with Ben, asking, "Sydney, who was that guy?"

"He works at a juvenile prison, connected with Roger's thing," I said, though it was hard to see how that was the case. Still, I didn't want to get lost in details with Ben present. "I'm hoping he can give us a lead on Carly. But he does *not* need to see you. Got it?"

Addy put on her tough face and carefully avoided looking at Ben as she said, "At this point, *nobody* needs to be seeing me. Can I take a shower now?"

My hand shook slightly as I waved toward the back of the house. Maybe I didn't need a caffeine top-up after all. "Have at it," I said.

She stalked out of the room, and soon I heard doors opening and closing heavily—the guest bedroom, the bathroom. Back and forth. Then finally quiet. I was still standing next to the coffee pot and felt its magnetic pull. I hadn't had *enough* caffeine yet, I justified as I poured. The shaking was withdrawal.

Meanwhile, Ben had started foraging. "Syd, your fridge is pathetic," he said, with his head inside it.

I reached past him for more milk, then pushed the fridge door shut. "So is my electric bill."

He didn't bite, but sat back down at the kitchen table and said, "You look worn out."

He was right; I was. And I didn't know why. I was used to working unusual hours and missing sleep. I'd also had more than my share of crazy stress over the past year, so you'd think I'd be used to that by now, too.

I gazed toward the sound of the running shower. I was worried about Addy. Yes, she was a pain in the ass, but she was a teenager. Being a pain in the ass was her job. And she didn't deserve this. Life was hard enough for someone with a reasonably normal upbringing. I just didn't see how she could come out of the chaos she inhabited now—and everything that had come before it—without being so far behind she'd never have a chance. Roger was an amazing guy, but even he had his limits. Especially now.

"Sydney," Ben said.

I realized I'd been tapping my spoon against the counter in a way bound to annoy anyone with functioning ears.

"Sorry," I muttered, but couldn't rein in my mind. I jammed my hands in my pockets to keep them from banging silverware.

Would I see Amos Weber again before he died? I hoped we'd brought Roger's father some measure of peace. But what about the families of the boys buried on that land? Would they feel better, finally knowing, or had they given up so long ago we'd only be opening old wounds? Maybe there wouldn't be any family left.

And what about the bad guys, the men who'd either actively participated or turned a blind eye to the decades of abuse at the Reform Center? How would they feel about those old wounds opening, and the people who opened them? Had Pinky Guy somehow gotten wind of what we were doing there? Maybe through something we'd filed, though that was all recent. Through some other prep we'd undertaken, or the corrections grapevine. Hell, even through someone at Mr. Weber's nursing home—

"Syd!" Ben said, more sharply. "Are you okay?"

I looked at him, then down at the small, thin key in my hand I'd been tapping against the counter. Almost as bad as a spoon. Not as loud but with a tinnier sound. But the key didn't belong to me...

From the Reform Center. On the floor of the admin building. I must have pulled it from the pocket of my dirty jeans while fidgeting. "What does this look like to you?" I asked.

"A key," Ben said, in a tone that suggested he couldn't decide if it was a trick question or if his neighbor had finally progressed from *eccentric* to *time to call the loony bin.*

"But for what?" I pressed. "Maybe a filing cabinet?"

Ben shrugged. "Doesn't go to a car or a house. Beyond that, I can't say I've ever really paid attention to keys."

I raked my hands over my face. I was overthinking it, except for the ability to think part. I tossed my sandwich crust into the trash and rinsed my plate before drifting to the fridge. "You're right," I said, peering inside, "that's just pathetic. You free for an hour or so?"

"Yeah," Ben said. "What do you need?"

I closed the fridge hard enough to make it rock slightly, then surveyed my cabinets. It was not pretty. "You mind hanging out with Addy while I make a grocery run?"

He didn't immediately answer, so I glanced over my shoulder, but I couldn't read his expression. Then it hit me. What was I thinking? She'd already run out on him once. What kind of masochist would he have to be to sign up for babysitting duty twice?

"Sorry, Ben. I shouldn't have asked. Maybe I can drop her off with Ralph and Diane," I mused, then smiled. That was something I'd dearly love to see, Addy going toe-to-toe with Ralph's wife. It'd be good for her to spend some quality time with a strong, black woman.

"It's okay, Syd, I don't mind," Ben said, transitioning to awkward shuffling. "I just didn't know if you'd trust me with her."

"Don't be a dumbass," I said, my version of a gentle dope slap. Maybe with a little physical one as well, before grabbing my purse. "Thanks, kid. And don't answer the door."

"Yeah, and don't forget to get groceries," he countered. "And be careful. While you're doing whatever you're really leaving to do."

"Did I say you're a dumbass? I meant a smart-ass." But the kid knew me too well.

32

There was someone I should have checked in with days ago, if she was still around.

Ralph had introduced me to Ginger Ratnor back when we worked together at the Public Defender's Office. She ran a cleaning service at the time, employing young women who had few prospects that didn't involve lying on their backs. In addition to employing them, she helped with housing, saw to it they attended substance abuse and mental health counseling, got their GEDs, and anything else that might get and keep their lives on track. But she played a little fast and loose with the rules to help the girls (occasionally underage). I was afraid it would eventually catch up with her.

Ginger and Ralph had had a falling out a few years ago and no longer spoke, but I didn't know the details. Something about her testimony in a case. I'd never wanted to get in the middle of it. I hadn't seen her much since then, but when I did last, she wasn't doing much of the actual cleaning anymore. About Ralph's age and a chain-smoker, she wasn't in the best of health. I hoped I'd find her in the office today.

With its wonky hub-and-spoke traffic layout, I often felt like nothing was very close in Tallahassee, but nothing was ever that far away either. The *Spotless Reputation* headquarters was tucked in one of the mixed residential-commercial neighborhoods downhill (on my side) from the crest that was the main portion of downtown. The business occupied one side of a single-story brick building with concrete accents, a realtor in the other. I pulled into the small, shared parking lot a little too quickly and winced as Cecil's underside squawked against the poorly graded entry.

I strolled past the realtor, and a bell dinged when I entered *Spotless Reputation*'s office. The front area was clean and simple, the only decorations a framed print on a wall and a vase of dried flowers on the counter. However, unless things had radically changed, I knew the shoji screens next to the counter concealed Ginger's slovenly sins from view—cases of cleaning products and other supplies, a desk piled with paper as a consequence of a filing *system* that pushed the boundaries of the word, a coat rack hung with clothes that were never worn or discarded. Ralph had joked she left them to feed and clothe the downtrodden moths.

The woman who lifted her eyes from the checkout computer screen at the sound of my entry was in her early twenties, dressed in a light-blue uniform with yellow piped trim that should have made her look like a nurse in a children's ward, and yet she pulled it off. It helped that her eyes were almost the identical shade of blue as her uniform, and her pale skin and dark, pixie-cut hair brought to mind... well, a Celtic pixie.

"Can I help you?" she asked, not unfriendly but not smiling either.

"Is Ginger around?" I asked.

She looked me over briefly, then said, "Out back. You know where?"

She returned her attention to the monitor, muttering under her breath at misbehaving numbers as I strolled behind the counter. I discovered that things had, in fact, radically changed—the only item behind the screen now was a floor buffer; even the desk was gone—before continuing down the short hallway.

"Out back" was actually through the side door, out of view of both the front entrance and parking lot, and thus out of view of any customers. The garbage used to be kept there, but that seemed to have changed as well. One thing, at least, had not.

Ginger sat at a green plastic patio table, doing her best to fill a large glass ashtray she'd probably emptied last night. Presumably she slept sometime, but sitting out here smoking was the only time I'd ever seen the woman still. Slim arm and long, agile fingers extended, smoke rising from her cigarette in a slow, sensuous cloud, Ginger reminded me of a classic Hollywood film noir actress.

If the leading lady had been black with a box braid bob.

Ginger glanced up at my approach, stabbed out her cigarette and jumped to her feet. She wore a dress version of the younger woman's uniform, with high espadrille sandals that made her skinny legs look even skinnier, but still barely reached my own not very impressive height.

"Sydney!" she exclaimed, throwing her arms around me so hard my purse slid from my shoulder and whacked me in the knee.

I am not the huggiest person, but I pick my battles, and not hugging Ginger was one I'd never win, even if I'd wanted to. She was all bones—thick, heavy ones, not delicate spindles—bones and sinew and energy. The cigarette smell was fainter than I'd expected, and I wondered how many times a day she changed clothes.

"It's so good to see you, Ginger," I whispered in her ear, and meant it. I hadn't realized how much I'd missed her.

"Come sit with me," she said, voice husky as always. She looped an arm through mine, dragged me to her table and indicated the upwind chair before lighting another cigarette.

"When I saw behind the screens, I thought maybe you were cleaning up your act," I said, then stared pointedly at the cigarette in her hand. "Obviously I was wrong."

Ginger narrowed her eyes in world-class stink-eye before flipping me the bird with her non-smoking hand. Had I gone too far, too fast? She burst out laughing at the expression on my face. "You know I love you, right?"

I raised my middle finger and said, straight-faced, "I love you, too," before breaking out into a big grin.

We sat for a moment, the sounds of birds, the occasional passing car, and the light roar of heavier traffic in the distance settling around us. Ginger's mouth seemed frozen, slightly open, as though she'd started to say something and thought better of it. And then she didn't. "How's Ralph?" she asked.

I was expecting the question, but not so soon. "You know Ralph," I said lightly. "Same old, same old."

She stared down at her lap, brushing something from her skirt, as she nodded. "The clean-up—the Purge, I call it—was all because of him."

"How's that?" I asked, at a loss.

Her head lifted abruptly (surprised I didn't know the details of what had happened?), and I noticed new gray at her temple. Her lips pinched together in the center, as though reluctant to speak. "Let's just say he made sure I was under a lot more scrutiny, from everyone and for everything."

"I'm sorry," I said awkwardly.

"Don't be. Ultimately it was a good thing. I'd gotten sloppy about... some of my business practices. And it's better to be beyond reproach than it is to be sloppy when you have the kind of employees we do." Her words were magnanimous, but her smile was strained when she continued, "But I'm sure you didn't come here to talk about Ralph. What can I help you with, Sydney?"

I pulled the photo of Carly from my purse. "I don't suppose you've seen her."

She didn't take the photo, asking instead, "How old is she?"

Disappointment pierced my chest, but it wasn't Ginger's fault. I'd told myself I was being neutral, but I'd disengaged entirely during what was apparently a traumatic reshaping of her life. At the hands of someone close to both of us.

"Ginger, I'm not trying to trap you, I promise. I'm trying to help her," I said gently. "Besides, I'm up to my neck in glass houses at this point, so I can't afford any stones."

Her mouth returned to its unhappy pucker, but she set her cigarette in the ashtray and took the photo in both hands, looking at it long and hard. "No, I'm sorry," she said. "I haven't seen her. You think she's in trouble?"

I sighed, slumped in my chair, and tilted my head over its plastic back to peer through oak branchlets exploring the air above us, brown and creased as mummified fingers.

"How bad?" she asked.

The sharp curve of my arched throat made it difficult to answer. I swallowed hard and admitted to Ginger what I wouldn't admit to anyone else. "My gut says she's dead."

I closed my eyes and listened to Ginger blow out smoke in a big exhale before she said, "Your gut isn't always right."

My neck protested as I nodded. The sky seemed too bright, even through closed lids, so I covered my eyes with my fingers. "TPD picked her up for something. Not sure where she went from there."

"It happens," Ginger said, in a tired voice that has seen everything.

But she couldn't afford to be tired. And neither could I.

I stretched my arms overhead as I sat up, my shoulder giving an unsettling pop. "Happen any more than usual lately?"

She stabbed out her cigarette, using it to rearrange the rest of the butts as she considered. "Hard to say. Arrests seem to go in cycles, whether it's drugs, prostitution, trespass sweeps, whatever. And it's not unusual for ladies to move on to different pastures—they're never any *greener*—when they're released."

Her words had slowed toward the end, and I prompted, "But..."

"There's nothing solid I can put my finger on, and I haven't had anyone I know go missing," she reiterated. Unlike Ralph, Ginger didn't immediately jump to conspiracy conclusions. "*But* there's a definite sense of unease, especially among the younger girls, the ones who often think they're invincible. I'd say they're scared."

"Any idea of what? Or whom?"

"A boogeyman."

I raised a brow and she continued. "All folk story and no fact, so I don't know what else to call him. Scar on his face. Someone evil you'll never escape, but even if you do, you'll wish he'd killed you."

"You think he really exists?" I asked.

"He wouldn't be the first. But I have no evidence one way or another."

I shook my head. "Forget evidence. What's your gut say?"

She wheezed a heavy sigh. "Probably." Ginger braced herself against the table, balancing carefully on her shoes as we stood, then gave me a sad smile. "Remember, we can't save them all. Be careful out there, Sydney."

33

I had one more stop to make before the grocery store.

Cooper's was open, but it was too early for a crowd. A youngish guy in a heavy metal shirt was working at the bar, but he slipped behind the curtain as soon as he saw me. By the time I made it to a bar stool, Glenn had emerged from the back.

"The usual?" he asked.

I sighed. "The usual when I'm being no fun."

He rested his elbows on the bar, and one side of his mustache curled more than the other as he smiled. "Darling, you are the rare creature who is fun both sober and intoxicated."

I felt myself blush. "Thank you, Glenn."

His smile turned wicked as he pushed himself away from the bar. "Of course, they're different kinds of fun," he added suggestively, pouring an uncorrected Coke over ice.

The previous guy had left a dishtowel on the bar, and I threw it at Glenn. "You're in good spirits," I said.

"I like Mondays." he said.

I waited to see what he'd pour for himself, but he stopped at handing me my drink. "So you're not working tonight," I said.

"And what makes you think that?" he asked.

"Educated guess."

"Show off," he said, but didn't contradict me. "If you're not here to drink, what brings you to my humble establishment?"

"Same thing that always does—you." I'd skipped the innuendo, but was pleased to see my honesty still brought some color to his face. "Sorry about the other night."

"Remember, we already did that. Nothing to be sorry for," he said. "You find anything over the weekend?"

I nodded and winced at memories of disturbed ground, and at the images my imagination supplied of my old friend Laney, working to disturb the landscape even more. In that way, our jobs weren't so different.

"Found one of the head honchos Turtle was talking about, alive but losing his marbles," I said, unwilling to feel any sympathy for the man. "And maybe a graveyard full of dead kids."

Glenn's caterpillar brows rose. "No shit?"

"No shit," I affirmed.

"You see the Tar Shed?" Glenn asked, voice low.

I shook my head. "Thank God. But I don't doubt it went down the way Turtle said. That place is dark... all the abandoned buildings and equipment. Makes my skin crawl. And I don't know how the hell we're gonna make anything stick to anybody."

I stared down at my Coke, swirled it in the glass and wished it was something stronger. "That place got in my head."

"Yeah, well, don't let it live there."

"I even—" I stopped, embarrassed that I'd been so scared at the farmer's market. Except something seemed off about the idea.

"What?" Glenn asked.

"That was before we went to the center," I muttered. I looked up to find Glenn's eyes on me, intense. "I thought I saw Turtle's nemesis, the pinky guard."

He didn't laugh. "Who says you didn't?"

"Me," I said, and made a rigor mortis-like expression that was supposed to be a smile. "Unless he was running low on scented chakra candles."

"You are many things, Red, but an unintentional fabricator is not one of them."

My soft laugh at his use of *unintentional* came easily. Glenn smiled and said, "Trust yourself." Tossing the dishtowel under the bar, he went on, "I gotta follow up with Turtle sometime this week, see how he's doing."

"Don't tell him what we found." I amended, "Or might have found."

"'Course not. But I'll let you know if he remembers anything else that might be helpful." Glenn huffed and dropped to rest one elbow on the bar. "Hell, he probably won't even remember we were there."

Maybe he was better off that way. Him and Mr. Dickey, which is why the latter man's memory loss pissed me off. He should have to carry the horrible things he'd done with him to the grave. "Sorry to bring you down," I said, touching Glenn's hand briefly.

He stood. "No, Red. It might not be rainbows and buttercups, but don't ever be sorry for bringing the truth."

As was often the case, something about Glenn helped ground me, and I felt better when I left Cooper's a few minutes later. My subsequent grocery store odyssey took longer than I'd expected, wandering the aisles with no list, but I had a sense of—not *hope* exactly—*resigned calm?* as I drove home with a couple of bags of food. The piece of candy I grabbed in the checkout line didn't hurt.

But dark chocolate serenity is apparently as fickle as any other kind. A hint of annoyed anxiety took its place as I approached my street and all of the things I had to do, all of the decisions I had to make. When I saw my elderly neighbor Mr. Ginley waving frantically from his mailbox, the hint of anxiety bloomed into the pre-vomit stage.

A breeze lifted a silver section of comb-over hair, making Mr. G look even more like a lunatic than usual. I pulled close to his curb—not too close, because he'd once accused me of trying to run him down—and rolled down the passenger window to yell across the seat at the stooped man. "Mr. Ginley, is something wrong?"

"Cops!" he spat. Literally.

"I'm sorry?" I asked, leaning across the empty seat while looking for old man spittle. Maybe it had hit my door.

"There was a cop right outside your house, not five minutes ago," he yelled, waving a flimsy sales circular and setting his pine-colored cardigan to flapping.

Crap. Since it was tantamount to admitting I was harboring a runaway, I didn't dare ask my nosy neighbor if the officer had left with Addy in custody.

"Thanks, Mr. Ginley," I said, ignoring whatever else he shouted as I swung into my driveway.

Lurching to a stop, I left everything in my car and fumbled with the lock. At least there was nothing nestled in the space between the doors, no official-looking notification (*Sydney Brennan, your life as you know it is about to end*). I staggered through the door into the kitchen.

The house had that late-day, shady neighborhood dimness conducive to napping. Maybe that's what Addy was doing. Maybe she hadn't even heard the cop knocking on the door.

Except I'd left Ben with her.

I rushed into the living room... and wished I hadn't.

Ben and Addy were on the couch. *Together.* Ben sat at the end, turned sideways so one leg stretched partway down its length. Addy sat astride him, tongue presumably down his throat. Their faces were locked together, buried beneath her loose, still-wet hair. One of Ben's hands was on the back of Addy's head and the other was on her lower back beneath her shirt.

And I thought Mr. Ginley was going to make me vomit.

"What the hell is going on here?" I demanded.

They both flinched and scrambled upright. Addy would have fallen onto my coffee table if Ben hadn't caught her. He glanced down at his hands, holding her ass, then at my angry face. To his credit, his eyes never left mine as he wriggled and set her on the couch next to him.

"Syd, I can explain," he said.

A moment earlier, Addy had appeared a combination of scared and penitent and embarrassed and every other flavor of the blushing teenaged rainbow. But as soon as Ben opened his mouth, the emotional landscape shifted. "There's nothing to explain," she countered. "*No reason* to explain."

I moved toward her, banging my shins on the coffee table. "Are you serious? I find you having sex with—"

"We weren't having sex!" She jumped to her feet, ping-ponging the table between us so it struck the same spot on my shins.

"You weren't having sex *yet*—it's a good thing I skipped the produce aisle!" I yelled.

Before remembering what had gotten me so upset to begin with. *A cop at my house.* Let's see… what else could make a cop show up at my house? *Me yelling loud enough for the neighbors to hear.* I'd never quite worked out whether Mr. Ginley was with me or against me on the cop thing, so he could be dialing 9-1-1 right now.

I stepped back, taking a deep breath to calm myself. Instead, I found I needed another breath, and another—

"Syd, what's wrong?" Ben asked, moving around the end of the coffee table.

Don't hyperventilate, dumbass, I told myself, closing my eyes briefly. *Breathe in, breathe out.*

I opened my eyes and turned to Ben. "Did you happen to hear a knock at the door while you two were getting busy?"

He blushed and clenched his jaw and Addy started to sputter, but I held up a hand and asked, "Did you?"

"No," Ben said.

"Probably because Addy's tongue was in your ear," I snarked, showing poor restraint.

"Hey!" Ben took a step closer, without quite crossing the line into my personal space. "You said not to answer the door anyway, so what's the difference?"

"It was a cop," I said, before he had a chance to get worked up.

Ben looked confused, but Addy went from ruddy righteous indignation to pale-faced terror so quickly I was afraid she'd pass out.

"It's okay," I said, moving toward her... and banged my sore shins on the table again. "Dammit!"

I pulled my leg back and almost kicked the stupid thing, but sat on it instead, rubbing my shin. Addy dropped heavily on the neighboring couch. I touched her knee gently, just my fingertips. When she didn't flinch, I repeated, "It's okay. He's gone now. But I think you should probably get your stuff together."

Dazed, her fingers went to lips that were still puffy. Her face was slightly abraded, but she looked so young, so vulnerable. "Okay," she said, and rose and disappeared down the hallway.

I sighed, and felt Ben standing over me. "Syd, what's this about?" he asked.

"You need to shave," I said. "Addy looks like you loofahed her."

"Dammit, Syd—what's going on?" he demanded.

I stood, trying to think straight. I'd told Addy she'd need her stuff, but what did I need? Besides possibly a new career.

"I don't know what's going on," I admitted. "Law enforcement shouldn't be looking for her yet—honestly, they shouldn't care. They normally don't when it comes to runaways. But for some reason this time they do, and if they find her, they'll take her."

"Take her where?"

I shrugged. "I don't know, but I'm guessing a juvenile facility."

A juvenile facility. Maybe like the one Carly went to, that Eleanor Dickey and Blake Tucker ran.

Suddenly, I was feeling a lot less laissez-faire about leaving. "Well, shit."

34

I had Addy and an overnight bag in the car, sharing space with the bags of groceries that never made it inside, but no destination. Driving the opposite direction out of my neighborhood from my usual route, I pulled into a shopping center and parked in front of a pet superstore. It had gone dark, and the city seemed particularly shadowy outside our parking lot puddle. Streetlights appeared as faint, decorative strands in the distance, engulfed by tree canopy.

"Are you mad at me?" Addy asked.

I'd pretended not to watch as she kissed Ben on the cheek good-bye, and it was the first time she'd spoken since we left my house.

"Not really," I said.

"Yes, you are," she said gently.

"Maybe a little bit," I admitted, voice as soft as hers had been.

"Why?"

"I don't know. Maybe I don't like guests making out on my furniture before I get a chance to," I joked. "It's a new couch."

Relatively new. I'd gotten it after a madman had nearly killed Ben and me in my living room, so I'd owned it a year or less.

And maybe it was that simple. Not that I was jealous of the physical act, but that I was jealous of having the opportunity to act. I rarely got to see Mike in the flesh. I was also jealous of my time and space, of sharing it with anyone. Although if that were the case, making room for Mike in my life would be a challenge as well.

I sighed and returned to, "I'm not mad at you."

A dark-skinned boy grunted as he pushed a cart with a huge bag of dog food past our car. His head barely reached the handlebar, but he was determined. I couldn't make out his dad's expression, but imagined he was hiding a smile. Their SUV flashed and bee-bopped as they approached, and the dad popped the back hatch.

"I like Ben," Addy said.

I could tell, I thought, but didn't say out loud. The coming hours and days would be long enough without me being a smart-ass.

"Is that why you're mad?" she asked.

"I said I'm not mad. You're both adults." I paused. "Sort of."

"But you don't think I'm good enough for him," she said, voice caught somewhere between challenging me to confirm her belief and fearing that I would.

I turned to Addy, able to distinguish the shape of her face and a portion of one cheek in the dark. "Did I say that? Don't assume you know what people think about you. And even if you do know what they think, *never* believe they're right. *Ever.* Who you are is your decision to make, not theirs."

She shifted in her seat, back pressing against the door as if to create distance without quite bolting from the vehicle.

"Don't worry," I said, slouching and attempting to let go of the unexpected energy she'd awakened. "I just hit my lecture quota for the month. How are you with sleeping in cars?"

"I've had a fair bit of practice," she said, looking over her shoulder at a pillow in the back seat, then settling for slouching against the window with her hood.

It was still early, though. I tried to remember what I'd bought at the grocery store, whether anything qualified as instantly edible without causing us stomach upset.

My cell phone rang, and I fumbled for it in the dark. Roger.

"Hey," I said. "How's your dad?"

"I left Deidre with him," he said. "Where are you?"

"In a parking lot," I said, blinking against another SUV's head-lights. Someone else with a chew toy emergency. But I'd bet the store closed at nine. Everything closed early in Tallahassee. "Who's open twenty-four hours? Walmart?"

"Like I would know. Is something wrong, Sydney?"

I sighed. I felt like I was doing a lot of sighing tonight. I debated not telling him, but Roger was in this up to his eyeballs, too, and he wouldn't thank me for keeping him in the dark. "A cop came by, looking for Addy," I said.

"So you weren't there?" Before I could answer, he continued, "You didn't speak with them, and they didn't serve you with anything?"

I reviewed all of his questions in my mind. "That would be no, no, and no. But it's complicated."

Now it was Roger's turn to sigh. He sounded as exhausted as I felt. "Of course it is. Why don't you come tell me about it in person?"

"I'm not sure that's a good idea," I said.

"You've spent the night before and left with your virtue intact," he reminded me. "Well, as intact as it was when you arrived."

I smiled. "That wasn't what I meant and you know it. My virtue is not alone."

"Let me worry about the rest," he said. "I'll even let you use the fancy shower again."

"And make me breakfast?" I asked.

"Don't push your luck," he said, trying to keep his voice light.

I glanced over at Addy. She'd already dozed off, head against the car window. I said, "We'll see you in fifteen."

ROGER and I sat at his rustic dining table, its wooden top nearly as thick as the massive front door. Addy stood at Roger's fancy stove, stirring a saucepan of milk and chocolate on one of its gazillion gas burners. He'd had sandwiches waiting for us, and Addy had offered to make hot chocolate before bed.

"That is... worrying," Roger said. The master of understatement.

"The cop, or Blake Tucker?" I asked.

"Do I have to choose?" he asked, sipping at a glass of Macallan. "The big question is, are the two related?"

He'd offered me a drink, but I was holding out for hot chocolate. Still... I reached for his scotch, and he was too dumbfounded to stop me from taking a sip. It was malty, oaky, liquid amber burning down my throat, with a hint of sweetness as I settled back in my chair. "Wow."

His mouth wrinkled at my heathenness as he moved his glass out of my range.

"Alcohol is sterile," I noted. "Or is it *sterilizing*?"

Roger ignored me and went on, "I can't see how the juvenile facility and the appearance of local law enforcement are related, but you know how I feel about coincidences."

I knew, because I felt the same way. "That they're the universe's way of saying, *Hey dumbass, look what's going on around you.*"

He smiled. "Succinct as always. So what is the universe trying to tell us?"

I didn't know, and I was tired of not knowing things. It made me cranky. "Devil's advocate," I said. "We don't even know the cop was there about Addy."

"True," he said, raising his glass and giving it a careful swirl. "But have you ever been served for anything work-related at home? Or had the cops show up at your house at all?"

"No on the former," I said, then grimaced with remembrance as I added, "Yes on the latter."

Roger leaned forward. He obviously wasn't going to make the connection on his own, and I dearly wanted to grab his glass again and toss it back like a shot of tequila.

I lowered my voice. "The dead guy in my living room."

His gaze drifted toward the ceiling as he reviewed all of the craziness we'd been involved in together over the past year or so, none of it involving dead guys. *That he knew about.* Finally, Roger's eyes grew wide with realization and he set his glass on the table. "The Thomas case. I'm sorry, Sydney."

I shook it off. "There's no reason you should have remembered—you weren't involved. But my house being a crime scene is the only time I can think of that cops have shown up there. I could call John Driscoll at the TPD and ask—"

"No," Roger said. "Bad idea. As of now, they have no way of proving what you do or don't know. Let's keep it that way as long as we can. And do you even know it was TPD?"

My mouth opened, closed, opened again. "Good point. For that matter, do we even know it was law enforcement? Ben and Addy both said they never heard a knock."

I hadn't told Roger the condition I'd found them in, not wanting to embarrass Addy. But being familiar with law enforcement persistence, it was hard for me to imagine them not hearing a cop knock at the door when they were still fully clothed.

Ben was my go-to for house stuff when I was out of town, but I also had Mr. G's number in my Contacts, just in case. He was not happy to hear from me. "Mr. Ginley, this is Sydney Brennan—"

"I know that," the elderly man crabbed, as though I were an idiot, or thought he was one. "I have that caller thingie. What do you want?"

"I'm sorry to bother you, but it'll just take a minute. I was wondering what kind of cop you saw outside my house today."

"What do you mean, what kind of cop? I didn't talk to the man." His voice dropped conspiratorially. "I waited until he left to get my mail."

"Did you notice what kind of car he was driving?" I asked.

"I don't know—just a car! But he was wearing a uniform."

"What color was his uniform?"

"Light brown," he said, before announcing, "I'm hanging up now."

And he did.

"Well?" Roger asked.

I shook my head. "Doesn't sound like he was a LEO. Mr. G didn't notice a regulation vehicle, and his 'uniform' was light brown."

Roger nodded. "TPD is navy, and Leon County Sheriff is dark green."

"I haven't stolen any picnic baskets or done anything else I can think of to piss off a park ranger," I said. Roger didn't smile.

It could be someone who didn't bother to change after work, or someone who figured they'd go unnoticed as an individual while wearing an official-looking uniform. And we both knew khaki was a common color for corrections uniforms.

"You think he was looking for me after all?" I asked.

"I don't know," Roger said. "But I don't like the not knocking. So far as he knew, no one was at home—correct?"

I nodded. "Car was gone."

"Maybe he left because he saw the neighbor watching him."

And what if he hadn't? What if he'd broken into my house and unexpectedly found Ben and Addy there? An image flashed in my mind of what had happened to Ben the last time someone had found him in my house, looking for me, and Roger's fancy scotch threatened the back of my throat.

"Whatever his purpose," Roger continued, "I think it's best for both of you to stay here."

I swallowed (*everyone's okay*), threaded my fingers through my hair and gripped my skull, but didn't gain any insight. "Agreed. Where do we stand on..." I hesitated as Addy approached with a couple of steaming mugs. "...the rest."

She sat across from me, hoarding both mugs. "If you can't trust me to hear about the things that directly affect me, you probably don't want to drink this. I might have confused salt and sugar because I couldn't read the containers."

Roger waited until I nodded for him to continue. He said, "Since we decided we were better off if I worked with everyone behind the scenes rather than being your official attorney, Juliet Sanders filed to be your *guardian ad litem*."

Addy's brows wrinkled as she slid a mug across the table to me.

"What's that mean? That I'm supposed to live with her? I don't even know her."

Roger shook his head. "It just means she'll be your lawyer in court, the one person who's looking out for nothing but your best interests. The approach is a little unorthodox, and we're doing everything we can to maintain a wall between us and her."

"So she doesn't know I'm here?" Addy asked.

Roger's mouth curled in a wry smile. "Among other things. But Sydney, I need you to write up an affidavit tonight about the Spencers hiring you. I'll walk you through the specifics. Tomorrow you'll deliver it to Juliet, along with a copy of the Spencers' motion to have Addy placed with them pending the custody determination."

"Got it," I said, wincing initially (whiskey-milk clash) but ultimately sipping chocolate appreciatively from my mug. The kid did good, with a hint of cinnamon.

"Wait a minute," Addy said. "Are you working for my aunt and uncle?"

"Not exactly," Roger said.

"In fact," I added, "the fewer people who know about Roger's involvement, the better."

Roger rose, taking his scotch with him. "I need to make a couple of calls. Syd—"

"If you're not back by the time I've finished my beverage, I'll start the affidavit." I'd brought my laptop, and I knew what he'd want. These things were more about what you *didn't* say than what you *did*. Like the fact that Addy was my roommate.

"Sounds good. I've got someone who can come over and notarize it," he said, topping up his drink, then turned to Addy. "If I don't see you again before you retire, sleep well."

A bit of milky foam in the corner of her mouth made Addy's smile asymmetrical. "Thanks, Roger."

She watched him head down the hall and disappear into his office, closing the door behind him. Her eyes dropped as she stirred the settling chocolate in her mug. Staring intently at the dark swirls,

Addy said, "He's not going to get in trouble for this, is he? For helping me?"

"Roger is an adult who is capable of making his own choices and taking care of himself," I said, before choking down the thick chocolate slurry at the bottom. "And no, he won't get in trouble. No one is going to get in trouble for helping you."

My voice was so confident, I almost convinced myself.

35

Roger's sister was staying with him as well, so the kid and I shared a room. Addy was asleep long before Roger and I finalized the affidavit and the rest of our plans for the next day. I finished prepping in the wee hours, and she didn't stir when I came to bed.

I didn't stir when Addy *left* the bed the next morning, either. In fact, I didn't wake until she nudged me. Strongly. Multiple times.

I'm not sure what proportion of the words that escaped my mouth were profanity, but since I'm not a morning person, I don't believe I can be held accountable for any of them.

"Sorry," Addy said. "But Roger told me to wake you at seven. And to tell you there was coffee."

I'd curled into a defensive ball under the comforter, and my head reluctantly emerged from its cotton shell. "Is he still here?"

"No."

In other words, I wasn't required to engage in coherent conversation yet. "Then shower comes first. Coffee after."

I'd dressed, had my half cup of coffee, and was slathering cream cheese on a wheat bagel when I finally noticed Addy wearing an unfamiliar pair of high-end yoga pants under her sweatshirt. "Where'd you get the pants?"

She had waited to have breakfast with me and said around a mouthful of bagel, "Deidre said I could borrow them."

"She's here?" I scanned Roger's kitchen and living room as though I'd somehow missed her. I'd worn Deidre's clothes before myself, so I knew Deidre was considerably shorter than the only Weber sister I'd actually met, but she was at least human-sized.

"She left before I woke you."

She had probably come home to shower and change. The quick turnaround time did not bode well for Mr. Weber. "You know about their dad, right?"

Addy fidgeted with her butter knife as she nodded, then asked, "Do you think I could talk to my aunt and uncle?"

I swallowed a chunk of bagel before replying. "Absolutely. But I don't know if that's a good idea at this precise moment, depending on what's happening legally. Let me check with Roger and see where things stand—say this afternoon."

I didn't mention that the Spencers were playing hard to get lately.

"You sure you'll be okay staying here by yourself today?" I asked. She'd said she would be last night, but I couldn't help feeling some anxiety.

Addy managed a wry smile as she said, "This place is practically a mansion. I won't run away again, if that's what you mean."

It was in part, but she didn't need to know I had lingering trust issues. "I just don't want you to die of boredom."

"I think I can last for twelve hours. Roger's got good cable, and he said to make myself at home."

"Except his office," I countered.

"Except his office," she agreed, with only the slightest eye roll. "And there's plenty of food. I swear his fancy fridge is bigger than the bathroom at my last home."

I rose and rinsed my crumby plate in the sink. "The courtyard out back is fine—"

"But don't go out the front door," she finished. "And don't answer the front door."

I gathered my pile of stuff to leave, much as I would have any normal morning at home. Then I handed her a list of phone numbers, including mine and Roger's cell. "If anything comes up, use the landline in the living room."

She tucked a strand of blue hair behind her ear as she skimmed the numbers. "Ben's not on here," she said, fighting a smile.

"Ben's in school. As you should be," I said, scratching down his number anyway. If something went sideways and she couldn't reach me or Roger, Ben was the next best option.

"No school last week," she said, "so this is only the third day I missed this semester."

"Uh-huh," I said, dubious but distracted as I poured coffee into a travel mug and headed for the door. "You met Deidre, but if a gorgeous, busty Amazon lets herself in, that's another one of Roger's sisters. He has a few. I'll check in midday."

Addy followed me, saying, "I've got it, Syd."

I tried not to take it personally when she pushed the heavy door closed behind me as if securing a line of defense against the hordes.

Roger's house had no garage, just a brick horseshoe driveway with a fountain in the center. There was no reason to assume I'd crash here versus with any other work colleague, and I suspected Roger guarded his home address more carefully than I did my own. Still, why make my presence obvious? Last night I thought I'd parked so the fountain's lush landscaping shielded my car from casual passers-by, but in daylight I revised my opinion. If I stayed here long, I'd need a rental car that wasn't as easily identified as my Cabrio Cecil. Could I bill that to the Spencers? And if I did bill them, could they afford to pay it? Being a private investigator would be so much easier, and more lucrative, if I didn't have scruples.

My first stop of the morning was Roger's attorney friend who'd filed to be Addy's *guardian ad litem*. She had an office downtown not far from my own but in a multi-occupant office building—high-rise by Tallahassee standards—rather than a separate space. I risked parking illegally on the street for what should be a quick in and out, hoping the universe would watch over me for helping the underdogs. Yeah, because that *always* happened.

Juliet Sanders's third-floor office was relatively small—just two closed doors behind the empty lobby and reception area. The decor was somehow both sophisticated and child-friendly. Scandinavian-inspired modern furniture made the space feel larger, and a gold chandelier, little more than metal framing and bulbs, gave it warmth. One corner was devoted to a recreation area with books and magazines and simple non-electronic toys. The rug there mimicked layers of wet sand that ranged in color from dark brown to pale gray. Presumably it was juice box-proof.

An attractive woman a few years older than me emerged from the smaller office to the right as I entered. Her short, dark hair was styled but not overdone, and her makeup was likewise—you knew she was wearing it because no one looks that flawless naturally, but darned if you could point to it on her face. The fabric of her charcoal gray suit was something between velvet and silk that shimmered slightly as if it were recently alive.

Her smile at my approach was genuine, not the lawyer-shark kind, and the crinkles at her eyes made me revise her age up a little, closer to Roger than to me.

"Sydney Brennan, I presume?" she said, motioning me toward her office. "Come on back."

I ignored the compulsion to touch the back of her suit jacket as I followed. I hadn't anticipated speaking with the lawyer personally and was glad I'd worn slightly wrinkled slacks rather than jeans.

"So Roger called ahead?" I asked, sitting in a lightly padded, spindle chair that was more attractive than comfortable.

"Late last night," she acknowledged. "He said to expect a redhead, and here you are. That's for me?"

"Yes," I said, handing her a packet of papers as I surveyed her office.

A hint of lemon emanated from a multicolored ceramic mug that could have been middle school homework or outsider art. Windows behind her offered a view of the street below and the hint of a green park beyond. There were no shelves of law books, but the requisite diplomas and licenses took up most of one wall. The opposite wall held photos of children and families that did not appear to be her own.

"How is Roger doing with his father?" she asked, in a voice that had lost its crispness.

It was not the question I'd expected, nor was her obvious deep concern. I shrugged. "You know Roger."

She gave a small laugh, almost more like a sigh. "Yes, I do."

My eyes were drawn back to the wall, to a photo at the far end of a dark-haired couple... I rose for a better look. It was a much younger Roger and Ms. Sanders, smiling with their arms around each other in front of a courthouse. They both wore suits, but their joy—and the bouquet—were a dead giveaway that the occasion was not work-related.

"Oh my God," I said, my mouth having no gatekeeper as usual, and sat heavily.

"You didn't know?" she asked.

I shook my head, and her smile held a hint of sadness.

"I was the first former Mrs. Weber." She amended, "Not that I ever changed my name."

I grinned. "I would dearly love to buy you a drink or five."

She leaned across her desk conspiratorially. "I'll bet you would. Maybe someday." She rose and said, "Obviously I can't talk to you about the substance of Ms. Hastings's case, but I will say the judge's assistant assures me they'll schedule a hearing by the end of the day."

She walked me through the still-empty lobby to the front door. "I'm glad I finally have a face for the name," she said, handing me her business card. She'd written her cell number on the back in a beautiful upright hand. "Keep an eye on him. And let me know if he needs help."

"I will," I promised.

～

My own office looked sorely neglected after seeing Juliet Sanders's space. It smelled it, too—one of the drawbacks of an old converted house with no central heating and cooling in Tallahassee's humid climate. It gets funky fast when I'm not there to air it out.

I left the front door open as I carried my mail to my desk. But first, my voicemail. I had messages from my exterminator (time to nuke the palmetto bugs again), a political fundraiser doing a cold call, and the Spencers' friend Faith Halliway. I crossed my fingers and gave her a call back.

She answered on the second ring and asked me to wait a minute. It took her about that long to return to the phone.

"Sorry," she said, voice low, "I didn't want the busybodies in the teacher's lounge listening in. Deborah ended up in the hospital over the weekend. She had a bad reaction to some medication, but Clint says they're fixing it and she'll be okay. I guess he forgot his cell phone, and he was dealing with her and their kids—anyway, he wanted me to call you and let you know what was going on."

"And they still want custody of Addy?"

"Of course they do!" she huffed, as if offended I would even ask. "They signed the papers, didn't they? But there's something going on. I think Addy's been reported to somebody, but it wasn't by the school. Unfortunately, I also think they know I'm feeding information to Clint and Deborah, because it's getting harder to find out anything."

That was a lot of *theys*, but I got the gist of her slightly paranoid confusion. I asked her to keep an ear open anyway, and to let Clint and Deborah know their niece was safe and thinking of them.

Speaking of paranoia, I quickly flipped through my stack of mail, wary of lingering in my office. A bill from one of the Clerks of Court for copies, some junk mail, and a regular letter-sized envelope with no postage or even address, just SYDNEY BRENNAN in bold block handwriting. I told myself the blood from any body part small enough to fit in an envelope still would have soaked through the paper by now (*ewww*), but nonetheless used my letter opener rather than a bare finger to get at the contents.

Inside were a half dozen folded pages of photocopies with a square Post-it on top that read simply:

She's gone.

—BT

Blake Tucker from Brummel. He must have dropped the papers off early this morning. I wasn't sure whether to be grateful or regret that I'd missed him. Mr. Tucker did not waste words, and I wondered if I could have gotten more out of him in person. Probably not.

Who was gone?

Carly Whitmore. Intake and discharge forms from the Brummel Youth Academy. I skimmed the pages and checked my desk calendar. She'd been released three weeks ago. I couldn't see anything to indicate where she was now, or why she'd been released, but the inventory of her property indicated she'd been wearing a pair of size 6 jeans and carrying a pink purse when she left.

Gee, that was helpful.

I was shoving the folded pages in my purse when my cell phone rang with an unfamiliar number.

"Sydney Brennan Investigations," I said, in my professional voice.

"Wow, someone who didn't know better would think you actually know what you're doing," said a woman's voice with a hint of humor.

A moment later, I connected the dots. "Laney?"

"Took you long enough. Is getting phone calls that insult your PI prowess a regular occurrence?" she asked, quickly adding, "Don't answer that."

"Ha, ha," I said, in my best you-think-you're-funny tone. "I can't imagine why we're not still housemates."

"Geography," Laney said. "To share a house, the commute would kill one or both of us."

I started Cecil before asking, "You staying in Tallahassee now?"

"No," she said. "We're in a shitty motel closer to the site. But I was hoping to see you."

"Why, so you can insult me in person?" I held the phone awkwardly as I reversed, then pulled down to the street.

"That, and I was hoping we could put our heads together about this place," she said. "Syd, there's something *off* around here."

I felt a tug in my chest. Laney was not an alarmist. "Something other than a decades-old graveyard of unidentified dead kids?"

"Yes," she said simply.

I looked down one end of the street, then up the other. At nothing. This time. Took a deep breath. "Okay," I said. "I'm on my way."

36

Laney's vague forebodings weren't my only motivation for heading west. Tracking down relatives was a priority; the last thing Roger and I wanted was for the victims' surviving family members to learn the fate of loved ones on the news. Of course, we didn't yet have identities for the bodies—we didn't even have bodies. But I'd begun compiling a list of the likely deceased from lawsuits and news reports.

It was a multistep process, identifying potential victims, then naming possible family members and tracing where those family members might be. I'd been running relatives' names through an online tracking service as I got them rather than batching, so I already had a dozen or so potential addresses in that area of the Panhandle. Meeting Laney would give me an opportunity to do some ground-truthing. I wasn't speaking with anyone yet, but I could at least make sure we knew where to reach them should that time come.

That said, I'm not an idiot.

I mean, everyone is an idiot sometimes. But being an idiot is not my default state. Not anymore. I've vowed not to do dumbass things on my own—and definitely not without telling anyone—if I can help it. That's why I stopped at the hospice on my way out of town to touch base with Roger.

He stood in the hallway outside his father's room. Peeking inside, I glimpsed the back of Deidre's blonde head, sitting at Amos Weber's bedside. Her father appeared unconscious.

"We don't expect him to make it through the night," Roger said.

I opened my mouth to say something heartfelt but useless, but stopped when Roger shook his head.

He appeared to be maintaining control emotionally, but was also as exhausted as I'd ever seen him. He ran a hand through hair that alternated between flattened and standing straight up. I seized the elbow of his offending arm and led him down the hall to a chair in the warm lounge.

I sat next to him, close enough that our arms pressed against each other, so I could speak as softly as the place and occasion seemed to require. "Something at the Reform Center has Laney Singh spooked."

There was a moment's delay as his mind shifted from his father's dying body to his father's dying wish. "Considering her vocation— the woman has excavated war zones—I wouldn't think she'd spook easily. Any idea what?"

"She wouldn't say on the phone. I'm heading that way now, figured I'd run down some of the potential family addresses and meet Laney at the site afterward."

Roger blinked slowly and turned to face me. "Are you sure that's wise?"

"I'm not an idiot." If I say it enough times, maybe people— including me—will start to believe it. "I doubt there's any real danger with a full forensic team at work, but Mike can tag along. Safety in numbers."

"Good," he said, nodding. "And Addy? Will she be okay?"

"Unless she burns your house down nuking a burrito. I'll check in with her, but I should be back at a reasonable time this evening. Don't worry about Addy," I said, rising. "Or me. This is where you're needed."

I reached out to fix Roger's hair, and he let me. "Mrs. Weber Number One asked about you," I said.

He smiled for a moment, before saying, "Juliet is a good woman." He brushed my hand from his hair, but said, "You're not so bad, either. Thanks, Sydney."

BETWEEN THE TRAVEL west and my list of addresses, I had hours of driving ahead of me. I did my best to avoid being maudlin, but it was hard not to think about Roger's father slowly dying, about what that would mean for Roger and the rest of his family. I didn't know the details of the double-digit children's adoptions, how long or from what ages they'd been raised together. Roger obviously felt protective of his sisters, but how close were any of the siblings? With both parents gone, would they still feel connected to each other? Assuming they ever had.

My sister Lisa and I had always struggled with our relationship, and even more so after my brother died in our teenaged years. As I prepared to exit the interstate for equally boring secondary roads, I wondered how much harder it would be without... not necessarily the genetic connection—that didn't matter unless your kidney failed and you needed a new one—but the lifelong reinforcement of identity. The minutes and hours, day and years of knowing you're stuck with each other, until you finally accept it.

The white letters of my exit sign swam a bit. I blinked to focus and the sign announcing highlights for the subsequent two exits came into view. *Brummel Youth Academy*. Hunh, I'd never noticed before that it was so close. What a happy coincidence. I ignored my turn and continued on for another mile and a half before exiting there instead.

Brummel was on the main road not far from the interstate. I couldn't have missed it unless I'd closed my eyes, which admittedly was tempting when passing any correctional center. Built in the past ten years, the two-story brick facility was huge, and the morning sun flashed against glass from numerous windows.

The complex lacked any fence at all, much less the bad-ass, *you're screwed* razor wire and guard towers I associated with maximum security prisons. It should have looked like a school, maybe even a community college, albeit one closed for a holiday or bomb threat with no students visible on campus. And yet, some indefinable essence brought to mind every jail I'd ever visited.

There were fewer cars in the parking lot than was typical at adult prisons. I chose a spot and passed through glass doors reminiscent of a bank entry. Continuing the institutional patchwork, the reception area felt like a doctor's office. If, that is, your doctor had the option of detaining you until you paid. There was seating for a dozen people, but at the moment only an elderly Latina woman sat there, clutching an enormous black leather purse on her lap. She stared straight ahead, ignoring the magazines and a toddler's bead and wire maze toy on the end table next to her.

A man and woman dressed office casual rather than in uniform sat behind a high reception desk adjacent to the waiting area. A restricted area began behind them, a combination of safety glass and good old-fashioned walls and doors that simultaneously gave a sense of openness and of being watched. The man's ready posture belied a purely administrative role and suggested security. The woman spoke to me politely, while still conveying her skepticism about my success when she asked me to wait.

I sat the customary buffer seat away from the waiting elderly woman. She appeared uncomfortable, continuously adjusting the shoulders of the print top she wore over blue slacks. Her lipstick was a bold peach, freshly applied and probably one of the items in her massive purse. I considered warning her—if she was here for visitation, they'd never let the purse inside. It had room enough for a grappling hook, a body double, and a rocket launcher besides.

Soon the woman behind the desk called me over and motioned me toward an entry hallway, buzzing me through. A parallel path with metal detectors led into the bowels of the facility, while this one gave access to administrative types, including the director, Eleanor

Dickey. (Their rebranding needed some work; my brain still said *warden*.)

"Ms. Brennan," she said, rising from behind a spotless black lacquer desk to meet me. "How can I help you?"

"Ms. Dickey," I replied, shaking her cool, elegantly manicured hand. Her nails matched her burgundy suit, one of many reasons that even when I was dressed for lawyer-visiting, the woman made me feel like a hobo. She motioned me to a guest chair far more comfortable than my own office chair, and I wondered what my chances were of absconding with it.

I made her wait while I took in her otherwise unremarkable office—white walls with the requisite framed documents and glad-handing photos, cheap gray carpet, and white plastic blinds covering the single window overlooking some other interior space, now closed. The desk and chairs were incongruous, such high quality she must have purchased them herself.

My smile wasn't entirely friendly when I said, "I'm sorry—should I call you Ms. Powers? It must be exhausting, choosing the appropriate identity for a given situation."

Her chin dipped as she mirrored my smile. "I suppose I had that coming. What do you want to know?"

"Why this?" I asked, spreading my hands and looking around to indicate *why here/corrections*, versus *why lie to me*.

Her mouth curled as she said, "It used to drive my mother crazy, the way my father talked to me about his work. But he had ideas about the ways the correctional system could be different, better. And I soaked them up."

She traced the edge of her desk with long fingers. "Eventually my mother sent me to boarding school, rather than have me live on the reform school property. But it was too late; I was hooked. I went the education route—even got my Master's in Business Administration—but this is where I wanted to be."

"How long have you worked in corrections?" I asked.

The self-consciousness about her age seemed forced when she admitted, "Over twenty years."

"And when did you find out the truth?" I asked. Her brows wrinkled inquisitively, and I clarified, "About your father, and the way he ran the Reform Center. That his talk of reform was just that—*talk*—while he oversaw egregious, institutionalized child abuse."

Eleanor glared at me with flushed cheeks and clenched her hands. Rocking forward slightly in her chair, she admitted, "A few months ago, Father began saying hateful things, things so horrible I couldn't believe they had any basis in reality. Until I found you and Mr. Weber in his living room. I still don't know they're not some cruel manifestation of the dementia that's turned him into a stranger."

A metal file drawer slammed shut in a neighboring office while we stared each other down. "So Brummel doesn't have a Tar Shed?" I pressed.

Her face cleared, expression blank as she said, "I don't know what that is, but I assume it's not associated with building maintenance." When I didn't elaborate, she pivoted to, "How are things going at the Reform Center? Have you found anything of interest?"

Shrugging, I said, "As you know, there's currently a forensic anthropology team on site, but they haven't made enough progress to report yet."

"Nothing at all?"

I gave her a wry smile. "You know how these scientific types are, unwilling to commit to anything unless you back them into a corner and beat them with hoses."

She leaned back in her chair, which—if my own seating was any indication—was more comfortable than my bed. Crossing her legs, she laced her fingers over her flat stomach. "Yes, I do know."

"I haven't had a chance to review them yet, but I appreciate you sending your father's records with Mr. Tucker."

She inclined her head in a royal nod. "I don't know how useful they'll be. He used to have a room full of boxes, but my mother burned most of them before she died—called them his mistress."

"Who knows?" I agreed. "But as a gesture of good faith, and because things were set in motion so quickly, I wanted to share how the forensic team became involved."

I scooted my chair stiffly across the industrial carpet and propped my elbows on her desk. She'd probably wipe it after I left. "We found something that may be a grave, at a location that's consistent with Mr. Amos Weber's recollections."

She sat up. "Where?"

"In the fields beyond the buildings. I believe they were in cultivation—that children were working those fields—when your family was there," I said, careful to keep any judgment out of my voice.

She tented her hands and rested her chin on her thumbs, as if she were praying, and closed her eyes for several seconds. I took the opportunity to tease out the faint floral scent in the room. Gardenia, but I wasn't certain if it was emanating from an item in her office or from her person.

Finally, she said, "You're probably right about the farm, but I'm afraid I can't say for sure. As I told you, once I started school I didn't spend much time at the center. When I was there, my mother was very careful about me wandering around the property."

"Do you know if the center was used for anything after the official shutdown? Or if, perhaps, it took longer in reality than on paper to close the buildings?"

"I don't believe so, but I can't say with any certainty. My father had retired by then, so any information I received at the time was second-hand," she said, apologetic. "Why do you ask?"

"For the forensic analysis," I riffed. "It saves time if they know when the property had regular traffic, so they know when items were likely to have been introduced or transferred."

"Ahh." Her distracted tone suggested she believed me about as much as I did, but wasn't much bothered either way. "Well, if that's all..."

I took the hint and rose, adding, "I was surprised to find Mr. Tucker outside the door of my home yesterday. Was that your idea?"

"He didn't mention where you'd spoken," she said, smoothing her skirt as she joined me. "But Blake can be very persistent. And... protective."

I didn't doubt that. "Well, please thank him for me as well. I appreciate him checking on the young woman."

"Was that for Mr. Weber?" she asked.

I winced apologetically. "Another client, but I'm afraid I can't say more than that."

"Of course," she said, waving me out ahead of her. "I just wish we'd been able to find something to help you."

"Oh, you did," I replied, pausing in the hallway. "Investigation is like dark matter. You can tell something is there, even when you can't see it, by looking at the effect it has on everything around it."

Her cordial mask slipped and her voice was cool as she said, "Goodbye, Ms. Brennan."

37

I spent much of the next four hours squinting for address numbers, waving cars around me as I crowded onto secondary road shoulders, and occasionally staring at empty fields where supposedly someone used to live. Somewhere in there I also hit a disappointing drive-through. How bad does fast food have to be to disappoint you? Bad enough to not finish it and hope you don't get sick.

Those tasks left my mind free to obsess about whether I'd butchered quantum theory with Eleanor Dickey. Probably, since my understanding was based on half-heard snatches of a TV program in the background at Roger's the night before. That is, when I wasn't trying to figure out Eleanor Dickey.

Was it suspicious that she had treated me like a human being this meeting? How about that she hadn't asked more about Carly Whitmore, or about the potential grave at the Reform Center? (I hadn't mentioned the graveyard possibility.) Maybe. She could have been playing politics, something I sucked at and occasionally needed assistance navigating. Or maybe she didn't ask questions when she already knew their answers.

It was a relief to finally make my way toward the Reform Center.

The pine corridor bordering the juvenile facility was now familiar enough to anticipate the compound's nondescript driveway and slow accordingly. The gate was pushed shut but unlocked and unmanned near the end of the work day. I passed the pair of live oaks and the rotten palm and bore right at the split in the road by the admin building. Then I parked in the same spot Roger had first occupied Sunday, stepped out of my car and stretched.

Having seen Laney work—and perhaps more importantly, lived with her—I knew she ran a tight ship and would likely work until dusk. I'd arrived a little early and she was nowhere to be seen. Mike wasn't either, but he'd been wrapping up a deposition in the opposite direction and would join us soon. Maybe I should call Laney and let her know I'd made it. I dug around in my car for my cell and lifted it to the sky, shielding my eyes. I had half a bar of reception, depending on which way the wind blew.

"Hey! What are you doing here?" a man shouted.

A young man with dirty blonde hair in a long-sleeved T-shirt and cut-off olive cargo pants made a beeline for me.

I tucked my phone in my pocket and held up a hand in greeting. "I'm looking for Laney—Dr. Singh, I mean. She asked me to meet her here."

"And you are?" he asked, skeptically. He must be a grad student, but a small smear of dirt across his youthfully unlined forehead made me think of a child playing with dump trucks.

"I'm Sydney Brennan."

He stared blankly for a moment, mouth not entirely closed. Obviously, Laney hadn't mentioned to expect a woman, which sounded like something Laney would intentionally omit. I almost felt bad for him. Living with Laney had been challenging enough; I'd hate to think of her giving me grades for something other than cleaning the toilet. (C+, and for the record it was spotless.)

Pulling a walkie-talkie from his hip, he said, "Sorry. We can't be too careful. Believe it or not, a reporter tried to bribe me. I'll tell her you're here, but she's out in the field, so…"

"So she'll be here when she gets here," I said, smiling agreeably. "See, I do know her. Half an hour?" I guessed.

His face relaxed a little. "Yeah, that sounds about right."

"No problem. I'll be in my car, or wandering around somewhere."

He didn't look thrilled at the idea, but didn't object, either.

I added, "Oh, and another friend is dropping by, too. Mike Montgomery. So if you see him, don't cuff him."

He gave me a brief sideways stare, as if he didn't quite know what to make of my humor. Yeah, working for Laney must be difficult for him. Poor, earnest soul.

I ambled on the patchy brown grass toward the remains of an old pallet, nudging a piece of wood with my toe. The short bursts of conversation between the grad student and another popping, staticky voice faded into the distance. Once he was out of sight, I grabbed a light jacket from my car, stuffed its pockets with semi-larcenous, PI-type accessories, and headed for the abandoned admin building.

Assuming the front door was still locked, I picked my way through the scattered trash and vegetation to the back. The familiar cheap laminate door greeted me there, but the metal security bar brace was empty. A quick search revealed the two-by-four leaning against the wall amongst the weeds, a good ten feet or so away. Probably a safety precaution.

The door must have been used since I'd last opened it, or maybe the humidity was lower. The wood gave more easily than I remembered, though still emitting a piercing squawk that made me cringe and look around guiltily. I didn't see anyone, and no one ran to stop me, so I pushed the door closed behind me, far enough that no one passing by could see inside but not quite latching. Or squawking.

The door may have been slightly more forgiving, but the hallway carpet smelled and looked just as scuzzy as I'd remembered. I pressed my forearm against my nose to suppress a sneeze—unsuccessfully—as I pulled a pair of latex gloves from my pocket. No way was I touching the nasty walls and surfaces with my bare fingers this time.

I wriggled my fingers into my gloves as I stood at the threshold of the first room. The detached door, resting partially on the twin-sized mattress on the floor, made me uneasy. Granted, the vision of a mattress on a floor rarely gives you the warm and fuzzies, but this struck me as particularly *off*, to use Laney's word.

I stepped inside gingerly and got out my pocket flashlight for a better look. One hinge was still attached to the door (the same cheap laminate as the back), while the other hinge remained secured to the doorframe. I didn't see any obvious metal stress. Had the door fallen off, or been literally torn from its hinges? I couldn't tell—must be another course I'd slept through in PI school.

Grunting, I dragged the top portion of the door off the mattress. The pad had the cheap industrial look one might expect in a correctional center, but aside from some overall dinginess and an oval, yellowish stain near one edge, the design's blue vertical stripes were the only obvious marks upon it. It still had crisp rectangular corners, and no craters worn into its surface.

Dust motes swam in my anemic flashlight beam and I sneezed again, so suddenly I couldn't cover my face. My sinuses constricted and I waved my hand in front of my face as I stood breathing through half a nostril, as if that would clean the air.

No way had the mattress come from the Reform Center, or at least, no way had it been *used* there. I scanned the room's corners, but saw nothing except dead palmetto bugs and one of the door hinge's missing screws. No trash, no food, no condoms. It seemed unlikely anyone squatting would have cleaned up after him- or herself so thoroughly. Nor was it the most romantic place for someone to bring a John, even one with kinks. So what the hell had been going on here?

My hand moved to my pocket, fidgeting with the key as it had in my kitchen yesterday. *Soon.*

I made my way down the hallway, thankful my slacks were a forgiving navy and my shoes were flats. The natural light was dim to nonexistent, so I panned my flashlight over the floor debris—a wheel from a chair or cabinet, scraps of wood, a doorknob—but none of it looked either personal or recent. The rest of the doors off the hall were, as I'd experienced the previous time, closed and locked. Presumably one of the rooms was a bathroom, but I was happy to skip a years-abandoned institutional toilet.

It was later in the day than my previous visit, so the front office/reception area was darker this time and, if possible, even creepier. A framed group photograph hanging near the hallway caught my eye. Black and white, it was the posed kind that depicts an entire class arranged in rows. The building in the background looked like one toward the rear of the property that was now collapsing, and the few dozen boys of various ages were all white. I didn't see a date, but most Florida schools hadn't really begun desegregating in practice until the mid to late 1960s.

Male staff stood on the row ends, sometimes doubled up, wearing short-sleeved, white dress shirts with dark slacks. A handful of men near the front wore full suits. I squinted to see if Milton Dickey was among them, but I would have needed a magnifying glass and better light to distinguish individuals.

I glanced up when a shadow passed across the nearest window, like someone walking by outside. The structure was raised, so the few windows in the office were set high relative to the ground, and the glass was painted, not just filthy as I'd originally thought. Still, I knew I hadn't imagined the flicker. It could have been a bird or a vehicle or a Sasquatch (Florida is too warm for Yetis), but it was more likely Laney or her put-upon grad student.

On a whim, I grabbed the picture from the wall and set it on top of the metal desk while I rifled through the drawers again. The flashlight didn't reveal anything I'd missed the first time around, which left the bank of filing cabinets. The ones that had been itching at my brain since finding the key in my pocket last night.

Shoving an overturned chair out of my way, I thought I heard an answering scrape at the rear of the building and stopped to listen. Echo? Paranoia? Cat-sized palmetto bug?

I shivered at the thought before re-checking the filing cabinets as I'd done with the desk. Six empty drawers, each long enough to hold a toddler lying flat, screeched and rattled on their metal runners as I opened and closed them. No bets on humans, but surely I'd just summoned every dog in the Panhandle. I focused on preparing my excuses to settle my shallow breath and the tickling sensation between my shoulder blades.

Holding the key for the remaining locked cabinet, my anxiety was replaced by a child's giddy anticipation. I clenched my hand into a fist to keep it from shaking and grinned as the key turned easily and the oval lock popped out like a button.

The top drawer stuck, either with rust or disuse, throwing me off balance when it came free. I stretched on tiptoes to peer into the recesses, but there was nothing inside except dust and the original metal hanging folder frame, one side off-kilter where it had been dislodged. The middle drawer stuck almost as badly and was just as disappointing. Its metal hanging bars had been removed and lay inside, along with a small, rectangular piece of paper with the slight sheen of a thermal receipt. I pored over both sides with my flashlight, but couldn't distinguish any print and I dropped it back inside.

Hand on the pull for the bottom drawer, I took a deep breath that made me cough into my shoulder sleeve. Probably asbestos. The only things I'd neglected to bring with me were a bottle of water and a star wrongful death litigator.

Clearing my throat, I swallowed hard and braced myself. But the final drawer slid open as easily as wrapping paper on Christmas. Inside was a single unexpected, incongruous item: a small, purple, woman's bag, not much bigger than a clutch. Something about it made me shiver and glance over my shoulder, confirming I was still alone.

Something about it also said, EVIDENTIARY VALUE, as clearly as a neon sign with an arrow and exclamation points. If that was the case, what the hell was I supposed to do? Leave the bag where it was? Call law enforcement? Which agency? Federal, state, or local? It took me a moment to recall which county I was in. And what would I say? *I'd like to report a found purse. Was it stolen? No idea, but it's sitting here looking lonely.*

As much as I hated to bother him, this required a Roger consult.

Even at half capacity, he could see the big picture like a satellite, which was not one of my strengths.

I slid the drawer shut before moving to one of the windows. The fraction of a bar of reception I'd had by my car was now gone—could I blame the primer covering the windows? I stared at the filing cabinet. I hated to leave the purse behind, but it's not like anyone was going to sneak past me into the abandoned building while I called Roger from outside.

Suddenly a *skreeck!* rang out from the back of the building.

Someone was closing the door.

"Hey!" I yelled, even though it meant I was busted. "I'm in here."

Probably couldn't hear me, said my rational brain. While my lizard brain screamed, *Get the hell out! Now.*

I was learning to trust my lizard brain. Rounding the desk, I nearly face-planted in my treadless dress flats.

"Hey!" I yelled again, racing toward the back. "Wait!"

Down the hallway, then I slid into the door, slamming hard enough to drop my flashlight. The door didn't budge. The knob turned easily—it wasn't locked. I rammed my shoulder into the door again, this time on purpose. Nothing. I switched to the other shoulder. Still nothing.

Because someone had barricaded me inside.

38

J ust a mistake, not intentional, I told myself as I yelled, in a voice that would pass for calm to anyone not in my head, "Hello! You locked me inside. You need to open the door."

I paused to listen. No response. No sounds at all that I could hear, except the hammering that filled my chest and ears.

"Hey!" I screamed, pressing a gloved hand to the dirty door so I could pretend it wasn't shaking. "What's going on out there? Come on, somebody let me out!"

Pain shot through my wrists as I pounded on the door. "Hello!"

Don't be stupid, Syd. You need your hands. I took a step back, got into a side stance that would have made Vince and Glenn proud, and kicked the center of the door at brace height, about waist high for me.

I must have imagined a faint splintering sound because there was no obvious damage. I kicked again and lost my shoe. The outside brace was solid, but maybe I could get through the door itself. I slipped my shoe back on and kicked lower, but the strike was more desperate than deliberate. My hip twinged and I flailed for the wall as I lost my balance.

I left a small depression in the laminate surface, and slight buckling created a sliver of air space at the threshold. But I was not getting through that door.

No need to panic. Laney was meeting me. Mike was on his way, and he'd be looking for me. At most, I'd be uncomfortable for a while before they found me and teased me mercilessly for my singular ability to get locked inside an unoccupied building.

Unless someone had locked me inside on purpose.

But who would do that, and why? To keep me busy, keep me out of the way, keep me from seeing... what? Nothing good. And whatever it was could be happening right now, which meant I couldn't wait for someone to let me out.

Think, Brennan.

I grabbed my flashlight from the floor and rotated it slowly in my hands, end over end, focused on mastering its uneven balance until the shit-throwing monkeys settled down in my head.

Windows.

With enough ambient light to avoid running into the walls, I shoved my flashlight in my jacket and jogged methodically from room to room, ignoring the locked offices. But all the windows were painted shut, and no amount of yanking or swearing would open them.

The wood frame dividing the painted glass into small panes had held up surprisingly well. It would take serious effort to breach one and I didn't fancy climbing through shards of heavy glass. Not to mention, breaking a window seemed a little drastic for simply being locked inside with suspicions.

The front door. Wouldn't it be hilarious if the front door was unlocked and I'd never bothered to check? Hilarious in an *I'll laugh at this three years from now with my therapist* kind of way.

I'd forgotten the front entry was a pair of heavy wooden doors, secured by a pair of deadbolts mounted one above the other. I took a running start at it, as much as I could in my shitty shoes and with the desk in the way. A bit of hardware poked my side painfully on impact. Did I imagine a fraction of flex? Or maybe the give was in me and not the door. I switched sides and took another run, slamming hard enough into the split where they joined to thump the breath out of me.

Panting, I squinted at the doors. The sliver of light between them had probably been there before I knocked myself silly.

"Hello!" I yelled through the teensy gap, on the off chance that someone was standing on the doorstep. "Someone please get me out of here! Hello?"

No takers. I was still on my own.

I couldn't generate enough force to barrel through the front doors using running speed, but maybe I could put my legs to better use. I needed something to keep me from budging while pressing against the doors. The ginormous metal desk must weigh a couple hundred pounds, and with practically nonexistent legs it had a low center of gravity. Which was exactly what was called for. I danced from corner to corner, scooting each end a few inches at a time, struggling to move it close enough.

When the desk was eighteen inches from the doors, I climbed on top, raised my legs awkwardly into position, and *skreeek!* The desk shifted before I could even push in earnest. It needed some stabilizing as well.

Even empty, the metal filing cabinets probably weighed another hundred or so pounds apiece. I used the same walk-the-corners technique to haul the first cabinet into place. Cringing in anticipation, I gave the solid metal a shove. There was a moment of inertia before it fell, the impact rumbling through my feet and noise stopping my heart. Vision clearing, I saw the cabinet was still intact, so I knelt next to it and scooched it against the desk.

I stood, catching my breath before moving to the next cabinet, and even laughed as I imagined the look on Laney's face when she saw my contribution to the abandoned building's decor. But my laugh transitioned to a coughing fit. I buried my face in my elbow. Damn moldy dirt. Except, on a wheezing inhale, I began to wonder...

I closed my eyes (my *irritated* eyes) and muttered, "Please tell me there isn't—"

Turning toward the hallway, I saw wisps of smoke. And beyond the smoke, flickering light.

The building was on fire.

I staggered toward the back, arm over my mouth. Low flames like a Boy Scout's failing campfire attempt blocked the door. The smoke seemed to have opened my sinuses, and among the toxic fumes I tasted on the back of my tongue was a hint of gasoline.

I didn't know about its bones, but the building had a stucco, not tinder wood, exterior. I had some time before I was in imminent danger.

Or I would have, if the skanky carpet hadn't ignited at the back door.

"Sonuvabitch!" I slammed my open palm against the wall. Any evidence of whatever the back room had been used for was going up in flames. And if I didn't get out of here, so would I. After asphyxiating.

"Hello, somebody—anybody! Get me out of here!" I shouted, with no hope whatsoever of being heard.

Back in the reception area, I grabbed an old-school office chair with a heavy metal frame and veered toward the hallway. A piece of molding marked the end of the carpet. I jabbed at the strip with the chair legs until it split in the center and two-thirds came free. A little more jabbing and I had the corner of the carpet in hand. I yanked at the edge, but the tack strip fought me every inch of the way. My protesting back hit the opposite filthy wall when the other carpet corner came free.

With the leading end detached, the sides came more easily. I pulled and peeled the carpet away from the floor, revealing the once spongy padding beneath, coughing against nasty-smelling smoke that advanced from wisps to clouds. Sweat ran down my back and between my breasts, a product of the rising heat and the effort required to roll the carpet.

I'd hoped to get close enough to toss the carpet into the open office at the back, but in the past minute or two, the fire had found its purpose. And I was bringing its fuel closer.

Screw the combustible padding. It was time to beat feet.

I jogged with my trusty chair back to the reception area, to a side window facing the parking lot. It was the most visible to any idiot passers-by too blind to notice the building was on fire. My first strike at the window was too tentative. I broke a single pane of glass and didn't make any headway on the frame.

Panting, I rested my hands on my thighs, wiped the sweat from my face with my arm, and fought the urge to cry.

Think about who did this, Brennan. About who locked people in here so they could sleep on a mattress on the floor. The same kind of assholes who bury dead kids in unmarked graves instead of treating them like human beings. You gonna let those fuckers win?

I stood, seizing the chair back with shaking, rage-fueled hands. A banshee scream tore from my throat as I swung the chair like a base-ball bat, so hard it went through the window and kept going. My arms followed it through the glass, and I couldn't hold on. I watched the chair fly out of my hands, over the flames, and bounce to the pitted driveway.

Over the flames. Hunh.

In addition to the drop being farther than I'd expected (oh yeah, raised building), the ground was ablaze. Not an inferno, but enough that I wasn't going to jump in it unless that was my only choice.

"The building is on fire!" I yelled, ending with an angry-throated cough. Too bad I didn't have that water bottle. Or a bandanna.

I peeled off my jacket and tore off my sweat-soaked blouse. Then I zipped my jacket over my bra and tied my nasty shirt around my face, ignoring a dark smear on one sleeve.

The room's front windows were smaller than the side ones and set higher, but had the advantage of opening onto the portico, which didn't appear to be burning. The bottom of the window frame was chest height, maybe a little higher. I grabbed another heavy, metal-legged chair. My shoulder twinged as I swung upward, and when the chair bounced off the glass it nearly clubbed my head.

"Dammit!"

I climbed on top of the desk for a better angle. This time I swung the chair low, as hard as I could. The glass broke, splitting into large shards that cracked further when they struck the concrete outside. The chair caught in the window frame, and that's all that kept me from falling off the desk.

As the sound of breaking glass faded, I became aware of the dull roaring of the fire in the back. White noise that made my fuzzy, sweaty hair stand on end. And something else—had I imagined it?

"Sydney?" a man's voice called from outside. "Where are you?"

Oh, thank God. My chest hitched in an aborted sob as I dropped the chair over the back of the desk. I leaned toward the window, careful of the ragged glass and the gap, catching myself on the dirty wall. My shirt bandanna fell off my face as I screamed, "Mike, I'm in here! I'm trapped inside!"

Seconds later, he was racing through a smoldering black ring beyond the front steps, the grad student I'd spoken with earlier on his heels. Mike yanked fruitlessly at the front door before rushing to my window.

"Syd, are you okay?" he asked, reaching toward me.

"Careful of the glass," I said, jumping off the desk. "The back door is barred from the outside, and it's on fire."

"Go see," Mike said, and the younger man nodded and ran.

"Last time I checked, the side windows were a little warm right now, too," I said.

Mike rubbed the side of his face as he scanned the area. "Still are," he said. "Can you get through this one?"

It was the height and size of a typical bathroom window, barely wider than my shoulders. Shards of glass stuck to its frame like silica fangs.

"If I have to," I said. My fingers brushed the desk behind me. Moving that closer would help.

Mike nodded, then held up a finger as he walked toward the doors, disappearing for a moment. The center of the doors flexed the slightest bit before he returned. "I think I can pry these open. Can you wait that long?"

I glanced over my shoulder and blinked against flames that

advanced down the hallway, licking at the ceiling, but hadn't yet achieved its end. Gray smoke poured out the broad window I'd broken and was now being drawn toward the window we spoke through. "Yes, there's time—go!"

No way was I leaving without what brought me here in the first place. While Mike sprinted to his Jeep, I retrieved the framed wall photo and the purple purse from the filing cabinet. I shoved them both in a bright, cotton bag from my bottomless jacket pocket. I set the bag next to me on the desk and went back to work knocking out the remaining bits of window glass, just in case.

"Syd, you still there?" Mike yelled, returning with a pry bar. "There's not quite enough gap."

I dropped to sit on the desk and, gripping the desktop, placed my feet against the doors. One on each side of the split, I pressed with everything I had. My already angry back screamed, my legs quivered, and my eyes teared. One corner of the desk squawked as it slid an inch or two on the floor, but mostly it held position.

"Syd?" he called out again.

"I'm pushing!" I yelled back at him. Like some kind of hellish Lamaze.

There was another voice and words I couldn't make out over all the ambient noise. Was the roaring in my head, or coming from behind me? Exhausted, light-headed, I couldn't tell. The tongue that stuck to the roof of my mouth felt scraped with a wire grill brush. My blurring eyes focused on the ceiling above me, stained where it met the front wall, between blinks that grew longer and longer.

But the gap widened.

I felt a banging scrape through the wood as Mike wedged the metal lever between the doors and groaned with effort. Or maybe that was the sound of burning building behind me. The doors buckled outward another fraction of an inch.

"Almost there!" Mike promised, his voice grinding like the metal on wood.

The dim, vertical band of light between the doors grew wide

enough to silhouette the thick deadbolts, clinging desperately to their sheltered channels.

Suddenly, the whole thing gave way, doors bursting outward and me tumbling with them. The pry bar clanged on concrete as I slammed into Mike, bowling us over on the hard surface, me on top.

I couldn't move for a moment, just lay on Mike, lungs heaving and head swimming.

"Sydney?" He rose on his elbows beneath me. "Are you okay? Talk to me!"

I lifted my head from Mike's chest and watched his gaze alternate between my face and the smoldering building behind us. A shredded latex glove dangled from my wrist as I rubbed his cheek until the terror faded from his wide eyes. I grinned and said, "About time."

39

Laney sat next to me on Cecil's bumper in the parking lot while I sipped my third bottle of water. Mike's yellow Jeep was parked next to us, but most of the other non-law enforcement vehicles were gone.

She said, "You always swore you'd do anything to flash a fireman."

"No." I hugged my jacket more closely around me, adrenaline dump and evening temperatures getting to me. "*You* swore you'd do anything to flash a fireman."

The fire truck had left several minutes ago and the remaining crew was wrapping up, with law enforcement milling among them. We watched the activity intently, though likely for different reasons.

"Oh yeah," she mulled. "That *was* me."

I wasn't sure who I'd flashed—whichever first responder made me remove my jacket to clean and dress the cut on my arm. I'd put it back on for a few minutes while he administered oxygen I didn't think I needed, before I refused hospital transport.

Mike had loaned me a spare clean T-shirt from his gym bag, but I could really use another outer layer. One that didn't smell like a redneck fire pit. And I could use a shower. A long, hot shower, followed by a long, hot bath, and then maybe another shower...

"Syd," Laney said. "You there?"

I must have faded out while she was speaking. "Yeah?"

"This wasn't one of my people," she said.

I blushed, realizing I'd underestimated my friend. People tended to do that. Once. My excuse was that I hadn't seen Laney in years. I'd forgotten how well she guarded most of what went on in her brilliant mind.

"I don't think that's the direction the investigation is headed." I said, and nodded toward the building's exterior wall. Between the smoke stains and fire hose power washing, the freshly spray-painted words were barely legible: *GO HOME, ASSHOLES!!*

The firefighters had gotten the blaze under control quickly. Either the arsonist's intent hadn't been to burn the building to the ground, or he or she had done a poor job of execution. Someone had ringed the building with gasoline and lit a match, presumably after leaving the threatening message on the wall.

"But there was no one here except my crew," Laney said.

"And me," I said, swinging my feet to get my blood moving.

"We knew when you arrived," she countered. "We would have seen someone else."

I huffed something close to a laugh. "Maybe. No offense, Laney, but you're not exactly running Fort Knox."

"I didn't think I needed to," she said, rising. She tugged at the cuffs of her long-sleeved T-shirt and crossed her arms as if the evening chill was getting to her, too.

"Didn't you?" I asked softly. I pressed the heels of my hands to my exhausted eyes, then dropped them abruptly, unable to remember if I'd cleaned my hands. "Laney, why did you ask me to come here?"

"I'm sorry, Syd. I almost didn't," she admitted, twisting on her feet like a withdrawing twelve-year-old. "Thought I was overreacting. But now..."

"This isn't a court of law," I said. "Or a doctoral defense, or whatever your bone-digger analogy would be. You don't have to prove anything. Just talk to me. You said something felt *off*. Like what?"

"Someone's been here," she said. "Recently."

"Is that unusual, for a place like this?"

"No. Abandoned structures often get their share of clandestine traffic. But the people who use them don't usually clean up after themselves."

I hooked a thumb at the admin building. "Have you been inside?"

"Just the one time I found a familiar intruder," she said.

I told Laney about the mattress, likely now ash. She pointed excitedly before I'd finished. "Exactly the kind of thing I'm talking about! And signs of disturbance with very little actual destruction, or even rubbish."

"You mean around the parking lot?" I asked.

She shook her head. "Not just there, and that's what really concerns me. Someone has been going deeper into the property, even beyond our site. Why would one do that? It's not casual trespassing."

"Someone with a mission," I said.

The sky above was more dark than light, contrasting with several portable lamps set up in the parking lot. The air was smudged with a haziness born of residual smoke and humidity, and probably my irritated, leaking eyes. Laney's head swung toward an approaching figure. Even with impaired eyesight, I instantly recognized Mike by his height (ridiculous, standing next to me), and the silhouette of his broad but not beefy shoulders. They lacked the slight hunch they sometimes got, particularly indoors, and his long gait was faster than usual. He must have just finished his statement (Laney and I had already given ours).

"No wonder you don't need to flash a fireman," Laney noted in a low, appreciative voice.

Mike nodded to her but headed straight for me, arms extended, water bottle in one hand.

"I reek," I said.

He set his water on the car and pulled me to him. His breath ruffled my stinky, fuzzy curls as he said, "I remember. And I don't care."

I wished I could smell him—his shampoo, the stuff he squirted on his hair, his deodorant, even his B.O.—but I wasn't sure I'd ever smell anything again over the scent of char. He felt good, though, solid and warm and safe. I wanted to crawl inside his clothes and nestle against him, but I couldn't. Not yet.

"Didn't we do this already?" I asked, but couldn't bring myself to pull away.

"Tough," he said, and nearly crushed me before finally letting go. Mostly. He still hooked an arm through mine as he sat on the car next to me.

Laney was watching us. "I could loan you my motel room."

I could hear the embarrassment in Mike's voice as he said, "Sorry."

"Don't be," she said, grinning. "It's not every day a man rescues his lady from a burning building—you need to own it."

"Hey!" I protested. "I was already on my way out—"

Laney made a loud, penetrating shushing noise that stopped me in my tracks, as it always had. "Shut it, Syd. I need the romance."

I shook my head. "Fine. I take it you've met?"

Laney nodded and pointed. "Rather dramatically, outside that burning building."

Hers must have been the other voice I heard, not long before my escape. Everything after the doors burst open was a blur.

I had to clear my throat to ask, "What's the verdict? Are they leaning toward my 'detention' as inadvertent or intentional?"

"Hard to say." Mike paused, staring at me with an intensity that suggested something significant was coming. "I saw someone leaving."

"Holy shit," Laney muttered.

"My thoughts exactly," he said.

Mouth even drier, I reached for my water bottle, but it was empty. Mike handed me his before he continued.

"The guy was near the front of the building when I pulled in the parking lot. I didn't see much—dude in a baseball cap, jeans, long-sleeved shirt. Could have been anybody. He took off on foot that way," Mike said, pointing past the admin building, toward the other branch of the road that led deeper into the property. "I started to run after him, until I discovered we had more pressing concerns."

"So his waiting vehicle could have been somewhere between here and the grave site," Laney said.

"Seems that way," Mike agreed. "Not that I saw it."

"Neither did I. And I drove from that direction." Laney's head dropped suddenly toward her chest, a move I used to call *The Realization*. Her mouth twisted as she raised her head slowly, then inclined it toward a passing LEO. "They wanted to know whether there was another vehicle exit from the property—there isn't, that I know of. But I've only been here a couple of days, and I go straight from my parked car to the field. It does make me wonder, with the other signs I was telling you about, Syd."

I managed to find my voice again. Investigator mode. "What else did they want to know?"

"Who was here and who had access to the building—on paper, none of us. But in practice anyone could have, either from my crew or simply driving in off the highway."

"I thought you said you would have seen trespassers," I reminded her.

She took her seat on the bumper again, sandwiching me between her and Mike. "After some reflection," she said, "I'd prefer to think my team is naive about security to the possibility that my team is harboring an arsonist."

We sat in silence. Someone in an official-looking windbreaker passed close by, giving us a suspicious look, as if no one at an abandoned correctional institution could be totally blameless.

Once he was out of earshot, Laney said, "There was something else. They wanted to know if we usually kept the back door padlocked. I told them—like I told you—we had nothing to do with the buildings."

"Your field guy said there was a padlock when I sent him to check the back," Mike confirmed.

I closed my eyes and tried to recall the back door as I'd seen it the first time with Addy... the *then-empty* hasp mounted above the security bar. I shivered. It was getting hard to believe locking me inside was an accident.

And maybe a little hard to breathe.

Mike turned to me and said, "Okay, I think that's enough for now. If they're done with us, you're coming home with me."

Wouldn't that be nice? Even after years apart, I didn't need to see Laney's expression to read her provocative mind. I hated that I was about to disappoint both of us. That is, all three of us.

"I can't," I said. "I have to get back to Tallahassee."

Mike opened his mouth to argue, but closed it again and looked skyward. It was reassuring to see his brain was functioning at reduced capacity as well. "Addy," he said.

I nodded. "She's—" I stopped, not wanting to inadvertently involve either of them in yet another legally questionable drama. "It's complicated," I told Laney, who had leaned forward, waiting for me to continue.

"Fine, you're going back," Mike said. "But I'm driving."

"I can't just leave my car—"

"My students and I carpooled, so I'll drive your car to my motel. You'll probably be back here soon anyway," Laney said, then grinned. "And you know I'm an excellent driver."

She was anything but, at least during the time we'd lived together. I almost got sidetracked to argue—Cecil and I had been through a lot together, and I'd hate to see him harmed—but I didn't have the energy. Instead I asked Mike, "Are you sure about this?"

He threw his arm over my shoulder and pressed me to him. I nestled in gratefully as he said, "I can be there and back in three hours."

I surprised myself by saying, "Okay. Thank you."

Everyone stood so I could grab my emergency beach towel from a bag in the back, hoping to spare Mike's Jeep upholstery from my nastiness. His clothes weren't nearly as filthy as mine, but I doubted the slacks and button-down shirt he'd worn to his earlier deposition would be good for anything other than yard work.

Mike and Laney were talking logistics, but their words escaped me when I opened Cecil's driver door and saw on the floor, in addition to my purse, the blue batik bag of goodies from the admin building. I'd thrown it in the car after our escape and forgotten about it in the subsequent chaos. Glancing over my shoulder at the remaining law enforcement personnel, I swaddled the cotton bag possessively in my towel before slamming the door.

Laney followed us out driving Cecil, but stopped near the entrance to speak with someone in uniform. Mike watched in his rearview mirror until she'd finished, and at the first intersection we went in opposite directions. I cringed as she and Cecil drifted across the center line when she waved an arm out the window at me.

Mike turned the heat on, and I peeled off my jacket as the Jeep began to warm. Inside the pocket, I found—*yes, another pair of latex gloves.*

"What are you doing?" Mike asked, eyes mostly on the road.

Gloved up, I set the batik bag on my lap and ignored the framed photo to pull the small purse free. "This was in a filing cabinet in the office."

I stretched to turn on the vehicle's dome light for the search. No wallet or cards inside. Hard to say for sure, but the bag looked more fuchsia than purple to me now. I held it next to the steering wheel so it was in Mike's field of vision. "What color would you say this is?"

"Pink," he said, then shot me a look that suggested he was reconsidering helping me out of a burning building.

I sighed and closed my eyes.

"What?" he asked. "Syd, what's going on?"

I kept my eyes closed until I'd slipped the purse back into my fabric bag, unwilling to look at it. "I should have known you'd say pink. Because you're a man. Just like the corrections officer."

"What corrections officer?" Mike demanded.

"The one at Brummel Youth Academy." I pulled the pages from my purse, but there was no additional detail beyond "pink purse" on the property inventory. As much as I hated to, I'd have to check with Addy to be sure. "I think this bag belonged to Carly Whitmore."

40

I clicked off the dome light. With the odor of a near-death experience still clinging to me, it was easier to share the limited information I had about Addy's friend in a car in the dark. At least for me, though I may have been alone in that feeling.

"So let me get this straight," Mike said, gripping the wheel tightly. "Carly Whitmore is picked up for something relatively minor while still a juvenile. She's transferred to Brummel. You can't find any indication of a court hearing—"

"Not yet."

"—But she's released from Brummel. Before or after she turns eighteen?" Mike asked.

He'd interrupted me digging my filthy, creeping slacks out of my butt. (This afternoon had definitely exceeded their design specs.) I fumbled for my flashlight and flipped back and forth between the pages, skimming. "I'm not sure. According to Addy, before, but it looks like there are two different birth dates entered for her."

"Of course there are," Mike muttered. "So she's released from one juvenile facility—we don't know where she goes—but you find her purse in a different *abandoned* juvenile facility right before someone tries to burn it down. With you in it."

"If they really were trying to burn it down, it was a half-assed effort," I countered, suppressing a sudden, powerful urge to cough.

"Because he was interrupted," Mike said.

I had no response to that.

"Why didn't you give the purse to the authorities back at the site?" he demanded.

"Which ones?" I asked.

A passing car's headlights lit up Mike's face. It wasn't enough illumination to appreciate the full intensity of his pale eyes, but God, the man was sexy when he was pissed.

"Sorry," I said. "But I'm not just being lippy. Who even has jurisdiction? And over what crime?"

A low, frustrated rumble rolled from the driver's side. "*Lippy*," he snapped. "Is that another fucking word for evasive?"

His anger surprised me. Mike was usually the even-tempered one, the peacekeeper. I stared at his silhouette, wished I could see him, preferably without him seeing me. My own voice was as composed as I could achieve when I replied, "I was trying to call Roger when I realized the building..."

I faltered, wary of the tremor creeping into my voice. This was why I didn't do calm. "When the shit hit the fan," I continued, with my own edge of anger. "That's all I want, is to talk to Roger first."

"Of course you do," he said, words thick with insinuation.

"Are you jealous?"

"Not really, because you won't tell him everything either."

"What's that supposed to mean?" I demanded.

He paused as we approached a road sign. After we'd passed it, he answered, "It means you dole out bits and pieces to everyone."

"Bits and pieces of what?"

"Your life."

The words resonated with gravity and finality. My mouth hung open, senseless with shock. But that state didn't last. Silence rarely did for me. "This from the recent divorcé who didn't even bother to mention he was married? How much have you told me about your wife?"

"Ex!" he shouted, and silence rang out in the car as the single syllable faded away.

I turned my face to the cool glass, watched the grass margin at the edge of the road, occasionally swelling with a patch of weeds in our headlights. I knew nothing about Mike's family. Not that he was exactly well-acquainted with mine. (In my defense, I hadn't been well-acquainted with mine until recently, either.)

Was not knowing anything about each other's families a sign of something wrong with our burgeoning relationship? Maybe. I was inclined to think it more an indication of something "wrong" with us as individuals, or wrong with our relationships with our families. Was this wrongness something we needed to address? Probably. But not now, when we couldn't focus on any root issues, but could channel all of our anxiety about everything else in the world at each other.

I rested my hand on Mike's upper arm in the dark. "I'm sorry."

He pulled it to his lips for a quick kiss. "Me, too."

I thought he'd leave it at that, but a mile or so down the road, still holding my hand, he picked up as though he'd never stopped talking. "That's the second time—just in the past few months since we started 'officially' dating—I thought I might lose you."

I bit my lip to keep it from trembling.

"I don't like it," Mike said.

"Neither do I," I admitted.

"All right then. As long as we're in agreement." And he adjusted his grip so our arms rested in the center, hands intertwined the remainder of the drive to Tallahassee.

IN A GESTURE of good faith openness (and maybe a touch of *you're on your own legally—you're the one who wanted to know*), I admitted to Mike that Addy and I were staying with Roger. Instead of dropping me off there, I had Mike take me to get a rental car. With so much happening, I didn't dare risk being without a vehicle for a moment.

Plus it seemed like a good idea to be driving something unrecognizable.

It occurred to me on the way to Roger's house after picking up a car that I should have called ahead to Addy since I didn't have a key. I wasn't afraid she'd run off (okay, maybe a teensy tinsy bit), but she might be in the shower or sleeping.

There were two cars parked on the brick drive when I arrived, Roger's and a sedan I didn't recognize, so it seemed at least gaining entry wouldn't be an issue. Good thing—the stone facade looked unassailable, almost primeval with the flickering gas sconces. As I approached, my meager belongings wrapped in my beach towel like a hobo for easier carrying, I flashed back to the first time I'd been to Roger's house with Ralph. Hard to believe it was just last year. I smiled as I remembered Ralph asking if he needed to bow.

I was still smiling when the door swung open to reveal an exhausted, red-eyed Roger. His hair was wet, as if he'd showered recently, and I could swear his shirt was misbuttoned.

"What happened to you?" he asked, stepping aside to let me in.

Oh yeah, speaking of disheveled. "Long story," I said.

I'd thought to head straight for the shower, but Roger stretched his arm across the narrow space, barring my way. My exhausted brain fixated on the wall beneath his hand. Was it the same color as the flooring (slate), or did it just look that way at night with the recessed ceiling lights? It made me feel like I was in a cave that would be blissfully, reassuringly cool to the touch.

"Sydney," Roger said, snapping me back to attention, "Give me the short version."

I tried to come up with an answer that wouldn't unduly alarm him—after all, the danger had passed—but for some reason, my brain wouldn't cooperate. I blurted, "Somebody tried to burn down the administration building at the Reform Center with me in it."

Roger blinked slowly, ran his hand over his face and seemed to find a patch he'd missed while shaving, rubbing that spot again. "That *was* the short version," he conceded. "Are you okay, and what do I need to know now?"

Standing in the foyer, I suddenly became aware of the unnatural, expectant hush in the house. My heart sped up as I asked, "Where's Addy?"

"She's fine. What about you?"

"No harm done," I said, gesturing at my intact body while I once again attempted to marshal my thoughts. "Something else has been going on at the Reform Center, something that might involve Addy's missing friend. Give me a day and I'll have more for you."

Roger lowered his voice. "You think she's dead?"

"I don't know," I said, getting a glare in return. But I wasn't avoiding committing; I truly didn't know. "It's a definite possibility."

He leaned back against the wall, bumping a piece of artwork I'd never bothered to look at and couldn't see now, except for its ornate frame. He pinched the bridge of his nose, muttering, "This goddamned world."

I glanced down the hallway toward the kitchen and living room, straining my ears for voices. I thought one of them was Addy's.

Roger straightened and said, "Don't tell her tonight."

I almost asked, but knew why when Roger wouldn't look at me— his father had passed. "Roger, I'm so sorry."

He nodded, staring at his feet, which still wore dress shoes. "I know, Syd. Addy's in the kitchen, with Deidre. She's not doing well. Deidre, that is. But Addy's helping. That kid... both parents gone at her age. Well, years ago, so even younger. Can you imagine?"

"*I* can't," I said significantly. But I suspected Roger's story wasn't so different.

He shook his head, voice cracking slightly as he said, "Amos and Loretta were my mom and dad, the only ones I ever needed." A sad smile crossed his face as he finally lifted his eyes. "Addy likes hot chocolate because her mom taught her to make it before she died. And now she's making it for Deidre. I know Addy is rough around the edges, but she has a generous spirit."

"Kind of like a man sheltering a runaway while his father's dying?" I asked.

His face flushed slightly, but I couldn't tell if he was embarrassed or trying not to cry. "Go get cleaned up, Syd," he said. "Before you mess up my furniture."

ddy and I sat at the dining table the next morning. We had just eaten breakfast, our earth-toned ceramic plates and coffee mugs still cluttering the table. Bananas and apples and oranges filled a large, matching bowl.

I knew they were real—I'd eaten an apple the night before—but the bright bag resting on the table somehow made the fruit look plastic.

"Where did you get it?" Addy asked, staring at the purse.

The color had drained from her face so quickly, Addy's lips were indistinguishable from the cream cheese smeared in the corner of her mouth. I was afraid she'd vomit her bagel.

"Is it Carly's?" I asked.

I almost protested when Addy reached for the bag, but couldn't bring myself to make her put on gloves. Its evidentiary value was questionable already, and if it was her friend's, Addy had probably handled it before.

"It used to have a skinny strap," Addy said, running her fingertips lightly over tiny, triangular clips at the sides. A fold-over flap secured the bright bag with a magnet-type button. Addy opened it slowly, as if hesitant to invade her friend's privacy. Or perhaps afraid of what she'd find.

I'd thought there was nothing inside the purse, but I hadn't searched it in daylight, and I hadn't known its owner.

I didn't often see Addy's hands, hidden away in her sleeves and pockets, and I was surprised how adult they looked, even with her nails short and unpainted. She unzipped a small compartment inside. Digging one-fingered, she pulled something free from the pocket, a bobby pin adorned with a tiny enamel daisy.

"She got this from me," she said, swiping a tear from her face as she stared at the hairpiece. "Who had her purse?"

"I don't know. Remember that building we went inside at the Reform Center? I found it in a drawer there," I hedged.

I hadn't told Addy about the fire. She hadn't seen me before my shower and was in bed by the time I retired, though in the dark she had asked about the lingering smoke odor in my hair. Hopefully my pillow didn't stink and this morning's second shower had finished the job.

Addy tucked the pin back inside, closed the purse and set it gently on the table. "Why?" she asked. "Who would have put it in that creepy place?"

"I don't know," I admitted, rising to bus my dishes. "There's a bigger picture that I can't see yet. But I'm working on it."

After rinsing my plate I topped up my coffee, then stood with the shiny refrigerator door open, wasting electricity. The assortment of milks in Roger's vast fridge baffled me. Had he purchased one of everything to accommodate his guests, or did he actually consume skim, 2%, and half-and-half on a regular basis? Removing the 2% revealed almond milk in the next layer back. The only thing missing was goat.

Or maybe I was just focusing on Roger's strange gastronomic habits to avoid talking with Addy.

I sighed and returned to the table, settling carefully next to Addy in my chair. My lower back and shoulders ached from the previous day's adventures in furniture moving. I winced as my jeans brushed against a cut on my shin that had needed more bandage power than I'd found in Roger's guest bathroom. Which was to say nothing of the gash on my arm.

I'm working on it, I'd said. And how exactly was I doing that?

My natural inclination was to do a deep records dive, looking for patterns in arrests and releases and missing persons. Were there more young women unaccounted for? Yes, because there were always young women unaccounted for. But was there a connection among those women? If so, was that connection prior- or post-arrest? Or did it lie within their incarceration?

Accessing those records from multiple agencies would be next to impossible, and it would take time I didn't have. Plus, like Addy, I needed to keep a low profile around said agencies. I needed a new approach.

I closed my eyes and recalled the back room in the admin building, presumably scorched beyond recognition now. The moldy, dusty funk that made my chest tight, and the mattress on the floor that made it even tighter. Its condition, and that of the room generally, suggested no one spent much time there, that it was a place of transition. Which might also suggest individuals were there voluntarily, on their way to—what they thought at least—was something better.

And yet, there was the bar on the back door. The window painted shut, and no handy chair to break it. The door removed from its hinges.

Absent more detailed information from Brummel—and I wasn't holding my breath—it seemed pointless to try to figure out where Carly was now. But if, as I suspected, Carly was not an isolated case, the pattern might not begin with her arrest. What had she done, or where had she been, that clued someone in that she was susceptible? That she could be used. That she could be enticed—or forcibly taken—to that abandoned building.

Someone had to have heard something. Word travels like gas-fed fire among the vulnerable, especially when it's something new to fear. Ginger said she'd sensed an uneasiness among the girls and young women, but didn't know the source beyond some fabled, disfigured boogeyman. I'd been to some of the shelters often enough lately to be an honorary staff member, and I didn't think I'd get anything more from them. So where else should I be looking?

I opened my eyes and found Addy staring into the distance.

For many people, "homeless" conjured dirty old men looking for handouts, so I phrased my question to her carefully. "Where do young people who are... *between places* hang out?"

Addy turned to me, but seemed unfocused, as though she'd also been lost in thought and was having trouble finding her way back. Like me, she wore no makeup, and she bit her naked lip so hard it made a white and pink checkerboard. Instead of answering, she asked, "Do you think Carly's still alive?"

I wasn't sure whether I was sad or relieved she'd gotten there on her own. Probably both.

"I don't know," I said. "I'm afraid Carly got tangled up with someone who makes a habit of taking advantage of people like her. Girls and young women who don't have anyone else to watch out for them. The problem is, I don't know where Carly stayed before she was picked up, or where she went when she got out."

"So figuring out what other girls like her do is the next best thing," Addy said.

"Bingo."

"I don't know. I haven't been here long enough." She went back to chewing her lip, but a moment later realized, "I'll bet I know someone who has."

I thought back to my recent visit to the house where Troy was crashing. "The chick who gave you a ride to Cooper's and then ratted you out," I guessed.

Addy nodded.

"She owes me now—she won't talk to you, but all I have to do is call her. On one condition." Gripping the edge of the table, she said, "I'm going with you."

"No, you're not," I said, shaking my head firmly. "Someone might see you."

She threw her arms up and scoffed, "Like I'm on *America's Most Wanted*."

It's true, Roger and I had discussed the unlikelihood of any organized effort to find her. The Department of Children and Family Services wouldn't exactly reroute satellites and send SWAT teams to bust down doors anytime soon. It would require coordination among multiple agencies in multiple jurisdictions to find Addy, and the sad fact was that *no one* stopped everything they were doing to try to track down a runaway.

But my discussion with Roger was before yesterday's events at the Reform Center when I found Carly's purse and nearly became a crispy critter. With the motive behind the arson unknown, I had to ask myself if anyone knew of Addy's connection to Carly. For that matter, who knew of her connection to me?

"Sorry," I said, "but we can't risk it."

Addy sprang from the table, nearly cracking me in the head with her empty plate and juice glass as she passed. "*We can't risk it*," she mocked in a whining voice. "It's my choice."

I set my mug down carefully, leaned back and crossed my arms. "Actually, it's *my* choice who tags along with me. And you bitching about it won't change that."

Her heavy plate rang as she slammed it in the stainless steel sink. "Fine. Then as soon as you're gone, I'm leaving. Maybe I can't go with you, but you can't make me stay here, either."

I jumped from the table as abruptly as Addy had, in her space before she could say boo. "I get that you don't care about me, but what about Roger? What do you think happens to him if you get picked up, and where you've been comes out?"

She looked away, her face flushing a color that nicely complemented the streaks in her hair.

"After everything Roger has done for you?" I pressed, but she didn't reply. "Yeah, that's some generosity of spirit all right. Fine, make your goddamned call. We leave in ten minutes."

42

"Don't touch the radio," I warned.

"I was trying to figure out the heat," Addy said, voice almost apologetic. She leaned forward, staring through the windshield at overcast sky peeking through heavy tree canopy. Back to wearing her own sweatshirt and pants, she tugged the sleeves over her hands.

I've spent enough time on the road to be an old hand with rental car climate controls, though windshield wipers still sometimes give me fits. I flipped a switch, adjusted a dial and heard the rumbling rush of warm air, followed by Addy's soft, *Thanks.*

I tried not to be angry with Addy. And I wasn't. Not really. She was a pain in the ass (and an excellent argument for using birth control), but I would have done the same thing in her circumstances. And yet, my mind kept returning to Roger making funeral arrangements with his sister at this very moment. The last thing he needed was more drama, and I couldn't help feeling Addy was going to bring exactly that.

We sat in the shade on a street dominated by single-story residences that had been converted to low traffic businesses—accountants, attorneys, etc. I'd parked next to a therapist's modest gray bungalow that currently appeared unoccupied. A small magnolia, barely the height of the building's roof, bloomed in its front yard. I'd cracked my window, and if the wind shifted, I'd asphyxiate from the overpowering sweetness of its broad white flowers.

Opposite lay one of Tallahassee's many designated green spaces, this one not large enough to merit a parking lot. Several young people (there was that old fogey feeling again) lounged against the metal bars of a dome-shaped jungle gym, warming themselves in the sun and kicking at the wood chip mulch that had nearly disintegrated beneath it.

"You sure about this?" I asked.

"Yeah, no problem," Addy said.

Of course it was no problem—this was Addy in her element. With people her own age in similar lousy circumstances. Still, there were good guys and bad guys everywhere, and I'd feel like a total jerk if she ran into one of the latter.

"We're just looking for names of people they might be worried about, either because they're into something, or they haven't been seen for a while," I said. "Or anything unusual."

"Got it." She threw her door open. "Back in a minute."

Addy jammed her hands in her hoodie pockets and strode across the street like someone who wanted out of the cold, the way only a native Floridian can.

Distance and bulky clothes with hoods and knit caps muddied gender, but it appeared three of the figures were female and one male. The man wasn't much taller than the women, and his pallor gleamed, even from across the street. He retreated to the back of the jungle gym as Addy approached, threading his legs through the bars. Two of the women, dark-skinned and alike enough in bearing and physique to be sisters, drew closer to each other. The other bounced easily away from the metal frame and stood with legs apart, tugging at a ponytail so blonde it was almost white.

The blonde abruptly stepped toward Addy and postured, in a black puffy jacket and red scarf, like a lead singer bitching about her ex in a music video. It didn't seem to faze Addy, who stood with her hands still in her pockets. Soon the blonde settled back against the jungle gym bars. I wondered if the sun had warmed them or their metallic cold still pressed through her jeans.

They chatted for a minute or two—with her back to me I surmised Addy's participation—until Addy shook her head. She turned toward the other two women, who sat on the same horizontal bar pressed against each other from shoulder to knee. Even bundled from the chilly night, they were both so tiny their mismatched layers blended to give the appearance of a single broad person. They seemed to shrink even smaller under Addy's scrutiny.

Addy shook her head again and turned to leave, until the man slipped deftly through a triangular gap in the bars, walking beneath the dome and sticking his head through on Addy's side. He said something, and the blonde yelled at him indignantly, ponytail flying. He calmly raised his middle finger at her (*man after my own heart*), finished speaking, then sidled out the back of the metal frame as if he were boneless. He continued past a tight patch of azaleas, gaudy pink flowers mostly spent, and disappeared.

Head down, it was impossible to see Addy's face as she crossed in front of the car. She flung open the passenger door and flopped onto her seat.

"Well?" I asked.

Cheeks flushed from the cool morning air, she blew into balled hands before pointing at the heater. It wasn't *that* cold. I rolled my eyes as I started the car and obliged.

"Did you get a name?" I asked, both impatient and leery of making her feel guilty if she hadn't.

Addy ceased her hand-warming, and her lightly chapped lips spread in the kind of grin I hadn't seen since her chocolate dessert at the Italian restaurant. "I got two," she said proudly.

WE SPENT the rest of the morning checking out the other hangouts on our list, adding three more names for our trouble.

I'd also brought the framed photograph from the Reform Center with me, thinking maybe Frank could give me some pointers on tracking down Pinky Guy's identity. That is, until I remembered Blake Tucker watching me outside the Archives earlier. I didn't know if he was working with Pinky Guy or not, but I didn't relish either man seeing Addy while she went in the building with me or—even scarier—waited in the car. I'd give Frank a call from Roger's instead. Maybe he could pull some things together for me and, if I was extra nice, stick around after hours tonight if need be.

I didn't want to take Addy into a restaurant either, but our bellies were growling so we hit a drive-through for lunch. (One of the advantages of driving a rental car—Cecil wouldn't smell like onion rings.) We sat with the windows down in a corner of the parking lot that backed onto a patch of pine trees. In typical Tallahassee fashion, the temperature had easily risen twenty-five degrees since we'd left Roger's that morning, so we'd both lost a layer. I could have done without the button-down shirt that covered my tank top, too, or at least rolled up the sleeves, but didn't want to expose the poorly bandaged cut on my arm.

Addy balled up her burger foil and announced, "I hate Florida." Then she wiped her hands before pulling her hair into a ponytail and fanning at her neck.

"I don't think you'd do well in cold weather," I said, sipping at a cup more ice than soda. I couldn't seem to drink enough today, perhaps a residual effect of yesterday's fiery close call.

"True," she admitted, "but it's like North Florida can't decide. Hot or cold. Just pick one already."

The straw honked as I tugged it up and down, prospecting for more liquid. No luck.

"We headed back to Roger's?" Addy asked, as I started the car and pulled out onto the street.

"I want to make a quick stop first," I said.

We pulled into the gravel parking lot at Cooper's a few minutes later and Addy asked, "You buying?"

A weight lifted when I saw Glenn's truck in the parking lot. It was hard to imagine a place I felt Addy was safer than at Cooper's—or anywhere else—while Glenn was in residence.

"Yeah," I said, "I could use a shot or two. You can drive us to Roger's from here, right?"

Hope and suspicion warred on Addy's face, and I laughed. "I know you're not that gullible."

"You're wound so tight, you could use a few shots," she said.

"No doubt," I said, as I noticed a familiar blue sedan with plastic for its back window. It was parked between us and the front door, the driver still seated behind the wheel. I cleared my throat before telling Addy, "Stay here. I'll be back in a minute."

My legs moved stiffly as I crossed the fifteen or so yards separating us. Turtle had parked nose first and at a wonky angle. The plastic sheeting made him nothing more than a dark blur as I approached. I held my breath rounding the rear of his car and wondered if he was pointing a gun at me.

Just keep walking, Brennan. Keep walking.

The driver window was open, and Turtle's wiry, scarred forearm rested on the door frame. I felt him scrutinizing me in the rearview mirror, even though I couldn't see his face. I stopped at his door, an arm's length away. Turtle's long hair was unkempt, straying into red-rimmed eyes. I doubted he'd shaved since I'd seen him, and the miasma of body odor from his dingy cotton undershirt made me wonder if he'd showered, either.

His right hand rested below my line of sight. I monitored it with one eye as I nodded and said, "Turtle. You here to see Glenn?"

His intense stare made the space between my shoulder blades tingle. "What day is it?" he asked.

"Wednesday," I said.

"No shit?" he demanded, seemingly shocked by the calendar.

"No shit," I confirmed. I waited, but he didn't ask a follow-up question, and his moment of clarity faded. He almost seemed to forget I was there, treating me as transparent as a pane of glass. "Be right back, Turtle."

Addy had been watching from the rental car. "Who is that guy?" she asked, as I opened the back door.

"Someone you don't need to know," I said, grabbing the Reform Center photo from the floor. "You remember Glenn?"

"Of course," Addy said. "What do you think I am, an idiot?"

I ignored her attitude. "I need you to go into the bar and tell Glenn his friend Turtle is out here. And I need you to do it without even looking at that guy in the car."

"Okay," she said, voice rising at the end with girlish uncertainty.

"After you let him know, stay inside until one of us tells you otherwise. Got it?"

"Yeah, I got it," she said.

"Good. Go now." I told her. "And keep your hood up."

We left together, but I peeled off to circle Turtle's car from behind again, carrying the photo. I was hoping he'd focus on me since I was arguably the nearest potential threat.

"Turtle, you remember me?" I asked. When he didn't answer, I said, "I'm with Glenn. We came to see you."

He still didn't answer, and I added, "Me and Baby Bear."

That time something flickered in his face, for good or ill I couldn't say. I stepped closer, though the primitive part of my brain said I was within his strike range. "Remember, we were talking about the Reform Center. I'm trying to track down some of these guys. I was wondering if you recognize anybody in this picture."

I held the image toward him, but he wouldn't look at it. "Who are you?" he asked.

"You know me, Turtle; I'm with Glenn."

But he kept staring at me, so hard and constant I wanted to close his dry, bloodshot eyes for him, if only for a blink. He repeated, "Who are you?"

"I'm the one who's gonna get the motherfuckers," I said.

Turtle's lip curled to reveal his chipped incisor. "Now I remember; I liked you."

He took the photo from my rigid hand, resting it on the steering wheel while he pulled a pair of reading glasses from somewhere before hunching forward for a better look. My monkey brain screamed in protest as I drifted closer, and my jeans snagged on a jagged bit of rust when my hip brushed the metal door. Turtle ignored me, his index finger tracing slowly around the adult periphery.

"Dick, dickey, dickey," he muttered. I noticed a dark-purple spot on his nail when he pressed his finger to the glass, over Milton Dickey's much-younger form.

He continued tracing, once around the group, then again. Paused. "You were a peckerhead, too." He tapped a knuckle against the glass. "Wading into shit. Always wading into shit."

"Who?" I whispered, counting pale-white faces so I could identify the guard later. "What's his name?"

He didn't seem to hear me, and his voice faded in and out, barely audible. "From that nasty, fucked-up trigger setting off where it didn't belong, all the way up to your goddamn eyeballs, seeing what they had no business seeing. Always wading in."

Intent on the photo, both of us jumped when Glenn appeared and wedged his body between mine and the rearview mirror, forcing me to make room. "Hey, man. What's this?" he asked.

Turtle's lips bared the rest of his teeth. "Just in time, Baby Bear. We're gonna adios this asshole." Turtle turned to me and demanded, "Isn't that right?"

Glenn glared at me and his head twitched in a brief shake as I said, "I'll take care of him."

"You'll *take care of him*?" Turtle asked, his mocking voice grating across my tightly strung nerves as his eyes burned through his glasses. "Bullshit."

"Turtle," Glenn barked, pulling his eyes from me, "if she said she'll do it, she'll do it. Her word is my word."

Turtle's chest and throat vibrated with a crescendoing groan. I flinched as he suddenly lifted the frame, slamming it against the steering wheel to the sound of cracking glass. "I want to be there."

"Not happening, bud," Glenn said, calmly taking hold of the photo.

Turtle resisted, fingers clamped on the frame. Shards of glass shifted, a few falling free to Turtle's lap with a faint, grinding clink. Glenn tugged harder, and I winced as a stray sliver pierced the padding adjacent to his thumb. Blood trickled toward his wrist as he handed me the photo. He wiped his hand on his pants and gestured toward my car with his chin.

I nodded. *Understood—I'm out of here.*

I didn't look back, but I heard Turtle's voice raise as I hightailed it to the rental car. Addy was already there, presumably on Glenn's instruction. I shook the last of the glass onto the ground (*sorry, Glenn*), then handed the photo to Addy and fell into my seat.

"What the hell—" she asked.

"Later," I said, starting the car. Glenn was leaning into Turtle's window, still standing and with no shots fired, as we exited the parking lot.

My breath was mostly even by the time I reached the main road, but it caught in my throat when Addy said, "You know there's blood on this photo, right?"

"Yeah," I said. It was drenched in blood, whether we could see it or not. I just hoped Glenn's was the last of it.

43

The scene with Turtle made me uneasy, and my anxiety hadn't abated when we reached Roger's neighborhood a few minutes later. I pulled over a few houses away from Roger's and idled, watching.

"So Roger's rich, huh?" Addy asked.

"It certainly looks that way, doesn't it?" I said. With someone else, I might have made the distinction, *upper middle class*. For Addy, currently homeless and in foster care most of her life, *rich* would do. I wondered how Roger would describe his financial status.

Roger's neighbor on one side had fully enclosed his lot. The only break in the six-foot-high brick wall was a metal gate that—I'd noticed when I stayed with Roger previously—the neighbor's car barely squeaked through. On Roger's other side, the white columns of a large plantation-style house practically gleamed from the back of the lot. A single enormous live oak, one branch stretching nearly to the ground, broke up the expanse of immaculate, grassy yard. I'd never seen anyone there, never seen any vehicles emerging from its garage addition, but lights glowed in the early evening from a downstairs room. I suspected it was a widow(er) or retired couple.

"You know that's Deidre's car, right?"

"Yeah," I said.

The fire-engine-red two-door (one of those models that looked like a sports car, without the burden of actual high performance) was the only vehicle parked in Roger's driveway. No intruders lurked beneath the windows, and the curtains were closed.

"Are we going to sit here all day?" Addy asked.

A single, shiny black, high-end sedan had passed our vantage point, and only once. I sighed, reluctantly put the car in Drive and parked in front of Roger's house. The rental wouldn't go unnoticed there for long, but parking on the pristine street would attract even more attention.

I thought Addy would bolt from the car, but when I opened the driver's door, she still hadn't moved. "What's up?" I asked.

Her lips puckered like a kid about to try an annoying new noise before she asked, "Are we going to Roger's dad's funeral?"

I was appalled to realize I hadn't even thought about it. "Do you want to go?"

"If you think Roger would want us there," Addy said. At least, that's what her words said. Her fidgeting hands, her refusal to look at me, her low, child-like voice said, *Yes, I want to go.*

"I don't know when it'll be yet, but if we can safely go, we will."

She nodded, but continued avoiding eye contact. I was still missing something. And then it hit me—anxieties weren't always existential. Sometimes the social ones felt just as pressing.

"Don't worry," I added. "I don't have anything to wear, either. We'll figure something out."

The wrinkles eased from her mouth and forehead. "Cool," she said, trying for nonchalant, but tumbled from the car so quickly she nearly got hung up in her seat belt.

This time I had a key. We let ourselves in, dropped our stuff in our room, and headed for the kitchen. Deidre sat in the living room, feet tucked in the chair beneath her as she stared into the distance.

"Welcome home, ladies," she announced, lifting a sweaty lowball half-full of clear liquid. The glass's simplicity doubtless belied its price tag.

"Hey, Deidre," Addy said uncertainly.

"Maybe we should do a load of laundry while we can," I said. "Addy, why don't you gather up your dirty clothes?"

She didn't argue.

I settled at the end of the couch nearest Deidre and watched Addy retreat to our bedroom.

"You think I'm being a bad influence," Deidre said, sipping deliberately at her glass.

Her makeup was tasteful, if a little heavy. Deidre lacked her Amazonian sister's easy elegance (and height, which is how I'd borrowed her clothes), but she was attractive and dressed well. Her emerald blouse hinted at cleavage without shoving it in your face, and her slingback heels matched her beige, wide-leg slacks.

"Actually, I'd join you if I didn't have work to do," I admitted, sighing. I rested my head atop the seatback, then scooted my hips forward to ease the neck strain. "You holding up okay?"

"The funeral is Saturday," she said.

Would Addy have had a court date by then? Or a temporary order, or whatever was necessary to get everyone off our asses? Maybe I could sneak back to my house for some black clothes. If I knew what I wanted, or even what I had, Ben could get them for me when he fed my fish.

"You're the one who talked to Emma, aren't you?" Deidre asked.

"Yes, I am." I waited for her to comment about the evening I'd met her friend, and how we'd managed to start a brawl in the strip club. With a little help from Emma's cousin, John Driscoll (off duty at the time).

Instead, Deidre rose and said, "If Roger needs something, I'll be in my room."

She walked more steadily on her heels drunk than I could have done sober.

The guest bedroom had a small desk, but I camped out with my laptop and notebooks and paperwork at the dining table instead and began working my way through the names we'd gotten that day. I was cringing at my findings when Addy plopped down in a chair next to me a few minutes later.

"I would have thrown your pants in, but they're ruined," she said. "There was a hole in the leg, and some kind of stain, and they smelled like a dumpster fire. What did you do to them, anyway?"

I'd already tossed my torn, bloody blouse in Roger's trash. "That's the PI life," I said, though thankfully it *usually* wasn't. "But I appreciate the effort."

"No big. Any luck on the names?" she asked.

I hesitated.

"You know, you wouldn't even have those names without me," she said. "And I am an adult."

"Debatable on the former, wrong on the latter," I said. But Addy did have a vested interest. "Not much. Luck, that is. And I'm afraid the only news I have so far is bad. But I'm about to call a friend I hope can help."

My brief chat with Deidre had made me decide consulting John Driscoll was worth the risk, as well as giving me an in. But that didn't stop me from crossing my fingers under the table as his phone rang.

"John, this is Sydney Brennan. I don't have a current phone number for Emma, and I was wondering if you could give her a message for me," I said, feeling a pang of unjustified guilt for something that wasn't even a lie.

"Is this about her friend's dad dying?" he asked.

I blinked in surprise. "Yes—how did you know?"

"Emma mentioned it last night, said she might need to come to town if things went sideways."

"With Deidre?" I asked softly.

"Yeah."

My guts twisted and my eyes were pulled in the direction of Deidre's room. I lowered my voice even more and wished Addy wasn't watching me so intently. "Did Emma think that was likely?"

"I don't know," he said, wavering between empathy and distraction. "I guess she thought it was likely enough to give me and my couch a heads-up. Was there something else you needed?"

"Now that you mention it," I said, and ignored a sound that might have been John groaning on the other end. "Look, I've stumbled across an issue with some young women—possibly still juveniles—that may or may not be missing. And this might require investigating by you boys in blue, or I might just be paranoid. I believe a quick check could determine whether it's a complete waste of time, or whether it's worth you passing it up the line."

And taking all the credit was implicit. He didn't curse at me, didn't say anything at all for long enough that Addy bounced on her chair, wearing a big *what the hell's going on* face.

Finally he said, "Give me the names."

I read the list from my legal pad, slowly because John apparently recorded information by inscribing on stone rather than writing on paper. I dropped my eyes, put my own pen to paper so I wouldn't have to look at Addy when I provided the last name, and said, "I'm afraid she's dead. A body discovered somewhere near Quincy last month had the same name, but I couldn't find any more details."

I was too much of a coward to look up when Addy left the table.

"So she's not missing?" John said, as though unsure why I'd included a dead girl.

"Well, pending confirmation on the ID. And if there's a pattern, she might be part of it." I sighed and rubbed my suddenly aching forehead. "I'm not asking you to spend a bunch of time on this, but I'd appreciate anything you can tell me about them—whether you guys picked them up, whether they were officially reported missing, anything. I just... goddammit, I want to make sure if there's something here, we're not all missing it."

There was a lot of energy—a lot of *anger*—in my final words, more than I'd expected. I held my breath, wondering if I'd done the right thing calling John.

"Let me call you back," he said, and hung up.

I took my time starting a pot of coffee (not hard, since Roger's fancy chrome machine needed an advanced degree to operate), then followed Addy to our room. *Our* room—how many days had we been here? How many days had Addy been on the run?

I found her sitting cross-legged at the head of the bed, head down, picking at the seams of the quilt. The spread was simple out lovely, stars fashioned from scraps of warm red and brown fabric against a cream background. It was the kind of thing someone's grandmother might have made. I wanted to tell Addy to stop shredding it, but held my tongue.

"You always let the cops do your job for you?" Addy grumbled.

"No," I said patiently, the bed shifting slightly as I sat on the end. "But keeping people safe isn't my job. It's theirs."

"You're just passing it off. You don't care about Carly." Addy's chest heaved visibly with her breath.

I leaned forward, trying to force her to look at me, but she turned her head. "Addy, I do care about Carly," I insisted.

"No, you don't!" she yelled, and I saw the tears she'd been hiding. "You wouldn't even be here if it wasn't your job. Nobody cares about Carly! Nobody cares about any of us."

I kicked Addy's backpack on the floor, moving around the corner of the bed toward her.

"Nobody gives a shit!" was her final volley before she broke down, wailing. Sobs shook the teen's body so violently, it was as if she'd never cried before and all the heartache in her world was finally tearing its way out.

Addy struggled when I wrapped my arms around her. We were about the same size, so I sat on the pillow for a better angle, and her head slammed my chin. My teeth bit my lower lip, but I held on, held tight until Addy settled into rocking with me instead of grappling with me. Her body radiated heat, even through her sweatshirt, and she sucked air between sobs like she was running for her life.

"Shh, Addy. It's okay," I whispered, smelling Roger's shampoo as I rested my face against her hair. A traitorous tear snuck down my own cheek. "*I* give a shit. I promise."

44

I went to the kitchen to give Addy some space while she washed her face. Pouring myself a cup of coffee from the stainless steel carafe, my hands shook. I wanted so much to believe the kid would come out of this okay, but wide-eyed optimism was not my strong suit.

My cell phone rang in the midst of me stirring a truly obscene amount of sugar into my coffee. Setting the ceramic mug carefully on the counter and tossing the spoon into the sink, I dashed to my phone and snatched it from the dining table.

"John?" I guessed, though it seemed a quick response.

"Is he my competition?" Mike teased.

Relief filled me so completely, my legs gave out and I sank into the nearest dining chair. Mike had texted last night to let me know he made it home, but I hadn't realized how much I needed to hear his voice.

"Syd, you there?" he asked.

I nodded, then realized he couldn't hear my brains rattle. "Yes," I said. "John's more likely to be *my* competition than yours. After all, you've held the man in your arms."

A reference to the strip club brawl. I heard the metallic bang of the fire door's push bar at the bottom of the PD's office stairwell, and a moment later Mike said, "You mean John Driscoll? Him I threw over my shoulder. *Held in my arms* is reserved for you."

I told Mike about Roger's father dying, then briefed him on what I'd learned so far today, and what I'd hoped John could tell me. Just the act of sharing with him lessened the burden. For me, anyway.

Mike sat in his Jeep with the windows down, intermittent birdsong in the distance on his end. He blew out his breath. "And you think Addy's friend ..."

He didn't finish, but he didn't have to. "Yeah," I answered.

"Poor kid—poor Addy. Do you want me to come to Tallahassee tonight?"

"Tempting," I admitted. "But you've logged enough miles lately to get your commercial license."

"It's good to have career options," he said.

"In case Richard gets sick of you and gives you the boot?" Richard was the Supervising Attorney at the Stetler County Public Defender's Office, and the attorney Mike worked with most often.

"Richard can't fire me," Mike said. "But he might drive me to quit. He's been a real pain in the ass lately."

Mike didn't often speak ill of anyone, so Richard's behavior must be exceptional. I removed my shoe before guiltily tucking a foot up on Roger's chair and scratching at a spot on the knee of my pants while Mike shared about the latest office drama. There was something so normal, so breathtakingly ordinary about the conversation. I only wished we were having it in person.

I was still listening when Addy came into the kitchen, face pink and blotchy with crying and a fresh washing, the way mine tends to do. She retrieved milk from the fridge and a tin of chocolate from a cabinet. Being a trained investigator, I deduced she was making hot chocolate. Addy took cinnamon from a mounted spice rack—that's what was so familiar when she made it before. My mother wasn't exactly a genius in the kitchen, but she did do hot chocolate well, and always with cinnamon. Addy held up an extra mug, and I shook my head. She started to put the mug back, but hesitated, left and headed down the hallway instead.

I forced my attention back to Mike. It wasn't that I wasn't listening; it's that the sound of his voice was so soothing, sometimes I lost the actual words. "And you don't have any idea what's going on with Richard?"

"He won't say, and Angela hasn't invited me over for a while, so I couldn't ask her," Mike said. "He's been pulling old cases, too, on the sly. I think he'd tell me if it was an issue with witnesses, something systemic like a LEO or expert or something."

"Crisis of confidence? Evaluating what he did right, or wrong, in the past?" I guessed, but I didn't believe it.

Mike didn't either. "I guess he'll tell me when he's ready."

Perhaps, but Richard didn't strike me as the most forthcoming guy when it came to feelings. He might need some encouragement. "Maybe you should—"

I broke off when Addy came racing down the hall into the kitchen area, eyes bulging, mouth open and chest heaving for air. Her hands were balled into small fists, and she pulled her arms to her side, as if trying to crank the words stuck inside.

"Just a minute," I said to Mike. "Addy, what's wrong?"

One more deep breath, and the words finally tumbled free. "Deidre's on the floor, and she won't wake up."

I heard Emma's words, *in case things go sideways... Shit.*

"Mike, I gotta go," I said, hung up, and shoved my phone in my pocket and my shoe back on my foot. Addy raced ahead of me to Deidre's bedroom.

Deidre's lavender-walled space was a little girly-feminine for my tastes, but the decor may have saved her from a concussion. I found her lying facedown on the far side of a canopy bed, its gauzy white curtains gathered at the four elaborate dark wood posts. One curtain hung asymmetrically, as if Deidre had grabbed it as she fell, and she'd overturned a white, padded ottoman, draped with subdued, black dresses. I righted the ottoman and moved it to kneel at Deidre's head.

Strands of long blonde hair had fallen across her face and stirred intermittently with her breath. I spoke in the loud, clear tone of voice reserved for dealing with drunks and head injuries. "Deidre, this is Sydney. I need you to talk to me."

No response. I checked her wrists—no MedicAlert bracelets, and Roger hadn't mentioned any health issues. Her skin was cold and clammy, and her pulse was slow. "Deidre, I need to know what happened. Did you hurt yourself when you fell?"

I gently ran both hands over the back of her neck. There weren't any bones sticking out, and recognizing protruding bones was about the extent of my medical expertise. Deidre stirred at the contact, but didn't speak.

I glanced over my shoulder to see Addy hovering uncertainly. "Addy, I need you to check her purse, her nightstand, her bathroom, anywhere she might be keeping drugs."

"You think she overdosed?" Addy asked.

"I don't know, but if she did, we need to know what she's on."

Addy stepped carefully over Deidre's body, and I placed a firm hand on the semi-conscious woman's shoulder. "Deidre, sweetie, I need to know what you took. Roger's gonna be worried about you."

This time she moaned and moved her arm. "Deidre, I need you to talk to me. *For Roger's sake.* Can you do that?"

Another sound, one I chose to interpret as affirmative. "Good. Did you hurt yourself when you fell?"

"No, 'm okay," she mumbled.

That she most certainly was not.

"Syd," Addy said.

I looked up. The teen sat on the bed with Deidre's black leather purse in her lap and a prescription bottle in her hand. "Ativan."

I closed my eyes, trying to recall what I knew about the drug. It was a benzo, like Valium and Xanax, which meant it worked as a depressant. As did alcohol, and when you combined the two, they tended to take their jobs a little too seriously.

"Dammit. Deidre, I need to know how much you took, and when," I said, squeezing her shoulder.

Her head lifted slightly, and one leg shifted as if she were thinking of getting up. Her blue eyes were glassy and her mascara was smudged, but she didn't look nearly as bad as she would before she was done. Assuming she didn't stop breathing.

"Deidre, how many?" I demanded.

"Jus' a couple this morning, a couple-few this afternoon. Serious-ly," she said, garbling the word. "I'm okay. Jus' leave me alone."

Plus a fifth of vodka or whatever she'd been drinking. I could smell it on her. I didn't trust the woman's arithmetic, but at least it seemed she was reckless rather than suicidal. I pulled my phone from my back pocket and handed it to Addy. "Can you call 9-1-1 while I see if I can get her up?"

"No! No hospital." It was the most coherent thing I'd heard from her so far, too close to my ear and somewhere between a shriek and a whining squeal. She tried to crawl away from me.

"Deidre," I said, gripping her arm. She rolled onto her side and glared at me, face twisted in an ugly, angry scowl. "Deidre, we can't dick around with this. You could die. Do you understand me?"

Spit flew on the thick, dark-gray carpet as she yelled, "Screw you, bitch!"

Little tip—not the best way to get someone to do what you want. "Nice. You kiss your brother with that mouth? The brother who's going to kick both our asses if we don't get you to a hospital? Addy, make the call."

"No!" Deidre whined, and Addy hesitated, staring at my phone in her hand as if she didn't know how to work it. Deidre took advantage of her doubt, pleading, "Please... why can't *you* take me?"

Because it would be stupid. Because I'm not a medical profes-sional, and I didn't want her dying—or puking—in my rental car. But I held my tongue, appraising her. She was conscious. Her plea had only been slightly slurred. And I couldn't blame her for wanting to avoid the drama of an ambulance, at any time, but especially the day after her father died.

"Fine," I said. "If you can make it to the car, we'll take you. Addy, just hang on to my phone. And can you grab my purse and keys and whatever you need while I get her up?"

Addy rolled over the bed on her back to get past us, holding her feet high so she didn't mar the white bedspread.

Leaving me alone with Deidre.

On my knees, I reached beneath her armpits, grunting as I lifted, and we lurched toward the bed. Deidre landed facedown on the mattress, her naked feet in the vicinity of the floor.

"Just hang out there a second," I said.

A white wooden, built-in closet took up most of one bedroom wall, with hanging bars on one side and shelves and shoe racks on the other. It was about a third full, with more slacks and skirts and dresses than I owned, but the shoe selection was thin on anything not high heels. A pair of slip-on, red canvas loafers would have to do, even if they made an interesting combination with her ensemble.

I rolled Deidre onto her back and jammed the shoes on her feet without injuring either of us. Leaning over her, I gripped her arm and said, "Okay, we're going to stand now. But take your time."

I slipped a hand behind her back as she sat up and slowly rose. "Good job."

She started to smile, but her face suddenly went pale. Her eyes rolled in her head as her knees buckled.

"Shit!" I flung my arms around her and struggled to keep us both upright. "Come on, Deidre! Work with me here," I said, voice strained.

She never went down all the way, and gradually began to regain her footing and straighten. "'Kay," she said.

I waited until I was sure she wouldn't collapse again before we took our first step. It wasn't pretty, but it was in the right direction. Deidre's head lolled on her shoulders as we shambled toward the hallway like a pair of monsters joined at the hip and shoulders in a classic horror movie.

"All right, Dee Dee," I said, wedging us carefully through the bedroom doorway. "You're doing good."

Addy met us in the hall, my purse over her shoulder and my keys jangle-clicking in her hand.

"Addy, can you unlock the car for us? Make sure there's nothing in the back seat. And then lock up the house behind us."

The teen bolted out the front of the house, leaving the door open behind her so the outside world glowed like an unwanted beacon. I held Deidre's hand to keep her arm securely draped over my shoulder. Her fingers were cold, and her breath whistled slightly in my ear. She wobbled, and I heard something fall next to her with a bang (umbrella stand? vase?). Hopefully it wasn't priceless.

"Anybody ever call you Dee Dee? Anybody you didn't punch, I mean." She didn't respond, but I kept chattering as we tottered toward the door. "Personally, I think it's an awesome nickname. Dee Dee. Although it is dangerously close to Doo Doo for kids."

"Cam Nixon," she muttered. I wouldn't have heard her if her boozy lips weren't inches away from my ears.

We'd made it to the front door, and I blinked against the sunny glare. The threshold had a raised lip, and then a step down that concerned me a little. Addy hovered just outside, perhaps planning to break Deidre's fall by diving onto the bricks first. She might have to break both our falls. My own legs had a hint of jelly, and my arms and lower back burned with effort.

"Easy does it, Deidre," I said, watching as she deliberately lifted, then lowered her leading leg to the ground. "This Cam brat called you Dee Dee? Or Doo Doo? Though with a name like Nixon, life couldn't have been easy for him, either."

She panted lightly a few times before answering, "No, I punched him for calling me Dirty in first grade."

"What an asshole," I said, silently cursing Roger for his fancy driveway every time Deidre's toe caught the brick edges and threatened to take us down.

But we were almost there. Addy had opened the car door, and the last few steps went more quickly than they should have. I staggered under Deidre's weight, slamming into the metal exterior of the car, and Deidre fell inside, thankfully landing on the seat. Together Addy and I lifted and bent her legs to tuck her inside the car.

"You mind sitting back here with her?" I asked.

"So she doesn't choke on her puke?" Addy asked, and I was struck again by the teen's contradictory mix of experience and naïveté. "Okay," she said, before I could answer, and lifted Deidre's legs to crawl under her.

I ran around to the driver's seat and climbed in, nearly losing an eye to Addy's hand when it appeared next to my face. She held the car keys and my cell phone. I took the keys and said, "Dial Roger, please. He's in my Contacts."

I'd made it to the first intersection by the time Addy found the number. "Deidre is shaking all over," Addy said, as she gave me the ringing phone.

"Keep her from going to sleep. Talk to her, rub her neck, whatever you need to—"

"Sydney, what's up?" Roger finally answered. "Is something wrong?"

"It's Deidre," I said, pausing in the hopes that during that hesitation he would catch up with me, even anticipate my bad news. "She overdosed. I'm driving her to the ER now."

"I'm on my way," he said.

I hung up and tossed my phone into the console. Eyes locked on the rearview mirror, all I could see in the back was the top of Addy's head or her anxious face. At the next intersection, I swung right after barely slowing for a four-way stop, then held my breath, praying the dark-colored SUV half a block behind us wasn't a cop.

It wasn't. In my relief, I hardly even noticed that it also made a rolling right to follow us.

45

Addy and I sat facing the glass and metal entrance in the hospital's white, aseptic waiting area. Huddled against the hospital's frigid air conditioning, I kept hoping someone would walk near enough for the doors to open and let warmer air inside.

A whimpering boy with an injured ankle sat in his mother's lap to Addy's left, and an adult man with a bloody arm sat to my right. Soon a guy wearing the same construction logo hat and T-shirt joined the bloody man and asked questions from a clipboard in hushed tones. I rested my elbows on the tubular metal chair arms and pulled my sunglasses from the tangled hair atop my head. The fluorescent lights were giving me a headache.

"Deidre's lucky to have Roger," Addy murmured.

"Yes, she is," I agreed.

Roger had been waiting out front when we arrived and carried his unconscious sister until someone met us with alternative transport. He was allowed to accompany her for treatment—I had no idea what that entailed because we hadn't seen him since. Which is why we were still hanging around.

I was pretty sure Deidre would pull through okay, but I had gone out on a limb and called Juliet Sanders, aka Mrs. Roger #1. I got the feeling they had maintained a good relationship even after their marriage ended, and who else would have as much context for everything happening in the poor man's life right now? Roger might get pissed at me for interfering, but he'd get over it. As soon as Juliet showed up, we were leaving. Having Addy out in public made me paranoid and anxious.

I bumped her as I dropped my hands and rubbed my eyes. Addy hadn't complained about my physical proximity, or anything else. Maybe experience had taught her complaining was pointless. Or maybe, *just maybe,* she had as much reason for hating where we were as I did.

"Did your mom die in a hospital?" I asked.

Addy's intense gaze swung at me, face a mix of flush and pallor, just as her expression seemed equal parts anger and anguish.

"I'm sorry," I said, looking away before she had to. "It's none of my business."

I leaned back in my seat and watched the security guard hovering near the entrance. Being the person with the least emotional investment in anything happening around us made him the least painful person to watch. A big middle-aged guy, he carried a few extra pounds and had artificially dark hair, but the tan uniform that mimicked law enforcement fit him well. I wondered if he took what he saw and heard and smelled home with him. If it softened him inside, or made him harder.

"My brother died in the hospital," I said, still watching the guard. "When I was your age. I've hated hospitals ever since."

I cleared my throat, wished for a bottle of water. Or better, a cup of hot tea, sweet and creamy. "Not that anyone likes hospitals," I added. "Nothing good ever happens here."

I was surprised when, a good thirty seconds or so later, Addy answered matter of fact, "Babies."

"Ha!" I laughed, glancing at Addy and getting a bonus view of the mother to our right glaring at me as though I'd kicked her injured child. At least the woman didn't shush me.

Addy tucked her hair behind her ear, then shoved her hands in her sweatshirt. Had we been together long enough for the blue streaks to begin fading, or was I just used to them? The shape of her dark, unplucked brows over her button nose reminded me of someone, but I couldn't place whom.

I wished I could read her expression better, without projecting what I thought it meant or wanted it to mean. I believed the anger I'd triggered was gone, and the anguish was at least softer. Part of me (the tiny part that encouraged such behavior) wanted to give her a hug. And part of me thought she wouldn't thank me for it. So I kept my arms to myself.

Turning my attention back to the guard, I got the distinctive, creepy-crawly feeling that now he was staring at us. Intently. I faked a stretch to scan the room. I didn't see anything unusual, and none of the dozen or so miserable, stressed-out people behind us held a bloody knife or looked like a mass murderer about to strike. By the time I'd rotated to face forward again, the guard was gone, probably stepped outside to make sure no one was bleeding on a potted plant. See, just paranoid.

And yet, it was possible to not be paranoid enough.

I closed my eyes, drifted with sniffles and mechanical shushing and clicks as an auditory backdrop. Felt myself begin to doze and surrendered to it.

Wait a minute... Juliet...

I sat up so abruptly I nearly slid out of my chair.

Dammit!

Juliet Sanders, the woman Addy and I were waiting for, was not just the former Mrs. Roger. She was also Addy's *guardian ad litem*, or would be soon. And if she found Addy sitting here next to me, things were going to get very awkward very fast for all of us.

I nudged the teen and handed her my sunglasses. "Put these on. Time to go."

Addy shrugged and leaned on the chair arm, as if she needed every assistance to rise. Then she said next to me, in the same matter-of-fact tone she'd used to note that babies were good, "My mom didn't die in a hospital. She had a freak aneurysm, and somebody found her at home."

"I'm sorry," I said, but before I could offer additional words of comfort or be any kind of real human, my attention was drawn back to the entrance, which suddenly felt more like a blocked exit.

The security guard had returned, now with a Tallahassee cop at his side. My heart beat faster at the sight of a gray-haired man in plain clothes with a law enforcement bearing standing outside, and another navy uniformed TPD officer approached on the sidewalk. *Shit.*

I turned slowly, as though stretching my legs, and tried to maintain my casual demeanor as I said softly, evenly, "Addy, don't rush and don't panic, but I need you to put your hood up and slowly make your way to a bathroom. If someone wants inside, tell them you're sick, and wait for me to tell you to come out."

Her body went rigid as she processed my words, and her eyes widened as they took in the approaching officers.

"Got it?" I asked.

"Yeah," she whispered, pulling her hood over her head with shaking hands. She shuffled to the end of the row of seats like an invalid missing her cane. Sidling around the corner, Addy bumped a woman's knee and muttered, "Sorry."

The lead TPD officer strode purposefully toward us—no, toward Addy, because that's where his eyes were—with his partner a few paces behind and the security guard now lagging to bring up the rear. The older man in plain clothes must have remained outside.

I quickly stepped into the first officer's path.

"Excuse me," I said, bracing myself for impact, but he succeeded in stopping. I pulled up my sleeve and tore the bandage off the cut on my arm. I'd done a half-ass job applying it, and winced as I re-opened the wound. "Does this look infected to you?"

Slightly below average height (which still meant several inches taller than me), the officer's hatless, shaved black head shone from the humidity. He stated, patiently but firmly, "Ma'am, the receptionist can help you with that. I'm not a medical professional."

He tried to step around me, but I edged in front of him again. "Yeah, but you at least had First Aid, right? As part of your cop training? Just a quick look—"

"Step aside," he said. It felt as if his body carried a force field, one that pushed interfering citizens out of the way like a bulldozer. And he only had eyes for Addy. "Miss!" he called out.

Addy stood just a few paces from the bathroom, not that it mattered now. She looked over her shoulder, her face bisected by her hood so only half was visible. Her mouth dropped open and she froze. That's when I noticed another officer circling the row of seats at the far end to cut her off. Addy was trapped.

"She's my niece," I riffed. "She drove me here because I felt faint. But now I'm not sure if I have insurance, so maybe we should—"

"Adelaide Hastings," the officer said, "I need you to come with me."

"No," I protested. "You've made a mistake."

"Are you saying she isn't Adelaide Hastings?" he countered. "Or that you have documentation to support that you are her legal guardian?"

"I'm saying..." My voice faded as I fumbled for a way out, a way to wipe the terrified look from Addy's face. "I'm saying where's *your* documentation? Do you have a warrant for her arrest?"

He raised a hand toward the security guard, who in turn waved an official-looking sheet of paper in the air. I'd taken a single step toward him when Addy yelled, "I didn't steal anything! Sylvia Maddox is a lying bitch."

"Miss Hastings, please just stay calm and come with us," my officer said.

Addy shook her head with the desperation of an animal caught in a trap, hood sliding from her hair. She was panicking, and I was afraid nothing anyone said would get through to her. She'd make things worse, they'd take her away, and somehow she'd disappear. Just like Carly.

Think, Brennan. Think. And finally I came up with my Hail Mary pass—Mrs. Roger #1.

"Her lawyer!" I blurted. "Juliet Sanders, her court-appointed *guardian ad litem*, is on the way. She'll be here any minute. If we can wait for Ms. Sanders, I know she'll be able to straighten all this out."

The lead officer shot me a sideways glance that suggested I'd squandered most of my truth capital with the man already, but I thought I'd also caught a flash of recognition on his face at Juliet's name.

"I swear!" I said. "Juliet Sanders. I have her number. You can call her right now. And we'll all just sit calmly and wait until she gets here. Is there somewhere we can do that?"

"In my cruiser," he said, with a hint of skeptical drawl.

"Fine," I said. "So long as we wait for Ms. Sanders. But Addy doesn't consent to go anywhere without her."

Like consent mattered if they had a warrant. But throw enough legal buzzwords around often enough and sometimes one sticks, or buys you the time you need.

"All right," he said. Both of us looked to Addy as he extended an arm in her direction and said, "Miss?"

Come on, Addy, look at me, I begged wordlessly, praying I could get through to her. But she wouldn't. Her body vibrated like a tree at an approaching strong wind.

Come on, Addy, do the right thing.

But she didn't.

She bolted.

"Aww, girl," I heard an elderly onlooker say as Addy ran straight at the TPD officer nearest her. Taller than my guy, he was also thicker with a higher center of gravity. Addy did a head juke that would have made an NBA player proud, slipped past him and slid on the slick floor around the far end of the goggling row of people.

That left her half the waiting area, then the too-slow automatic doors to navigate, and for what? Pavement. Winding lanes for parking and medical buildings, streets she could maybe traverse to reach the patches of woods surrounding the hospital and scattered throughout the neighborhood. She wouldn't make it, and it would only make things worse for both of us. But it didn't matter. Instinct and adrenaline kicked in, and I had to try to help her.

Standing between Addy and the exit, with her officer hard on her heels, I did what any team player would do. I set a pick.

Putting myself in their path, I spread my feet a little, dropped my hips slightly and allowed a flex in my knees. My arms remained at my side—as much as I wanted to protect my chest and drop my ass lower, I wasn't a total idiot. I needed to at least attempt plausible deniability.

Addy saw what I was doing and cut close to my body as she scrambled past. The officer a half-step behind her didn't. He slammed right into me, elbowing my boob painfully and knocking me flat on my back on the terrazzo floor. I lay on the unyielding surface, stunned, until the cold seeped through my clothes and Addy's shrieking protests (*Let go of me!*) pierced my roaring ears.

Sucking in a deep breath, I curled an arm over the stabbing pain in my chest and rolled on my side. I couldn't tell the darker chips in the terrazzo from the spots swimming in my vision. Suddenly, a big navy blur seized me and flipped me onto my stomach, twisting my arms behind my back. My right shoulder popped as he slapped his cuffs over my wrists. I jerked my hands and the metal bit into my skin.

"No! Leave me alone, you perv!" Addy shrieked.

My face had settled to the floor (the coolness didn't feel so bad now against my cheek), and I raised my head. Between my hazy vision and the bad angle, all I could see was a nearby dirty shoe and a lot of motion, Addy flailing while both officers tried to control her.

I raised my head and said, "Addy, don't fight them! It'll be okay."

Of course it would be nothing of the sort.

"Sydney!" she wailed.

"Don't worry, kid. I promise, I will get you out of this," I said.

I watched them lift her, then let my forehead fall to the floor as the entry doors peeled back at their approaching motion. But wait...

My neck spasmed when I wrenched my head upright. Just beyond the doors, I'd seen him again. The plainclothes, gray-haired man. But now I recognized him.

It was Pinky Guy, Turtle's torturer.

"Hey!" I shouted, fighting a cough and weaving my neck painfully to see past all the uniformed legs. "He can't have her!"

"Keep it down," said the uniformed man standing over me.

"No, you don't understand," I pleaded desperately, waggling my head toward the door. "He'll hurt her. Don't let him have her!"

I twisted to look up at the cop, but the strain reduced him to a navy blur.

"Lady, I said take it down a notch!" he warned.

"But she's not safe with him! Addy!" I screamed, as his shoe pressed down on my back.

46

I'd gotten my promised seat in a TPD cruiser, though not alongside Addy. I'm not sure how long I'd been sitting there when the door opened, but long enough to calm down and for my head to mostly stop swimming. An auburn-haired officer, young and looking fresh from the academy, helped me step from the car and removed my handcuffs.

"Ma'am, you're free to go," he said.

Rubbing my aching wrists, I stepped back for him to close the door and nearly bumped into Roger. I hadn't seen him standing behind the officer. Roger had his court face on, the stony one that juries rarely saw and prosecutors feared. I hoped it wasn't directed at me.

"Where's Addy?" I asked.

"In custody," Roger said, handing me my purse. "Be glad you aren't."

"Where is she?" I pressed. My throat felt raw.

"TPD has her," he said. "She's safe."

His gray suit jacket was draped over the other arm, and it should have made him look GQ cover casual. Instead he looked as though he'd removed it to traverse hell.

"How's Deidre?" I asked.

He flinched slightly, the way you do when a bug hits you in the face unexpectedly, before resuming his stone face. "She's been admitted. She'll be okay," he said. "Come on."

I followed Roger deeper into the parking facility, all concrete and artificial light and rows of anonymous vehicles, and tried to remember where my own car was parked. I'd need it to do whatever came next. I had no idea what that was, but finding my car—hopefully *that* I could do.

Except I wasn't driving my car, I was driving a rental, and I couldn't remember what color the damn thing was. I stopped, rested my hand against one of the textured gray supports. Rough and porous and cool, but not as cool as the hospital floor had been. My breathing was too shallow and frequent. I swear the assholes forgot to include air when they built this car catacomb.

"Syd!" Roger called out. He stood next to his BMW, several slots ahead of me, and gestured for me to join him. "You coming?"

I took a deeper breath, nodded, and pulled the rental keys from my purse. A silver car beeped in the same row when I pressed the clicker. My rental. Crisis averted.

For now.

Sitting in Roger's vehicle was like crawling into a fine leather cocoon. But even its luxury interior lighting couldn't erase the jaundiced hue in Roger's exhausted face.

"Did Juliet show up?" I asked.

"You're the one who called her?" he demanded.

"Yes," I said unapologetically.

His jaw worked for a moment before he answered. "By the time she arrived, they'd already taken Addy into custody."

Nausea skewered my guts, and I found myself dry swallowing against rising bile. "There was a plainclothes guy, older than you," I said.

"I've heard that you thought so," Roger said carefully. "But the officers assured me, there was no one like that involved in her apprehension."

Had I hallucinated the Pinky Guy from the market? I pushed a strand of hair back from my face with a shaking hand. Putting aside the implications for my sanity, hallucination was the best-case scenario. Addy might be terrified now, but it was less likely she'd be harmed by the local officers than by the Reform Center boogeyman.

So said my rational mind, but I'd spent the past week tracking down details on kids dead by *someone's* hand. And there was that nagging promise to Addy that I'd get her out. "Where exactly are they keeping her?"

"I don't know," he said. "Neither does Juliet. She said she'd call when she finds out, but I don't know. I haven't seen her this pissed off since—"

His voice trailed off, leaving his previous offense against his ex-wife unspoken. Roger braced his arm against the door and rested his forehead in his hand. "Fuck, Syd. What are we going to do?"

I felt a stab of guilt that I'd involved Roger in Addy's drama. He should be focusing on his sister's physical and mental health, and his father's upcoming funeral. I dreaded hearing the details (I'd have to eventually), but knew Roger had prevented my arrest this evening. Not that any charge would have stuck, but fighting it would have been a pain in the ass. Of course, if Roger's sister hadn't overdosed, we wouldn't have been at the hospital in the first place.

That's right, *Addy and I wouldn't have been at the hospital.*

"Roger," I said slowly, thinking the words as I spoke them aloud, "how did they know Addy was at the ER?"

His head lifted from his hand and tilted as he considered. "I don't know," he admitted. "Someone must have tipped them off."

What if I was looking at this the wrong way around? What if Addy was picked up because we'd gotten her involved with *our* drama? I continued out loud, "Addy's a runaway, not important enough to be on anyone's radar herself. What if she wasn't really the target, she was just a means to an end?"

Roger turned to me, and I saw a little life return to his sunken eyes. "Another way to distract us."

I raised an eyebrow in acknowledgment of the possibility.

"But from what?" he asked.

WE DROVE BACK to Roger's house in our separate cars to wait for Juliet's call.

If Addy had been picked up to distract us from our work at the Reform Center, we had to be close to something important. Life and death were the highest stakes I could imagine, which suggested it was something about the boys who had died at the facility. What were we missing? There was nothing for it but to go back to the beginning.

Roger camped out at the dining table, as I had earlier, and I sat on the rug in the living room with boxes and folders and pages of notes scattered around me. I paused long enough to start a pot of coffee and give Mike a quick call, reassuring him after my earlier hurried hang-up that no one was dead. Mike understood sudden deadlines, and once I'd convinced him I still didn't need him to drive to Tallahassee, he left me to my files.

I hadn't yet reviewed the box from Eleanor Dickey's father, Milton, so I started working my way through that. It was a mess, a hodgepodge of file folders, of multiple colors and mostly unlabeled, piled in a stack rather than arranged upright. I tried to impose some sort of order as I removed them, putting likes together on the assumption that they were created close in time. I wondered if Ms. Dickey had found the box this way, or pulled the files from multiple different boxes? If the latter, where were the rest?

Tucked inside an orange folder at the bottom of the box was a hunter-green journal, its unlined pages filled with small, fastidious handwriting. It seemed Milton Dickey had kept his own ledger, the contents of which weren't included with any of the limited materials I'd previously seen from the center. Entries recorded summaries of the day's events in an abbreviated shorthand, sometimes with multiple entries per page.

On closer inspection, I could see faint horizontal pencil lines, as if he'd entered the data with a ruler. Not every day had an entry.

Consulting my notes, I found that none of my known dates of boys' deaths had entries. But there was another pattern. Those boys, or at least boys with the same last name and first initial, all appeared in entries within days of their death with the notation: *MB-2*.

A second pass through the book confirmed that several other boys had the same or a similar notation: *MB-1*. I pulled out my map of the facility. Buildings were outlined, but not always labeled. Of course, it needn't be a location. It could be anything, including a reference to a particular kind of twisted punishment.

Speculation was getting me nowhere, so I abandoned the ledger and moved on to the rest of the records. I flagged any references to boys I knew or suspected had died in custody at the center, and also to the other boys with the unexplained notation. Scanning for names, I couldn't help but think of the teenaged girls now missing, decades later, and hope their stories had happier endings.

Roger's ringing phone jarred me from my morbid task. He groaned as he rose from his chair, and I stretched my neck and straightened my crossed legs in sympathy. It had gone full dark hours ago, but we'd neglected to turn on the recessed ceiling lights, so Roger passed unhurriedly from lamp pool to lamp pool to answer his landline.

"Yes?" he said, and not much else. After a full minute of listening, he tried to interject, "I—" but must have been shot down. Another minute passed before he said, "Okay. I understand. Thank you."

Still standing, he stared at the receiver in his hand as if he'd forgotten how it got there. Or perhaps had forgotten where it belonged when it wasn't squawking.

"Any news?" I asked.

He carefully set the receiver in the cradle. "That was Juliet. Addy has a hearing Friday. We won't be allowed to speak with her before then."

"Where is she?" I demanded. "Did Juliet see her?"

Roger sat heavily in the nearest armchair, its brown leather seat crackling beneath him, and massaged the bridge of his nose. "Juliet wouldn't say where, but she saw Addy briefly, and she's calmed down now. Addy, that is. Juliet is still rather remarkably pissed."

He positioned himself carefully, forearms flush and palms flat against the armrests, then slowly closed his eyes. "I can't remember the last time I was so tired," he admitted.

Acid born of too much coffee and anxiety ate at my stomach. It was nearing ten p.m., and we hadn't eaten dinner. I doubted if Roger had even eaten lunch. I rose and headed for the kitchen, giving his arm a pat as I passed. "I'm sure you were under warrant."

Meaning the chaotic days and weeks leading up to a client's execution.

"Yes," he agreed, "I'm sure I was."

There were ham and turkey sandwiches in the fridge, and I found a bag of Zapp's chips in the pantry. I fixed us both plates and split a large bottle of Guinness between two glasses. It was a little heavy under the circumstances, but appeared to be the only beer in the house, though there was plenty of liquor and wine.

Roger opened his eyes easily when I nudged him, obviously awake. "Thank you, Sydney," he said, taking the plate and glass of beer from my hands and looking wistfully at the dining table buried under files, boxes, and his laptop.

"I won't tell if you won't," I said.

We ate silently in the living room with our plates on our laps. After rinsing the dishes in the sink, we went back to work. At two a.m., we finally retired to our respective rooms, bleary-eyed and no closer to finding the answer.

I stepped over Addy's backpack on the floor and wondered if she needed anything in it. Maybe I should drop it off at Juliet's office. My own cloth batik bag sat on the bed. It was hard to believe I'd shown Carly's purse to Addy just this morning, and the photo to Turtle this afternoon.

Flopping wearily onto the mattress, I carefully pulled the photo free from the remnants of its frame. Taking it had been a whim, really, wanting a better look even before I knew the Admin Building was burning down around my ears. I squinted at the black and white figures. How many of these boys were still alive, and of those that were, how many were irreparably scarred? It was taken a few years before Turtle's time, so he wasn't in it, but how many more Turtles had they helped to create?

I peered down at the men who would have created them, perched on the row ends in their white shirts. How many of them were still alive, still carried the burden of what they'd done or witnessed? Or perhaps the will to see their crimes remained buried? I counted faces to locate the man that had so disturbed Turtle. A couple looked miserable, hunched, but that young officer's chest was as expansive as if he were holding his breath.

There was something familiar about him, maybe the shape of his jaw.

Wading into shit... From that nasty, fucked-up trigger setting off where it didn't belong, all the way up to your goddamn eyeballs, seeing what they had no business seeing.

I sat up, zoomed the photo closer to my face, then spoke aloud in the empty room. "No. Fricking. Way."

Finger, not *trigger*.

"Roger!" I yelled, vaulting from the bed. "Roger!"

I almost dropped the photo when we collided in the hallway.

"What, Syd?" Roger demanded, grasping my shoulders. "What's wrong?"

I couldn't answer for a moment, transfixed by the dark, abundant chest hair his unbuttoned, flapping blue silk pajama top revealed.

"Sydney," he said, giving me a gentle shake. "Are you okay?"

"I, uh, yeah," I stammered. "Sorry—do you have a magnifying glass?"

Now it was his turn to blink. "A magnifying glass... in my office. Why?"

I held up the photo triumphantly. "Because I'm not crazy. And I know who the sonuvabitch was who tipped off the cops at the hospital."

Roger buttoned his pajama top as he led me to his office, where he sat at his immaculate desk and turned on a desk lamp.

"He's bulked up a little with age—mostly muscle, I'd say—but he still looks fit," I said, handing Roger the photo. "Moves like it, too, the little bit I've seen of him."

The lamp was one of two objects on the desk, the other being a blotter. Since no piece of furniture should be so clean, I sat on top, legs dangling. I reviewed my first sighting of Turtle's tormentor at the farmer's market, while Roger examined the photo with a brass-handled, Sherlock-worthy magnifying glass.

"Is that—"

"Yes, that's blood," I said, sharing the highlights of my recent interaction with Turtle.

Roger made a low noise, like a hum without a tune, then nodded. "Just because we're paranoid…"

"Doesn't mean they're not out to get us. I got that, Yossarian," I said. I was trying for flippant, but I have honestly never been so relieved by confirmation that I was a target.

"You really think it's him?" Roger asked.

"I know it is," I said. "Look how part of his right hand is tucked in his pocket, so you can't see the end of the pinky. Probably didn't even know he was doing it. Self-conscious force of habit."

Roger tilted his head at my argument that an absence of evidence was evidence.

"And Turtle said he had a fucked-up finger."

"Fine. But what about at the hospital?" he asked. "Why would he even be there?"

"He followed us," I said.

Roger lowered the photo, staring at me; his skepticism had progressed to disbelief.

"Come on, Roger. I wasn't exactly looking for surveillance while I carried Deidre to the car. The man could've been in your driveway and I wouldn't have seen him unless I tripped over him. And someone else ran a stop sign behind us—I just didn't think anything of it at the time."

Roger leaned back in his chair, and I braced myself for more cross-examination. "How did he know about Addy?"

"I don't know," I admitted. "But he did. And the cops were telling the truth; he didn't have anything to do with Addy's actual arrest. But I'd bet my PI license he told the security guard about her. Did you see what 'warrant' they had for Addy?"

Roger shook his head.

"I'll bet that came from him, too. Either it was fake and TPD played along until they got the real thing, or it was a valid document he kept handy."

Roger tilted his head back and forth, as though he were ambivalent about verticality. "Maybe," he conceded. "But that brings us back around to how he knew about Addy. Not to mention who the hell he is. We don't even have a name yet."

"He may not have been there when your father buried that boy, but we know he was up to his neck in the nasty shit that went on at the Reform Center. And tomorrow," I promised, "I will find his name. And then, I will find him."

47

D espite not knowing his precise identity, confirmation of Pinky Guy's existence helped me sleep well. Until my alarm screamed at me a few hours later.

I staggered to the shower and dressed in a tank top and button-down shirt over jeans that may have seen too many days without a wash. The coffee aroma hit me in the hallway. I found Roger in the kitchen, pouring himself a cup—I wouldn't hazard a guess at what number. The dining table was still covered with boxes, and he pointed at a plate of toast on the counter.

"Thank you. You look like crap, by the way," I said, taking in his sunken eyes without mentioning my own unusual use of makeup.

Roger's voice was deep and raspy, as though he was coming down with something or had gotten trapped in a burning building with me. "And here I'd forgotten why I enjoyed having you stay with me."

He gave a surprised look of mild annoyance when I hip-bumped him out of my way for a clean mug. Roger did not do superfluous physical contact. I smiled, picking up a piece of bread already slathered with some kind of French purple berry spread. "You know you'll miss me. Almost as much as I'll miss your little coffee cyborg."

He allowed himself a small smile. "I'll be sure to check that it's still here when you leave."

I stuck out a toast-laden, purple-smeared tongue.

After breakfast, Roger went to the hospital to check in on Deidre. I'd forgotten to ask him whether the lawyers representing the Spencers had gotten in touch with the couple about Addy's status yet. I supposed it didn't matter; I owed my clients a call either way. No one answered at their home (a moment of guilty relief for me), so I left a message explaining Addy's current status and that their lawyers would be able to tell them more about Friday's hearing.

That prompted me to call my office and check my own messages. I had an urgent one from my landlord. In all of the craziness of the past week, I'd forgotten to send my rent check. He was pretty understanding, but my life was not going to get less complicated anytime soon, so better to take care of it now. And movement would be good for me.

In retrospect, the degree to which I relied on muscle memory for driving that morning is frightening. I found myself downtown with no recollection of navigating Roger's neighborhood. In fact, I didn't even realize I was downtown until I shut off my car, having parked illegally in front of a tall office building. Juliet Sanders's office building, to be exact.

The elevator to the third floor gave me just enough time to realize what a bad idea it was to drop in on Addy's appointed lawyer. (The part where she was Roger's ex-wife probably wouldn't help, either.) I might have done the sensible thing and pushed the "Close Doors" button when they opened, retreating right back downstairs, if I hadn't seen her. The exterior wall of her office was primarily glass and almost directly across from the elevator. Juliet was crossing her reception area, wearing a black pantsuit and a scowl. Her expression only worsened when she saw me.

I sighed and stepped off the elevator, bracing myself for a tongue-lashing I totally deserved.

She waited, hands on her hips, for me to enter. As soon as the door closed behind me, she said, "You know I can't talk to you."

I nodded, not quite looking at her. "Yeah, well... I was wondering, if somehow, during the course of my investigation I came into possession of some of Addy's belongings... Would it be appropriate to pass those to you?"

I could hear her breath rasping in and out of her nose from across the room. *Inhale, exhale. Inhale, exhale.*

"What the fuck were you thinking?" she demanded, color rising in her cheeks.

I stood, open-mouthed, slightly surprised by her language in an office with a children's area. Not that there were any children in it at the moment. Once I got past the f-bomb (it's not like I didn't detonate my share), my frustration rose to meet her temper. "Roger—"

Was the one who insisted on knowing everything, on being in the middle of everything. On doing it his way. On caring for me and Addy. And these were all things I could not share with Juliet.

When she realized I was not going to finish my sentence, Juliet finished it for me. "Roger is a dumbass. And one of these days he's going to get himself disbarred."

"I'm sorry," I said, but I couldn't even say what I was sorry for. Not if I was going to maintain Juliet's integrity as Addy's lawyer. "Look, I know we can't talk about the case, but can you just tell me if Addy is okay?"

Juliet bit her lower lip (without marring an apparently magical shade of red) and fiddled with a small, heavy gold hoop at her ear. Finally she said, "It's fortunate that you stopped by now. I won't be around this afternoon because I'm seeing a client, and I'd hate to have missed the chance to chew your ass out."

My head dropped and my hand went to my chest in relief. "Will you tell her I'll be at the hearing Friday?"

Juliet drew herself upright and spoke in a firm, slightly lower tone —lawyer voice instead of human voice. "No, you won't be at the hearing because it's *in camera*, and only the parties present."

"Then I'll be waiting in the hallway, or the bathroom, or outside in the rain," I said, in my own, *You seriously think you can intimidate me? Bikers try to kill me* tone of stubborn, persistent nonchalance.

Juliet almost smiled as she replied, "Good."

BACK AT MY OFFICE, my mind strayed while I looked up my bank balance. Enough to keep rent from bouncing, plus a crucial coffee cushion. Tapping my pen on my checkbook, my eyes came to rest on the messenger bag that held my notes and some of my research materials. I'd spent several hours reviewing files last night, but I hadn't reviewed my notes. Time to remedy that.

The handwriting on the yellow legal pad was legible, but my improvised shorthand sometimes stymied even me. Flipping through page after page of notes, I didn't skim, but let the words flow past like water. I paused at the personnel list I'd made from the Archive records. Some of the staff were identified only by initial and surname —*J. Travers,* for example. Needless to say, those were individuals I'd been unable to track down. Pinky Guy could be in that group.

My notes on Milton Dickey's ledger had focused on tracking the fate of the children in custody rather than identifying the Reform Center staff. I pulled the green book from my bag. Dickey did occasionally include staff names, but much like my own jotting, his entries were fragmentary and inconsistent. They presented the reverse of the problem I'd had with the Archive records—here, identification was often only by first name, with the addition of a surname initial where staff shared their given name, like *John S.* and *John M.* In fact, there were three Johns. It was a good Biblical run all the way around, with Luke, Paul, David, Joseph... There were no women, or I'm sure they would have been called Mary. On the other hand, Larry didn't sound very Biblical. Neither did Wade, or Stewart.

But wait—*something* was there. I closed my eyes and let my chin fall to my chest until the tickling in my brain grew stronger. My interview notes were in a different notebook. I pulled it from my bag as well, and said a silent prayer of thanks to Ralph when I found what I was looking for in the final handwritten pages. He'd drilled into me the importance of recording people's words, as nearly exact and close in time as possible, especially when confronted by the unexpected.

Turtle had been a tough interview subject, and not just because he'd smacked me and put a gun to my head. He was unreliable, but not intentionally. I suspected even Turtle didn't know what Turtle knew. He'd been particularly agitated and rambling in the Cooper's parking lot. I'd heard most of what he was saying, but I hadn't under- stood it. The messed-up *trigger* instead of *finger* was the most obvious example, but I didn't think it was the only one.

Back at his house, he'd talked about Milton Dickey in an almost figurative way, saying he was a dick so they called him Dickie, that they'd made up songs about him. He'd spoken of the Pinky Guy in the photo with that same distant, not quite literal quality to his voice. *Always wading into shit...* According to my notes, Turtle had said some variation on that observation three times. *Wading... Wade.* Could it really be that simple?

And could I really be that naive, to think anything about this case would be simple?

I spent the next half hour aiming to prove or disprove my hunch. Twice, Milton Dickey had recorded Wade with a surname initial, *Wade Y.* (Both times occurred alongside one of the triple-Johns, so it was probably force of habit.) Not many surnames started with "Y," but cross-referencing with the Archive records, I found a W. Yates. Wade Yates. Cue the brass bands and pop the champagne. Too bad celebration would have been premature.

The goal was to track this guy down, but my subsequent back- ground checks on Wade Yates came up empty—no one fit Pinky Guy's profile. I was staring at my computer, considering sacrificing a barnyard animal to the PI gods, when John Driscoll called.

Speaking of requests for intercession, I'd been praying I'd hear from John, but still hesitated before answering—what if he knew about my incident at the hospital? More specifically, that I'd been harboring a runaway I'd gotten assistance from him to find. I took a deep breath and assumed my best hale and hearty persona.

"Hey, John, what's up?" I asked. "Do you have something for me?"

It took him so long to reply, my shit-flinging monkey brain started filling in answers, none of them good for my long-term career prospects in Leon County. But when John spoke, his voice was surprisingly thoughtful, even apologetic.

"Sydney, you were right about the missing girls. I'm afraid I can't get into details, but there's something going on."

"What do you mean you can't get into details?" I asked. "What's happening?"

He lowered his voice. "Look, I checked here and with Leon County and Gadsden Sheriffs. Most of the girls you gave me were picked up by one of us within the months before they disappeared."

There was that tightness again, the sensation of my heart beating too high in my chest. Playing devil's advocate, I countered, "That doesn't mean anything. If they were runaways, they were at high risk for being picked up already."

"True," John said. "But I began reviewing missing persons cases in the Panhandle for the past couple of years, and they weren't the only ones who disappeared soon after being released."

"What did Sutton say?" I prompted, betting that he'd called on Eugene Sutton from the Stetler County Sheriff's Department, one of our mutual acquaintances.

"He said it was time to call in FDLE when we hit the half-dozen mark," he admitted.

So the apologetic tone was because my favor had now been transferred out of his hands. "Fine," I said, trying to convince myself at the same time. "That's good. The whole point was to make sure somebody was paying attention."

"Yeah, well, they're paying attention all right. There's talk of looking at Georgia and Alabama, too, bringing in GBI and Alabama's SBI and maybe even the Feds." He paused, working his way up to the real reason for his contrition. "And there's talk about where I came up with this. Who was my source..."

I cringed reflexively. The last time I was on the radar of The Powers that Be, the results were pure pain in the ass professionally speaking: universal bad attitude in person, sluggish responses to record requests, and even more sluggish payment of my invoices. I hadn't done anything then except mouth off to a reporter. What would it mean to actually be associated with an investigation?

And yet, what was the alternative? I couldn't very well bitch in private about how the system was treating people and not back it up in practice. Not to mention, what better way to track down Carly than sic the big guns (with guns) on it?

"Fine," I said. Again. "You can tell them. On one condition."

"I kinda already did," John admitted sheepishly. "I figured you wouldn't care—you're not exactly shy about what you think. But the thing is, they need to interview you."

"Of course they do," I muttered. I did not have time for this. "Who's *they*?"

"I don't know yet," John said. "Representatives from multiple agencies. What was your condition?"

I told him this had all been prompted by Addy's friend Carly, who was currently missing. He took her information and promised they'd add her to the investigation. "But Sydney, they want you to come in for an interview now."

"I thought you didn't know who *they* were," I reminded him.

"I don't," he said, his former penitence rapidly transforming to impatient pissiness. "But I know my Chief, and *he* said they want to interview you. *Now*. At TPD."

"Sorry, John, but I have a previous appointment knocking at my door. I'll have to catch up with them later," I said, hanging up.

My fingers touched my parted lips, which had gone a little numb, maybe because all the blood was in my brain for once.

I was a fricking idiot.

A total fricking idiot.

This was why Addy had been picked up, this was what they wanted to distract us from. It wasn't about what happened decades ago; it was about what was happening *now*. Whatever the hell that was, because I still didn't know.

Picking up the phone, I called Roger, reluctant to do anything irrevocable without talking to him first. No answer—he was probably still at the hospital with Deidre. Next I tried Laney, in the hopes that she'd learned something new from the arson investigation. That now seemed even more likely to have been an attempt to destroy evidence. Laney didn't answer, either.

She wouldn't, if she was in the field. And she'd be in the field come rain or shine, so long as the police didn't shoot her for being on the property. Because that's where she'd find answers.

And I had a feeling, so would I. At the Reform Center.

Good thing the rental car had a full tank of gas.

48

Back in the car again, with ugly, boring, grass-bordered road passing by while I ground my brain gears. I retrieved my scratched, backup sunglasses from my glovebox, my good ones having vanished with Addy during the hospital drama.

I was all for investigative epiphanies—hell, who wasn't? Doug from self-defense class probably thought I had them every day. But as shiny as my most recent one was, did it hold up?

I was certain Pinky Guy was wrapped up in this, and I was certain I'd seen him at the hospital. But I'd also seen him when I was alone at the farmer's market, which suggested he was interested in me, not Addy. She was just collateral damage. Maybe I should have tracked down the hospital security guard, pressed him on how TPD had been tipped off to Addy. It would have been a waste of time, though. The guard would never have admitted if Pinky Guy was his source. Still, I might have at least been able to confirm his name. *So, about our buddy Wade Yates...*

Also on my list of possibly should-have-dones: I hadn't told John Driscoll about finding Carly's purse. It truly was an inadvertent omission, born of stress and sleep deprivation. And yet, I couldn't help wondering if my subconscious had been at work as well.

A few cops and prosecutors have proven themselves to me and shown they can be trusted. Then there's everyone else. Everyone else is suspect and, rightly or wrongly, that suspicion trickles up to infect the very structures and agencies they support. Rationally I know the vast majority of people on the right-hand side of the criminal court aisle do the right thing, that they're honest folks abiding by the laws they defend and trying to keep their communities safe. But working on criminal appeals, I often dealt with the exceptions, the cops who'd do anything to get a confession and prosecutors who'd do the same to secure a conviction, showing blatant disregard not just for defendant's rights, but also for truth and the integrity of the process.

So, should I have reported Carly's purse earlier, or my other suspicions, or even that I had Addy? Maybe. But, what if someone *was* getting to these young women? And what if that someone was connected with law enforcement or corrections? Talk to the wrong officer or the wrong agency, and I risked tipping off the bad actor(s). Then all the evidence would just go away, disappear like those young women. And unfortunately, unlike the missing women, I had a feeling the asshole (or assholes) would come back as soon as it was safe to do so.

Driving down the final stretch of fencing and pines bordering the Reform Center an hour or so later, I still felt pretty comfortable with the decisions I'd made so far. But I was no closer to knowing what I would find, or even what I was looking for.

Someone had gone DIY on the entrance security at the old correctional institute. The cattle gate had been replaced with another metal fence gate, this one a taller rectangle with vertical bars. They'd fixed plywood to the interior, making it impossible to see what was happening on the other side. The fence the gate tied into was the same old chain link that had been on-site for years, so the place wasn't exactly airtight, but at least it was more difficult to drive right in.

The young blonde guy who'd been on the scene a couple of days ago when I nearly became a crispy critter was stationed outside the entrance, wearing green cargo shorts dirty enough to be the same pair. He leaned against the gate, pencil scratching in a small yellow waterproof field notebook, the kind Laney used to leave lying in odd places in our house. The gate shifted as he stood, plywood banging raucously against the metal.

"Hey," he said, shoving his notebook into a ridiculously large pocket. At least they were functional, though his walkie-talkie had to be mounted on his hip. "You're Sydney, right?"

"That's me," I agreed.

"I'm Craig," he said, releasing the gate's catch and swinging it inward. Having a near-death experience had apparently made me an honorary member of their crew. "You might still be able to catch Professor Singh in the parking lot. She just left me here."

I lifted a hand in an appreciative wave and drove past him, toward the water- and soot-stained admin building. It was surrounded by a scorched ring of earth, but appeared to have come through the fire structurally intact. Window still open, my nose wrinkled against the lingering scent of gas and char, or was it an olfactory memory? Either way, the sensation twisted my guts like coffee from an all-night convenience store on an empty stomach.

I didn't immediately see Laney, but she must have driven Cecil to work that day. I parked next to my Cabrio and, if he'd had a tail, I swear he would have wagged it. I might have done myself. After a quick pat to his hood, I made a methodical circuit around my vehicle, squatting and peering, searching for new dents or scratches.

"I didn't break your car," Laney said. I glanced up and found her staring down at me, arms crossed. The posture was so familiar—as was the quality of her bottom drawer field attire—I flashed back and saw her ten years younger.

"I never said you did." Nagging aches from my furniture-moving fire escape prompted me to stand slowly, with an assist from Cecil's bumper.

"I didn't break your previous car, either," she said, leaning against Cecil and appraising me, noting every muscular hesitation. Laney didn't miss much.

"You never even saw, much less drove, my previous car," I said. "The car before that is the one you broke."

She grunted, adjusting her baseball cap. Her black hair hung down her back in a thick braid. "It was a piece of crap—"

"On its last legs, if cars had legs," I finished. It was an argument we'd had so many times it was no longer a conflict, just a performance piece. "How's it going here?"

"Slowly. Doesn't help that I'm short an able body at all times to watch the gate." She gave me a last ostentatious once-over. "Is that why you're here? To volunteer your less than able body to help out?"

Before I could make a smart-assed reply, Laney took my arm in hers and led me away from Cecil. My white button-down shirt hung open, and she brushed it back for a better look at what lay beneath it. "You are wearing a tank top," she pointed out.

"That means nothing," I countered. "I almost always wear a tank top."

"Come on," she said, guiding me to a beater sedan I'd noticed one of her students driving previously. "It'll do you good."

She was probably right, and it would give us a chance to talk. I followed her to the car. The door stuck a bit when I opened it, and I lowered myself cautiously into the passenger seat. Why was the second day after committing dumbassery always more painful than the first?

"Might want to roll down your window—the A/C doesn't work. But we're not going far."

She'd forgotten, I knew exactly how far we were going—I'd been there before.

Laney adjusted the rearview mirror before reversing out of the space more quickly than I would have done. I ignored her scowl as I clung to my shoulder harness. I was less successful ignoring the odd odor that permeated the car, a mixture of dirt and something it was probably better to remain ignorant about.

We headed briefly in the direction of the entrance before swinging around the building to follow the road toward the back of the property. Laney nodded significantly at the scorched structure. "So how are you doing? You been sleeping?"

"I'm fine," I said.

"Bullshit," she replied calmly, then repeated, "How are you sleeping?"

I sighed. "I don't know," I said honestly. "Who has time to sleep? Did I tell you Addy—the teenager—got picked up when we took Roger's overdosing sister to the ER?"

"Jesus," she muttered. "Seriously?"

"Afraid so."

"And you're trying to figure out how to get the kid released?" she asked.

We passed between the desolate pair of old dorms, a fenced sentinel on either side of us. The brick buildings depressed me so much I momentarily lost the power of speech. (*Where were they keeping Addy?*)

"Of course you are," Laney said, voice rough with the impact as we passed from pavement to gravel. "Released to whom?"

"Not me," I shot back.

"Easy," she said, taking her hands off the wheel in a conciliatory gesture that only made me more anxious about her driving. "Don't bite my head off. So why are you here?"

I didn't answer, concentrating on the side mirror. The thick, pale cloud rolling from our bumper was as mesmerizing as it was impervious. The world we'd left behind might as well be gone. Olive-green leaves of patchy, feral shrubs and needles of the occasional pine were milky with dust. We approached the next set of derelict buildings, and the bright smears of classroom chairs among the wooden debris were as discordant as I'd remembered. Laney slowed, and I braced myself for the bone-jarring ruts.

Finally, I said, "One of the things you mentioned before, when I asked you what was off about this place, was that someone was driving deeper into the property. Can you show me where?"

"I can try," she said. "Let me check in with my team first."

Soon we entered the familiar grassy field. Figures crouched and crawled and pointed and otherwise excavated in the distance. Three cars, all dusty and with the blush of youth behind them, were perched as close to the edge of the road as possible. Laney rolled up behind the last one and parked.

The sound of her door closing dissipated quickly in the open space. I waited in the funky-smelling vehicle, while Laney strode through knee-high grass on a now recognizable but still narrow path where there had been none just a few days ago. Her nearest students gathered round her, faces rapt with listening. Laney had once confided, in an unusual moment of quiet, sober reflection, that she believed her work brought peace to the dead. Is that all we were doing now for Carly? God, I hoped not.

Laney's face was somber on her return. Did she share my thoughts, or was it simply the proximity of the children's graves? She started the vehicle and squeezed past the other parked cars. Our tires crept to the edge of the road and beyond, and I gasped as the driver's side abruptly dropped six inches.

"Whoops," Laney said softly, leaning over the steering wheel for a better view. "Bet you're glad this isn't your car."

The other vehicles were still visible in the side mirror when the gravel and shell track narrowed. A taller variety of grass appeared in sporadic clumps by the roadside, along with a thin, weedy shrub that had also colonized the fields. I rolled my window up partway against the occasionally frisky vegetation as Laney veered around the worst of the potholes.

"What brought you out this far?" I asked.

"It's a huge property," she said. "Sold to the State for a song by one of those rich assholes whose granddaddy made his fortune in the slave trade back in the day. One day I guess I needed some space. And I was curious to see where the path led, but eventually I gave up and turned back."

"After you saw that someone else had been here," I suggested.

"Yes," Laney agreed. "It made me... uneasy."

"And you're sure it wasn't one of your people?"

"Positive," Laney said, slowing to a stop. She pointed off to the right and said, "There."

"I don't see—" I began, but then I did. A section of eroded road edge, with the vaguest hint of disturbance in the grass.

A woody branch flexed against my door when I opened it, and there was just enough room to step out into lingering dust from our car. I coughed as Laney made her way around the front of the car and joined me. It seemed likely the crumbled earth had been caused by a vehicle, but the dry ground had retained no tracks.

"Why the hell would anyone—anyone not avoiding her grad students—come out this far?" I mused.

Laney shrugged. "There was a rough circle in the grass, as if someone had turned around."

"Which way?" I asked.

Laney glanced at me in surprise, then grew quiet and closed her eyes for a few moments. "I'm not sure," she admitted. "I assumed they were going the same direction I was, but that's all it was—an assumption."

I put my arms up to act out the scenario. "I usually U-turn to the left," I said, "unless there's some reason not to."

"As do I, for what it's worth."

Which suggested at least the possibility of someone driving *toward* the excavation site from... who knew where in the opposite direction, and turning around before they were seen.

It was hot and sunny, but not yet summer hot, and sun snuck in at the top of my sunglasses. I wiped the sweat at my hairline before shading my eyes to stare off into the distance. Mike had seen someone running deeper into the property after the fire was set. "They ever figure out where our arsonist went after torching the admin building?"

"Not that I've heard," she said, "but I don't know how hard they were trying. I can tell you no strange vehicles passed my team out in the field, and none of our cars went missing."

Blake Tucker and Pinky Guy (I needed to train myself to call him by his name) both drove SUVs, so some low-level off-roading wouldn't be a problem for them. I turned to the beater sedan, and the less than Indy-caliber woman driving it. Did we dare?

Laney's dark eyes twinkled beneath her baseball cap as she read my mind. "Ready for some buccaneering?"

That's what we called our occasional late-night, no-men-allowed, bar-hopping adventures in college. A wicked grin twisted my lips as I climbed back in the car. "Aye," I said. "So long as there are no booty-surrendering jokes."

Twenty minutes later, I was shaking a persistent mosquito out of my ear, the sun's heat tight on my bared shoulders. The chances of my aching body crawling into a comfortable bed tonight sans sunburn were shrinking by the second.

"What forensic anthropologist doesn't keep a shovel in her car?" I asked.

"Not my car," Laney reminded, kneeling by the rear of the now-marooned sedan. "And they're all in use. Where's your long-limbed boyfriend when a car needs pushing?"

"If Mike were here," I said, dropping a pile of wood scraps near the front tires before ticking off on my fingers, "first of all, we'd have been in his Jeep, and we wouldn't have gotten stuck. Second of all, he'd have been driving, and we wouldn't have gotten stuck."

"Is there a third of all?" Laney asked, voice sharp.

And here I'd thought I was being kind by using the inclusive plural pronoun *we*. "Third of all, he'd probably know for sure if this car is a front-wheel drive."

Laney stood, tilting her head in consideration. "Good point," she said. "This car probably *is* a front-wheel drive, so we should place our traction aids accordingly."

We'd gone another slow mile on the gravel road, grass and weeds with aspirations giving way to shrubs and the occasional tree, before seeing a trail on the left-hand side. Theoretically, that direction led back to the Reform Center. So we'd followed it. Unsuccessfully.

In our defense, it was as broad as the "road" we'd just left, and it had obviously been used by vehicles before. But those vehicles probably had four-wheel drive, and were driven by individuals with experience in the increasingly sandy conditions.

We hadn't made it far. When the car got stuck, we'd walked an additional quarter mile or so, both paranoid that some important clue lay just out of sight. Or maybe we were just reluctant to deal with the stranded car and hoped it would magic itself free while our backs were turned. Either way, our stroll gained us nothing but more sweat and shoe grit, and a growing certainty that the road continued toward the admin building.

Since I couldn't easily dig a track, I piled the wood debris and a few small rocks behind the front tires, then topped them with the floor mats.

I swiped at my forehead sweat with my wrist to avoid muddying my face, and stood to find Laney holding out a bottle of water.

"Thanks," I said, taking a long swig. "Think it'll work?"

"It'd take a miracle," Laney said.

I smiled at the reference to our favorite movie, and Laney patted my arm as I leaned around her to toss the bottle in the car. Then I stepped back as she got behind the wheel. I closed my eyes against potential sand spray and, as the engine crescendoed, afraid of seeing our failure and contemplating the long hike back.

"Woo!" Laney whooped.

I opened my eyes to see she'd made it out and was reversing slowly toward the road, periodically popping her head out the open window. I followed her. It wasn't more than a tenth of a mile, but she stopped several yards short of their intersection. Uncertain how much oomph the sedan had in reverse, we needed to evaluate and possibly shore up the edge of the road before attempting it.

I high-fived Laney as she got out of the car and said, "I didn't think you had it in you."

"Neither did I," she admitted, dropping to the rough ground and lying back, knees raised, groaning with relief.

"Hey," I said, kicking her foot lightly as I stood next to her. "You did good."

She nodded, pulled a blade of grass from the edge of the path and began peeling it apart lengthwise, following the parallel veins. "Did you know graminoids grow from the bottom? That's why they're resistant to grazing. And fire." She tossed the blade away and stood. "This isn't just about the fire, is it? There's something else happening here."

I sighed. "I believe this place is somehow connected to a pattern of girls disappearing. Teenagers. Maybe runaways, maybe not."

"Shit. So, what? Serial killer? Prostitution ring? What are we—"

Laney stopped when a cell phone rang from the car. "Not me," she said.

I dove across the seat, grunting on my belly. "*Here* I have service?" Only barely. The phone crackled as I answered, "Yeah."

"Is that you, Sydney?" a woman asked. It took a moment for my brain to kick in and recognize her through the static—Juliet Sanders.

"Yes, I'm here," I said, crab-crawling back across the seat to stand. When I last saw Juliet, she was pretty pissed at me, and I couldn't recall her ever using my first name. I tried not to panic about why she was now.

"Have you spoken with Roger lately?" Her voice held an edge of strain, a trace of anxiety I wouldn't have expected in the seasoned litigator.

"No. Why, is something wrong?" She didn't answer, and the longer she went without answering, the more anxious *I* became. I demanded, "What's going on?"

When Juliet finally spoke, her words spilled out as if whatever held them back had fractured under the pressure. "She's gone. Addy is gone."

I leaned unsteadily against the car. Laney watched me, but held back when I lifted my free hand. "What do you mean, she's gone?"

Juliet didn't answer, again.

"Juliet?" I pushed off the car, paced away from it until, at the intersection of no patience and extreme apprehension, I snapped, "Where the fuck is she?"

Instead of being angry, Juliet's reply was soft and soothing, which made me even more paranoid. "It's probably nothing," she said. "Just a mix-up. When I went to see her, I was informed that she'd been transferred to another facility."

I held my breath for a few seconds, suppressing the shallow panting that kept creeping up on me. "Okay," I said tightly. "What about her hearing tomorrow?"

"Yes, well, the transport itself isn't necessarily unusual, nor is not informing counsel in a timely manner," said the voice of experience. "But the child wasn't transported locally. They took her to Brummel Juvenile Center."

Eleanor Dickey's facility. Where Blake Tucker works. My heart thumped in my throat, and I swallowed to unstick my tongue from the roof of my mouth. "When?" I croaked.

"I'm not sure," she admitted, irritated. "They're dragging their feet on the details at TPD. Sometime between when I saw her yesterday and when I showed up today."

My uneasiness vanished, replaced by a resolute certainty that this was not a simple miscommunication. "I'm leaving for Brummel now."

I was almost as good as my word. Laney and I got the car back on the road without further incident, and she left a dust cloud worthy of a post-apocalyptic movie in our wake, racing back to the admin building. I left my rental keys with Laney and took Cecil instead, promising to keep in touch.

The blonde guy—Craig—stood with the gate open for me, glancing around as though hordes of incensed protestors would bust through if I didn't pick up the pace. On that count at least, Laney had been lucky. Perhaps because the media coverage had been nonexistent. *Nonexistent…*

Craig nearly walked into Cecil, attempting to close the gate when I stopped halfway through.

"What?" he asked, annoyed. "You leaving or not?"

"You told me a couple of days ago that a reporter tried to bribe you. To do what?" I asked.

Craig leaned toward my window conspiratorially. "Well, he was feeling me out for details about what was going on, and what it would take for him to get inside."

"He the only one?"

"Only one that approached me," Craig said, "and I didn't hear about any others."

"Can you describe this guy?" I asked, both hoping he would and praying he wouldn't confirm my suspicions.

Craig shrugged. "Just a white dude. Maybe brown hair?"

Thus the criminal justice system's love-hate relationship with eyewitnesses. "Was he young or old? Buttoned-up, corporate-looking? Or more like you, laid-back?"

A heavy exhale made Craig's lips vibrate. "Older than me. And he never got out, but he definitely had a more corporate vibe."

"What kind of car was he driving?"

Craig winced. "I don't really know cars."

Presumably Craig was more observant when it came to dead people and their stuff. "Pickup? Hatchback?" I asked, thumbing at my own Cecil. "Or something in between? Was it red? White? Black?"

"It was dark and big. An SUV," he said. "He was a big guy. I don't think he'd have fit in your car."

Blake Tucker.

Guts twisting, I thanked Craig and continued on my way. At least the investigator gods were watching over me. The drive from the defunct juvenile center to the operating one should have been twenty minutes, but only took fifteen. I swung into a close spot and sat, gripping my steering wheel and telling myself to breathe as I stared at the glass-doored entrance. The massive brick facility loomed like a structure with a hundred more years of dark history under its belt rather than one still under warranty.

49

She's going to be okay, I told myself. *Addy's fine. Just stay calm, keep your head.*

I found a towel in the trunk and wiped at any sweat that hadn't dried in the car on the way over. Thank God I'd taken off my white button-down shirt before we dug out the stuck car. I put that on over my damp tank top. My jeans were dusty, so I did my best to brush them off. They'd been worn enough to stretch out and gape at the back, and grit had worked its way in there as well. At the last second, I remembered I was wearing a baseball cap. Tossing it in the back, I pulled my tangled red curls into a low ponytail, then strode confidently through the front doors.

The reception area was empty today, with two women behind the desk, one seated and one standing. Both had their heads down, focused on tasks in the rear of their pod. I knew they'd seen me enter, but had to clear my throat and wait for the standing one to deign to approach. Stocky and even shorter than me, her pleated khaki pants did not do her a kindness, nor did the hard face beneath her short, graying hair.

I set my driver's and PI licenses on the white counter. "I'm working with Juliet Sanders," I said, adding her business card to the pile. "I need to see one of our clients, Adelaide Hastings."

She sighed and reached for a clipboard.

"I'm not on there," I said. "Ms. Hastings is due in court in Tallahassee tomorrow. She was erroneously transported to this facility. I'm here to reassure her that we're aware of the situation and we're working to straighten it out."

The woman's forehead arched all the way to her hairline, but she didn't speak. Maybe she was mute. She stepped away with a swagger that suggested she was wearing a weapon, though I didn't see one, taking my identification with her. After they shared a few words, her trimmer, seated, black colleague glanced at me, expressionless. I gave a slight smile of the *I'm not a dick but I'm not a pushover either* variety before she looked away. Her fingers tapped away at the keys, and I fancied I could hear them over the hum of central air as she consulted her digital overlords.

I glanced at my naked wrist. I generally wore a watch any time I set foot in a prison, but I hadn't been prepared this time. Juliet was on her way, and if she'd driven as fast as I had, I figured she'd arrive in the next half hour or so. I wasn't sure how she'd react to me lying about our working relationship, but I really didn't care. I didn't care about much at the moment, except making sure Addy was okay.

The mute woman stared over her colleague's shoulder at the screen. Whatever they found on the computer made the typist purse her lips and reach for the phone.

"I'm still here, you know," I called out. They ignored me, and I shook my head and rolled my eyes, pretending I was frustrated. I wasn't. I was alarmed, even more so when, a minute or two later, the hallway door buzzed.

Eleanor Dickey emerged and said, "Come with me, Ms. Brennan."

She walked quickly down the hallway, her body shimmying slightly in an elegant black pantsuit to accommodate her high-heeled gait. I followed her into her office and before the door had closed behind me, demanded, "Where is Adelaide Hastings?"

She motioned me to sit, rested her elbows on her black, lacquered desk, and tented her fingers. "I'm afraid I don't know."

I shook my head and felt my molars grinding. "There's an awful lot of that going around."

She nodded and said, "I understand your frustration at the inconvenience—"

"Inconvenience?" I barked, incredulous. "You've lost a child!"

Color rose to her cheeks, combining with her makeup to make them glow too brightly. "We have not lost her. I'm just unable to say where she is at this precise moment." She inclined her head toward her monitor. "Ms. Hastings arrived here at 11:42 a.m., transported with one other female resident from the Tallahassee Police Department. The intake process was initiated for both young women, but there's a note that Mr. Tucker took custody of Ms. Hastings before she joined the rest of the residents for lunch."

My blood ran cold at the man's name. "And?" I prompted.

"And he probably simply failed to log her in when they arrived at their destination."

"Which would be?"

The normally composed woman's hands fluttered through the air like a dying moth. "The commissary or her dorm. A classroom..." her voice trailed off.

"So why don't we ask Mr. Tucker?" I suggested, fighting the impulse to climb over the woman's desk and choke the living daylights out of her. I didn't fight it too much, though. My anger was the only thing keeping me from panicking.

Ms. Dickey swallowed audibly before admitting, "I haven't been able to reach him."

I jumped to my feet and slammed my palms on her pristine desk. Hopefully the oils in my hands would eat through the fancy finish. "So do a goddamned search."

"That's underway now."

I leaned forward, ignoring the pain in my bending fingers. "And pull the security footage. It's a juvenile prison, for God's sake. What do you have—a hundred and fifty cameras?"

Ms. Dickey stood and placed her hands on the desk, inches from my own. She was taller than me wearing heels, but not by a lot. Up close, with her face finally exhibiting human emotions, her perfect brows and smooth, shaped bob looked artificial. They were too dark for her skin tone, and I realized she colored her hair. "Don't tell me how to do my job, Ms. Brennan."

"Apparently somebody needs to!" I shot back. My body vibrated with the need to smack her self-righteous face.

We both flinched at the sound of her office door opening. I didn't bother turning, assuming an armed guard was about to grab me by the waist and drag me from the building.

"Not now," Ms. Dickey growled, eyes still locked on mine.

"I'm sorry, ma'am," said an audibly uneasy woman behind me. "But there are officers from the Florida Department of Law Enforcement waiting to see you."

"Tell them—"

"Actually," a man's voice cut in, "we're not waiting."

Curiosity and self-preservation outweighed my need to win our staring contest. Hands still on the desk, I looked over my shoulder to see a man in a dark suit sidestep an anxious woman in business attire in the doorway. Average height and build with unremarkable brown hair, he had an everyman familiarity, but I'd never seen him before.

"Where is Mr. Blake Tucker?" he demanded.

50

I saw more FDLE guys and uniformed officers from the local Sheriff's Department when I was escorted from Ms. Dickey's office back to the waiting area. Another mute Brummel employee watched over me there. He wore black slacks and a short-sleeved, white button-down with no tie, splitting the difference between a uniform and business attire and evoking a mental facility doctor in a horror film. His glowering brows didn't help.

The few individuals who did speak with me were long on questions and short on information. With no watch and no clocks in evidence, I had no idea how long I'd been waiting for answers, but when yet another white dude in a suit dodged me, I hit the wall. Mostly metaphorically.

"Come on," I pleaded. "Are you looking for Blake Tucker in connection with the disappearance of Adelaide Hastings?"

"I told you, I can't comment on the investigation," he said.

I stepped close enough to catch a whiff of his cologne (cedar and citrus) and to confront the reality of his height advantage (easily eight inches). Glaring up at him, hands on hips, I said, "You need to get over yourself. All I want to know is who has custody of Addy Hastings, where she is, and if she's safe."

"You need to step back," he countered.

"Listen, asshole—"

"Sydney," said a familiar voice behind me, moments before Roger's hands settled on my shoulders. "Let's put our heads together elsewhere."

His arrival was a welcome relief that took the edge off my anger, but I gave The Suit one last dirty look before allowing Roger to lead me outside, arm over my shoulder.

"Who keeps you from being arrested when I'm not around?" he muttered, clicking his car unlocked.

I sat hard in the passenger's seat and said, "Maybe I only end up at risk of arrest in cases when you're involved. Ever think of that?" When he didn't reply, I asked, "What are you doing here?"

"Juliet," he said.

Leaving Deidre's room at the hospital, he'd noticed a message from his ex-wife and reached her already en route. He'd departed immediately and arrived at Brummel shortly after her. He inclined his head toward the facility and said, "Which reminds me—they took my phone, and I need to get it back."

Which reminded me... "Give me a minute."

I climbed wearily from my seat and retrieved my cell phone from Cecil, standing next to it while I dialed John Driscoll. He picked up quickly, but was reluctant to help.

"I can't talk to you," he said. "If you come in for an interview, I'm sure they'll be more than happy to share."

My laugh was short and bitter. "Yeah, right. Look, I don't have time for this! It's a simple question."

"No," he said. "It's not. Nothing is simple now. The FBI is all up in our asses—"

"John, I'm in the Brummel parking lot, and another girl just disappeared."

He blew out his breath on the other end, then admitted in a soft voice, "Yes, most of the missing girls were released from Brummel. Including the girl found dead last month."

"Thanks, John," I said, cutting him off as I hung up.

I barely had the strength to share the information with Roger when I got back in his car.

"So you think it's Tucker?" Roger asked. "You think he has Addy?"

The proposition made my skin crawl and a shriek creep from my mind toward my throat. "I don't know. It's possible—whatever the hell is going on, Tucker's involved—but something just feels off. Then there's Pinky Guy."

Roger looked momentarily confused.

"Fine, let's call him Wade Yates, since that's probably who he is. How does Yates fit into this? Is he working with Blake Tucker? If he is, I don't understand the interest in Addy, and I don't understand the sequence of events. Yates tips off the cops so Addy is picked up, just so Tucker can kidnap her from Brummel? That makes no sense."

Roger has an excellent poker face—it was one of the things that made him a powerful litigator—but we'd been through a lot together lately. Either he was masking less, or I was seeing more. In this case, a shadow in his face that had nothing to do with his grief or exhaustion. "What is it?" I asked.

He hesitated, then motioned again toward the juvenile center, still crawling with agents and deputies. "I heard them say something about the FBI."

I blinked, tried to navigate my way through jurisdictional issues far beyond my expertise. The FBI wouldn't care about Addy as a runaway. Even if there were allegations of kidnapping, I'd heard nothing about crossing state lines and she wasn't a child of "tender years," which is what usually triggered FBI involvement.

So if the FBI wasn't interested in Addy per se, what else did they have jurisdiction over? My gut said issues at juvenile facilities would be investigated by the Department of Justice rather than the FBI, but my gut was not equipped with a law library.

But they hadn't just appeared—or threatened appearance—at the juvenile facility. John had said the FBI was sticking its nose into their local investigation, too. And what were TPD and FDLE and everyone else gearing up to investigate? Not just a missing girl, but a *pattern* of missing girls like Carly, vulnerable young women with no real support network who disappeared. Who were taken or coerced into another life...

God, no. My face and feet went numb, and sound barely escaped my lips. "Human trafficking?"

"Yes, I'd say it's a strong possibility." Roger closed his eyes, clenching his hands into fists. His voice was bitter when he looked at me and added, "After all, Florida is a perennial worst offender, along with California and Texas."

"And somehow Addy's caught up in it." Or rather, we'd *gotten* Addy caught up in it. How long would it take to get her wherever they were taking her, to whomever had paid to take her? I pressed my fingertips against my forehead, pushing away vivid, visceral images of what might be done to her, even now. "What do we do?"

Roger looked away, as though ashamed he didn't have a better answer. "Juliet is in with them now. They'll tell her things they won't tell us. Though probably not much more."

"So what do *we* do?" I repeated, more forcefully.

"We wait for an update from Juliet."

I shook my head. "Not good enough."

He sighed and abused the bridge of his nose, squeezing until he winced. "Then what do you suggest?"

I didn't know. But I knew I couldn't remain here. Motion was better than sitting, and it would help me see things more clearly. "You stay here. I'm heading back to the Reform Center."

I STOPPED at a fast-food place for a quick bite and a bathroom break. It must have been an early day at school. The booths were filled with teens, boisterous with their recent release. Did Blake Tucker have kids? I didn't think so. Not that it necessarily made a difference, or gave me any insight into whether he was evil—evil people had kids, too. Of course, most people who did bad things weren't downright evil. They didn't start there anyway, though bad act after bad act might eventually land them in the Luciferous camp. But for someone who wasn't evil, selling kids would be a pretty big leap.

The metal-plywood gate stood open when I arrived at the Reform Center. I waited for an exiting car to pass, and Craig gave me a wave from the passenger's side as they did. The team must be wrapping up for the day. Craig, in turn, waited for me to enter the property and secured the gate behind me.

A gentle breeze tickled the strands of Spanish moss dangling from the live oaks flanking the driveway, but what should have been beautiful felt eerie. The rotting palm seemed apt. As I approached the road's fork, I could barely tear my eyes from the scorched admin building and surrounding area, now even more seedy in the warm, late afternoon sun. Presumably the structure would also be left to rot, as it had been to this point, but now the job was closer to done. My recent experience had given me a mild aversion to open flames, but part of me wanted to light a match and finish it off. In fact, I could have lain waste to the whole facility and slept better at night.

I whispered an apology to Cecil when a pothole jarred my teeth and his suspension. My rental car was the only vehicle remaining in the parking lot, and I parked Cecil next to it. Of course Laney would be last to leave, but I was a little surprised that everyone else was doing so with an hour or so remaining before dark. Laney had mentioned something about a piece of equipment, delayed ground-penetrating radar, that was supposed to arrive today. Maybe that had prompted the early finish.

I leaned against Cecil's back bumper and stared at the damnable structure. I tried to imagine it fifty years ago, when Mr. Weber had worked here, but the thought turned my stomach. The spot seemed, to put it bluntly, doomed for evil shit. The hip roof had lost a few more shingles with the recent fire. They lay scattered around the building, perhaps dislodged by firefighters wetting down the roof. I stared at the painted windows, the ones I hadn't been able to open or see out of.

Screw this, I thought. I rolled my neck and shook out my arms to dissipate the creepy-crawly sensations. Grabbing a flashlight, I headed for the building, picking my way carefully through the burned vegetation and rubbish. Whether sharp metal or melted, soft rubber, all objects now appeared equally charred, black and indistinguishable. My button-down shirt would probably finish the day no longer white.

I suppressed a shudder at what used to be the back door and was now a gaping, burned hole. Either the cheap laminate had been consumed entirely or its remnants were removed as part of the investigation, as was the hasp and padlock. Stinking chunks of black and gray rubble swished and chattered as I toed through them.

Pulling out my flashlight, I panned it around the doorframe and immediate interior of the building (looked solid enough) before stepping carefully over the threshold. Before, the building had been dimly lit at best. Now it seemed to absorb all light. I stood for a moment, getting my bearings, and heard an engine pass by outside. That explained Laney's absence; there must have been one last vehicle out in the field. Time to suck it up and see what I wanted to see, before she could come yell at me.

I'd forgotten to wear gloves, so I shoved my spare hand into my jean pocket to avoid mucking it up. A plasticky stench burned my nostrils and made my eyes water, and the floor felt tacky beneath my sneakers. The nasty pile of carpet had been mostly consumed (or removed) near the door, but a few fragments hadn't burned completely. The doors off the hall were blackened but remained closed in place, so those rooms had probably survived. The first, doorless room on the right, however, had been severely damaged by the fire. I hovered at its threshold, staring at the debris in the center of the room, scant remnants of the mattress and unhinged door that had rested upon the floor.

Blake Tucker, Wade Yates—someone had been using this place, until Roger and I started digging around. They'd left people, likely young women, in that first room. But not for long; the space hadn't been permeated by human body odor. Or waste for that matter, and presumably there was no functioning bathroom. So the... *detainees*, for lack of a better word, were there no more than a night or two at the outside. They could have used a bucket.

However brief the period, whoever had brought them here had locked the building from the outside. My thoughts returned to the hollow core door that had been lying on the floor. I fought the urge to kick around the debris to see if its hardware had survived. To see if something could tell me the story that had haunted me before the fire: who had removed the door, and from which side?

I squatted, elbows on my knees, and covered the flashlight with my other hand. The darkness enveloped me, all but the pinkish glow through my palm. "Did they keep you in here, Carly?" I whispered. "Did you make it out alive?"

A shuffling noise approached the doorway outside, startling me— Laney come to chew me out. I stood and winced against an ankle turn as I pirouetted and nearly over-balanced, attempting to retrace my original footsteps to avoid disturbing more probably toxic and definitely filthy nastiness.

"I know, I know," I said, stepping out into the hallway. "But you get to play in the dirt *all the time*, so the least I can do is—"

I broke off, looking up from the funky floor.

The glare from the world outside silhouetted a large figure that stood between me and the doorway.

It was not Laney.

I pulled my free hand from my pocket and spread my legs slightly so I was standing strong. "Hello, Mr. Tucker."

51

"Ms. Brennan," he acknowledged.

My racing brain snagged on the incongruity of the tenor voice coming from his massive body. If he'd been wearing a suit rather than casual clothes, the jacket's structured shoulders might have brushed both filthy sides of the hall. As it was, he simply blocked most of the light. And my way out.

"I think at this point, we might call each other by our first names," I said. My arms hung relaxed by my sides, except where one hand still gripped my tiny flashlight, now illuminating the mess on the floor. "Did you come to finish the job?"

"Which job is that?" he asked. His face was shadowed, but I could tell by his artificially flat tone that I'd struck a nerve.

Killing me, was the first response that popped into my head, but instead I said, "Burning this place down."

"That wasn't me," he said. "Though I might have liked to."

Blake's arms likewise hung by his sides, their bulk bowing slightly away from his torso. Bow-armed. If he'd been bow-legged, maybe I could have dived between his knees to escape. How much damage had Mike and I and the firefighters done to the front entrance? Were the double doors secured now? I wished I'd checked earlier.

"So it was your partner who nearly killed me?" I asked.

"No—" He caught himself, and I wondered what he'd been about to say. "My partner had nothing to do with it, either."

"What, it was spontaneous combustion?"

"I don't know what the hell it was," he said, resignation so thick in his voice that I almost believed him.

But what had happened in this building two days ago didn't matter, not right now. I asked him the only thing that did. "Where's Addy?"

"Who?"

His confusion sounded genuine. I nearly shined my flashlight in his face to see his expression, but didn't want to risk provoking him. "The girl who was with me until yesterday, the girl who disappeared from Brummel Youth Academy today."

I expected him to qualify his ignorance, as liars often did. Instead, a rumbling sound began in his chest, and his body went rigid as the noise became a low roar. He drew his elbows up, and his hands curled into fists.

"That sonuvabitch!" he growled, and twisted toward the wall. His massive fist was a blur, driving through whatever had survived the fire with a symphony of splintering cracks.

My mouth hung open. How could someone that large move so quickly? Blake's breath panted and ash danced around him in the light from the doorway, its corrosive stench irritating my nose and lungs. He slowly lowered his fist. The muscles in my calves and thighs tensed, ready for flight. But he came at me so fast I didn't have a chance.

Tucker knocked me sideways as he passed in the hallway. I bounced lightly against the filthy wall remnants, and when I'd caught my breath yelled after him, "Hey! What about Addy?"

"She won't go to prison," he muttered, head hanging low like a chastened grizzly.

What the hell was he doing? Why was he going out the front of a burned building when he was just—

But I realized he wasn't going *out* the front, he was going *to* the front. To retrieve something that was no longer there.

"You won't find it!" I called out.

My toe snagged on something and I nearly busted my ass chasing after him. One of the front doors was gone, and a slanting band of dim light illuminated the metal desk in the reception area, shoved to one side. Blake stood, staring where the filing cabinets used to be. I shone my flashlight at his profile, but he didn't react.

"The purse isn't there. I took it."

He spun on me abruptly, grabbing my shoulders so forcefully my flashlight strobed across the ceiling. "Where is it?" he demanded, fingers digging painfully into my clavicle.

Back in Tallahassee, on Roger's desk in his home office. Not that I was about to tell Tucker that. "Somewhere safe. Now let go of me."

He glanced down at his hands as if he wasn't sure how they'd gotten there, nodded and released me. "Okay," he said, and strode toward the gaping front doors.

By the time I marshaled my shaking legs to move, he was through the door and out of sight.

I found him standing behind his dark-gray SUV, now rendered almost unrecognizable by dust, parked a few car lengths from Cecil. The back hatch was up and Tucker pawed through piled belongings with his left hand, his right held to his side. A zipper burred, and a moment later he pulled a maroon towel from a fancy duffel bag of the same deep red.

The SUV shifted as Blake sat on its bumper and shook out his right hand. Like me, he wore jeans, and he shoved the sleeves of his waffle-textured, sand-colored Henley up to his elbows, leaving a dark smear on one cuff. It looked like he'd punched a coal bin. Damage and dirt were nearly indistinguishable, but I still winced at the sight of his abused knuckles. Sweat had gathered at his temples in his short brown hair, trickling down the side of his broad face, but his expression remained stoic as he rubbed the towel roughly across his injured hand.

"What the hell's going on at Brummel? And here?" I asked.

Flexing his fingers slowly, he responded with his own question. "Are there really people after me? Looking for me?" he asked.

"Seems that way," I admitted.

"And why are you here?"

"Looking for answers," I said. "Looking for Addy. You're the last person she was seen with, according to the records at Brummel."

"Bullshit," he said, shaking his head. "She never made it to Brummel."

"Then where the hell is she?" I demanded.

He stared down at his knuckles.

"Hey, asshole!" I shouted. When he kept ignoring me, I punched his thigh as hard as I could. It was like striking a wall.

Blake raised his head, and his dark eyes bored into me like the heat from the recent fire, their intensity taking my breath away. "Where is she?" I whispered.

"Give me your keys," he said.

I took a step back, gauged the distance to Cecil. Maybe thirty feet. I might get inside, but I'd never get the door shut in time. Best-case scenario: even if Tucker face-planted out of the gate, I'd never get Cecil moving before his fist or elbow came through the window. And yes, I know how hard it is to break a car window.

"You're the one who hid Carly Whitmore's purse, aren't you?" He didn't answer, but he didn't have to—I could see the affirmative in his face. "Why? Did you recognize her name when I asked you about her? Or maybe you didn't realize until you saw her records."

He dropped the blackened, bloody towel into the car next to him, closed the hatch, and advanced on me. He stopped so close that only the broader spread of his hips kept us from standing on each other's toes. "I said, give me your keys."

My heart slammed in my chest and my brain shut down for a moment, transfixed by a hand that could palm a beach ball, never mind my head. I shook the image from my mind and said, "I'll go with you."

"No, you won't," he said. The rough skin of his palm brushed over the back of my hand before he gripped my wrist and squeezed.

My knees buckled, just an inch or two, before I could stop them. "Yes, I will," I said through gritted teeth.

His fingers adjusted slightly on my wrist, then gave a quick twist.

I gasped as my fingers flew open of their own accord, dropping my keys into his other hand. "Asshole!" I squealed, shaking out my wrist, though I was more indignant at the man turning his back on me than still in pain.

He walked toward Cecil. "Your cell phone in there?"

I didn't answer, but he opened the door and rummaged in the console.

"It never works here," I said, which was mostly true. My phone looked the size of a paper clip in his hands as he took it anyway, backing out of my car and locking it. "What are you doing? Are you meeting Wade Yates?"

His head jerked toward me at the idea, but I wasn't sure if he actually recognized the name.

"What do you think I'm doing?" he said, returning to his vehicle. "Getting the hell out of Dodge."

"Not with my keys and phone, you're not," I protested.

I followed him to the driver's side, and before he slammed the door in my face, I heard him say, "But first, I can fix this."

I tried the nearest passenger door as he started his engine —locked.

"Hey!" I glared at Blake through the windshield and slammed my hands on the hood of his SUV, felt the *bang* resonate through my wrist. "You can't leave me here!"

His square face was resolute, as though he were looking through me. What was I supposed to do, jump on top? I considered it, but self-preservation prevailed and I stepped back as he reversed out of the space. I wasn't sure if the front gate was locked, but it was still closed. It didn't matter. When Tucker reached the split in the road, instead of heading toward the gate, he turned in the other direction, driving deeper into the complex.

Shit. I watched his dust cloud retreat into the distance. Blake was my only possible link to Addy. And what was he going to fix? Eliminating witnesses? Although you'd think that would have included me.

I had no cell phone to call for backup. No car to follow him. Except the locked rental, but I didn't have the keys for it, either. I could walk toward the excavation site on the assumption that Laney was still out there in another vehicle, or I could walk to the road on the off chance that someone passed by. The road was closer.

I walked toward the road.

At least I started walking, until I saw something that made me run.

The gate was moving, thanks to a man who'd removed his suit coat and rolled his pale-blue sleeves to his elbows.

"Roger!" I yelled, sprinting toward him.

"Sydney?" he said, brows wrinkling at the sight of a colleague apparently gone insane. "What's wrong?"

I shoved the gate from his hands, swinging it wide. "They find Addy yet?" I asked, panting.

"No."

"Then let's go! Tucker's getting away."

Roger didn't argue, just jumped in the car and accelerated into the property, leaving the gate open. "Right or left?" he asked, as we approached the split.

"Left," I said. "I don't know where he's going—maybe off-road, so slow down or we'll miss him." *Or die*, I thought, gripping the armrest on the door.

"So he has Addy?" Roger asked.

"No, but he has my phone and my car keys," I said. Roger's gaze shot at me, so I continued, "And he might know where she is. He definitely knows who has her. Honestly, I don't know what the hell's going on, but he's neck-deep in it."

I squinted at the cracked but still technically paved lane. The sun was low enough in the sky for me to drop the sun visor and wish I were a few inches taller or had my sunglasses on hand. Of course they were locked in my car. I leaned forward, eyes glued to the road.

There was still a trace of dust in the air, but no sign of Tucker. How familiar was he with this place?

We slowed to a crawl at the first set of buildings, the single-story dorms that had so appalled Addy. (*They locked people up here? Kids?*) What if they were keeping her there? But I didn't see an access point, and the only place for Blake's SUV to hide was behind or inside a building. "He's not here," I said, waving him forward. "Keep going."

Roger couldn't drive much faster. Soon the pavement fell away, and the abrupt transition to shitty gravel was jarring even in his BMW.

"Sorry," I said, when Roger cringed at a particularly hard jolt.

"That's okay; I'll figure out some way to send the State my mechanic's bill."

The looming pine trees felt even more threatening than previous occasions, and we were starting to lose the light. I wasn't sure if that would help or hurt us. Even if we saw the glow of headlights in the distance, that didn't mean we'd be able to find the path to reach them.

"Wait—there," I said, pointing ahead and to the left. "The palmettos."

Fanned bunches of long, straight green leaves formed a dense clump several feet high and thick. Saw palmettos are common in Florida; I had them in my own yard. But at the Reform Center I'd primarily seen them around the main buildings, and never before bordering the road.

Roger stopped and I clambered from the car for a better look. I waved a triumphant arm—it was another road, curving back at a sharp angle, which further disguised its appearance. I jogged a few yards and couldn't see the end of it. Recent tire tracks appeared as rough trenches, but the route seemed more solid than the one Laney and I had gotten stuck on earlier.

"What do you think?" I called out.

Roger scuffed at the ground with one brown, fine leather toe. "Let's go," he said, and we hurried back to the car.

Palmetto fronds tickled the driver's door as Roger performed a couple of quick reverse maneuvers to turn onto a road that felt smoother than the one we'd left.

"Tucker's got to be meeting someone," I said, still terrified for Addy and still desperately scrutinizing every inch of ground ahead of us. But Roger's arrival had opened a crack to let hope in. "He says he didn't torch the building."

"You believe him?" Roger asked, grasping the steering wheel tightly.

"Yeah, I think I do," I said, deciding as I answered. "Doesn't seem his style. Blake said it wasn't his partner, either. That I'm less sure about."

Roger said, "The other guy. With the pinky."

Poor thing—I'd broken him too.

"Wade Yates. Maybe it's him. Or maybe Blake isn't part of a meeting at all, maybe he's breaking one up." I pushed my hair back with an unsteady hand and fought to keep my voice steadier. "He put his fist through the wall when I told him Addy'd been taken. And I think he's the one who hid Carly's purse."

Roger's own voice was ragged when he replied, "So maybe he doesn't approve of selling girls, and he's trying to stop the hand-off. Got any ideas for when we catch up with him and whatever circus is waiting?"

"Call for help?" I suggested, and glanced away from the road to see if Roger's phone was handy.

"Left it with Security at Brummel," Roger said. "Hopefully Juliet will think to grab it when she gets hers."

The little sliver of hope narrowed, along with my airway. "Then I guess we'll have to wing it."

The pines on our winding path became shorter, bushier trees growing closer together, with scrubby vegetation filling in the gaps in the red needle-strewn carpet. I unhooked my seat belt and stuck my head and shoulders out the window, straining to hear or see Blake's vehicle without losing my head to a stray shrub. The chorus of insects and frogs created a low wall of buzzing, chirping white noise, punctuated by a persistent, trilling call.

Roger slowed as we approached a suspicious rift on the left side of the road.

"Good eye," I said.

He left the car idling while we followed the branching path and bent over it, as if we'd suddenly become forensic experts in the past half hour. The slightest hint of tread showed in some of the tracks. I spread my fingers to gauge the size.

"Smaller than Tucker's tires, so I think it's safe to assume his vehicle didn't detour this way," Roger said.

"Agreed," I said, waving at a humming mosquito circling my ear as I returned to the main path. "Looks like the smaller tires turned left here, heading the same direction as Blake, the same way we're going."

Roger nodded. "Okay, then—let's go."

My hand was on the door handle when the natural forest rhythms went silent and a gunshot rang out through the forest, shockingly immediate and loud. My heart stopped, then jolted ahead as a second shot ripped through the air. Its lingering echo made the hairs on my arms prickle.

Addy... I bolted down the road after Tucker.

52

"Sydney, wait!" Roger said.

I lost my footing and stumbled near the edge of the road, which was the only reason Roger caught up with me in his fancy shoes. Spinning around as he grabbed me, I slid in the loose dirt and fell to one knee.

"Sydney," Roger said, seizing my shoulders, "Don't be stupid. You can't help Addy if you're dead."

Panting slightly, I nodded. The gesture was intended to convey, *I hear you*, not *I agree with you*.

Spots of color stood out on his pale cheeks as he continued, "We don't even know she's here. We don't know who's here, or who's armed."

I nodded again.

"The gunshot sounded close. It's probably safer to go on foot, but let's not just sprint directly into someone's line of fire. Agreed?"

I nodded, and Roger said, "This time, I need to hear you say *yes*."

"Yes," I said.

Roger released my shoulders, his hand briefly cupping my fuzzy hair.

We ducked low as we trotted down the road, cutting from one

edge of the trail to the opposite one to stay out of sight when the path curved. Back and forth, my blood rushing so loudly in my ears I wouldn't have known if we mimicked a stampeding herd. The surrounding canopy thinned momentarily, and the penetrating sunlight lent a pinkish-orange tint to Roger's glowing shirt a half-step ahead of me.

The road finally straightened to reveal a dark luxury sedan similar to Roger's. It was parked a couple of car lengths ahead of Blake Tucker's SUV, and both faced the same direction. We drew closer, and I saw a figure kneeling at the edge of the road between the two vehicles.

Eleanor Dickey, still wearing her heels and pantsuit, held a gun in her hand.

Roger crept forward and, before my tongue could form words, he barked, "Stand up and drop the weapon on the ground! Now!"

Back to us, Eleanor flinched and slowly rose, tossing the gun away with visibly shaking hands.

"Oh, God!" transitioned to a wailing moan as she turned toward us.

I shuddered with apprehension at a long, dark shape on the ground, closer to Tucker's vehicle than to Eleanor Dickey's. Blake Tucker's body became distinguishable from the earth as I rushed toward him. The mound of his massive chest was unmoving.

Blake lay on his back, eyes open and face stiff, a roughly round and slightly bloody entrance wound just off-center in his forehead. A desperate, hiccupping sound escaped me as I quickly looked away, taking in the wound in his chest. It had bled more, dark against his pale, textured shirt, but not as much as I would have expected. I put my hand to his wrist, feeling a moment's revulsion at the certainty that the man was gone from this sack of meat, but went through the motions anyway.

Roger watched, standing with his arms around Eleanor Dickey. My fingers moved from Blake's wrist to brush the fluffy tips of his close-cropped hair as I said, "He's dead."

Eleanor Dickey's knees buckled, and she nearly took Roger down with her.

"Ms. Powers? Eleanor?" he said, endeavoring to hold her upright. "You need to tell us what happened."

Her voice trembled as she said, "I don't know. I don't know *why.*"

"Eleanor... Eleanor!" Roger finally shouted in her face. "Pull yourself together."

After a moment's hesitation, she gave her head a shake and stood under her own power, though still leaning heavily against Roger on awkward, unsteady legs and wobbling heels. "I'm sorry. I just—I don't understand any of this. Blake asked me to meet him here."

"Why?" I asked, echoing her earlier statement as I knelt next to Blake. Her eyes flicked at me briefly, then quickly away.

"I don't know why. I know I shouldn't have met him, that I should have reported the contact to someone in authority. But Blake and I have been together for so long. I couldn't help thinking there'd been a misunderstanding. That I could convince him to come in on his own and straighten things out."

"But you still brought a gun?" I asked.

She blinked, mouth moving wordlessly for a moment, then said, "My father's daughter. I always carry a gun with me."

Roger gently disengaged himself from her, creating a handsbreadth of space between them. "What did he want?"

"I—" She stopped herself, releasing a hiccup similar to my earlier one, and her hand flew to her mouth. "I almost laughed. Can you believe it? The idea of saying *I don't know* again made me want to laugh."

"It's shock, Eleanor," Roger said. "What did he want?"

She pursed her lips against the automatic *I don't know,* then answered, "He seemed to think someone had given me something. But he wouldn't say what, and he wouldn't say who the person was. He just acted like I already knew, that I was playing games with him."

She glanced over when I stood, then turned back to Roger and continued, "I think he was insane. Truly, clinically insane. He said he was going to kill me. And he would have."

Eleanor hadn't once mentioned Addy. Where the hell was she?

I walked around Blake's SUV, peering in the windows and standing on tiptoes to inspect the back. My cell phone was on the passenger seat, so I grabbed it, but there was no Addy. I hadn't expected her to be there, but I had to check. In fact, I had to check everywhere.

I walked toward Eleanor and Roger and asked, "Ms. Powers, may I have your keys?" She hesitated, and I added, "I'd just like to reassure myself that Mr. Tucker didn't put something in your car without your knowledge."

"Okay," she said, though still sounding uncertain. "The keys are in my car."

As expected, her car was unlocked with no one inside. It beeped at me until I pulled the keys from the ignition. The trunk release was mounted next to the steering column, and the pop when I pulled the lever made me flinch as badly as the gunshots had done. The metal trunk lid slowly floated up to fill the back window.

"What are you looking for?" Eleanor asked.

I ignored her and let Roger answer, ignoring him as well.

Five. That's how many steps it took me to round the corner of the trunk, sneakers leaving drag marks on the gritty ground... holding my breath as the hollow, interior space came into view.

Empty. No body.

My legs didn't want to hold me. I grasped the bumper, riding out the unholy mix of relief and disappointment that surged through me. The air I inhaled stuck at my upper chest, leaving my lungs hungry. Fighting the desperate need to gasp for more, I focused on the flat odor of musty synthetic carpet and the sharp tang of windshield wiper fluid. When I could see straight, I examined the trunk more closely with pulsing eyes and shaking hands. Nothing unusual that I could see in the dim, built-in bulbs and fading dusk. I missed my little flashlight.

So where was Addy? And what was really going on here?

Slamming the trunk shut, I shook my head as I met Roger's eyes, recognizing the same mix of relief and disappointment there.

"What is it?" Eleanor asked, gaze shifting between us.

I don't know how Roger answered; I was too busy staring down at Blake Tucker's dead body, wishing he could talk. Blake had said he was getting out of Dodge. Was running away an impulse or planned? I remembered a duffel in the back, but that could have been his gym bag. I circled his SUV and lifted the hatch again. Just the one bag, but a flash of color caught my eye. It was a triangular, red flag on a flexible metal shaft, the kind you might attach to a bike. I was certain it hadn't been there when Blake was tending his knuckles.

"Sydney," Roger called, I had a feeling not for the first time. He rounded the SUV and said, "You locked Eleanor's car. She asked me if I'd call the police, but we need the keys to get her cell phone."

Roger stood next to me, touched my elbow gently. "Sydney?"

The man who'd taken my keys less than half an hour ago was frightening, but not insane. I met Roger's eyes and pointed at the flag. His chest expanded with a deep inhale, but he didn't speak.

I closed the hatch and walked toward Eleanor's car. "Sorry about that. Eleanor, the police will need to examine your gun to corroborate your story. Do you have something we can use to preserve the evidence? Maybe a plastic bag?"

She hesitated. "I, uh, yes. I keep garbage bags in the glove box—"

"I'll get them," I said. "You have gunshot residue on your hands. If you want this resolved quickly, it's best to avoid contamination. And I'll get your phone, too."

"Fine," she said, but didn't sound crazy about it.

"Eleanor," Roger said sympathetically, returning to her side, "once we've notified the authorities, is there anyone else you'd like to call?"

I got in the passenger's side for easier access, and the car muffled their conversation. The glovebox was unlocked, and I discovered Eleanor and Roger were cut from the same anal-retentive mold. A roll of small, white plastic bags was tucked next to an empty, leather gun holster and a quart Ziploc bag full of plastic handcuffs. I peeled a bag free and shoved a couple of the restraints in my jean pocket. Her cell phone was in the center console. I slipped it in my back pocket and climbed into Eleanor's back seat.

"Did you find it?" she called out.

I shoved my hand in the crease where the back support met the bottom—nothing—and stuck my head on the floor to peer beneath the seats before shoving my hand in there, too. Beneath the driver's seat, was a small, cheap cell phone.

I heard Roger making excuses ("probably couldn't hear you") as the two of them approached the car. I slipped the cheap phone in my pocket, trading it out for the one from the console.

Backing out of the car, I said, "Got it. It had fallen on the floor. Here, you can call it in."

I handed the fancy phone to Roger with an infinitesimal head shake, one I hoped Eleanor couldn't see and Roger understood. Then I approached Blake's body and Eleanor's gun. I turned the rustling plastic bag inside out to pick up the weapon, as if it were a pile of dog poop. Eleanor had drifted in that direction as well while Roger called 9-1-1, his words precise and his calm voice reassuring.

"Eleanor," I said. She was staring at Blake's body, lower lip trembling, and I waited for her attention to turn to me. Her face was tear-streaked, mascara slightly smudged at the outside corners of her eyes. "How did you get here?"

She looked pointedly at her car, as if to suggest this was a poor time for jokes. "I drove."

"How did you find it?" I asked, voice carefully neutral. "Had you been here before?"

"No, never."

"So Blake Tucker gave you directions?" I asked.

"Yes. But I didn't bother writing them down. They were simple— just one turn directly off the highway past the entrance. And"—she pointed at her head—"I've always been good with those kinds of things."

If he'd set up the meeting, why take the longer route through the main part of the complex and risk being seen? Devil's advocate: he had to go that way to retrieve Carly's purse, not knowing I'd already taken it. But where had he picked up the red flag? It wasn't in the back of his car when he'd left the admin building, so logically he'd picked it up on the way to meet Eleanor. I imagined him stopping at the vegetation-obscured turn, then getting out and retrieving the flag to prevent me—or someone far scarier—from following him.

So the better question than where Blake had picked up the flag was, who had set it out to mark his path?

Blake had quickly transitioned from confusion to anger when I told him a girl had disappeared from Brummel. *That sonuvabitch*, he'd said, which usually referred to a man. But moments later, when I was chasing him down the hall and asked about Addy, he'd said, *She won't go to prison*. I'd assumed he was answering my question, and that he meant Addy.

Even earlier, I'd asked about his partner nearly killing me, and he'd caught himself, carefully avoided using a pronoun. I'd *assumed* (there was that word again that means I made an ass of myself) the partner was Wade Yates. A *he*, not a *she*.

And who had spoken to Blake already and warned him that people were looking for him?

We often have a cultural bias against suspecting women of masterminding criminal enterprises rather than being their victims, especially where children are concerned. But look at Addy's foster mother, cycling through vulnerable children for checks, with no real regard for their welfare. I'd seen far worse at the Public Defender's Office and later working criminal appeals, where the breadth of venality among the fairer sex was staggering.

And yet, for all their mercenary actions, on my more generous days I couldn't help feeling a trace of pity for most of these women. Their deeds were born from desperation, from poverty, from hopelessness.

If Eleanor Dickey was involved in this, her behavior was motivated by greed. And maybe by something darker.

Roger moved to stand alongside Eleanor Dickey, the cell phone in his hand. His lips pursed, adding an edginess to his haggard face. I looked to him, and he gave a slight nod. *No idea where you're going with this, but I trust you*. At least, that's what I decided he meant. Then he said, "They'll be here soon and asked me to stand by for their follow-up call."

"Ms. Dickey," I said, "Where is Addy Hastings?"

She blinked, head tilting with disbelief. "You mean she still hasn't been found? Wait... you think Blake had her?" A hand went to her mouth. "Oh, dear God. That poor child."

I turned my back on her as she closed her eyes against her tears.

How much time had passed between the gunshots and Roger and I stumbling on the scene? Maybe a minute or two. So what had Eleanor been doing when we arrived? I walked to the edge of the road, broke off a branch from the nearest leggy shrub, and poked it through the vegetation, shoving aside grass and leaves.

It didn't take long—white plastic flashed in the dim light.

Blood rushed to the surface of my skin and I felt my face flush as I picked up my sunglasses. I'd loaned them to Addy in the hospital, and they must have been among her effects when she was arrested. I held them high, rotating for the best light. A couple of long hairs hung from one hinge, straighter than mine and darker. My anxiety probably conjured the hint of blue.

"My God," Eleanor said, "he really did have her."

"But she isn't in his vehicle, so where would he have taken her?" Roger asked as I approached them and dropped the sunglasses into the bag with the gun.

"I don't know," she said. "I've never even been to his house."

"Really?" Roger asked. "Because he'd been to yours. Or at least to your father's. Did he have a relationship with your father?"

"No. He came there for me. We were working." She shook her head with confusion. "Why are you asking me all these questions?"

Roger began scrolling through her recent calls. "Blake Tucker called her ninety minutes ago."

"That's what I told you. Please," she pleaded, "can you tell me when someone will be here? I just want this to be over."

"What's Blake Tucker's number, and the exact time of the call?" I asked, and watched Eleanor as I pulled out the cell phone I'd found under her car seat. She didn't react at all.

Roger read out the number, while I scrolled through the other phone's recent calls. *Bingo.* "Blake called you because *you* called *him* two minutes earlier, on this burner phone. He was calling you back, per your instructions."

"That's not my phone," Eleanor said calmly.

"It was in your car," I said, handing it to Roger, who scanned its directory.

"Then Blake must have left it there," she countered.

"Before or after you shot him?" I asked. She didn't answer. "Who's your other partner?"

She stared at me blankly. "I don't know what you mean."

"Is it Wade Yates?" I asked.

I hadn't thought it possible, but her face became even emptier. Like a mannequin. It was creepy. "Where's Addy?" I demanded.

"I wish I could tell you," she said, in a flat, noncommittal tone that matched her expression. Did I imagine the taunting edge when she added, "She obviously means a great deal to you."

My hand cracked across the woman's face, hard enough to send a shooting pain up my wrist and set my fingers and palm buzzing.

Eleanor touched her cheek, where my handprint was already visible against her pale skin. Her mouth had dropped open with the impact. She licked her lips before they curled back in a smile, gone as quickly as it had appeared.

"Don't hurt your wrist," Roger said, then indicated a contact on her phone identified merely as *#3*. "Look at this. She called the number this morning and last night and regularly for months prior to that, usually on Thursdays."

"Try it," I said.

Eleanor began, "You have no right—"

I shoved a finger in her face. "Back off."

She did, raising her hands and looking at me as though she were innocent and I were a psycho.

Eleanor's firearm hung heavily in the bag by my side as I angled my head toward Blake's body and his SUV, sensitive to the unlikely possibility that his phone would ring. No electronic sounds broke the relative stillness of the woods, but someone picked up on the other end. I banged against Roger, leaning in to hear.

A man's angry, whining twang said, "You're late. Where are you?"

Roger hung up.

He had her. Wade Yates, Pinky Guy, or whoever the hell it was on the other end of the line, some motherfucker had Addy. I just knew it.

Stepping back, I pulled Eleanor's gun from the bag, barely able to sense its textured grip beneath my still-tingling hand. I pointed it at Eleanor and said, "Get on your knees."

53

There's something clarifying about holding a gun on someone, especially when it's her gun.

"Sydney…" Roger warned, as Eleanor protested, "You know I'm the victim."

"You admit you just killed a man," I pointed out. "Forgive me for restricting your movements until the authorities make their own determination as to what happened here. So get on your knees."

Eleanor slowly lowered to one leg, then both, with the poise of a CEO doing her 2:45 desk yoga. I tossed Roger a set of plastic restraints. He hesitated.

"Roger," I said, "Addy doesn't have much time. Do it. And then call it in. For real this time."

He threaded the plastic cuffs awkwardly, then pulled on Eleanor's hands to make sure they held. Digging an agent's card from his wallet, he said, "FDLE," and paced behind Eleanor.

I wanted to shake him—*Dumbass, bullets don't always stop with one body.* And Eleanor Dickey was inviting a bullet. Maybe more than one.

The revolver in my hand was smaller than Turtle's with a shorter barrel. I popped the cylinder and confirmed it was fully loaded, with the two shots that killed Blake Tucker the only cartridges fired.

"Right now," I said to Eleanor in a low voice, "I don't give a shit whether you go to prison or not. I just want Addy, safe and sound."

Hands restrained, Eleanor's body swayed slightly when I pressed the muzzle to her temple next to a prominent vein that looked like a river on a map. "Maybe I should have mentioned, I don't give a shit whether *I* go to prison, either. Now where is she?"

The pressure against the gun's muzzle increased, as if Eleanor was leaning into it, and her mouth curved into a mirthless smile.

Blake was right. Eleanor would never allow herself to go to prison. If she couldn't escape prosecution, she'd take her chances with the jury, probably even take the stand. And with her word against a dead man who was twice her size, she had a decent shot of winning. So she wasn't about to make a deal with anyone in law enforcement, or an admission to any civilian who might testify against her.

Eleanor's eyes danced with excitement, but she never spoke. And she was never going to.

I tugged at her hands, doing my own safety check. "Please, pull hard and cut off the circulation. The only thing better than you in prison is you in prison sucking your food through a straw."

"Sydney," Roger said softly. I wasn't sure when he'd come to stand next to me. "They're on their way."

I watched Eleanor's face as I asked, "They looking at Brummel staff?"

She blinked, but her expression didn't change.

Roger said, "They were doing that hours ago."

Depending on how far any underlying trafficking investigation had gone, FDLE or the FBI or somebody may already have suspects in mind for conspirators. If not, a deep dive into the center's records would probably point them in the right direction. Either way, it would take time to get any answers from that angle. Time Addy didn't have. Especially since I doubted Wade Yates worked there.

I wasn't worried about Eleanor making a break for it—an escape attempt would be a damning admission, one difficult to explain to a jury. I walked to the other side of her car so I could pace without looking at her. Eleanor was less afraid of dying than of going to prison. How could I use that to help Addy? *Think, dammit, think!*

My relentless footsteps brushed away scattered pine needles, revealing the sandy ground beneath them. What else did Eleanor's messed-up mind state tell me? Maybe something that would give me insight into her role in this criminal enterprise. I channeled my inner mean girl and my inner psychotherapist, and tried to recall all the ways Eleanor had pushed my buttons. Was there a pattern there?

She was dismissive of women, like her administrative assistant. She'd also been rude to me at our first meeting and mostly ignored me to interact directly with Roger. She worked in a male-dominated field, even more so than me. Her closest confidants—did she have such a thing? Her closest *associates*—seemed to be men. Blake Tucker, for example, and it looked like Pinky Guy/Wade Yates as well. Did she surround herself with men because they represented power, or because she could better control them? At her father's home, she'd initially been protective and respectful of the man, but ultimately dominated him. *Ellie* had some serious daddy issues.

So she wasn't just dismissive of women; she was dismissive if not contemptuous of other people generally, unless they were useful to her. And she sometimes gave the impression that she was playing a part, imitating emotions instead of feeling them. In short, she was a sociopath.

I glanced at Blake's dead body. He might have been a good source of insight into the woman, and I couldn't help wishing I'd spoken with him longer, convinced him to come clean. I covered my eyes, heels of my hands pressing against my cheekbones, and breathed into the darkness for a moment. If wishes were horses, I'd hook Eleanor's ankle to a saddle and drag her sorry ass behind one.

But she might like that; my hunch was that she was an adrenaline junkie. The photo of the helmeted skydiver in her dad's home—I'd bet anything it was Eleanor. And the photo of the blonde child...

I stopped in my tracks. That was it. Whatever genetic defects had nudged Eleanor toward being a psycho, her childhood had solidified her nasty, sadistic core. A shiver ran through me, recalling Turtle's words when he put a gun to my head and nearly killed me. *Was it you?* he'd asked. *Were you the one watching at the window?* And I'd made the same blind, sexist error I'd made with Blake.

Roger stood near Eleanor, revolver by his side and her cell phone at his ear. He had the expectant expression of someone waiting on hold rather than listening to another human being. Eleanor had slipped off her spiky shoes and seemed comfortable sitting on her heels. I ambled toward her, teasing my fingers through my curly, red hair, wincing at the tangles. Her short, dark bob still had body where it was shaped in back and hung smoothly toward the front.

"Humidity's a bitch," I said.

Eleanor raised a narrow, perfect brow, but didn't comment.

"You're a natural blonde, aren't you?" I asked. I'd caught her off guard, enough to get a flicker of reaction. She almost seemed pleased that I'd noticed. "Were you afraid people wouldn't take you seriously as a blonde?"

"Something like that," she said.

"I get it," I said. "Though it's a shame to lose the incongruity of an innocent, angelic blonde doing not-so-innocent things."

I had her attention, gaze tracking me as I dropped to one knee next to her. "Especially when she's a child. Did you know they knew you were there? Watching through the window? Because they did know."

Her eyes widened slightly, lips parted. I continued in a husky, conspiratorial voice. "You suspected, didn't you, Ellie? That's what made it so exciting."

I leaned in, so close to her ear my breath lifted fine hairs as I whispered. "So addictive."

Eleanor blinked slowly, and a rough sigh escaped her.

"But somebody reported you, or maybe Wade Yates just caught you in the act. Did he punish you?" Eleanor's pupils dilated. It might have been my shadow's influence, but I didn't think so. "Uh-huh.

That's when he knew he'd found his soulmate, even if you were just a child. Because age is nothing more than a number."

She smiled, much like she had with a gun to her head. I noticed in my peripheral vision that Roger had hung up and focused his entire attention on me. On us.

"And now, the girl is waiting for you, for her punishment. But you won't be there to watch it, will you? Or to take your own." I drew back until I could see her face, but still close enough to count her lashes if the light were better. "You know he won't wait for you, don't you? He doesn't need you anymore. You were. Never. In. Control."

Her smile spread, baring her white teeth. "I am *always* in control."

"Then where's the girl, Ellie?" I whispered.

"Don't worry," Eleanor said. "She won't have long to wait."

I envisioned Eleanor's blood staining those pretty, perfectly spaced white teeth while I considered her words. *Not long to wait.* Someone was coming for Addy. Someone besides Eleanor.

"Did you hear that?" I asked Roger as I stood.

"Yes, I did," he said, voice vibrating with anger, his gun hand shaking with restraint.

Her smile faded, replaced by her spooky, blank Stepford expression.

Who was coming for Addy? And where?

I led Roger away from Psycho Bitch and Blake Tucker, not so far that he couldn't easily shoot her, but far enough that he wouldn't be so tempted. "Okay," I said, "We don't know who has Addy, and we don't know who's coming for her."

"If someone has her," Roger countered. "She could be securely detained, alone."

I considered. "That's our best-case scenario, since it means fewer players. But someone is coming, and Thursday is the day she uses the burner phone with this guy."

"So it could be the hand-off day," Roger said. "The day they pass off girls to buyers."

I pressed the back of my hand against my mouth to keep angry, desperate tears away (*I'm coming, Addy*), then cleared my throat. "But this is all speculation. As for where... Eleanor said she's always in control. How long ago did we call the partner?"

"A few minutes," Roger said, looking down at the screen. "Seven," he corrected.

"If she is calling the shots, and he doesn't hear from her again soon..."

Roger nodded, jaws grating as he looked past me at Eleanor.

"Did they ever text?" I asked.

"Yes," he said.

I held out my hand for the phone and scanned their communication. They never used specific names or places, which meant tricking the location out of her accomplice was risky and unlikely to succeed. Instead I focused on the style of Eleanor's texts, whether she used complete sentences or obscure abbreviations. And then I imitated her.

Got interrupted, I typed. *I'll be on my way soon.*

I felt a moment's fear masquerading as regret when I hit *Send*.

Roger and I stared at the blank screen in my hand. Waiting. Wondering if it even went through.

Voice low, Rogers said, "That doesn't much help if—"

The phone buzzed and the screen flashed. *Okay. Hurry up.*

"—we don't know where they are."

Roger was right; the clock was running. I shoved a hand in my hair and tugged it away from my forehead, hoping the mild pain would clear my racing mind.

"Maybe they can trace his phone," Roger said.

Maybe "they" (some component of the LEO alphabet soup) could, *when* they arrived. *If* they could tap into whatever technology was required remotely. *If* we had time we didn't have.

"Let's assume Eleanor did set up the meet with Blake, and she did it last minute," I said.

"Tying up loose ends," Roger said.

I nodded. "It sounds like the guy on the other end is already expecting her. With a schedule that tight..."

"She would have asked Blake to meet somewhere she knew and

could control, but also somewhere close to where she was meeting Wade," Roger finished.

"Exactly."

Roger circled a finger in the air. "On the extended property?"

"Maybe. Somewhere they'd used before." I ran through possibilities in my mind.

The admin center was out, and not just because of the recent fire. Whatever they'd been doing there had to have gone on standby once the excavation started. Same thing for any place the forensic crew would pass daily, which encompassed most if not all of the still-habitable buildings. I certainly hadn't seen anything on the site plan that fit the bill.

"Do you think I could beat it out of her?" Roger asked.

He wasn't kidding.

"I think she'd love you to try. And if I thought it would work, I'd make you stand in line. What about this road? It has to lead somewhere."

"But will we see where?"

Fair point. We were losing the light, and if they'd taken steps to mask the entry the way they had this one, we'd be hard-pressed to detect it. Assuming there was only a single turn, and that we'd even recognize our destination when we got there.

The phone rang in Roger's hand. My throat constricted, only easing slightly when he looked at the screen and said, "FDLE again." He answered, and an indistinct voice echoed from the other end. "I'm sorry, you need to repeat that."

Eleanor still sat on her heels, seemingly checked out, but Roger continued watching her while he talked on the phone. I planted my ass on the hood of Eleanor's car, hoping she'd make a run for it. Then I could launch myself at her and stomp her to the ground.

I was certain Addy was somewhere nearby. But with Eleanor mute and Blake dead, who else might know where?

Eleanor's father was at least an hour away and wasn't aware what century we were living in. I doubted he or his daughter inspired deep loyalty in his household staff, but I also doubted Rosa or anyone else there would be privy to their secrets or vulnerabilities. And the man holding Addy was probably the only person around who'd been part of their lives back in the Reform Center days.

God, that was creepy. Wade's connection with a young Eleanor had been a shot in the dark, but it had definitely hit its mark. I couldn't blame her twisted adult actions entirely on Wade Yates, but the man had a lot to answer for.

And not just when it came to Eleanor...

I pulled out my cell phone and scrolled through my Contacts, but couldn't get enough signal to connect and I didn't want to use Eleanor's burner and inadvertently pull someone else into this. Sliding off the hood of the car, I grabbed Roger's arm. "I need that phone."

He didn't argue, just said, "Look, I've gotta go; call me when you actually know something," to the person on the other end, hung up, and handed me Eleanor's device. I punched the digits in and, after several torturous seconds of hesitation, heard a ringing *brrr*.

"Who's this?" demanded a gruff man's voice with shades of Sam Elliott.

"Glenn, it's Sydney."

His voice grew closer to the phone, more intimate. "Darling, I hope you're not in the shit, because I guarantee I am many miles away from helping you."

Something between a profanity and a sob choked out of me. This had been my last, desperate long shot to find Addy. Before it was too late.

"Hey, easy, Red. Tell me what's going on."

I drilled a knuckle into my forehead. "I'm at the Reform Center. I found Turtle's kid voyeur. From the Tar Shed."

The line crackled and his voice echoed at the end, but Glenn's surprise was still unmistakable as he blurted, "Are you kidding me?"

"All grown up now and as much of a bitch as you'd expect," I said. Eleanor was watching me closely, and I gave her an emphatic one-finger salute. "You remember Addy?"

The line crackled again while he considered, or maybe it was a lag in the connection. "The teenager you brought in my bar?"

"Yeah. She's in trouble. Believe it or not, the grown-up kid and the sadistic guard with the fucked-up pinky stashed her somewhere." I dug in an extra knuckle to get through the next part without breaking down. "I gotta find her, but I don't know where she is."

When he didn't answer immediately, I thought I'd lost him, but he was calculating. "I'm at least two hours away, but if Turtle and I leave now—"

"Turtle?" I cut in.

"Yeah, he kinda went off the rails after your last conversation, so I had to take him somewhere. Somewhere safe."

I laughed and maybe even cried a little with relief.

"Syd, you okay?" Glenn asked. "You still there?"

"Yeah, I'm still here," I said, swiping a tear from my eye with the heel of my hand. "But I wasn't calling to ask for your help. I'm asking for Turtle's."

54

"Are you sure about this?" Roger asked. I'd switched on Eleanor's headlights, and the shadows they cast made his face look cadaverous. "Because I'm not."

"Yes," I lied, rummaging in Blake's SUV for anything useful to take with me. "Look, we gave FDLE the information like good boys and girls. And if they get there first, fine. I'm happy for the pros to do their job. But I'm not going to just sit here and wait, not knowing. We've wasted too much time already."

Getting answers on such a sensitive subject from a jonesing Turtle (Glenn was doing his best to get him clean) with Glenn acting as go-between took longer than I would have liked. But now we had a potential location.

The Tar Shed would have been the most poetic choice, but it was no longer standing. When pressed, Turtle had remembered there were two medical buildings, a main one in the compound for everyday accidents and sickness, plus one down the road. It was old, not supposed to be used anymore, but that's where they'd taken serious cases, boys they didn't want outsiders to see. The boy's rotten foot he'd described was from Turtle's time in the other infirmary. And Pinky Guy/Wade had regularly taken the boys he'd punished there.

"But they're on their way," Roger said.

"Yeah, the good guys *and* the bad guys," I said. Blake hadn't been carrying a gun that I could find, but I helped myself to his lug wrench. *Lesson learned, Glenn.* Maybe I'd get to use it this time.

"If she's even there," he said.

"If she's not, it doesn't matter anyway. Except we'll be able to check one place off whatever list the cops are working from. I'll just see if it's occupied." Shielding my eyes from Eleanor's headlights, I slammed the SUV door and held up my phone. "I'm not stupid. If there is anyone, I can dial 9-1-1 to report it and any carrier will pick it up."

One of those reassuring nuggets I'd picked up in my many hours on the road.

"I should go," he said.

"Why—because you're a man?" I spat, out of patience.

"Because no matter how much of a monumental pain in the ass you are, there's only one of you," he snapped, short on patience as well. He raised his arms toward the sky. "Wait, what am I thinking? We should both go."

I tucked my phone in my pocket, then thumbed toward Eleanor. "You really want to risk leaving her alone? What if someone else is supposed to meet her so they can ride off into the sunset together?"

"We take her with us," Roger said. Eleanor hadn't spoken, but she'd sat up straight and seemed to be following our conversation as Roger continued, "Who knows? She might be useful."

"As a human shield?" I asked, and saw a tiny, secret smile cross her face. "Fine. But I'm driving."

Roger didn't argue, nor did Eleanor when he grabbed an elbow and helped her stand. She walked willingly (and barefoot) to climb in the back seat of her car. Too willingly. I wished I knew the woman's endgame.

The car's engine purred when I started it, softer than Cecil's. I adjusted mirrors and the seat, then twisted to look behind us. I shuddered at the red taillights ghoulishly illuminating Blake's body like a cheap horror novel. It was stupid—the man was dead—but I felt funny leaving him behind, lying alone on the ground in the growing darkness. I closed my eyes and whispered a quick prayer for him and for Addy, then set off past him and his vehicle, down the trail toward the highway.

At least I hoped we were headed toward the highway. All we had on that count was Eleanor's word, before she'd accepted we were onto her.

We'd determined Roger should sit in the back with Eleanor, lest she try something, but I could have used his help with navigation. The car crept at a geriatric snail's pace as I scanned the edges of the trail for the route Roger and I had discovered earlier. I made two false stops before it finally came into view on the right.

Now that I knew where we were going, or at least we were pretending like I did, I leaned forward to pick up the pace.

"Easy," Eleanor said from the back seat, right before the car bottomed out in a hidden divot.

My teeth clicked together, and Eleanor gasped in the back seat. "You got your finger on that trigger, in case she makes a break for it?" I asked.

"Absolutely," Roger said.

Of course he didn't. A jounce like that last one was as likely to shoot us as it was Eleanor. And we knew there was nothing wrong with the weapon.

"How did you kill Blake Tucker?" Roger asked.

When Eleanor didn't answer, I said, "I'm guessing one to the chest, then the headshot after he was down—you'll remember the delay—but I'm no expert."

"Yes," Roger said, "but he was a big man. And why didn't he see it coming? Surely he didn't trust her."

A snort-like sound of disbelief escaped me. "Easy," I said, watching Eleanor as I answered. "He underestimated her."

She looked away, but not before I saw confirmation in her eyes. *Men.*

"Did Blake tell you I have Carly Whitmore's purse?" I asked.

Eleanor's eyes shot back at me in the mirror.

"So he didn't?" I said, smiling wickedly. "Did you even know he took it before tonight?"

She turned away, toward the side window rather than facing Roger.

"I guess Blake wasn't as stupid as you thought he was. How does that make you feel? He's going to help send you to prison from beyond the grave. Roger, she's going to need a good lawyer. Think you can help her out?"

"Even I have to draw the line somewhere," Roger said.

Eleanor hissed at the scraping sound of the undercarriage snagging some brush—the result of me trying to watch both of them, and our path, at the same time.

"I am curious," Roger said, "did you always intend to kill Mr. Tucker?"

When she didn't answer, I did. "Of course. You can't leave your scapegoat alive to tell his side of the story. I'll bet you even counted on him being seen when you told him to follow me."

And I'd bet Addy had never met Blake—as he'd said, maybe even never made it to Brummel. I didn't know how she'd faked the intake records, but who better to do so than the woman in charge? Maybe her fabrications wouldn't hold, but if Roger and I hadn't happened on the scene, they wouldn't have had to—no trial for a dead perpetrator, and no one to look that closely.

I admit, I was surprised when I saw clear twilight sky ahead— we'd actually made it to the highway. A final steep, earthen incline gave me some palpitations. Even with the transmission in Low, we spun a bit at the end. There was no traffic on the highway, and I took a moment to get my breath and make sure I was merging into the proper lane in the proper direction.

Apparently, Roger was surprised as well. "I'm going to call FDLE and let them know what we're doing so no one shoots us. Accidentally, I mean."

I ignored Roger's phone conversation, my eyes on the road except when I monitored Eleanor in my rearview. I often found her watching me as well.

I had only the vaguest idea where I was going or how far away it would be. Turtle had said they'd put them in a van and it was "pretty close." I suspected it was about half a mile beyond the Reform Center entrance, back in the direction of Tallahassee. I'd noticed something there the first time I'd driven here alone, when my eyes were searching everywhere for my destination, but had paid no attention on subsequent trips.

The sky had gone from blushing to bruised, and even Eleanor's fancy headlights weren't much help. I slowed and squinted at the entrance to the juvenile facility, now coming up on my left. The gate still appeared closed, but I pulled across the empty traffic lane to be sure. I left the car idling while I jogged to the gate and gave it a quick yank. The familiar banging of metal and plywood cut through the murky dark. Laney must have locked up when she left.

My hands vibrated on the steering wheel, and the rhythmic repetition of the highway's broken center line—*flash, flash, flash,* in the windshield—made me even edgier.

I will get you out of this. That's what I'd told Addy at the hospital. I didn't like breaking promises in general, and I *hated* breaking promises to people who weren't used to promises actually meaning something.

If someone was already waiting at the medical building, I'd keep driving while Roger notified the authorities. Anything else was likely to put Addy in more danger than she already faced.

But there was a problem with that plan, I realized, as a driveway materialized ahead of us on the right. "Roger, I can't see."

He leaned forward in the back seat as I slowed and came to a complete stop at the head of the driveway instead of making the turn. The pale shape of a single-story structure appeared, a near-twin to the torched admin building across the road. A row of coniferous trees appeared as a line of loosely connected shadows, blocking our view.

"The back corner of the lot looks empty, but I can't see the rest," Roger agreed.

"Okay, I'm going in," I said.

Torquing the wheel hard while eying a dark ditch next to the driveway, I learned Eleanor's car had an excellent turning radius. The building's windows reflected milky white in my headlights, paired like the admin had been. The parking lot was empty. But one window seemed to glow slightly from within.

"Is that a light?" Roger asked.

"I think so. I'll turn around," I said, swinging wide to make a U-turn. It would be less dangerous—for Addy at least—if I came back on foot for verification.

This property had less ground cover than the main one, and it was hard to distinguish the weathered parking area from the surrounding earth. As my headlights swung across the surface, I realized what I had taken for grubby ground was not.

I hunched over the steering wheel. "Dammit!"

"What is it?" Roger asked.

"The parking lot goes around the back of the building, not just the side. Someone's here."

If someone inside saw our headlights and we left, they'd know they'd been made. They'd take off for parts unknown, and they'd have little reason to not kill Addy first. Risk it and leave, or stay and... what?

These thoughts flashed through my head in a millisecond, and before I could decide what to do, my decision was made for me.

The parking lot wasn't the only difference between the two similar buildings. The admin building across the street had an exit on the far end. This one had an exit *near* the end, but on the side facing us. The door swung out, and my headlights blinded a white guy in a tan uniform carrying a camping lantern. He pulled his cap down against the glare.

"Shit!" Panicked, I almost ducked behind the steering wheel. "Should I gun it?"

"No time," Roger said.

He was right. The man had seen us, so racing away would only make things worse. And he still held the door open, so I had no chance of running him down before he got to safety. Assuming he wasn't just a state employee working overtime.

He lifted his free arm—had he pulled his weapon?—and waved an acknowledgment before stepping back inside.

I let out the breath I'd been holding, and I heard Roger do the same. We were in Eleanor's car; the man thought we were Eleanor. Crisis averted. For maybe thirty seconds. I backed into a spot across from the door and cut the headlights.

"What are you doing?" Roger demanded.

Grabbing the lug wrench, I ordered Roger, "Get up here— through the seats, don't open the door!"

"What the hell—"

"Stay with Eleanor," I said, and pointed at the building. "As soon as that door closes behind me, drive back out to the road—*headlights off*—and do whatever it takes to make sure the good guys know where to find us."

"Sydney, this is crazy—"

"I know. But it's Addy's best chance," I said, and jumped out of the car, adding, "And for God's sake, don't let anyone without a badge near you."

I trotted to the back door, lowering my head as a battery-powered motion light flicked on above it. Blinking, I tested the latch; he'd left the door unlocked. I held the wrench pointing down, flush against my leg as I slipped inside. My eyes registered a figure in the hallway facing the other direction, so I dodged quickly to the right.

I found myself in a pocket of space that deeper shadows in one corner—boxes?—suggested had been used for storage. The enclosed offices began less than ten feet from the door, on either side of a central hallway. The only light came from the hall, a lantern carried by the figure I'd glimpsed, presumably the man who'd waved from the door.

The man's drawling voice called out, "Goddammit, Eleanor, it's about time! You know that little bitch tried to bite me?"

I stood poised along the wall with the wrench, pointing the

curved bit away from me and gripping the other end tightly. (*Not too tight, Syd,* Glenn whispered in my head.)

The dim light grew slightly brighter as he approached, illuminating a cardboard box by the door. It had once held paper towels, but was now labeled in fat black marker, *MB-1*. The same notation I'd seen next to murdered boys in Milton Dickey's ledger.

An extra jolt of fear ran through me as his mass came into view, and I swung backhand at his center as hard as I could. The stocky, five-eight or so officer (Corrections, not Law Enforcement) grunted and stumbled backwards with me on his heels. His lantern strobed the desolate, institutional interior as it fell from his hands.

"Who the fuck—" he gasped.

I let out a banshee shriek as I swung again. He twisted sideways, and my forehand glanced off his shoulder. The lug wrench smacked the wall next to me on the follow-through and seemed to snag there, the bar falling from my hands to the floor. I scrambled, found the wrench, but fumbled it in the shadows as the man started to straighten and reach toward his waist. *Weapon.*

Dropping to one knee, I drove a hammer fist into his groin. A screaming wheeze clawed from his throat as his legs buckled, dropping him to his knees. I grabbed the lug wrench and landed another solid shot to his shoulder that might have clipped his head as well. He toppled, falling against a nearby doorframe, then backwards through the open door. His head slammed the bare concrete floor hard, and he moaned and wheezed but made no move to get up.

The room he lay in was illuminated as far as his waist by an angled beam from the hallway lantern, but the rest was shadows. I high-stepped carefully around his legs and stood over him, panting, wrench at the ready. He would get up eventually, and he would come after me again. And he wouldn't hesitate.

I could finish him now.

I shook my head, tried to stop the buzzing and clear the haze from my eyes. The wrench clanged when I dropped it on the floor to keep my hands free. I didn't need to kill this guy, but I did need to disarm him. First, I took the flashlight from his duty belt. It was easier to handle than the lantern and made a decent weapon in a pinch. By its light, I saw he wore a semiautomatic handgun clipped to his hip in some kind of plastic, molded holster (definitely not Department of Corrections issue). The fit was snug and the angle was weird. He groaned but didn't move to stop me as I struggled to pull his gun free. I nearly elbowed him in the nose before finally tossing the firearm past his feet.

In addition to the handgun, mounted in front just off-center of his crotch (thank God I hadn't hit it) was a Taser with a bright-yellow grip that could have been mistaken for a kid's toy gun. It probably was DOC issue, but looked similar to one Vince had shared with our self-defense class. I drew it and held onto it, knowing it was one trigger I'd have no hesitation in pulling.

The man's nearest arm twitched, but he still seemed out of it.

"Stay the fuck down," I said, before removing a black, extra-long cuff key hanging from a clip and jamming it in my jeans pocket. I didn't see his set of cuffs—were they already in use?

"Addy?" I called out.

I heard a banging in response from one of the rooms down the hallway and yelled, "I'm coming!"

The jerk on the floor kicked out, sweeping both my legs from beneath me. I landed hard on one hip and felt the pain shoot all the way to my skull, just before my head banged against the wall. The flashlight bounced away, but I held on to the Taser. He was up and almost to his knees, little more than a hulking shadow, when I pulled the trigger. *Dammit—safety!* I flipped it up and pulled the trigger again, so damn hard. *Come on...*

It finally popped, the darts shooting out the end. He yelped and toppled like a tree as they crackled softly. Five seconds, and I enjoyed every moment of his seizing agony. My hip pain faded into the distance.

"Asshole," I said, standing over him and pulling the barbs from his shirt. I hit the safety before squeezing to release the cartridge and tossed the wire tangle away from me. The dart cartridge only worked once, but I could still use the device as a direct contact stun gun.

I wriggled my remaining plastic cuffs free from my jeans pocket. They fell to the floor, along with the CO's handcuff key, but I didn't have the spare breath to curse. The flashlight hadn't gone far. The CO groaned but didn't move as I knelt next to him. In his mid-thirties, his face was pale in the flashlight's beam, with sweat and maybe a trace of blood muddying the hair by his temples. "Mess with me, and I'll zap you again."

Except I had to shove the stun gun into the back of my pants to manage him, and I still needed more hands. My button-down shirt tangled in it, and I yanked the fabric free to hang loosely over the device. I tucked the flashlight between my chin and shoulder so I could see to prep the plastic cuffs. My hands shook with adrenaline, and maneuvering the loops and edges wasn't easy. Finally, I lifted his heavy arms, flopping at the elbows, and gathered his wrists on his belly to secure his hands. Maybe a little too tightly, but he didn't complain.

I intended to stand, but my arms and legs turned to water, so I kneed away from him, then sat on my feet, hands resting on my thighs. For just a second. Just long enough to catch my breath. The flashlight slipped from my tingling fingers—again—rolling down my leg to the floor.

"Dammit," I muttered. But I didn't rush to pick it up. I could still see.

Why could I still see?

I froze. If I turned to identify the source of light behind me, I didn't have a chance. The Taser at my back required contact, and I'd lost track of the CO's gun.

I had no choice. I let my head and shoulders drop, as though overcome by exhaustion, thinking I had a better chance staying low and lunging.

"Stay down." The man's voice was deeper than the CO's, deeper than Blake Tucker's, with the rough edge of advancing age. "Hands on the back of your head."

One of my arms screamed as I raised it, the shoulder protesting my recent lug wrench handiwork. My palms only made it as far as my ears before the pain outweighed the risk of noncompliance. My fingertips traced the knobby bones at the base of my skull through my thick, fuzzy hair.

"You must be Mr. Yates," I said, voice almost steady.

"You must be stupid," he said.

And then he shot me.

55

F alling forward, I collapsed into a protective tuck.

I didn't feel the bullet when it penetrated my flesh, but the gunshot resounded throughout my body in the enclosed space. My ears rang with it, even though my hands had been and were still covering them. Eyes closed... I was afraid to see the damage, what additional punishment awaited me.

Come on, Red, Glenn growled in my head. *Suck it the fuck up, or you and Addy both die.*

So I did.

I saw blood, much more than had wept from the dead Blake Tucker, wet and lurid in the stark cone of white artificial light. But it wasn't mine.

The CO's wide eyes saw the same blood seeping across his khaki uniform as he looked down at his chest. His mouth moved, but if sounds came out I couldn't hear them. And I didn't want to. Blood frothed from his mouth and his head rolled back as he heaved for air. The blood on his chest seemed to bubble.

The second shot reverberated, and the CO's body rocked with it. Another to his chest, and it stopped heaving. A moment later, the light disappeared.

Huddled on the floor in the dark with my hands to my head, fingers hard as stones grabbed me by the arm and pulled me to my feet. Pressure and sound warred in my ears, roaring and ringing.

"Come on," a man said, the voice sounding unnaturally distant as he dragged me out of the room into the dim hallway. He barely paused as he deftly nudged the forgotten lantern upright with his foot, now our only source of illumination.

I was too stunned to resist, just tried to keep my legs under me and moving. Average height, chest broad under a dark uniform that looked familiar, but *off*, with no agency insignia. Short gray hair, solid jaw... not half as solid as the arm dragging me down the hall. My hand pressed against it as I came to my senses. He stopped, jerking me around to face him.

"Don't fuck with me," he said, his voice slightly echoey, but the message of the gun pointing at me unmistakable.

The same gun that had just killed the man I'd beaten. How was that for one-upmanship? My legs went watery again. To keep my knees from buckling, I focused on the gun's trigger, not the barrel. Or rather, the hand—the *fingers*—on the trigger guard.

He followed my gaze and grinned, extending his bottom fingers. "That what you're looking for?"

It was subtle—at least in this light—like his pinky had no nail. You really had to stare to recognize it was missing the final joint. Pinky Guy.

If I'd been Vince or Glenn, I probably could have taken advantage of that moment, seized it to seize the gun. But I wasn't Vince or Glenn. I tried not to dwell on what that augured for my future.

He tapped at one of his ears where something protruded from his ear canal. "Trying to keep what hearing I got, and supposedly these still allow conversation. Also means I got no reason to hesitate," he said. "Can you hear me?"

"Mostly," I said, voice cracking until I cleared my throat. "Helps to watch you speak. Wade Yates?"

"Jonathan. So my momma christened me." A pale line of teeth

split his shadowed face as he grinned. "But it's true, I've always gone by my middle name. Jonathan Wade Yates."

"Sydney Brennan," I said, as though we were meeting at the worst business convention ever.

He nodded. "I've been to your house before, but you weren't home. Goddamn nosy neighbor was, though. You're the redhead." He tilted his head and squinted at me. "Hard to tell in the dark. We'll fix that in a minute, because we've got a lot to discuss. But first, I'm gonna show you something. And I need you to keep your head, or I'll blow it off for you. Honestly, I'd much rather know what you know, but killing you won't keep me up tonight. Got it?"

"Got it."

I glanced down at his duty belt. Unlike the man he'd just killed, Wade's featured only his gun holster and his heavy flashlight, hanging low down his opposite leg like a six-shooter. "Can I use your flashlight?" I asked.

"Hell, no." He motioned me to walk ahead of him. "Head for the first open door on the right. And remember what I said."

My hip ached, and I staggered close to the dirty wall, tracing it with my fingertips to maintain my balance. Its funk, overlaid by a hint of sulfur from the gunshots, irritated my sinuses. Coughing into my elbow only made my throat feel more raw.

Approaching the room, its interior slowly came into view as an expanding wedge. A cheap plastic, battery-powered camping lantern, twin to the one in the hallway, rested on an overturned milk crate alongside a wall. Near it stood an industrial metal stool—unoccupied, with a water bottle on the floor next to it. But I sensed something, just at the edge of my humming hearing... something that might have been a human whimper. I walked faster, turned the corner, and what I saw made bile rise in my throat.

The small room also contained a cream-colored metal chair with worn black vinyl padding. The chair rose from a pedestal base, and a foot pedal sprouted from its back like a forked tail. A wall-mounted, round metal lamp seemed poised to swing into action for interrogations, but instead, light came from another lantern perched upon one of two tiny porcelain sinks below the lamp.

It was an antique dental chair setup, straight from a torture museum.

And Addy sat in it.

Her hair hung loose over her shoulders, almost indistinguishable from a dark V-neck shirt and matching pants reminiscent of goth scrubs. Her knees were raised slightly, feet atop a platform extending from the base of the chair. Her bare arms were secured to spindly armrests positioned on Y-shaped supports like dinosaur wishbones. Her head balanced against an equally spindly headrest, invisible behind her skull except for the metal bar it perched upon, and she'd been gagged by a long piece of cloth.

Addy squealed desperately through the gag, and wet tear tracks shone on her face.

Wade's hand clamped down on my aching shoulder, fingers digging into muscle and tendon and bone with a sadist's instincts. Pain knifed through to my skull and my spine and my hip, and I fought my buckling knees. *Motherfucker, I am not going down.*

The barrel of his gun pressed against my back. "Remember what I said. Get stupid, and I got no use for you. Either of you."

I tried to nod, but something about his grip had short-circuited those muscles. Instead I said, "It's okay, Addy. I'm here, and you're gonna be okay."

Wade said something I couldn't make out and directed me to the metal stool across the room. "Sit," he said.

I did, while he loomed over me, leaning against the wall. "What do you need to know?" I asked.

"Everything you know. Everything the cops know."

I swallowed, throat dry with fear and filth, calculating what would keep us alive long enough for Roger to return with the cavalry. Assuming he'd driven away and Wade hadn't already killed him. "When did you get here?" I asked, pointing at the floor.

"Don't fuck with me—"

I raised placating hands. "I'm not, but a lot has happened in the past hour or so. *Everything* could take a while, so I'd just as soon skip what you already know to save us some time. Where were you?"

He narrowed his eyes but answered. "I've been babysitting with dipshit for the past half hour."

I avoided looking at Addy, or in the direction of the dead man Wade Yates had killed. He also hadn't intervened in our altercation. "Including since I got here?"

He shrugged. "I hoped you'd kill the sonuvabitch and save me the trouble."

"Sorry, I did my best." It seemed he didn't know about Roger and Eleanor in the parking lot. "So the two of you were waiting for Eleanor Dickey?"

His chin dipped in acknowledgment. "Where is she? Don't make me wish I'd finished you off in that fire."

"I don't know," I said, reminding myself down to the core of my duplicitous bones that I really didn't know, so I wasn't lying.

"Bullshit," he said, shifting restlessly against the wall.

"She killed Blake Tucker."

His brows arched as if to say, *Duh.* "Well, that was the plan."

With those words, I had no doubt he was going to kill me and Addy. And I didn't know how to stop him. I babbled, "Eleanor's idea, right?"

Wade Yates was in my face before I knew he'd moved. He had to be pushing sixty, but the quick burst suggested a much younger man. "I don't know what kind of game you think you're playing, but unlike the dead dipshit, this ain't my first rodeo." He hooked a foot under one of the stool's crossbars and flipped my seat, sending me with it.

It was so unexpected, there was nothing I could do to break my fall. Just a split second of my heart in my throat before I hit the concrete floor flat on my back. Something stabbed sharply into one kidney on impact, and my head bumped down as an afterthought, but I was sucking wind so hard I barely felt it. The room went dark.

Don't panic, Brennan. You've felt this before, and you didn't die. Just breathe.

Wade was speaking again, but I couldn't hear him over the roaring in my ears and my wheezing gasps. *Breathe…*

My vision finally started to clear, black to lighter gray, and he bent over me.

"I guess you missed that. I said, since you seem to think we got so much time for dicking around, I'll be over here getting to know your young friend a little better." He straightened and advanced on Addy, stroking himself slowly through his pants as he said, "You know, dicking around."

I rolled onto my side and yelled, "Wait!" I coughed so hard I thought my eyes would burst, but choked out, "Tell you everything."

"That's more like it," he said.

His return gait was splay legged to accommodate his arousal. I'd only put off the inevitable by however long I could talk without pissing him off. Which was probably also how long I had to live.

He righted the stool, then picked me up by the arm just as easily and dropped me roughly onto the round seat. "Okay, let's have it."

"They know everything my team knows," I croaked. Wishing I had a team.

"Who's they?" he asked.

"Don't have names—I was supposed to go in for an interview but never made it yet. FBI. FDLE. Maybe GBI and SBI. At least three county Sheriff Departments." I paused, fought my irritated throat to swallow.

"Fuck," he said. "So what is it they know?"

"About now or forty years ago?"

"Now," he snapped. "Who gives a shit what happened forty years ago?"

Amos Weber did, I thought. *And if he hadn't, we wouldn't be having this conversation.* "They haven't worked out the details, but they're working on a list of girls you trafficked—"

"They find any of them yet?"

"Just one of the dead ones. There are stories going around among the street girls, but they think you have a scar," I said, and cleared my throat. "But law enforcement knows who you are."

"How?" he demanded.

"I gave them your name."

He inhaled deeply through his nostrils as his eyes widened. I thought he was going to shoot me. When he didn't, I added, "I figured it out from some of Milton Dickey's old files."

He rubbed his nose, considering, as I'd hoped he would. "Do they actually have any evidence against me?"

My hands strayed to massage my back as I considered. I winced and shed a genuine pained tear as I probed the Taser still tucked in the back of my pants. In one piece, though I wasn't sure I could say the same for my back. Sliding the safety off, I carefully positioned the weapon for a better draw. Then I brought my hand to my chest and throat, took a shallow breath and coughed before continuing.

"I don't know the specifics on the physical evidence, but they had something." I cleared my throat again. "Maybe when you burned the admin building?"

He waved a hand dismissively through the air.

I thought about the vehicles driving beyond the excavation site, how we'd never pinpointed their destination. It obviously wasn't here, across the highway. A horrific thought struck me, one so horrible it had to be true. "What about when you buried the bodies?" I asked.

He shook his head. "It was just the one girl here, and that was all dipshit's handiwork."

I covered my mouth, disguising an involuntary sob as a cough. It had to be Carly. "But Blake Tucker kept her purse."

His hand shot out, and the heat of his fingers on my throat made me instantly ill. "You're lying," he said, and squeezed just enough for me to feel the pressure in my head and see blurring at the edges of sight.

I suppressed a powerful urge to cough—or vomit—as I whispered, "I saw it. It was purple."

"Goddammit!" he said, shaking his head. But his hand released my throat to point in my face. I was transfixed by his unfinished pinky and decided he'd bartered it to the Devil. "I told her Tucker wasn't buying all her shit, but she didn't want to hear it."

I fought the impulse to shield my neck from further abuse. "He told me he gave it to her." Cough. Swallow. "He also said—"

And I was overcome by hacking. Wade blustered something, but I couldn't hear him and clutched at my throat. The water bottle, a heavy cylinder likely from the same supply store as the lanterns, had been knocked over when he'd flipped me on my back, but it hadn't rolled far. He picked it up and handed it to me.

I unscrewed the cap with shaking hands and sipped slowly, carefully. The water was nasty, a metallic tang barely discernible beneath the heavy funk of an unwashed microbial wonderland. If I survived this asshole's gun, his germs still might kill me.

"What else?" he demanded.

"What do you think?" I asked, before taking another nasty sip, visualizing exactly where the stun gun rested against my back all the while. *You can do this, Brennan, you can do this.* "That Eleanor Dickey was going to testify."

He didn't flinch at her name, but went still. It wasn't enough. I let the bottle fall from my clumsy, trembling hands, and barely heard the ring of it striking the floor, tumbling end over end to dump its water. *Look at it, asshole. Look away from me!*

Pinky Guy's eyes never left mine. Not for an instant. I couldn't tell if he was on to me or just single-minded, but I wanted to cry. After I cut out his liver.

"She'd never do that," he said. "She'd never turn against me."

"Why, because she cares so much about you?" I asked, sarcasm dripping from my raw voice.

He shook his head slightly, just a twitch. He had a crooked smile to match when he replied, "No, because even if she testified—look at what she's done!—she couldn't walk away. Any kind of deal would still mean her going to prison, and she won't do that."

His words echoed Blake's, and I believed them both. I glanced at Addy. Her eyes were closed, mouth twisted to cry soundlessly through the gag. I was out of options, and so was she.

"That's assuming she only testifies *against you*."

Wade laughed outright. "Eleanor may have a high opinion of herself, but even she knows her 'contacts' would kill her before she could set foot in a courtroom. Especially after seeing them kill that girl," he said, waving vaguely in the direction of the admin building.

His lingering humor faded abruptly, and his face became what it always was—a thin veneer of flesh and skin over something dark and ugly and twisted. "I thought you didn't know where Eleanor was."

Movement behind him caught my eye. It was Addy, shifting in her chair, straining to twist her head... She'd heard something. I hadn't, and apparently neither had Wade.

"Hey," he said, leaning over me. He grasped the shoulder that already held his fingerprints and bent his head until our foreheads were almost touching. His gun, pointed at my chest, was so close. "Where is she?"

"I don't know, exactly," I said, swallowing. Praying for anyone out there to stop taking their goddamn time. I continued, "But I can guess. The last time I saw Eleanor, she was handcuffed in her own car. She's probably in custody by now."

His body tensed.

"Telling stories about the man who abused her. The evil pedophile guard who beat and fucked little boys and made her—"

He hit me in the face, just a quick, short pop—from his hand or his gun, I couldn't tell—that left me gripping the edge of the stool to stay upright.

"All this was her idea! It's always her idea. She's the one who learned from Daddy how to take her cut from the man and the contractors and everybody else. How to double-dip and stretch out sentences and use what you got... cheap, fucking labor. 'Cuz some things never change."

He shook his head. "The bitch give you my name?"

My head swam and I let him see it, swaying on the stool. My hand crept behind me as I sagged forward, stretching my waistband.

"Did she give you my name?" he demanded, so close the acidic tang of old coffee on his breath made me dizzier.

He froze abruptly. I still didn't hear anything, but I watched his eyes track to the parking lot. Away from me.

My hand slid up my back, drawing the Taser free. Ignoring the pain in my shoulder, I whipped my arm forward and up, jamming the Taser into his neck as if it were a gun. Then I pulled the trigger and held it.

Rapid snapping pops sliced through the air inches from my head, much louder than the earlier soft ticking of the barbs' current. Wade jerked back, howling with rage, but I rose with him. Pressing the prongs to his neck, I grabbed at his other arm, but he dropped his gun before I could reach it. We hit the wet patch from the water bottle and both went down, limbs flailing and his head slamming the concrete floor. I fell on top of Wade, and my finger released the stun gun trigger. How long had I zapped him in the neck? A second? Two? Not long enough.

I fumbled on top of him, kneeing him in the groin as I shoved the stun gun just below his clavicle. I wasn't sure my finger had the strength for the trigger pull. Finally, his body tensed and a noise rumbled from his chest as I counted out three seconds, but he didn't fight his way free.

Crouched atop Wade, I stretched out my leg and kicked his gun away before pressing my fists into his chest to sit. My ears still hummed, and when I spoke, my words echoed in my ears. "I will kill you before I let you touch her. But only after I cut your dick off and feed it to you."

Addy was straining against her bonds in the chair, trying to sit up and vocalize.

"It's okay, kid," I said. "You're gonna be okay."

Either my hearing was fritzing again, or I was hearing something else. Somewhere else. I shook my head. It didn't matter. I slid off Wade onto the floor and sat next to him. I needed to secure the man before freeing Addy, but I needed to catch my breath first. Stop shaking.

His eyes weren't entirely opened or closed, just slits, and I hoped he could hear me. "By the way, Eleanor Dickey didn't give me your name, asshole. A little boy named Turtle did. And he says hi."

The distant noises I'd heard suddenly grew louder and coalesced into shadows, dark figures covered head to toe, with even darker weapons that seemed to absorb the light. Their barked words blurred together, first in the hall, and then breaching the doorway.

I tried to raise my hands, but my burning, aching arms wouldn't cooperate. Slumping with exhaustion and relief, I said, "About time."

56

There's nothing like being in a stand-off when you're too exhausted to actually stand.

I sat on the floor, back against the wall, stroking Addy's hair, separating out blue sections for no good reason except they were there. The (supposedly good) guys in black had freed her right about the time they'd taken Wade into custody. Addy had collapsed into my arms, then both of us onto the floor, and we'd been there ever since. She'd finally stopped crying, but she hadn't spoken yet, and neither of us was inclined to move.

"You can't have her until you tell me where you're taking her," I said. For the second time.

"Ma'am," began the officer who must have drawn the short straw. He'd taken off his protective headgear, but not the rest of his body armor, and his blond hair was slick with sweat.

"Don't fucking *ma'am* me! You're the ones who *let her* be kidnapped in the first place."

"Ma'am, that was American Correctional Enterprises, not the Sheriff's Department—"

"You can't have her!"

I said that being fully cognizant of the fact that Addy and I were the only people in the tiny dentist's room—probably in the entire building—who weren't armed. I'd even surrendered my Taser as evidence, so good luck backing up my ultimatum. I was banking on them not wanting to cause a scene with an already traumatized teenager. That is, a bigger scene.

The officer was clearly out of his depth, hand brushing sweat from a face that was concerned and confused, with a chance of irritation. He opened his mouth, but before he could muster another, more magically persuasive argument, a Latino officer entered the room. I couldn't see a difference in their gear, but body language suggested he was the blonde's superior. The new arrival spoke in the other officer's ear.

The blonde nodded, then said, "Ma'am, we have a counselor here to speak with Ms. Hastings."

"That sounds like an excellent idea," I said, "but what I want to know—"

I broke off as Addy flinched and hid her face against me. A dark-haired woman in a suit had appeared in the doorway.

"It's okay, Addy," I said to the crown of her head. "It's not her."

Addy lifted her eyes, and her rigid body relaxed, as did mine, when she recognized the woman.

Juliet Sanders held up a few creased sheets of paper. The slacks I'd seen her wearing that morning were equally creased, and I wondered if she'd made it back to Tallahassee, only to turn around again, or if she'd still been occupied in the area with Brummel issues.

"Addy," I asked gently, "is Ms. Powers—the director—the one who took you from Brummel?"

I winced when her nodding head pressed against one of my bruises, but leaned into the pain to hear her soft response.

"Her and one of the guards. Not the scary old guy, a different one. Unloaded the van, and took everyone else inside but me," Addy's voice grew stronger as she continued. "The guard, he wasn't exactly Prince Charming, but the woman said things... told me things she was going to do to me, that she'd done to other girls... I think her and the scary guy together."

Addy sat up. Her bottom lip trembled as she said, "That bitch better be going to prison." She pointed at the blonde officer to add, "And you assholes better not be taking me back. I'll die before I go back to that place."

"Ms. Hastings," Juliet said, "I have a court order here granting me your interim custody. That means you can go home with me, if you want."

Addy gave me a questioning look. I pushed her hair back from her tear-streaked face, revealing a pink and puffy nose and lips. She appeared so young and vulnerable, and yet her core was more resilient—downright bad-ass, honestly—than most adults.

"There's no way they'll let you go home with me. And Juliet may not be the toast mistress I am," I said, eying Juliet over the top of Addy's head, "but she won't let you starve. I think she's the best offer you're likely to get."

Addy sighed heavily, then said, "Okay." She stood, brushed off her pants, and helped me to my feet.

Definitely bad-ass.

We separated as we exited the building, from the front this time, which was disorienting. It was dark outside, but flashing, silent strobes passed by intermittently on the highway, and officers were setting up tall, portable lights. I watched Addy and Juliet walk away, Juliet venturing an arm over Addy's shoulder. A female officer approached, then took her place on Addy's other side to lead them... somewhere. Somewhere safe.

My knees wobbled descending the handful of steps at the raised entrance. An officer offered me a supportive arm, saying he was taking me to give my statement, but I found it hard to focus on his words.

"I'm sorry, but before I say anything else, I need to talk to my attorney—"

"Sydney!" yelled a familiar man's voice.

Squinting at the sound, I said, "Speak of the devil's advocate."

The parking lot wrapped completely around the building, but with no highway exit. That explained Wade Yates's unseen vehicle.

The white blur of Roger's shirt streaked toward me from that portion of the dark lot.

"Mr. Weber, wait!" yelled a man trailing Roger, almost indistinguishable in a dark suit, the jacket flying behind him.

My escort stepped in front of Roger, but something passed between the men in uniform, and a moment later he allowed Roger to pass.

Roger slammed into me and clutched me to his chest, painfully. I might have complained, but I wasn't sure he'd hear me over his own muttering. The only word I could make out was *stupid*, probably because he repeated it so many times. His heartbeat pulsed against my cheek, and my fingers traced the sweat-soaked pleat on the back of his dress shirt.

He murmured directly into my ear, "Just play it straight. I trust your judgment on what to say. And don't worry about anything—Juliet's taking Addy with her."

I nodded—obviously I knew that—but his confirmation helped my preeminent source of dread collapse, and I nearly did too. Making me the one clutching him painfully.

"Sydney, are you all right?"

I nodded into his chest.

Apparently a speechless Sydney is cause for alarm. Roger took hold of my shoulders and dropped his face to mine. "What's wrong? Say something!"

I swallowed, this time against incipient tears rather than lung-wrenching coughs, and said, "Did you think you'd have to bail me out again?"

"Oh, Sydney," he said, releasing his pent-up breath. "I've learned my lesson. When it comes to you, that is now the least of my fears."

OUR REUNION WAS BRIEF. Roger and I weren't allowed to speak in depth until we'd given our statements. We were, after all, both witnesses in an investigation it wasn't exaggerating to call remarkable.

In the past couple of years, I felt as if I'd given a lifetime worth of statements to law enforcement. (Not to mention the times they would have loved to talk to me, had they known of my involvement in dubious matters.) It was liberating this time, not having to keep my lies straight, not even ones of omission. Of course, no one was interested in Addy's whereabouts before she was incarcerated, which was where the truth became... complicated. And maybe omitted.

On the other hand, between a quick medical check (they said I'd live, though I may not feel like it in the morning) and the not-so-quick questioning, it took *forever*.

I had a premonition Roger and I wouldn't get away until the wee hours, and they didn't object to my quick *I'm alive* call to Mike, particularly after I'd explained that otherwise he'd show up at the crime scene demanding to be admitted. I promised Mike I'd be in touch the next morning. I also let Glenn know Addy and I were okay. (Turtle being my source was one of the few things I'd omitted from my statement.)

Roger was waiting for me when I finished. His hair was as mussed as I'd ever seen it (translation: still more put together than mine on a normal day), and one of the dark stains on his shirt sleeves looked suspiciously like blood. An officer had retrieved his car and parked it by the medical center entrance. Cecil remained at the Reform Center because my car keys were still missing in action, presumably squirreled away in Blake's SUV. I hoped they weren't on his dead body; I knew it was stupid, but that creeped me out and I didn't want to have to get new keys for my car.

We strolled toward the highway, mostly ignored by the various law enforcement cogs, uniformed and otherwise, doing their bit to make sense of the world. The moon was muffled by clouds, but there was enough ambient light from the activity around us to walk to Roger's car, so long as we kept our eyes on the pale, gritty ground. My mind wasn't so easy to safeguard.

I felt horror at the nameless CO's murder, at the visceral fact of it and the man's helplessness in the face of it. But, although I'd been the one to bind him, my horror was not coupled with guilt. Blake Tucker, on the other hand... the man wasn't perfect, but the notion of him lying dead on the ground was a yawning, dark hole I needed to avoid. At least for tonight. Should I have seen that coming? Could I—could *we*—have done something differently to avoid it?

"Eleanor Dickey is in custody," Roger said, his elbow bumping me as he pulled his keys from his pockets.

"You think she'll get what she deserves?"

He gave a short, bitter laugh. "Not in this lifetime."

Settling in his car, I asked, "Will she go to trial or plead out?"

"It depends," he said, glancing toward the activity at the facility. "SWAT moved in when they did because the Feds were coming at this from the other direction."

I rubbed at my face. My hair was making it itch, but I didn't have a tie or a hat. Had I had one at some time? "You mean, the FBI was working the trafficking angle. The big shots Eleanor was hooked up with."

"So my inside source tells me," Roger said. "For several months."

My exhausted brain tried to pull up the little bit I knew about human trafficking. "So who was she working with? The Mexicans? The Chinese?"

Roger started the car and his A/C came to life. Maybe it could clean some of my stink out of the air. He said, "It sounds like she was involved with at least mid-ranking individuals in homegrown organized crime."

Homegrown... *damn.* That brought to mind another relatively recent case that had gone gruesome. "You got any names?"

Please don't say Moreno...

"No."

I was struck by another less-than-pleasant thought. "Please tell me we didn't somehow mess up their investigation."

I occupied enough spots on enough shit lists already; I did not want to be on the FBI's as well.

"No," Roger said, "this time we're in the clear. If anything, we helped them."

"Because now they can leverage Eleanor Dickey," I said. I felt nauseated as the conversation came full circle, approaching the possibility I'd suggested to Wade Yates.

Roger continued, "I suppose if someone's in a lousy mood, they could blame us for missing a chance to turn Blake Tucker, too."

"Maybe," I said. "But I doubt Blake knew much about the trafficking."

Roger finally merged onto the highway, leaving that godawful place behind. My body sank lower and lower in his luscious seat, until only the seat belt was holding me upright.

"That's how they could set him up to be their fall guy, because he didn't know the big picture," I continued. "Wade Yates said something about all of the other things Eleanor Dickey was into, how she'd learned to work the system from her father. That's probably all Blake knew about."

"He gets a cut from that side, and it's enough to have some power over him," Roger mused, "plus keep him close, so he couldn't betray her before she betrayed him. It's a plausible theory. It'll be interesting to see how it plays out, with Wade Yates part of the equation as well."

I nodded in the dark and wondered, "How much does Yates know about the trafficking?"

"If your theory is right, and Eleanor is the power at the center, probably not as much as he thinks he does. Though I imagine he's well-versed in the rest of the correctional center corruption. The question is which cases will take precedence. Unfortunately, depending on how much Eleanor Dickey knows about the larger trafficking operation..."

"She may not serve real prison time for everything else," I finished.

"Alternatively, she may take her chances with the jury after all. I suspect she'd relish the attention." Roger's voice grew deeper, even portentous as he added, "Or she may not live to do either."

Did hoping for the final option make me an evil person? If it did, I wasn't sure I cared. "What about us? You think we'll both come through all this with our licenses intact?"

Roger answered too quickly, in a hale and hearty voice that belied his words. "Sure. Smelling like a rose."

"For a defense lawyer, you're an awfully shitty liar."

"Didn't seem worth the effort," he said, squinting against a set of approaching headlights. "It might be a little bumpy, but I do think we'll both be all right in the end."

I hoped he was more convincing this time because he believed what he said, not because he was making the effort to lie better. "So where are we going now?"

"I got us a hotel room," Roger said.

I sat up and attempted face divination in the orange-red glow from the instrument panel.

"Two rooms," he clarified.

Then why was he smiling?

The nearest motel was simple (to put it kindly) and only had about a dozen rooms. Half were undergoing renovation, and Laney and her crew occupied the rest. Roger had instead booked us into a decent hotel in neighboring Stetler County, half an hour away.

I was fading by the time we arrived. I might have dozed off at the reception desk because I don't remember anything that transpired between the glass front doors and Roger handing me a key card. I'd started stiffening up already and felt so zonked I couldn't even muster mortification at my reflection in the elevator. I closed my eyes.

"Hey," Roger said, nudging me gently. "We're almost there. Fourth floor. Coming right up. We'll be neighbors."

I opened one eye. "What's going on? Why are you so... small-talky?"

Roger does not do small talk. It's one of the things he hires investigators for.

I reluctantly opened my other eye when the elevator stopped and dinged. The doors remained closed, as if they were waiting for Roger to answer as much as I was.

He sighed. "I did something and..."

The doors opened and he waited for me to step out before continuing. "You might not like it. I hope you're not mad at me."

Now we stood outside our respective rooms, key cards in hand. "If you are mad, tough shit. And I'll see you in the morning."

He entered his room without another word.

Weirdo. We hadn't talked about the financial arrangements for our accommodations. Maybe he'd upgraded me to something particularly luxurious I would never purchase myself. Seemed unlikely in Stetler County, but a girl could always dream.

My key worked on the fourth try. I entered my dark room with no purse, no pajamas, no toiletries, no spare clothes—I checked my pockets—and three dollars in cash. The bathroom was right next to the door, so I went straight to the loo and peed for the first time in... a lot of hours. I mostly ignored my dirty, haggard face in the bright vanity mirror while I drank a glass and a half of water. Maybe I'd have another one in a minute. Maybe I'd even wash my face.

But, *damn*, I was tired.

I flipped a light switch and was vaguely aware of a table lamp illuminating on the far end of the room, then flicked the door latch across the top. Finally, as I turned, I saw a figure sitting in the dark. Waiting for me.

I screamed. Fumbled with the damned metal loop. Too hard—it bounced back. Pushed the damn door handle down, but couldn't seem to pull the door open at the same time. It finally came free and caught on my foot.

"Sydney." Then a hand on my shoulder and more light.

I threw an elbow, spun around... Both hands on my shoulders...

"Sydney," Mike said. "It's me. It's just me."

And then I could breathe again.

57

I sat in an armchair, still warm from Mike's body, feet tucked beneath me. All of the lights in the room on. And I was calm. Really, I was. Mike and Roger, not so much. They were arguing by the bathroom, trying to keep their voices down so Roger didn't have to work his magic smoothing things over with the hotel again. My hearing had recovered well enough to follow their bickering.

"You just left her there? Alone?" Mike demanded, dumbfounded. Taller than most people, including Roger, for once he was showing his full height. "What were you thinking?"

"She's right here," I muttered, not that either man heard me.

Roger looked away. "You don't think I know how stupid I was tonight? How absolutely fucking stupid? She could've been…"

He didn't finish.

Stupid. I sighed with a realization: when we first met after the Wade Yates interaction tonight, Roger's muttering had been chastising himself, not me. My second realization: it was time to be the stable grown-up in the group.

I groaned as I rose from the chair, but neither man heard me. Mike was on the offensive again, voice rich with a mix of emotions beyond simple anger. "Then how in God's name could you leave her there?"

Both men seemed closer to breaking down than to hitting each other, but I stepped between them just in case, putting a hand on each chest. "Hey, we're all okay. Everybody's okay," I said. "Including me. Including Addy."

Neither man would look at me. I turned to Roger. "I put you in a tough spot, and you did exactly what I asked. Thank you for trusting me, and for deferring to me." I smiled. "I know that doesn't come naturally for you."

Biting his lips, the corners curled into an attempt at levity.

"Did you invite Mike here?" I asked.

Roger still couldn't look at me. "I'm sorry, Sydney. I should have told you. I wasn't thinking—"

"It's okay," I interrupted. "Nobody got hurt, nobody kicked us out, and I appreciate the thought. Thank you. Sleep well," I said, giving Roger's shoulder a pat, "and I'll see you in the morning."

Roger nodded. "Okay. Good night, Sydney."

I watched him leave, then faced Mike, who was also avoiding my gaze. Not that difficult a task when there's nearly a foot of height difference between you. He wore his favorite math joke T-shirt, jeans, and sneakers—he obviously hadn't taken the time to change when Roger told him where we were headed.

"It's good to see you," I said.

Mike's face whipped toward me. He'd left his glasses on a nightstand next to the chair, and his eyes shone with anger and unshed tears. "What the hell were you thinking?" he asked.

"No," I said firmly, striving to not match his temper. "We're not doing that. If you want to have a sensible discussion tomorrow or some other time, fine. But at least two people tried to kill me tonight. And Addy—"

I broke off. If I thought about what the teen had experienced, and how much more worse it could have been, I'd melt down completely. I continued, "I do not have it in me to deal with dysfunctional shit, and I doubt either of us can speak rationally about what happened at the moment. Understood?"

Mike's hands dug into his hips as he fought some internal battle. Finally, his face softened. "Fine." He gently placed his hands on my shoulders and bowed to rest his forehead against mine. Smiling, he said, "I brought you jammies."

I glanced at the bed, where a couple of clothing items were folded, including my Red Sox jersey nightshirt on top. I laughed. "Oh, how much do I love you," I said flippantly, before pinching his cheek. "I'm going to take a shower."

I took the jersey with me and started the shower, letting it get hot and steamy. I'd burned through my adrenaline long ago, and relief drained me like an above ground pool. My bruised hip ached, as did my head, and my muscles burned with some sort of crazy shit hangover. I was nasty, with filth ranging from field dirt and work sweat acquired salvaging cars with Laney, to abandoned building grime and stress sweat from trying to save Addy. Stepping into the scalding water, I placed my hands against the tasteful, gray tile and watched slightly discolored water swirl down the drain. Not nearly as dark as I'd expected.

I'd reacted to potential danger in my room, but I hadn't gone deep into the crazy train. My body hadn't triggered all of the physical and psychological responses it often did. That was good. And now I succeeded in shutting off my brain, blocking out all thoughts of the evening. Mostly. Except for the man waiting patiently for me outside the door.

I dried off, blotted and squeezed my wet, kinky hair with the heavy towel and hoped for the best. Then I donned my Red Sox jersey nightshirt and went out to join Mike.

Sitting in the same chair he'd been reclining in when I'd arrived, he jumped up when I exited the bathroom. "I'm sorry I fell asleep and frightened you. I'm the one who asked Roger not to tell you I was here. He had to put my name on the—"

"Mike," I said, seizing his face and pulling it down to me. "Shut up."

And I kissed him, long and hard and deep, until I couldn't breathe but didn't care. The scent of him after a long day (sandalwood deodorant, a hint of sweaty oil on his face, his hair still a trace of shampoo), and the unexpected kid taste sweetness of root beer on his tongue—those were more critical to me than oxygen.

I didn't come up for air so much as tilt my head like a freestyle crawl, our faces still touching. I pushed Mike backward slowly, toward the bed.

"Hey," he muttered against my lips. His hands grabbed my face, pulled it inches away from his and held it there. "Hey—are you sure about this?"

I gave him a gentle nudge, so he sat on the bed facing me. The white bedding gleamed against a high, dark wood headboard, and the mattress seemed to go on forever. It took a moment to get my breath. My aches were forgotten, and the tingling in my chest and nether regions made me shiver.

"Here's the thing," I said. "I have been known to ride adrenaline waves into bed throughout my life. And that is perfectly fine. Except I want more with you."

"Exactly," Mike said.

I pinched his lips with my fingers and found I was nibbling my own. *Focus, Brennan. Words first. Fun bits second.*

"But, even with all the crazy shit that happened tonight, that adrenaline is long gone now. And let's be honest. We have been taking it slow, but weren't we both not-so-secretly planning to have sex last weekend?"

Mike raised his brows and shrugged his shoulders in embarrassed acknowledgment.

"So we should penalize ourselves?" I climbed up onto Mike's lap, a knee on either side of his hips. My fingers slowly traced the back of his skull while I brought my lips close to Mike's and grinned. "Are we really going to let the forces of evil win?"

He grinned back at me, the tip of his nose softly brushing mine. "That would be downright immoral, wouldn't it?"

His breath and his words tickled the sensitive skin on the side of my neck. I pressed my body against his, nestled close until he got the hint and followed up with his lips.

"Your hair's wet," Mike murmured into my throat, lips making their way down to the crew neck of the shirt. His voice turned playful as he nuzzled around the fabric edge. "And you're not wearing a bra."

I wrapped my legs around his waist and teased, "That's not all I'm not wearing."

His eyes went wide as his hands slipped beneath my cheeks. The bottom ones, that is.

"Gee whiz," he whispered, checking the veracity of my words.

Hopefully my laugh—and any subsequent sounds—didn't wake Roger next door.

58

I finally roused around nine a.m. the next morning, and I wouldn't have done even then if Roger hadn't called and woken me.

I vaguely recalled Mike untangling himself from my limbs and the sheets a couple of hours earlier, kissing me goodbye with a promise to come to Tallahassee this weekend for our long-delayed visit. After a quick wake-up shower, I threw on clean clothes: T-shirt, pair of jeans, and even clean underwear—all items I'd previously left at Mike's house. How many times had I stayed with him? And yet this was the first time we'd, in the immortal words of Shakespeare, made the beast with two backs. (And a front and a back, and some other permutations more difficult to describe.)

We'd managed a decent amount of sleep, but that's when the aches had really settled in, and exhaustion clung to every molecule of my body. I noticed a hint of a shiner on one cheek, but avoided looking at the rest of my body. I walked gingerly to the elevator with Roger. And yet I grinned the whole time, on the inside. I tried not to let it show on my face, but Roger's occasional head shakes suggested I was not successful.

Daydreaming, I was a little slow following him off the elevator, and Roger glanced back at me. "Seriously?" he asked. But even he was smiling.

We grabbed coffee from the lobby, and I snarfed half a bagel on the way to Roger's car. He'd gotten a call that my cell phone (found in the hallway at the medical center) and car keys were available at the Sheriff's Department and would drop me there on his way back to Tallahassee.

"Are you sure you don't want to ride back with me?" he asked.

"Thanks, but I'd still have to get my car." I reached for his arm. "Let me know if you need anything. If I don't see you before then, I'll see you at the funeral tomorrow. Okay?"

Roger nodded and squeezed my hand.

I had a long wait at the Sheriff's Department, even though the deputy who spoke with me swore my timing was perfect. (I'm not sure if we had different understandings of *time* or of *perfection*.) He handed over my cell phone and keys, but also needed me to sign my statement, a detail that had somehow been overlooked the previous night.

The deputy left me seated while he attempted to locate my statement. His desk was reasonably clean, the cheap brown laminate surface uncluttered. It sat in an open plan area with a half dozen or so other desks, a few of them occupied. On the far side of the open area were a couple of offices and what I guessed was a detention or interrogation room with a much larger, picture-type window (blinds closed).

It was hard to keep my mind on Mike, on the world outside, on anything positive, while sitting in the law enforcement den. My mind kept drifting in an edgy, exhausted spiral back to the Reform Center. Back to what had happened there on so many days and nights decades ago, and what had nearly happened there last night. What had been their plan for Addy?

Perhaps she was going to be passed along their trafficking network, like so many young women before her. But I thought it more likely her fate was linked to Blake Tucker's. If Roger and I hadn't happened along after Eleanor killed Blake, Eleanor could have left his body in the woods. Then she and Wade were free to do whatever they wanted to Addy, before killing her and blaming it on Blake. Might get a little messy, but it was doubtful time of death forensics could reliably contradict such a theory.

We'd probably never know the truth of their world, Blake Tucker and Wade Yates—

And Eleanor Dickey.

An officer raised the blinds before exiting that third room I'd been eyeing, and there she was. Eleanor Dickey sat at a table inside, dressed in a blue jumpsuit with her cuffed hands resting on the table. It appeared she was alone.

I waited for the officer to leave before negotiating desks to cross the broad area. A uniformed man and woman didn't even look up as I passed. I opened the interrogation room door before I had a chance to reconsider.

"Hello, Eleanor," I said.

She sat up straight, smiling slightly. Her hands had been secured to a waist chain as well, and she dropped them to her lap to sit up straight. "Ms. Brennan."

Foot wedged in the threshold (wary of being locked inside), I stretched my arms to their limit to lower the blinds. Then I leaned against the doorframe. "How was your first night in jail?" I asked. "First of many incarcerated, that is."

"I slept like a baby, thanks for asking," she said, smile never slipping but an intensity in her eyes that said she'd wrap that chain around my neck given the chance.

Or maybe I was projecting.

"See, most *normal* people wouldn't sleep like a baby after killing someone." Her smile faded. I leaned forward and watched her carefully. "Especially someone they considered a good friend and trusted colleague. That's something you might want to work on before you get to the jury."

I was sure I saw a subtle reaction on her face, a slight relaxation, perhaps? But it was very damn subtle.

"So you're not going to the jury after all?" I guessed. Yep, slight crinkle at the corners of her eyes. "You got one of those FBI agents wrapped around your finger, the way you did poor Blake Tucker? And... what was his name?"

I shook my head slowly, snapped my fingers, but she simply raised her brows as though inviting me to continue. I shrugged. "Guess I didn't get his name before I hit him in the dick."

Her brows narrowed, but she didn't respond.

"And then there's always Wade Yates, the wild card." I glanced over my shoulder through the doorway and saw a deputy—young, buzz-cut, and eager—approaching fast. "Emphasis on *wild*, huh? You've got your kinks, don't you, *Ellie*? But I think you'll find it's not nearly as much fun when no one respects your safe word."

She must have observed my reaction to the approaching officer. Her eyes went to the door before she said in a rush, "Excellent point, Ms. Brennan. It never pays to assume we're safe, does it?"

I suspected she'd have said more—the woman really was a master of mind fucks—if she'd had more time. The deputy stopped an arm's length away from me and assumed a relaxed but ready position.

"Ma'am, you're not allowed to interact with the prisoner," he said, in a deep, even voice he'd no doubt practiced while wearing his uniform. "You need to step away from the door now."

"Sorry, Deputy. I was looking for the bathroom," I said, meeting Eleanor's eyes one last time. "Something over here smelled full of shit... My mistake."

LANEY JUMPED at the chance to pick me up from the Sheriff's Department and take me to the Reform Center to retrieve Cecil.

"Let me guess." I said, climbing into yet another beater car I hadn't ridden in before and dropping the plastic bag that held my dirty clothes on the floor. "They won't let you onto the property because they're still processing... something."

"In a manner of speaking," Laney said, then reached over to pat my leg gently. "But I also wanted to see you. You're moving like an old woman again this morning."

She started to pull away from the curb, but suddenly did a double take, turning her attention back to me.

"What?" I asked, trying desperately to keep my face straight while she scrutinized it. Apparently, I didn't succeed.

Her eyes popped, and the car lurched as she smacked my arm with both hands.

"Laney!" I yelled, pointing in the general direction of all the driving controls (steering wheel, pedals, gear shift) she was ignoring.

She rolled her eyes and put the car into Park. "You finally did the deed with tall, dark and handsome—you lucky skank!"

We were still sitting in front of the Sheriff's Department entrance, and a uniformed man with an unhappy face approached. Laney waved vacuously like the ditz she was not, before muttering and pulling away from the sidewalk. She otherwise held her tongue and focused on driving until she'd merged onto the highway.

Laney glanced over at me, back to grinning. "Is he limping today, too? Did you ride the poor man until he begged for mercy?"

"No!" I yelled reflexively. Then I relaxed and added, "But I promise, I did my best."

Our eyes met briefly, and we burst out laughing.

When Laney left Tallahassee, I hadn't done very well replenishing my non-work-related social network. Noel Thomas and I were making inroads, getting past the awkwardness of our initial client-employee relationship. But I'd forgotten what it was like to have a close female friend who shared everything with you.

"I've missed you," I admitted, hoping it didn't sound maudlin.

"Me, too. Give us another week and our periods will be synced again," Laney said, wiping at an eye. "And I'm happy for you. In addition to being a tall glass of yum, Mike seems like a really good guy."

"He is." I smiled. Or rather, realized I was still smiling. It might be one of those days.

Laney looked at me again, long enough for me to point (ignored again) at the road. "But you might want to dial back the bedroom routine until you get used to it. You do look rough."

I sighed. So much for smiling all day. "I can't exactly blame Mike for that," I said, and gave Laney a thumbnail of the previous evening.

Laney grew quiet next to me, but it was a rich, textured kind of quiet. Experience said it was the lull that foreshadowed her sharing something insightful.

The edge of town was marked by a narrow, wooden church with pointy, arched doorways and windows, a couple of years past needing a fresh coat of white paint. Laney slowed as we passed it, and for a moment I thought she'd pull over. Instead, we continued onto the mostly dull, mostly stark road that led to the Reform Center. Grass and gravel and asphalt, occasionally relieved by a body shop or clump of washed-out pines.

"So," Laney said, "their intent during the fire wasn't clear, but in the past week you've been nearly killed twice. Assuming we count all of last night as one incident. Is this unusual for you?"

"Yes!" I said defensively. Then I paused to consider. "I mean, it's not regular."

"Meaning it—mortal peril—has occurred before?" she asked.

"Yes," I admitted. "More so the past eighteen months or so. I mean, crazy things happened before, but now it's like I'm on the universe's radar for the truly bizarre."

Laney hummed an acknowledgment. "You know I don't go in for the woo-woo, magical thinking crap. I do believe in patterns. It could be what you're experiencing is a result of something external, though I'm not a big believer in conspiracies either. More likely, it's a result of something you're doing."

My mouth fell open. "Are you saying it's my fault?"

Laney's eyes shot at me. "Don't be silly. I'm saying think about how you've changed, and what's changed about the way you interact with the world, during that time. Maybe you're simply more engaged. Or taking more risks. Maybe... I don't know."

She slowed on the last straight stretch before the Reform Center and pulled over on the narrow shoulder. The sky was overcast and glaring, the air heavy with the threat of rain, though that may be all it was. This far west, drought had been prevalent lately, and I could smell the parched grass.

"I could be way off base," Laney said, "in which case, ignore me. But there's something else I need to tell you about the facility."

I blinked, having trouble moving past her big-picture observation. "Go on."

"I do want a peek at what's happening there now," she said. "As you can imagine, I do not take being barred from a site — even temporarily—without a fight. Did you tell them about what we were doing yesterday?"

Brain still sluggish, I said, "Getting a car stuck in the sand and swearing at each other?"

"I don't think I ever technically swore *at you*," she countered. "But yes, specifically what we were looking for."

"Which was?" I asked. Even though I already knew the answer. I'd gotten it from Wade Yates last night.

Laney tilted her head, face radiating the compassion her quick wit often hid. "The tidbits I've gathered from my discussions with law enforcement, about what they need and what we can expect... I think one of the reasons they kicked us out today is that they're looking for a fresh grave. Or at least one more recent than would benefit from my expertise."

My shoulder protested when I covered my eyes and slowly ran my hands down my face.

"Syd, are you okay?"

I nodded, but my breath juddered as I exhaled. "I think I know who it is."

"If it helps," Laney said gently, "in my experience, it's always better to know."

I had to agree. But if I was right, if it was Carly, who would be the one to tell Addy?

59

Laney had called ahead to be let in, but the officers on duty at the Reform Center kept us on a tight leash. We both drove away from the facility within minutes of our admittance, no wiser than when we'd arrived. At least I got Laney to agree to take care of the rental car for me.

I headed back to Tallahassee, mind spinning just enough to keep me awake, with the help of a giant, over-sugared coffee drink I picked up at a convenience store.

Carly's potential fate aside, I wondered how Addy was doing. The hearing previously scheduled for today had been pushed back to Tuesday, and I wasn't allowed contact with the teen before then. The whole *me being with Addy when she was apprehended* situation couldn't have helped. I wasn't sure if Juliet was still mad at me about that, or if the rescuing her from the bad guys thing had bought me some forgiveness. I was hoping for the latter, but Juliet was a tough woman. (Not tough enough to stay married to Roger, but tough enough to marry him in the first place.) Either way, I kept my distance from them at Mr. Weber's funeral on Saturday.

The service was held graveside, with Amos Weber being buried next to his wife in a modest but pleasantly pastoral cemetery just outside Tallahassee. I wished I had a parasol, as did my fluorescent-white skin. The black jersey dress I'd found in my closet (worn, but reasonably presentable) absorbed the sun like a hungry solar panel. Fortunately, a gentle breeze kept it from being oppressively hot and the ceremony was brief.

The pastor was the sole speaker, though for a moment Roger looked poised to do so as well. Several people I took to be siblings gathered on one side of him. I'd met Bridget the Amazon before (her light-brown hair was longer now) but didn't recognize the rest. Deidre stood on Roger's other side, arm linked in his. She was pale, but didn't appear to be in danger of imminent collapse. And she still, a day after being released from the hospital, walked in heels on the grass better than I did.

Addy stood next to Deidre, their shoulders touching. Deidre may have reservations about me, but something about the teen's attention had touched her, and Deidre seemed to appreciate having Addy around. Juliet was on Addy's other side, then a dozen or so mostly older couples.

Mike had gotten hung up in Stetler County and wouldn't arrive in Tallahassee until that evening. Not wishing to prompt drama with Juliet, I stood in the back with Ralph and his wife, Diane. I didn't approach Roger until we took our place in the informal receiving line to offer our condolences with everyone else after the service.

Roger's siblings represented a range of ages, builds, and even races, but they were recognizable by their grief. None of them lived in Tallahassee and they hung back, comforting each other and leaving Roger to represent the family. We waited and encouraged others to go ahead, and I watched as Roger accepted the kind words and hand-shakes and cheek kisses from the men and women. In fact, we waited so long that my heels worked their way into the ground and I nearly tripped at Diane's nudge.

I'd worn sunglasses, but kept my eyes down anyway. It seemed respectful, it helped obscure what the makeup hadn't of the bruise on my face, and it was a great way to avoid pissing off Juliet, or at least avoid seeing that I'd pissed her off. Also, I'm not good at grief. I know, no one is. But I don't do *comforting* particularly well, especially the wordy bit. I hate greeting cards, and when I found myself staring at Roger's shoes, it was no surprise that the flowery language from one didn't spontaneously arise in my mind.

Leaning in awkwardly for my cheek kiss (another social nicety I struggle to perform), I whispered, "You did good."

Roger pulled me against him roughly and spoke into my hair, "No. *We* did good."

He released me, and then Deidre shocked me with a hug as well (less awkward since we were nearly the same height).

I'd literally been the end of the line, so the initial groups had dissolved and were reforming as everyone settled their subsequent plans. Having ridden with Diane and Ralph, I blinked in a fog of emotion until I found them a short distance away, enjoying the shade of a lonely oak tree.

Ralph had his hands in his pockets and practically harrumphed when I joined them, but Diane reached out to take both my hands. Her deep-brown skin crinkled around her eyes with a hint of a gentle smile. Maybe her anger toward me was finally softening.

"Are we ready?" Ralph asked abruptly.

Diane was a woman who *did* do comfort well and had the patience of a saint—one of the saints who actually had to be around people instead of getting to sit in a cave. Still, she shook her head at her husband and muttered something that sounded suspiciously like *cretin* as she pulled her keys from her purse.

Before we could make our escape, I was surprised to see Juliet and Addy approaching. Juliet wasn't glaring, but her immobile face belonged in a sculpture museum. I took a deep breath, in case one breath's worth was all the verbal defense I'd have time to muster.

Addy's hair was pulled back in a low ponytail, and the bright sun bleached a blue streak until it was almost gray. She wore a hint of makeup and a short-sleeved black dress much nicer than mine. Juliet must have bought it for her; Addy was closer to my build than Juliet's, and her clothes wouldn't have fit so well. I envied Addy her chunky-heeled shoes, too. Less likely to get stuck in the turf mire.

Addy glanced at me, her eyes more hazel than brown in the sunlight, and flashed a quick smile. Flushing slightly, she mouthed, "Hey, Syd," while Juliet introduced her to the Abrahams (the lawyer ignoring me like a pro).

"I, um," Addy began, speaking to Ralph. I could see her chest heave as she took in a deep breath, much as I had moments ago. Then she continued, in a more confident, more adult voice, "I understand you'll be working on the lawsuits. With the old kids' prison, I mean."

Diane stared at Ralph, then glared at me. I held up my hands—it was news to me, too, though not particularly surprising. Presumably, Juliet had learned of it through the grapevine, i.e., her ex-husband. Ralph avoided both our gazes as he said, "Well, I worked on some of the old wrongful death suits, back in the day, so they asked if I could help out again. If things go forward."

"Good," Addy said, nodding. "I just wanted to thank you for that, since they can't."

She hurried away, shoulders hunched, but straightened as Juliet put an arm around her and said something we couldn't hear. The teen had left us speechless, and I felt a shiny but perilous sliver of hope stab my chest. Maybe she'd be all right after all. At least she hadn't dropped "the n word" at Ralph and Diane.

I carried that uncertain optimism with me back to the Abrahams' house (though Diane didn't invite me in), and then driving Cecil across town back home. It really was a beautiful day, sunlight dappling the road through heavy live oak branches as the Spanish moss swayed gently with my passing. I had the whimsical notion that the grayish-green, curling tendrils were whispering secrets to me. I could hear them, if only I listened closely enough.

≈

I ARRIVED HOME TO, for once, a *pleasant* surprise—a bright-yellow Jeep in my driveway. Mike sat on the steps by the kitchen door, waiting as I stepped out of my car.

"Thought you couldn't make it until tonight," I said, voice as close to giddy as was possible while still wearing funeral garb.

"And yet, I'm here," he said, smiling with an edge of sadness as he took in my clothes. "Come on. Go get changed, and we'll do something fun."

And we did, driving down to St. Mark's Wildlife Refuge to hike the sandy, piney trails, heckling alligators and armadillos for hours while we shared aimless stories, then getting steak sandwiches and beer at a riverside cafe. I suffered a mild case of sunburn on our excursions, which was a perfect excuse for extensive aloe vera slathering.

Not wanting to get the rest of my furniture sticky, we stayed in bed all weekend.

60

I sat at my office desk Tuesday morning, sipping a cold drip iced coffee from around the corner. It was sunny outside, but a breeze teased the branches overhanging my office and flowed through the screen door. Coupled with the ceiling fans, my space was downright comfortable. In short, I was still riding my weekend-with-Mike high, when John Driscoll called from the TPD to threaten my beautiful state of mind.

Where did we stand, I wondered? I'd given John a tip that may have helped apprehend bad guys and advance his career. Of course, then I may have made him look bad by ignoring a "request" to come in for an interview to further the investigation. Hmm... In these situations, I find it's best to let the caller demonstrate his intentions first.

"So, a SWAT raid, huh?" he asked.

John didn't always have the most vigorous sense of humor. Was he joking, or was that the initial question in an official interview? I took a chance and assumed the former. "Sorry—should I have called? Or do you only do strip club brawls?"

I liked to think I made him smile, albeit briefly. Hard to say. After a moment's hesitation, he got straight to his reason for calling.

"Since Blake Tucker resided here, TPD has been involved with some of the follow-up investigation around him," John said.

"Interesting stuff?" I asked.

"I thought it might be to you," he said.

So on balance, I'd landed in his good column, or I'd landed in *someone's* good column. John didn't seem nervous about sharing with me.

He continued, "It appears Mr. Tucker has been supplementing his salary with unreported income for years."

Definitely someone else's good column. I doubted John would have this kind of big-picture access this quickly. "How much?" I asked.

"It varied," John said, "but nothing dramatic, ten K or less annually."

The sudden metallic plink of mail being dropped in the box mounted outside my door startled me. I waited until the postal carrier's shadow was gone to ask, "And where was he working?"

"Brummel for much of it, and previously at an adult facility, also under Eleanor Powers."

"Imagine that."

"We don't have access to all of his bank accounts, so the numbers could change. There is talk—outside of TPD—of an additional account with substantial recent deposits."

Moderately interesting, but I felt like that alone would not have been worth the call. "And?" I prompted. "There's more, isn't there?"

John lowered his voice, but he sounded excited over secret-sharing rather than anxious over secret-hiding-from-my-superiors. "A packed bag at his house, tucked away in his closet, with five thousand dollars cash. An anonymous draft letter on his home computer, written a few weeks ago. So far as we can tell, it was never sent, so we don't know if it was intended to be emailed or posted."

"Saying?"

"Take a look at inmate releases from Brummel and another juvenile institution. Also named a few local businesses, including a particular cab company that seems to magically get all of Brummel's unaccompanied departures."

"Who else did he name?" I asked, but was pretty sure I knew the answer.

"No individuals, if that's what you're getting at."

In other words, not Eleanor Powers.

I leaned back precariously in my chair after John hung up. He wouldn't share their working theory, but I didn't need it; it all fit the one I'd shared with Roger. That Blake was shady, involved in low-level institutional graft for years. But when he discovered the trafficking, Blake found his conscience. And Eleanor and Wade found their scapegoat.

What had Blake expected to happen when he went to meet her that evening? At least information about what was happening. Had Eleanor promised a last pay-off? He hadn't entirely trusted her, especially after our interaction. But so far as I knew, he hadn't taken a weapon, other than his large male self. He'd underestimated her, just as everyone else had.

TUESDAY WASN'T DONE RAINING on my parade, or at least making me stop and consider whether a parade was an appropriate choice of entertainment in this day and age. Versus... I don't know, gladiators skewering puppies.

My first thought when Roger called that evening was to wonder how time had gotten away from me. I'd intended to be home by dark, so I sat hunched over my files with a single desk lamp burning, squinting in denial.

My second thought was one of guilt. Despite all my concerns and good intentions, I hadn't spoken to Roger since his father's funeral.

"How are you doing?" I asked.

"Busy," he said, in a typical Roger-avoids-emotion non-answer. "Things accumulated at the office the past couple of weeks. And I'm Dad's executor, which I'm learning is a whole job of its own."

"How's Deidre?"

He paused, and I knew he was worried about her, whatever words would follow. "Better," he said cautiously. "She's staying with me for a while. You should come over some night for dinner. She likes you."

"Really?" I asked. He must have heard my skepticism.

"Yeah, I can't explain it either," he said, deadpan. I thought he'd leave it at that, but he continued. "Sydney, what you did for Dad, and us... Deidre will not soon forget it, and neither will I. Thank you."

Either he got choked up at the end, or I was projecting my own emotional state. I said roughly, "You're welcome."

"So, dinner tomorrow night?" he asked hopefully.

"Sure," I said. "Sounds great."

"Good—Deidre will be glad to hear it. Now that we've got that taken care of, do you want the good news or the bad news?"

I sighed, rubbing my forehead as I felt any tatters of my weekend high slipping away. "I hate when people make you choose. It's like that little bit of agency somehow makes you complicit in whatever shitty thing they're about to tell you."

"Wade Yates is dead," Roger said.

"Is that the good news or the bad news?" I asked, having difficulty assimilating the idea. I was stunned. He'd seemed in pretty good health when he tried to kill me a few days ago.

"I'm not sure," Roger admitted. "Let's just call it *news*."

Which presumably meant there was still both good and bad news to come. I might have to stop answering my phone. "What happened?" I asked.

"Found hanging in his cell," Roger said, voice flat. "He'd been working in private security for years, but they'd placed him in protective custody because of his corrections history. You met the man. What do you think—was he suicidal?"

"No, he was *homicidal* at the time. But he knew he was low man on the make-a-deal totem pole, and he was looking at serious time as a high-value target inside. And the man had some intense mental health issues, especially around control and dominance. Which path that would have made him choose, I couldn't say." I shook my head.

"But it's awfully damned convenient, for people we can't even begin to comprehend. Not to mention how he pulled it off."

"My thoughts exactly," Roger said. "Not that there's any question what the death inquiry will conclude."

"Well, on that bright note," I said, "why don't you go ahead and give me the bad news."

Roger paused long enough for me to hear either sound or absence of sound in the background that made me think he was also alone in his office. Finally he said, "They've recovered the body."

My mind briefly went blank. After all, ours is a relationship built around dead bodies. Half a second later, Laney's words *fresh grave* flashed in my head. I asked softly, "Is it Carly?"

"The preliminary identification is Carlotta Whitmore," he said, "but that won't be officially released until they have confirmation."

A day's worth of coffee turned to acid in my stomach, and my throat burned with it. I carefully pushed my most recent cup across my desk, the bitter, milky smell nauseating. "Does Addy know?"

"Juliet just told her."

So Roger was getting his information straight from the source. Poor Addy. A small, cowardly part of me was glad I hadn't been the one to break the news.

"She's upset, but doing surprisingly well," Roger said. "I think you'd done a good job preparing her for the possibility."

Is that what I'd done? I bit my lip, felt tears trickle down my cheek, and I couldn't say why. It was a tragedy, but I'd never even met Carly, and what was Addy to me? I swiped at my face, but watched a drop hit my desk blotter anyway, leaving a broad wet spot on the paper.

"Sydney," Roger said patiently, kindly. The man whose father had just died. "Are you ready for the good news?"

"Hell, yeah," I snorted.

"The Spencers got temporary custody of Addy today. Juliet says, if everything goes well, they shouldn't have any trouble keeping her indefinitely."

My poor lips were taking some serious abuse, but I stopped

chewing them long enough to say, "That is good news. Very good news."

"Mrs. Spencer is taking her home to Ocala tomorrow, but I think she wanted to stop by your office on her way out of town, if that's okay." When I didn't answer immediately, Roger added, "If you'll be around."

"You bet," I choked out.

"I'll have Juliet let them know," he said. "And don't forget dinner tomorrow night."

After he hung up, I sat staring across my desk at the white, wood-framed windows, the individual panes threatening to blur together. It was late enough that I couldn't see the trees or the street, just the darkness outside and the vivid, round ball of my desk lamp reflected like a mirror. I was a shape in its orbit, but of no more distinction than the furniture.

The pressure built inside me. It was non-partisan—neither purely positive or negative—just a physical force, a corporeal reaction. It rose in my chest, then through my throat and into my skull, until finally I dropped my head to my desk and sobbed. My shoulders rocked like the unseen branches outside.

61

I was nervous the next morning, agitated. I couldn't decide what to wear and finally chose my fallback tank top, button-down shirt, and jeans. At the last minute I added my cowboy boots, even though it was too warm for them.

My first half hour at the office, I glanced up every time a car parked on the street, but eventually I settled down. Like Roger, I'd lost some ground on other cases the past couple of weeks and was still playing catch-up. So when Addy knocked on my screen door, I nearly flipped my rolling chair rushing to get up.

Not that I do that on a regular basis or anything.

"Hey," I said awkwardly. "Come on in."

Addy looked over her shoulder and lifted her hand. The angle was bad, but I saw a woman's arm wave an acknowledgment from the street below us. She sat behind the wheel of the same light-blue sedan I'd seen Clint Spencer drive.

"My aunt Debbie," Addy explained. "She'll be in soon, but she wanted to give us a minute."

I nodded and led Addy to a chair at my desk. "Can I get you something?"

"No, thanks," she said, sliding down in her chair. "We just had a *huge* breakfast with Juliet. Oh my God, I ate so much."

I noticed Addy was wearing new denim pants and asked, "Juliet find you those jeans, too?"

"Yes!" Addy said, half-standing again to demonstrate that they fit her hinter regions. "And they're so comfortable. I didn't even try them on, somehow she just knew what size to get me."

"Maybe I can get her to find me a pair," I said, with a hint of irony.

Addy raised a brow, transforming from teen to adult in a moment. "Give her some time," Addy said. "It's not like she hates you."

The morning was warm but not sweltering, and atop the jeans Addy wore a simple, pale-green T-shirt that brought out the highlights in her eyes. The flesh beneath them looked a little dark, but not bad considering. No more than you'd expect on a teen any given day. And yet I heard myself ask, "You sleeping okay?"

Addy dropped her head and stared at her hands gathered on her belly. "Mostly," she said. Her gaze flicked up at me. "You?"

I shrugged. "Mostly."

We shared a sardonic smile.

Addy rolled her eyes. "They say they've got someone for me to talk to."

"Good," I said. "Do it."

"Are you?" she challenged.

"No," I admitted. And why wasn't I? Because I was stupid, or hardheaded? Not precluding the possibility of both. Again, like an out-of-body experience, I heard myself say, "I'm not yet. Roger knows people. I thought I'd ask him for a recommendation tonight."

Addy's face lightened momentarily at the mention of Roger, then grew somber. "How's Deidre doing?"

Because—my own amateur psychologizing—she could not imagine *Roger* doing anything but well.

"She's hanging in there. I'll see her tonight, too." Addy opened her mouth and I added, "I'll tell her you said hi."

"Thanks," she said, blushing.

"Anyone else you want me to say hi to?" I asked, giving her a sly sideways glance.

I was surprised that didn't earn me another eye roll.

"If you're referring to Ben," she said, in the self-conscious tone of a teen imitating an adult, "thank you for the offer, but I have his number already."

My stomach lurched at the thought, just a little. *You're a friend, not a mom. To either of them.* So I went for my default non-confrontational response, "Good."

Addy grew quiet. She hadn't brought up Carly, but the poor girl lingered in the air between us like a ghost. I didn't push Addy—I'd leave that to the people with degrees. Still, she might have said more if it hadn't been for the knock.

I watched Addy for signs of anxiety as I went to the door, but didn't see any.

The woman standing on my office porch was probably around my age, but looked older. Drained. Kids might do that to you, likewise recovering from hospital stays. She had the brownest of brown hair, shoulder-length with soft, simple bangs, flipping a little on the ends. Her face would have been unremarkable, plain even, save for the button nose she shared with Addy. Mrs. Spencer's had a bit more upturn at the end. As with Addy, it reminded me of someone, but I still couldn't recall whom. Probably a romcom star.

"You must be Mrs. Spencer," I said. "Come in."

"Miss Brennan," she said.

She made it almost as far as my desk before taking my proffered hand and standing, trance-like, as if she'd forgotten why she was there. I hoped she was okay to drive.

"Please, sit down," I said, waiting for her to release my fingers.

She blinked, looking embarrassed as she dropped my hand. "Thank you, but we can't stay. Addy, we really should be going."

"Oh, okay," Addy said, rising slowly.

She didn't seem afraid of Mrs. Spencer, or reluctant to leave with her. I felt a lump in my throat as I realized Addy's reticence was about saying goodbye to me.

"Thanks, for everything," Addy said, walking slowly past us toward the door.

"You're welcome," I replied, going for warm-hearted but not mushy.

Then Addy changed her mind, swinging back toward me for a sudden embrace. It felt both strange and familiar to hug someone my own height, and I was glad she couldn't see me wince as I raised my arm, pissing off my still-aching shoulder.

"Can I call you some time?" she asked, voice little more than a whisper.

"Absolutely," I said, before noticing that Mrs. Spencer, watching us closely, seemed to have mixed feelings about the prospect. "Whenever the Spencers say it's okay," I added.

She nodded, and Mrs. Spencer put her hand lightly on Addy's shoulder as she walked her to the door. Then she handed Addy her car keys. "Go on, sweetie. I'll be right there, but if you get too hot, you can turn the A/C on."

I waited, leaning against my desk, until Addy was gone, then said, "Mrs. Spencer, your husband and I already settled the financial arrangements."

I didn't believe that was why she'd sent Addy ahead, but hoped it would encourage her to admit why she actually had.

She shook her head and said, "You really don't recognize me, do you?"

"I'm sorry. Should I?" I asked, though I had the most unsettling feeling that I did. "I thought your husband said you didn't know me."

Specifically, that she didn't even know my gender, if I remembered correctly, though she had wanted to hire me.

"Not by this name," she said. "I might not have recognized you either, if Addy hadn't mentioned your red hair. That planted a seed. And then your father... well, it doesn't matter. It's been so many years."

I stared at her, confused, vaguely uneasy, though I couldn't have said why. In fact, I doubt I could have said anything.

She continued, "I just wanted to thank you, in person, for helping bring Addy home to us. Because that's what she'll have—a home. And not just because she's all I have left of Beth..."

Beth... *Bethany*. Whatever words she spoke after that were lost to me. My lips and fingers went numb, and if I hadn't been leaning against my desk I'd have dropped to the floor. My knees started to go anyway.

Deborah's voice came from far away, and I didn't realize she was saying my name until I felt the seat of the chair she'd slid beneath me. "Miss Brennan? Are you all right?"

She disappeared, and some time later handed me a can of Coke that must have come from my refrigerator. "Here, drink this," she said.

I managed a few sips without choking, and the cold, fizzing sugar-packed liquid slowly did the trick. I set the can carefully on my desk and watched my hand reach for Mrs. Spencer, finger extended like someone looking for God. But I was looking for answers.

"Deborah?" was the only question I could vocalize. I hadn't thought of her in so many years, I'd forgotten that was the name of Bethany's sister.

She didn't sit, wouldn't stand close enough for me to actually touch her, but smiled stiffly as she confirmed, "Deborah. You really didn't know. I should have. *Sydney*... in retrospect the name is a dead giveaway." She shook her head. "You and Bethany."

My mouth fell open, and if I weren't already sitting, this time I would have fainted. Addy... *Adelaide.*

"Addy," I whispered. "Is she..."

I couldn't finish. But I didn't need to.

My big brother was a baseball star in high school. It carried him into college, and when he dropped out, he'd planned (so much as he had a plan) to play minor league. But surfing had been his first love.

We grew up near Orlando, more central than coastal Florida, and with his other commitments it was hard for Allan to get water time. But when the waves really went off, he'd drop everything to catch them. Sometimes he'd sneak me away, too, until he started dating Bethany. I didn't begrudge her—she never tried to exclude me, and she made him happy. Young as I was, I still recognized how deeply unhappy my brother could be.

And sometimes, surf or not, they went and took me with them.

Addy had said, *Mom told me my dad loved the ocean. She didn't tell me much about him, but she said that more than once, so it must be true.* She was right.

We'd lie on the sand, Bethany's head on his shoulder and me covered in copious quantities of sunscreen and beach towels, listening to Allan daydream about Australia. Telling stories about the surf, about kangaroos and crocs and what it would be like when we lived there.

He'd ask us to pick our city. I always chose Sydney, and Bethany always chose Adelaide. Because we liked the sound of them.

I took a deep breath, then another sip of Coke. I wondered what Deborah was waiting for, what she wanted me to say. What came out was, "Thank God neither of us picked Darwin."

Deborah smiled, but it was a pinched smile that seemed to resent itself. "Beth always thought you were funny."

My eyes burned. I wanted to stand, but still didn't trust my legs. "Your sister was very kind to me. I'm so sorry. I didn't know. About her, or Addy. I didn't know."

"I believe you," Deborah said, but as though she wasn't sure it mattered. "But your family..."

"Why do you think I changed my name?" That didn't seem to buy me any points, either. I continued, "We've been estranged, it feels like, since Allan died. But Lisa... she's pregnant now—her first. And we're trying to get to know each other again."

Deborah nodded. "You need to talk to your father."

"My dad?" I asked. As if he bore none of the familial responsibility or guilt. He never seemed to, and I never asked myself before why that was.

Deborah turned for the door, and I staggered to my feet. "Wait!"

She stopped with her hand on the screen latch, but wouldn't look at me, as if she knew what I was about to ask.

"Will you tell her?"

"I don't know," she said. And she left.

I listened to the whooshing springs and shuffling, scraping metal of the closing screen door, but I couldn't hear her departing footsteps on the concrete steps. A little while later, a car door closed, but its engine noise was indistinguishable from the ambient downtown noise.

My head felt hollowed out by the past few minutes, and past two weeks. Sure, there were little buzzes around the edges about my father and what he knew, then and now. About my mother's involvement, and the story my sister Lisa had carried with her for so many years. About my brother gone too soon, and Bethany raising her daughter alone, stranger to her own family and ours. About lost years.

But mostly, one thought echoed through my head, crowding out everything else and pulling my cheeks back in a giddy grin.

I sat down behind my desk, looked at the phone. Things might get complicated with everyone else, but I wanted to tell Mike. Couldn't wait to share. But I just sat a moment, reveling in the unexpected gift the universe had handed me.

I have a niece.

And no one could take that away.

ACKNOWLEDGMENTS AND HISTORICAL NOTE

First, the heavy stuff.

The characters in this book are of my invention, but the inspiration for my fictional Florida Youth Reform Center is the Arthur G. Dozier School for Boys. The juvenile detention facility was plagued by federal and state investigations throughout its history, from its opening around 1900 to its shutdown in 2011. In addition to acting as a labor camp, allegations of wrongdoing at the facility included torture, rape, and many heinous acts similar to the ones I describe within *Grave Truth*.

Dozier's horrifying and heartbreaking spectre has been lodged in my mind since I first learned of it nearly twenty years ago. My hope, in treating a fictionalized version of this as the distant backdrop of *Grave Truth,* is to present a glimpse of what might have been—and may still be—without sensationalizing the real harms that were done or intruding upon stories that are not mine to tell.

Now, on to the appreciation. Thank you to my usual, indispensable crew: developmental diva *(as if)* Alida Winternheimer, copy connoisseur Calee Allen, and bestest beta readers Sandy Mom and Paul. When time got tight, my crew of awesome advance readers also caught tears in Sydney's space-time continuum. And special thanks to my husband for his patience (and to dogs for face-loving) when the story took me to dark places it is difficult to leave behind.

Thanks also to you, the readers who followed me to those dark places. The next Syd still won't be all rainbows and buttercups, but I promise any graveyards will be zoned, above ground and clearly marked on a map.

ABOUT THE AUTHOR

A recovering criminal attorney, Judy K. Walker has enough spare letters after her name (and student loan debt) to suggest that insatiable curiosity is something fictional private investigator Sydney Brennan inherited from her creator. Fortunately, Judy's curiosity rarely involves murders.

Judy also created the *Dead Hollow Trilogy*, an Appalachian thriller series with a touch of the paranormal that taps into her West Virginia origins.

She writes from her home in Hawaii, where she is surrounded by husband, dogs, cat, and assorted geckos. If she's not tapping away at her computer, she's probably sweeping tumblepuppies (the piles of accumulated critter hair).

Learn more about Sydney Brennan's world and connect with me online at:
www.judykwalker.com